"Good mor..... ..issed the excitement."

She eyed him with misgivings. "What excitement?"

"The chef's done a runner, so I'm filling the breach. Builders, bangers, and egg-and-toast soldiers, on the way."

She frowned. "In English, please?"

"Armand's gone. I took it upon myself to assume breakfast duty." He removed the bacon to drain on a layer of paper towels. "Tea, sausages, and soft-boiled eggs with toast."

"That sounds very . . . bracing," Phaedra said. "Thank you. But why has Armand left? Has he gone to the grocery store? Are we out of eggs? Is he coming back?"

"No. Not until, and this is a direct quote translated from the French, 'Hell freezes over.' End quote."

"Oh no." Phaedra sank onto a chair at the table.

"Evidently Mrs. Overton insulted his meringues as well as his knife skills after dinner last night. I came in for a coffee and tried to persuade him to stay, but he packed up his knife roll along with his pride and slammed out the door."

"What'll I do?" Phaedra groaned. "We need a chef!"

"What about Hannah?" he asked. "Surely she can pinch-hit until you find another chef."

"She could," Phaedra agreed, "if she was still here." She rose and went to the fridge to retrieve a tray of scones waiting to be baked.

"A problem cropped up at the embassy," she told him as she set the oven to preheat, "and Hannah had to catch a flight back to D.C."

Mark scratched his chin. "I make a decent breakfast," he said doubtfully, "and I can manage the odd sandwich or cheese toastie, but as for the rest . . ."

Before Phaedra could answer, before she'd even formed a coherent thought, a high-pierced shriek echoed across the lawn and shattered the tranquil late summer morning.

She dropped the tray of scones to the counter with a clatter as another scream pierced the stillness. Racing to the kitchen door, she flung it open.

The garden. The scream had come from the garden.

Leaving Mark and the warm, fragrant kitchen behind, Phaedra plunged out into the chilly air and raced down the path, long skirts flying, until she reached the kitchen garden. Her heart pumped wildly as her gaze swept the neatly spaced rows of herbs and marigolds.

Normally, she'd pause to breathe in the heady scents of thyme, basil, lavender, and oregano, or listen to the splash of water in the stone fountain nearby. But today, her eyes went straight to the herbaceous border.

Someone lay faceup in the rosemary. Which, had one of the guests imbibed too much sherry the previous evening and passed out, wouldn't have been quite so alarming.

But this particular guest had an arrow in her chest.

Berkley Prime Crime titles by Katie Oliver

PRIDE, PREJUDICE, AND PERIL
A MURDEROUS PERSUASION

A
Murderous
Persuasion

A Jane Austen Tea Society Mystery

Katie Oliver

BERKLEY PRIME CRIME
New York

BERKLEY PRIME CRIME
Published by Berkley
An imprint of Penguin Random House LLC
penguinrandomhouse.com

Copyright © 2023 by Katie Oliver
Penguin Random House supports copyright. Copyright fuels creativity, encourages
diverse voices, promotes free speech, and creates a vibrant culture. Thank you for buying
an authorized edition of this book and for complying with copyright laws by not
reproducing, scanning, or distributing any part of it in any form without permission.
You are supporting writers and allowing Penguin Random House to continue to
publish books for every reader.

BERKLEY and the BERKLEY & B colophon are registered trademarks and
BERKLEY PRIME CRIME is a trademark of Penguin Random House LLC.

ISBN: 9780593337639

First Edition: January 2023

Printed in the United States of America
1 3 5 7 9 10 8 6 4 2

Book design by Alison Cnockaert

To Bentley, my favorite canine fan. This one's for you.

Facts or opinions which are to pass through the hands of so many, to be misconceived by folly in one, and ignorance in another, can hardly have much truth left.

JANE AUSTEN,
PERSUASION (1817)

One

It began, as so many unwelcome things do, with a loud banging on the door.

Phaedra Brighton swam up out of a beguiling dream, in which she and Mr. Darcy shared a picnic on the banks of the river Thames, and sat up abruptly in bed. The digital numerals on the alarm clock informed her it was eight a.m.

She tossed back the covers, sending her well-worn copy of *Pride and Prejudice* tumbling to the floor with a thump and a flutter of pages, and bent down to retrieve the book.

Perhaps if she waited, her visitor would go away.

"Phaedra! I know you're in there. Open up!"

The banging resumed, and she realized the person on the other side of the carriage house door wasn't going away. She hurried down the stairs, leaving her cozy loft bedroom and dreams of Mr. Darcy behind.

She flung the front door open and regarded the slim woman with short, angular black hair. "Lucy?"

Lucy Liang, professor of post-modernist literature and her closest friend on the Somerset University faculty, brushed past Phaedra and unshouldered a backpack.

"The flea market," she said, answering Phaedra's unspoken question with the patience of a preschool teacher. "No classes until fall term. Freedom from academia until mid-August." She tossed the backpack on the sofa.

From his perch atop the back of the sofa, Wickham, Phaedra's Himalayan cat, regarded the backpack with blue-eyed disfavor. This was his domain, where he kept vigil over the driveway and front lawn and monitored the red-and-blue flash of blue jays and cardinals winging by.

Phaedra headed for the kitchen. Her hair, woven into a dark gold braid down her back, was coming loose, and her dream of Darcy and the sumptuous picnic they'd shared began to evaporate. She needed a bracing cup of Keemun, stat. "Tea?" she inquired.

"Coffee, please. How could you forget?"

"That you prefer coffee?"

"That we had plans. And what is that you're wearing?" Lucy slid onto a seat at the kitchen island.

Phaedra glanced at her long, flower-sprigged night-gown. "What's wrong with it?"

"Nothing, if you're Catherine Morland, traipsing around Northanger Abbey with a guttering candlestick and a pounding heart."

"It got chilly last night." Phaedra filled the teakettle and the coffee maker with water. "And the only pounding was you, banging on my door."

"Then grab another blanket," she pointed out. "Or better yet, a male. Both work wonders to keep a girl warm."

Phaedra didn't bother to correct her. Lucy knew her feelings on that matter. Instead, she filled the basket with fresh-ground beans and started the coffee maker. "Why are we going to the flea market? And so early? Remind me."

"Because your aunt's threatening yet again to put the Laurel Springs Inn up for sale," Lucy reminded her, "and you convinced her to hold off—"

"By promising to host a Jane Austen Murder Mystery week at the inn next month." Phaedra groaned as it all came back to her in a rush.

A great, big, *what was I* thinking *of* rush.

Yesterday morning, she'd seen a real estate sign planted in front of her aunt Wendy's bed-and-breakfast, the Laurel Springs Inn.

FOR SALE.
HISTORIC BED-AND-BREAKFAST.
OFFERED BY BERKSHIRE HADLEY.
BY APPOINTMENT ONLY.

She'd rushed across the lawn separating the carriage house from the inn, a Queen Anne whimsy bristling with turrets and gables and elaborate gingerbread trim, and marched up the wide wooden steps to the porch.

Inside, the front desk was empty. She glanced past the ornate 1920s brass counter bell and the numbered cubbies where room keys and telegrams were once tucked away, and faced the staircase that divided the first floor.

"Aunt Wendy?"

The door at the end of the hall leading to the kitchen swooshed open, releasing the smell of burnt toast and a string of French invective as Chef Armand scolded a server for some unknown infraction. A teakettle began to shriek.

"Someone, please take that kettle off the stove!" Wendy Prescott snapped. "Before you burn the place down."

The shrieking abruptly stopped.

The door whooshed shut, restoring quiet as Phaedra's aunt approached the lobby. She paused as she caught sight of her niece. Normally groomed to the nines in elegant but comfortable clothes and bright cherry-red lipstick, Wendy looked fashionable but frazzled. She tucked a strand of hair, recently cut and streaked with caramel highlights, behind one ear and gathered her niece into a hug.

"You saw the sign." Wendy drew back. Her hand strayed to the chunky necklace encircling her throat. "I wanted to talk to you first, but . . ."

"You can't sell the inn. Tell me you're not serious."

"I'm afraid I am." Glancing back at the kitchen door, her aunt took Phaedra's arm. "Let's go in the front parlor. We can talk privately there."

". . . and that's the long and the short of it," she finished a short time later. "Business is down and so are profits. We've limped along for six months, but I can't keep this place going at a loss any longer."

"But *selling*?" Phaedra leaned forward on the sofa. "There has to be another way."

"There isn't. I've cut staff, sourced cheaper produce, taken out ads . . . it's not enough. I know how much this place means to you, but I'm out of options. I'm sorry."

"What about hosting seasonal events?" Phaedra, grasping at any straw, suggested. "Like the Spring Fling open house at the Poison Pen."

Every spring, her father's bookstore sponsored a week's worth of book giveaways, guest authors, contests, and prizes, along with plenty of free nibbles.

"I run a B and B," her aunt said. "Not a bookstore."

"The principle is the same. You could host a . . . a Halloween-themed masquerade party, for example, or a *Titanic* tea. Or . . ." She thought of the pile of cozy mysteries on her bedside table. "A murder mystery week!"

Her aunt sniffed. "A gimmick, you mean."

"Call it what you want, but special events appeal to guests." Phaedra eyed the pocket doors separating the front parlor from the back. "We could throw a 1920s dinner dance." She warmed to the idea. "Flappers and gangsters, bathtub gin, everyone doing the Charleston and swigging champagne—"

"Spilling booze and cigarette ash all over my Persian rugs?" Wendy shook her head firmly. "No, thank you."

"Okay." A thoughtful expression settled over Phaedra's face. "What about something a little more elegant?"

"Such as?"

"Such as," she mused, "a Jane Austen immersive event."

"And what's that, exactly?"

"Just what it sounds like. Guests immerse themselves in the Regency period and leave their cell phones behind. They'll dress in period costumes, play card games, discuss Austen's novels, drink tea, dance, and stroll through the rose garden."

"Sounds dull. And the rose garden needs pruning." Wendy frowned. "What would people do? Besides drink tea and wander around in long dresses?"

"We'll have archery on the back lawn," Phaedra said, warming to the idea, "and tea in the dining room, with tea cakes and sandwiches. And maybe an Austen quiz, with a prize for the winner."

"What sort of prize? I can't afford more than a box of notecards at this point."

"And to make it even more fun," Phaedra rushed on, "what if we sponsor a murder mystery week?" She leaned forward. "Jane Austen inspired, of course. With a staged murder, a victim, and suspects. We could do a *Persuasion* theme," she mused. "With each guest assuming the role of a character in the novel. Whoever solves the murder first wins a prize."

"You keep saying 'we,'" Wendy said. "I hate to throw water on the fire, but who's paying for all this? Who's arranging the costume rentals and hiring actors to take part in the murder? It sounds complicated. And expensive."

"Elaine Alexander manages the Laurel Springs Players. We met at UVA years ago. She's opening a costume shop next door to the Poison Pen, and she's desperate for business. She'll jump at the chance to produce a murder mystery." Phaedra's enthusiasm quickened. "And perhaps I can persuade Clark to give us a write-up in the *Clarion*."

Clark Mullinax, a reporter for the *Laurel Springs Clarion*, was brash and pushy, with a knack for turning up looking for a story at the worst possible times. They normally gave each other a wide berth.

But a piece about the immersive Austen event in the *Clarion* would be sweet local publicity . . . not only for Elaine, but also for the inn.

"Armand does an excellent dinner," her aunt said doubtfully, "but a tea? All of those scones and watercress sandwiches and fussy little cakes . . ."

Phaedra stood up. "I'm sure he'll be up to the challenge. I'll meet with him and come up with a menu. Leave the details to me. And the cost."

"Absolutely not," her aunt said. "I won't allow you to do that. More to the point, why would you *want* to do it?"

"Memories." Phaedra's gaze softened as she glanced around the room. "Who could forget all the parties, New Year's Eve, Christmas—raiding Great-Aunt Hester's old trunks in the attic . . . And Halloween! Your costume parties were epic."

"We once shared an entire carton of Chunky Monkey," Wendy reminded her. "Do you remember?"

"How could I forget? It was right after Donovan dumped me for Emily Endicott."

"Donovan," Wendy added darkly, "was a rat. Handsome as the devil, but still a rat."

"Every spring you hid Easter eggs on the lawn for Hannah and me to find. So. Much. Candy."

"I let you and your sister get away with murder. If your mother only knew the half of it . . ."

"But she didn't. And that's why we loved you. Well, one of the reasons." Phaedra sighed. "Please, don't give up on the inn. Let me help."

Wendy threw her hands up in surrender.

Now, Phaedra regretted her impulsive promise. How could she deliver a *Persuasion*-themed murder mystery event in less than a month, with all that entailed . . . and save her aunt's bed-and-breakfast in the bargain?

Pressure? Not much.

Lucy glanced at her wristwatch. "The flea market opens in ten."

"I'll wear my sprigged muslin," Phaedra decided, and set her mug down. "It's lightweight."

"You're dressing in costume? On a *Saturday*? You don't usually do that."

Phaedra shrugged. "Why not? It'll be fun."

"Okay. But it's warm outside," Lucy pointed out. "And sunny. Bring your bonnet."

Professor Brighton was a familiar sight on the campus of Somerset University, strolling across the quad or lingering to chat with one of her students, dressed head to toe in Regency attire. Wearing an Empire-waist gown, with a silk shawl draped around her shoulders and ballet slippers on her feet, she felt her clothing was both a teaching tool for her students and a nod to her favorite writer, Jane Austen.

As Phaedra hurried up to the loft to change, Lucy dropped a slice of bread in the toaster. "What is it we're looking for, anyway?" she called up.

Halfway up the stairs, Phaedra paused, her head dancing with visions of antique china teacups, old books, and lace tablecloths. "Possibilities," she said.

One hour, two boxes of Regency romance novels, an armload of tea-length dresses, and a dozen mismatched vintage teacups and saucers later, Phaedra and Lucy returned to the carriage house.

Lucy got out of the car and shaded her eyes against the sun. "Hey. Over there. What's going on?"

Phaedra slid out of the car and followed her gaze.

A police vehicle was parked halfway down Main Street, in front of the Poison Pen bookstore. No flashing lights or crime scene tape, but still, not a reassuring sight.

"Why's a police car parked in front of your dad's bookstore?" Lucy wondered.

"I'm sure it's nothing. It's probably just routine."

But even as she said the words, Phaedra's throat tightened and her thoughts ran rampant. Had someone broken

into the store? Vandalized it? Such things were largely un-
heard of in Laurel Springs, but the Poison Pen had been
robbed once before, when two of her father's first editions
went missing.

"Go check it out," Lucy said. "And call me later."

"I will."

Lucy grabbed her backpack. "Okay. See you Monday."

Phaedra nodded. The Jane Austen Tea Society held their
book club meeting on the first Monday of each month. "I'll
be there."

As Lucy left, Phaedra pocketed her key fob, drew in a
calming breath, and headed to her father's bookstore to find
out what was going on.

Two

The Poison Pen was doing a brisk business when Phaedra arrived.

The bookstore's flag, with its eye-catching image of a black quill pen silhouetted against a splotch of blood, flapped in the summer breeze as she went up the porch steps to the front door.

After retiring from criminal law, her father, Malcolm Brighton, converted the first floor of their inherited Victorian town house into a bookstore, stuffing its shelves with mysteries, police procedurals, noir, cozies, and true crime novels, along with comfortable armchairs tucked in every available nook and cranny. He and Phaedra's mother, Nan, lived upstairs with their pug, Fitz.

Phaedra shut the door behind her and surveyed the store. Customers lingered in front of shelves, floorboards creaking beneath their feet as they browsed, while others waited at the counter to pay for their books and magazines.

Her father narrated the opening sentences of the latest legal thriller by Charlottesville's own John Grisham, his voice drifting out from the reading room, and the rich

scent of Guatemalan coffee—today's featured blend—
wafted on the air.

Although her dress and bonnet earned her a quizzical
glance or two, most of the locals were accustomed to her
Regency garb. The sight of Phaedra in a high-waist Empire
gown and silk slippers, a reticule dangling from one hand,
elicited nothing more than a nod or an indulgent smile.

Her mother glanced at her from behind the cash register
as she rang up purchases. Phaedra, relieved all seemed
normal, edged past a knot of customers to seek out a man
standing by the cozy mystery section.

His dark, watchful eyes scanned the room, missing
nothing as he lingered in front of the shelves. He looked as
out of place as a cat in a bathtub.

"Hello, Detective," she greeted him.

Homicide detective Matt Morelli glanced up. "Professor Brighton. How's the murder magnet?"

She'd jokingly assigned herself the title after helping to
solve two murders during filming of a reality show at the
historic Marling estate the previous spring.

"I'm fine. What brings you here?"

"I can't stop in and browse the bookshelves?"

"Yes, of course you can. But I've never seen you in here
before. Need something to read on your next stakeout?"

"Maybe. Any recommendations?"

She didn't hesitate. "Ed McBain and Joseph Wambaugh.
For police procedurals, they're your guys." She eyed him.
"Is this an official visit?"

"We've had a few robberies in town. I'm letting shop
owners know and warning them to take extra precautions."

"No first editions missing, I hope." The bookstore had
suffered the loss of two rare volumes the year before, neither of which had been recovered.

"A few items from the hardware store, and fifty bucks
from Brennan's cashbox. Small stuff."

"The bakery next door was robbed?" That was a little
too close to home.

He nodded to someone he knew. "We're asking folks to keep their eyes open and report any suspicious activity."

Phaedra wondered who the town thief might be. Break-ins were unusual, and serious crime was practically un-heard of in the quiet mountain town. "Are the thefts drug related?"

"Doubtful. Laurel Springs isn't exactly a hotbed of oxy users."

"Who, then?"

"Kids, probably. They got in through an overhead air duct. Someone small enough to fit into a narrow space."

Her phone rang. "My sister," Phaedra said with an apol-ogetic smile. "Thanks for the update."

"No problem. Who were those authors you mentioned again?"

"McBain and Wambaugh. First aisle on the right."

"Got it. Thanks."

"Hannah," she said, turning away and speaking into the phone. "How're things in D.C.?"

Her sister worked as a pastry chef at the British em-bassy, where in just two years she'd wowed guests and *Washingtonian* magazine alike with her delicious and cre-ative confections.

"Good. Busy. Which is why I'm calling."

Phaedra unhooked the velvet rope at the bottom of the staircase that led up to her parents' private living quarters above the bookshop. "Hang on." On the other side, she clicked the rope back into place and headed upstairs.

"Is the bookstore crowded?" Hannah asked.

"*So* crowded," she said as she entered the second-floor kitchen and took a seat at the island. "I'm upstairs now, so we can talk in private."

"Hold on." She covered the phone. "Eggs over there, please. Sorry," she told Phaedra. "I have some vacation time coming up. Thought I'd come and spend a few days."

"Great." She stood up to put the kettle on. "When?"

"Not sure. Probably sometime next month."

"Perfect! You can help me with the murder mystery week I'm planning for Wendy."

"Murder mystery week? You're kidding."

"Dead serious." She smiled as Hannah groaned. "Sorry. Pun not intended. Business is down and she's threatening to sell the inn. Again. But I think this time, she means it."

"Sell? She can't! No way. I had my first kiss in the guest cottage."

"What? I never knew that."

"There's a lot you don't know," Hannah said smugly.

"What about Charles? Is he coming with you?"

"No, why would he? We're dating, Phae. We're not joined at the hip."

Surprised by Hannah's reaction, Phaedra put the kettle on to boil. "Sorry. I just thought, since his sister, Karolina, lives nearby, he might want to visit her."

"No idea when he'd find the time. No idea how he even finds his desk at the embassy, to be honest. It's covered in files and paperwork."

"I'm sure things will ease up."

"Maybe." Hannah didn't sound convinced. "I'll get back to you with specific dates. No, Sandrine," she exclaimed to someone nearby, "leave it! The mirror glaze isn't set." With a heavy sigh she returned to the phone. "Sorry, but I've gotta run. Talk soon, okay?"

"Hannah, wait—"

But her sister had already hung up.

One down, sixty-seven more to go, Phaedra thought as she left the costume shop an hour later and headed for the *Laurel Springs Clarion* office.

Relieved that Clark Mullinax, local reporter and not her biggest fan, wasn't at his desk, she placed an ad with Sage, the receptionist.

"When do you expect Clark back?" Phaedra asked.

She shrugged. "Who knows? He's out on a story," Sage added, finger quoting "story."

"Would you let him know I'd like him to do a piece on my aunt Wendy's B and B? We're having a Jane Austen–themed murder mystery week next month."

"Leave me your contact info. *Laurel Springs Clarion*," she said crisply into her headset without missing a beat. "How may I help you?"

"Thanks," Phaedra mouthed, and departed.

I need a list, she decided as she returned to her car. Correction, *lists*. She'd need tea, china, and silverware settings for six, a menu, ingredients . . .

The place settings and china shouldn't be a problem; her mother's pink chintz Spode, inherited from Gram, would do nicely, and Wendy had a linen closet filled with antique lace tablecloths. She'd order the teas online.

That left the menu. Not to mention renting archery equipment, creating a challenging—but not *too* challenging—*Persuasion* quiz, finding suitable prizes for the winner and runner-up, and sourcing a dozen quill pens—

"Hey, Professor."

Phaedra looked up to see a teenaged boy, as tall and skinny as the rake resting on his shoulder. "Billy! Hi. What're you up to today?"

"Earning money. Or trying to." He eyed her. "Does your aunt need any work done at the B and B? Painting? Grass cut? She'll need the yard raked soon. Lots of trees there."

"Those trees," Phaedra agreed, "are both a blessing and a curse." She reached for her handbag. "There's a rusted hinge on the screen door that needs replacing, and a warped floorboard on the side porch. Someone's going to trip if it isn't fixed. What's the going rate?"

He hesitated. "Forty?"

His shirt, she noticed, was worn, and one of his tennis shoe soles had separated from the upper. She peeled off three twenties and handed them over. "Consider this a down payment for keeping the yard raked in the fall. I know I can count on you to do a good job."

"Yes, ma'am." He flushed. "I mean, Professor."

She smiled. "Tell Wendy I sent you. She'll get you started."

"Sure. Great. Thanks." He pocketed the money and took off in the direction of the Laurel Springs Inn, tennis shoe sole slapping against the sidewalk.

Billy's father had died six months earlier. Everyone in town knew of Joe Roberts's struggle with lung cancer. His death had left his wife, Angela, with a teenaged son to raise and a mortgage to pay.

"Well, well," a voice behind her drawled. "If it isn't Phaedra Brighton, doing her good deed for the day."

"Clark." She turned around. "Just helping a neighbor out. You should try it sometime."

He chuckled. "Sorry, but I'm not much of a do-gooder, Prof. I'll leave that to you." He glanced back at the *Clarion* office. "Sage tells me you want a write-up on your aunt's B and B. Something about a murder mystery week?"

After filling him in on the details and securing his promise to cover the event, she rented targets and archery equipment from the hardware store and stopped at Brennan's for one of their chocolate chip cookies.

She deserved a treat.

Phaedra returned home, pleased with her progress and enjoying the warmth of the summer day, and let herself into the carriage house. The rough brick walls and tall arched windows never failed to bring a familiar rush of comfort and pleasure.

Wickham leaped down from his spot along the back of the sofa and greeted her with a deep-throated purr. She knelt to stroke his silken fur and smiled as he pawed at her skirts. "Hungry?" she asked.

He looked at her with blue-eyed reproach.

"Of course you're hungry. What a question."

She went in the kitchen to rustle up some kibble and a

can of tuna, when the phone rang. Phaedra set the dish down for Wickham to pounce on and picked up her phone. "Hello?"

"You'll never guess who I just ran into," her aunt Wendy said without preamble. "Brian Callahan! My old high school flame."

"Didn't you two go steady for three years?"

"Yep. Right up until I left for JMU and he went into his father's real estate business. That was that." She heaved a wistful sigh. "I met Jack, got married, managed the B and B, and . . . well, you know the rest."

Two years ago, Wendy found out Jack not only was cheating on her with the inn's receptionist but also had been skimming money from the books to invest in a "sure thing" that turned out to be anything but.

"Brian must know you're a free agent," Phaedra teased. "News travels fast in Laurel Springs."

"Actually, he's in town for a meeting at Berkshire Hadley and he saw the 'For Sale' sign. He's a real estate broker."

"I see." Phaedra tossed the empty tin of tuna in the recycle bin. "What about the Jane Austen Murder Mystery week? I've already placed an ad in the *Clarion*, and rented archery equipment, and Elaine's providing costumes and a cast for the murder. We agreed—"

"We agreed I'd give you a chance," her aunt assured her, "and I will. But we both know it won't be enough."

"Oh, ye of little faith." Phaedra, her good mood deflating as she sank down onto a seat at the kitchen island, watched Wickham pad to the back door, where he eyed her expectantly. She stood to let him out.

"He asked me out to dinner tonight," Wendy added.

"Are you going?"

"Yes, I'm going. He wants to discuss a possible business opportunity. Speaking of which, what should I wear? I haven't seen Brian since high school." Her voice rose to a wail. "I haven't been on a date in eighteen years!"

After assuring her aunt that she'd stop by and help her choose an outfit, Phaedra ended the call and sighed.

Those teas and quill pens wouldn't order themselves.

In the dining room, she opened her laptop and navigated to the search engine page. Before tackling the tea offerings, she took a quick look at the *New York Times* bestseller list and saw the usual suspects, along with a new entry, *The Duplicitous Duke*, by Harriet Overton.

As an avid reader of Regency romances and cozy mysteries, Phaedra had read several of Ms. Overton's books over the years. And now the Richmond, Virginia, author had found national success.

She took out her planner and jotted a note to provide a few Regency romances and Austen novels in each of the inn's guest rooms, along with a reminder to invite Ms. Overton to attend next month's Austen event. Having the author stay at the inn as a guest would be a real coup.

Publicity, as Elaine often said, was priceless. And Harriet Overton had an active social media presence. If she stayed at the inn, it could lead to future reservations.

Next, she typed "tea, Chinese" in the search bar.

Her aunt's assertion that Brian Callahan wanted to discuss business over dinner that evening left Phaedra unsettled and more than a little apprehensive.

What if Wendy's former flame made her an offer on the bed-and-breakfast? An offer her aunt couldn't refuse?

"Don't borrow trouble," Phaedra muttered, studying the dozens of hits her search turned up. After a few dates and shared memories, her aunt's ex-boyfriend would bid her adieu, and things would return to normal.

At any rate, Phaedra realized as she ordered oolong, Yunnan, and gunpowder tea leaves, the pressure was on. The upcoming Jane Austen Murder Mystery week at the inn had to be unforgettable. Something guests would talk about long afterward.

And she had less than one month to make it happen.

Nope. No pressure at all.

Three

M ore tea, Professor?" the footman inquired.

Phaedra nodded as Dave Kowalski, a member of Elaine's acting troupe, replenished her tea. It was Saturday, the first day of the inn's Jane Austen Murder Mystery week, and she presided over breakfast on the side porch, ensuring the guests seated at the linen-draped table enjoyed their repast of eggs, bacon, sausage, and toast, as well as Hannah's peach scones, still warm from the oven.

"I'd like more, please." Harriet Overton nudged her cup forward and simpered as the footman, clad in frock coat and breeches, filled her cup with fragrant Sencha.

"Thank you," she cooed as he withdrew.

Phaedra suppressed a smile. She suspected Mrs. Overton's admiration had less to do with the young man's tea-pouring abilities than his strapping physique.

"Have you tried the scones, dear?" her husband, Tom, asked. Like the footman, he wore Regency-era clothing. But there any similarity ended. His bony limbs, earnest expression, and eagerness to please his wife rendered him less Mr. Darcy and more Mr. Collins.

"My sister made them," Phaedra told him. "She's a pastry chef at the British embassy in Washington, D.C."

"Please give her my compliments. They're delicious."

Harriet turned to Phaedra. "What's on our itinerary today, Professor Brighton?"

"I'm glad you asked." Phaedra placed a slice of lemon in her tea. "After breakfast, we'll tour the grounds and stroll through the garden, then try our hands at archery. Afterward, we'll have a picnic lunch on the lawn."

"Sounds lovely." Felicity Penrose, a technical editor with a passion for all things Austen, smiled. "I must confess, though, despite living on a farm in Oregon for several years, I'm not much of a sportswoman. Croquet is more my speed."

"Croquet? Hardly a Regency pastime," Harriet sniffed.

Felicity sipped her tea and favored the woman with a bland smile. "What a good thing it is that, unlike games, good manners never go out of style."

Harriet narrowed her eyes but did not reply.

"Say cheese for the camera, everyone."

They looked up as Clark Mullinax, Nikon held aloft, snapped photos of the assembled guests in their colorful Regency attire as they sipped tea and buttered scones.

"Who are you?" Rollo Barron, a journalist writing a feature about the inn for his Richmond newspaper, eyed Mullinax with suspicion. "And why, exactly, are you photographing us?"

"Clark's a reporter for the *Laurel Springs Clarion*," Phaedra said. "He's covering our murder mystery week."

"How exciting." Felicity looked at Clark expectantly. "May we have a copy of the article when it's published?"

"Sure." He lowered his camera. "I'll be prowling around all day. Pretend I'm not even here."

"Such a beautiful house," Elaine said. "All these trees! Hard to believe Main Street is just over there."

The bed-and-breakfast, set back from the road and painted a pale buttermilk yellow, was shaded by pin oaks and surrounded by a white picket fence. The wraparound porch welcomed guests with rockers and wicker furniture. Wisteria climbed a trellis at the far end of the porch, its scent lingering on the air like a sweet memory.

With pursed lips, Harriet surveyed the porch. "Lovely, yes. But the house is Queen Anne. Not Georgian."

Rollo spread a layer of raspberry jam on his toast with a flourish. "The house, dear lady, is a bed-and-breakfast. Surely it can be forgiven if it was built too late. We're here for a Jane Austen event, after all. Not an architectural summit."

Phaedra bit back a grin. Rollo was sociable, inquisitive— one might even say *nosy*—yet she suspected that beneath his lively exterior, he was as sharp and ruthless as a prosecuting attorney.

"Verisimilitude is everything, Mr. Barron," Harriet replied. "As a journalist, you should understand that." She added pointedly, "Or perhaps not."

"Sticks and stones, Mrs. Overton. Sticks and stones."

"Do you two know each other?" Phaedra asked.

"Unfortunately, yes," Harriet said with a curl of her lip. She did not elaborate, nor did Rollo.

Before Phaedra could pursue the matter, a vintage dark green Triumph TR5 pulled up at the curb. She laid her napkin aside and stood as a tall man unfolded himself from the car and paused to survey the house.

"Mark," she called out, her voice warmed equally with surprise and delight. "Come and join us for breakfast."

"I've eaten, thank you. But I wouldn't say no to a cup of tea." His smile smoothed the angles of his face and tempered the intensity of his gaze.

"Yes, do join us," Harriet said. Her eyes devoured him as if he were a scone topped with Devonshire cream. "How charming he is," she observed. "Such a handsome young man. And that British accent!"

Phaedra poured him a cup of tea as he slid a backpack strap over his shoulder and made his way up the walk to the porch. "Welcome, Professor."

"Thank you," he said as she handed him tea. "For this. And for inviting me."

She turned to the others. "This is Mark Selden. Like me, he's a professor at Somerset University. He's not much of an Austen fan. But he's a noted Shakespearean scholar."

There was a flurry of welcome as Phaedra introduced him to each of them in turn.

"How delightful!" Harriet pressed a dimpled hand to her throat. "We must endeavor to improve your opinion of Miss Austen's work. With such an impressive background, Professor Selden, I do hope you'll consider taking part in our planned murder mystery theatrical."

"I'm afraid not," he replied. "My participation will be limited to observing. I'm here to work. Publish or perish is the byword for us academics, you know."

"I admire your devotion." Harriet's face brightened. "You'll join us for dinner, at least, I hope?"

"I'll make every effort."

"It seems we have something in common, Mr. Selden," Elaine said. "I'm here to manage and mount the amateur theatrical. I'm not quite a guest, either."

"You most certainly are," Phaedra protested. "Even though you're not staying with us."

Elaine turned back to Mark with a grin. "Like I said, hired help. Now, if you'll all excuse me, I need to get the costumes ready for our murder mystery rehearsal on Wednesday night."

The thwack of arrows hitting their targets echoed across the back lawn that afternoon as the first annual Jane Austen archery contest officially got underway.

"Whoever hits the most bull's-eyes," Phaedra announced, "wins a free weekend at the inn." There was a smattering of enthusiastic applause as Dave the footman handed out bows and quivers of arrows to each guest.

As the first round of shots was fired, he chased after

wayward arrows while Eve, his wife, carried plates and silverware to a cloth-draped table in the shade of an oak. When he returned, the archers resumed shooting.

Everyone, Phaedra noticed, but Felicity Penrose. She sat alone at the table.

"Not participating, Ms. Penrose?"

"Felicity, please." She shook her head. "As I said, I'm really not a sportswoman. And without my glasses, I'm more likely to hit a guest than a target."

Phaedra joined her at the table as Clark, camera in hand, wandered up.

"Time for refreshments?" he inquired hopefully.

"Have you taken any photos?" Phaedra asked him. "You're here to work, if you recall."

He gave her a wounded look. "You won't begrudge a hardworking journalist a crust of bread, surely?"

"Let me see what you've got on film first."

With a sigh, he sat down and began to scroll through the accumulated digital photos. "Here you go. You have first approval on the photos, of course," he added.

She had to admit that Clark had captured the whimsy of modern men and women dressed in Regency garb. Her favorite was a photo of Harriet traipsing across the lawn, skirts billowing and one hand on her bonnet, juxtaposed against a telephone pole in the background.

"These are good. Really good."

"Don't sound so surprised." He took the camera back as Eve poured them each a cup of black currant tea. "May I?"

"Help yourself," Phaedra said. "You've earned it."

She stood and returned to the archery range. Rollo, with his short stature and distain for all things athletic, couldn't hit the broad side of a barn, but laughed good-naturedly as his shots went afield. "No threat to Robin Hood here," he observed.

Harriet's husband, Tom, on the other hand, acquitted himself well. He released each arrow expertly and sent them sailing straight into the center of the target.

"Good job," Phaedra said as he hit another bull's-eye. She couldn't quite keep a note of surprise from her voice.

"I was on the archery team in college."

"Oh, don't boast, Tom," Harriet scolded him. "No one cares about your college glory days."

His face fell. "Of course not. Sorry, dear."

As he turned away and lifted his bow to fit the arrow to the bowstring, Wendy shouted across the lawn.

"Stop! Everyone, please, stop at once!"

Four

Startled, Phaedra saw her aunt approaching, a man and a woman in her wake. "Is everything all right?"

"Fine," Wendy called back. "But I don't want my new arrivals getting shot on their way to the guesthouse."

"Of course." Phaedra signaled for everyone to hold off on firing their arrows.

A man, solidly built and just this side of stocky, approached and thrust out his hand. "Brian Callahan." He had a genial face and a head of cropped fair hair. "As long as no one mistakes us for targets, we're good."

"Phaedra Brighton." Wendy's former flame had blue eyes and an affable smile as he took her hand firmly in his. "Are you joining our little house party?"

"I'm afraid not. I'll be in the guesthouse. Working."

A twentysomething brunette in a pencil skirt and silk blouse trailed behind him, her high heels sinking into the grass, a portfolio in one hand and a mutinous expression on her heart-shaped face.

"This is Victoria Sutton, my administrative assistant," he said. "I couldn't get a thing done without Tory." He winked at the young woman. "Isn't that so, Tory?"

She didn't answer.

"She'll be staying in the main house," he added. "But we have some business to take care of first."

"I hope it doesn't take long," Tory grumbled. "I'm starving. And I need to unpack." Her glance strayed to Dave, leaning over to pick up an arrow in his servant's livery. "At least the scenery's nice." She smiled as he straightened and caught her studying him.

He reddened slightly and turned away. His wife, Eve, however, lasered a glare of blue-eyed fury on Tory.

Harriet approached. "Harriet Overton. Lovely to meet you both." She turned to Brian. "And you are?"

"Brian. This is Tory, my administrative assistant."

Harriet nodded and turned back to Callahan with a pensive frown. "You look familiar. Have we met?"

"If we had, I'm sure I would've remembered."

Phaedra indicated the cloth-covered table under the tree. "We're having tea soon. Why don't you both join us?"

"Can't, I'm afraid," Brian said. "Work to do."

"Will we see you at dinner?" Wendy asked.

"Wouldn't miss it." He favored her with a roguish grin. "See you then, doodlebug. Come along, Tory."

With a put-upon sigh, she followed Callahan.

"I'm sure I know you," Harriet called after him. "I never forget a face."

He gave her a genial but dismissive wave as the two headed to the guesthouse, a gray-shingled cottage on the property's far edge. Salvia and begonias filled the window boxes with bright splashes of red and purple. Slate steps led up to a flagstone patio outside the front door.

"Doodlebug?" Phaedra echoed as Harriet left to join the others.

"That was Brian's nickname for me in high school. I drove a VW."

With a nod from Phaedra, the archery contest resumed. Wendy followed her back to the table. "We have a problem."

"We do?"

"Harriet brought her cat. I told her there's a 'no pets' policy. I also told her, politely but firmly, that she needs to board the cat for the week or leave."

"And yet she's still here. And the cat, too, I assume."

"She raised such a ruckus that I gave in."

"I think that's her standard operating procedure."

"If it were up to me, I'd throw her out, cat and caboodle. But Bella's an Instagram star, if you can believe it, with ten thousand followers."

"I'm guessing Bella is the cat."

Her aunt nodded. "Should I let her stay?"

"Unless she scratches the furniture or wanders the halls, I don't see a problem."

"Harriet?" Wendy raised her brow. "I'm sure she's house-trained."

"Oh dear," Mrs. Overton exclaimed, all aflutter as Wendy and Phaedra returned. "My arrow's gone astray."

"I'll go and fetch it," Dave said.

"No, no, I'll get it. I could do with the exercise." She handed Tom her bow, batted her lashes at Dave, and marched off toward the guesthouse.

As Wendy returned to the house, Phaedra took a seat at the table. Eve set out a three-tiered silver stand laden with a tempting array of nibbles.

"Sandwiches or cake, ladies?" she inquired.

"Nothing for me." Felicity rose. "If you'll excuse me, I need a little nap. The trip tired me out."

"Wait, please," Phaedra said. "You forgot your card."

"My card?"

"Elaine's given us each a role to play for the week." Phaedra retrieved a small envelope from Felicity's place and handed it over. "I'm Elizabeth Elliot, Sir Walter's oldest daughter. Open yours and tell us who you are."

"Very well." She slid a finger under the flap and withdrew a cream-colored card. "Oh! I'm Anne Elliot."

"The heroine of *Persuasion*," Phaedra said approvingly.
"And the love of Captain Frederick Wentworth's life.
Lucky you."

Felicity smiled faintly. "How nice."

As she departed, Phaedra couldn't help but wonder at
her marked lack of enthusiasm. For heaven's sake, she had
a lead role. Perhaps she didn't like being in the spotlight.

Twenty minutes later, as Clark reappeared with his camera, Dave announced, "We have a winner."

"Not me." Rollo shrugged. "I only hit the target once."

"The winning archer," Dave said, pausing as his glance
flicked over their avid faces, "is Mrs. Harriet Overton."

"I won!" she crowed, and accepted the trophy, a statuette
of Emma Woodhouse, bow in hand and arrow drawn back,
as Clark snapped her photo. "You may be an expert marks-
man, Tom, but *I* won the contest. Not you."

For a moment so brief Phaedra wondered if she'd
imagined it, a curdled expression darkened his face before he managed a smile. "Well done! Congratulations,
dearest."

As Harriet marched toward them, trophy in hand and
her husband in tow, Eve's gaze narrowed.

"Not a fan?" Phaedra asked.

"Of her books? Never read one." Eve set a plate down
with a thump. "She's certainly a flirt. Tory, too."

"I wouldn't worry. Dave's not flirting back."

"He'd better not." Eve laid a protective hand on her
stomach, slightly rounded under the black servant's dress.
"He's already taken."

A smile warmed Phaedra's face. "Congratulations."
She indicated the heavy silver tray Eve had carried out. "I
hope the servant role isn't proving too much for you."

"Not at all. I run every morning and keep myself in
good shape. And it's only for a few days." She yawned.
"Sorry. I don't sleep very well lately."

"If you'd like a quieter room, we can move you—"

"No, our room is perfect. We have it until Monday. Then it's back to our apartment."

"Oh? Why's that?" Phaedra asked. Wendy wasn't charging the pair since they were working the event and acting in Wednesday night's planned rehearsal.

"Someone's reserved it. Newlyweds, your aunt said."

"How delightful!" Harriet thrust her trophy at Tom and joined them, surveying the tiered stand of goodies.

"I'm surprised she took her attention off my husband long enough to notice the food," Eve muttered.

Harriet took her seat and studied the offerings with a covetous eye. "It all looks delicious. Where to begin?"

"Perhaps a sandwich," Eve suggested. "We have cress and egg, cucumber, roast beef with pimento cheese, and mini chicken salad croissants with . . . pecans—"

She turned a waxy shade of pale.

"Are you unwell?" Harriet inquired.

"I'm fine," Eve mumbled. "Excuse me." She bolted back to the house.

Harriet shrugged and chose a croissant as the others joined them. "Find your places, please," Phaedra invited. "It's time to get on with our planned murder mystery."

"What's this?" Rollo took his seat and picked up a small envelope beside his plate.

"There's an envelope at each place setting," Elaine explained, "with a name inside. You'll each assume a role as a character from Jane Austen's novel *Persuasion*."

Harriet reached for hers. "I deserve a starring role."

"Every role is important. One of you is the victim, and one the murderer. The killer's identity won't be revealed until the cleverest among you uncovers the clues and correctly guesses the guilty party."

"How are we to do that?" Tom asked.

"You may ask three questions of each guest," Elaine answered. "I'd suggest you choose your questions wisely and make note of the answers."

"What a pity that handsome Shakespearean scholar isn't taking part in our theatrical," Harriet said.

"Professor Selden," Phaedra said, "is determined to work on his monograph all week."

"What a waste." Harriet heaved a bosomy sigh. "He'd make an excellent Captain Wentworth."

"Yoo-hoo! Is there room for one more at the table?"

Victoria Sutton, high heels clasped in one hand, left the guesthouse to join them. "I'm so hungry, even those little lettuce sandwiches look good."

"They're watercress," Phaedra corrected her.

"Oh." She frowned. "Are they gluten-free?"

"Yes." Thank goodness Chef Armand had prepared options for those with dietary restrictions.

"Perfect." Tory took a seat, helped herself to an egg-and-cress sandwich, and dug in.

Harriet tore her envelope open and regarded it with a frown. "Lady Russell," she said. "Anne Elliot's godmother." She turned to Elaine. "I deserve a bigger role, don't you agree? Anne Elliot, for instance?"

"'Bigger' being the operative word," Tory muttered.

"Sorry, but that role is Felicity's," Elaine said.

"Then I'll switch roles with her."

"Please don't." Exasperation flickered over Elaine's face. "It's a game, Harriet, not a Broadway production."

"But you're wasting my theatrical qualifications."

"*You* were in the theater?" Tory plainly didn't buy it.

"Not to brag, but yes, in my younger days I was a professional actress. I once trod the boards."

"I hope the boards were sturdy," Tory mumbled. Rollo turned his snort of laughter into a cough.

Harriet glared at him. "And who, Ms. Sutton," she asked with venomous sweetness, "are you to be?"

"To be?" Tory echoed blankly.

"Or not to be," Rollo quipped. "That *is* the question."

"Your envelope," Harriet prodded. "Open it and tell us which character from *Persuasion* you'll be playing."

"I'm here to work. I don't have time to play games."

"You have to join in. We all do. Open your envelope."

With a long-suffering sigh, Tory complied. "Louisa Musgrove." She tossed the card aside. "Whoever she is."

"Louisa is Charles Musgrove's younger sister. She's young and flighty and foolish." Harriet smirked. "Perfect casting, if you ask me."

"No one did," Tory retorted.

"Louisa is injured," Phaedra explained, "when she jumps down from the harbor wall in Lyme Regis."

"Why would she do that?"

"Because she had her eye on Captain Wentworth," Harriet said. "She counted on him to catch her."

"And did he? Catch her, I mean?"

"The first time, yes."

"And the second time?" Tory prompted.

"She jumped too quickly and caught Wentworth off guard," Phaedra said. "She fell to the pavement."

Tory sucked in a breath. "Ouch."

"Ouch, indeed." Rollo grimaced. "Speaking of pain," he added as he turned to Harriet, "I finished reviewing your latest book. Not your best. Two and a half stars from me."

She said nothing but tightened her grip on her teacup.

"You can read the review in the Sunday *Times-Dispatch* tomorrow. I've already turned it in. Or I can share it with everyone now, if you like."

"Can I stop you?" she snapped.

"'Harriet Overton, at her mediocre best.'" He took a sip of tea. "You really did phone it in this time."

"You have a nerve, you scurrilous little cretin—" Aware of everyone's eyes on her, Harriet swallowed her fury.

"Sorry, Harriet, but the only way this book is flying off the shelves is if your readers throw it off."

"Wow. That's cold," Tory said. "Even for you."

He shrugged. "That's the power of the press."

"Now, see here, Mr. Barron," Tom Overton sputtered. "Your behavior toward my wife is most unchivalrous."

"Haven't you heard, Mr. Overton? Chivalry is dead."

"I'd like to see *you* dead," Harriet snapped.

Rollo shrugged. "You just might get your wish, if I end up as the fictional murder victim in our little Austen theatrical. As for me, I sincerely hope the role goes to you, dear lady. You so richly deserve it."

With that, Rollo excused himself, stood, and strode back to the house.

Five

"What is it you do, Mr. Callahan?" Harriet asked at dinner that evening.

Brian, a thin slice of rare roast beef halfway to his lips, paused. "I'm in real estate."

"Yes, of course." Her face cleared. "No wonder you look familiar. I've seen your photo on dozens of 'For Sale' signs."

His gaze slid away. "I'm a broker these days."

"And a very good one, too," Tory chimed in.

"I have no doubt." Harriet turned back to Brian. "Do you know, Mr. Callahan," she confided, "I once listed a house with your company, Callahan Real Estate. You won't remember, I'm sure. It was years ago, but I distinctly remember having the pleasure of meeting your—"

Brian let out an oath as he knocked his wineglass over, spilling purple-red Malbec across the tablecloth. He pushed his chair back and grabbed his napkin.

"Oh, dear." Harriet regarded the rapidly spreading stain in dismay. "It didn't get on your clothes, I hope?"

"No." He dabbed at a spot on his tie. "Most of it landed on the tablecloth, I'm afraid."

"It's washable," Phaedra reassured him. "We can launder your shirt if you wish."

"I'm good. Just embarrassed." He chuckled. "That's what happens when someone like me sits down to a fancy dinner."

Conversation resumed and Phaedra studied Callahan. Despite his words, he didn't strike her as the ham-fisted type. Far from it.

"Professor Brighton?" Dave prompted. "More wine?"

She nodded. "Yes, please."

As he refilled her glass, Brian gave her a roguish grin across the table. Maybe she should cut him some slack.

After all, everyone had an off night now and then.

After dinner, Phaedra followed the clatter of pots and pans through the swinging door and into the kitchen to convey her compliments to Chef Armand.

He dismissed her thanks with a curt nod and barked, "Service, s'il vous plaît. Dessert is plated and ready."

Wendy placed a selection of individual meringues filled with lemon curd and topped with fresh berries on a tray and handed it to Dave. "Take these out, please. I'll bring the coffee in a moment."

As Armand followed Dave out to greet the diners, Wendy collapsed into a chair. "What a day! I'm exhausted."

Phaedra poured her a cup of coffee. "At least it's nearly over. In the meantime, this'll help."

"Thanks." She took a rejuvenating sip and studied her niece. "What do you think of our guests so far?"

"Let's see. Miss Penrose is antisocial, Rollo's a stitch, Tory's a flirt, Brian's charming and very suave—"

"Until he knocked his wineglass over," Wendy tutted. "Malbec *everywhere*."

"—Tom's terrified of displeasing his wife, and Harriet is an absolute stickler for the Austen canon."

"I'd like to stick *her* in a cannon," Wendy said darkly. "All she does is complain and find fault."

Phaedra shrugged. "She's a typical Austen fan. 'Verisimilitude is everything.'"

"I can't even pronounce 'verisimilitude.'"

The kitchen door swung open and Eve appeared. "The guests are asking for their coffee, Ms. P."

"I'll be right there." With a sigh, Wendy stood and picked up the tray. "Time to head back into the lion's den."

Phaedra stood as well. "I think I'll slip over to the carriage house. I need to check my email and return a few phone messages. And let Wickham out," she added.

Wendy paused at the door. "Be sure you're back in time for sherry in the drawing room at eight."

"Wouldn't miss it. See you then."

"One more glass, Professor?" Mark Selden asked Phaedra later that evening.

He'd joined them in the drawing room for sherry following dinner, after working on his monograph all day. Everyone sipped a glass or two of amontillado, conversing and nibbling on almonds roasted with sea salt and rosemary before disappearing upstairs to their rooms for the night.

Phaedra started to refuse; sherry was an acquired taste that she'd never acquired a taste for. But with the last of the guests gone upstairs, she deserved—no, needed—a nightcap before heading back to the carriage house for a bath and bed.

"Very well." She held out her glass, and he topped it with more of the amber liquid. "But first I need to go next door and let Wickham out. Will you excuse me?"

"Only if you promise to come right back."

"If I'm not back in ten minutes, you can send out a search party."

As she made her way through the darkened yard and

across the dewy grass, Phaedra paused to breathe in the cool night air. The humidity had dissipated, and a scattering of stars winked overheard. The pungent scent of wild onions teased the air.

She'd just arrived at her back kitchen door when a flash of something pale and diaphanous caught her eye.

Phaedra paused to study the inn's adjoining grounds, encased now in deep shadows. What had she seen? Her gaze searched the still, silent garden and the sloping expanse of lawn, but nothing out of the ordinary presented itself.

She shrugged and moved to unlock the door when she heard the muted crunch of footsteps on gravel and a low, throaty giggle.

What in the world?

Soundlessly she crept to the edge of her terrace and peered into the darkness. Her gaze came to rest on the guesthouse on the far side of the lawn.

The door creaked open. But the interior lights were off, and she couldn't discern who the visitor was, only that she was female. She slipped inside, the door closed, and all was still, save for the crickets.

Aunt Wendy, Phaedra decided, and bit back a smile. She'd worn a pale green dress during drinks in the drawing room, and Brian could scarcely keep his eyes away from her.

She glanced at the luminous dial of her watch. It seemed her aunt had decided to pay a late visit to her old flame, Brian.

"Good for you," Phaedra murmured. After a bitter divorce and the stress of keeping the inn afloat, Wendy deserved to grab whatever happiness she found . . . even if she didn't exactly approve of her aunt's erstwhile suitor.

She opened the kitchen door. Wickham shot straight out and into the yard and, having done his business and decided there was nothing of interest in the hedges, returned inside almost at once.

She refilled his water dish and he tolerated a ruffle of his ears. "I'll see you later, Wicks."

Suit yourself, his attitude of supreme indifference said. *As for me, I'm heading for bed. Don't make too much noise when you come back.*

"I was just about to send out that search party," Mark observed as she returned to the inn's drawing room a short time later. "Thought you weren't coming back."

"Sorry. I let Wickham out and I got distracted."

"Oh? By what?"

"Nothing," Phaedra said lightly. "Seeing ghosts in the shadows." She didn't mention her aunt's visit to the guesthouse. Wendy's fling with Brian was a private matter, after all.

He took her cue and changed the subject. "Tell me, what do you think of Harriet Overton thus far?"

"Very demanding. But very knowledgeable about all things Austen."

"I don't think your aunt Wendy is a fan."

"I don't think anyone is a fan." She frowned. "Did you notice that Elaine let Harriet have Felicity's role as Anne Elliot? Didn't you find it odd?"

"I did, a bit. But Felicity didn't seem to mind. And Elaine could hardly refuse. Not after Harriet badgered her about it all evening."

"Still, I'm surprised Elaine gave in so easily. She's normally very strong-minded. And stubborn."

"Sounds like someone else I know."

Phaedra's smile was swallowed by a yawn. She was too tired to parry his verbal thrust.

Mark set his glass aside. "You look knackered, Professor."

"Knackered?"

"Done in. Exhausted."

"Why do you do that?" she asked. "Use different words for the same thing. It's confusing. And so . . . British."

"But I am British." A smile warmed his words. "Surely I can be forgiven for that."

"I'll think about it." She regarded him sleepily. "Aren't you tired?"

"I often stay up late," he said. "Unless I'm teaching an early class. I get my best work done then."

She nodded and let her eyelids, suddenly so heavy, close. Just for a moment.

Later, she had a vague recollection of gentle hands arranging a velvet throw pillow behind her head, lifting her feet to the sofa, and draping a blanket over her as a quiet voice wished her a good night.

Then exhaustion claimed her, and she slept.

The smell of bacon lured Phaedra awake the next morning. She found herself lying on the parlor sofa beneath a blanket with no recollection as to how, or why, she was there. The events of the night before rushed back, and she sat up abruptly.

She smoothed her skirts and hair and left before the first guests came downstairs looking for their breakfast.

When she arrived in the kitchen, feeling disheveled, she halted in the doorway. Professor Selden stood at the stove, frying bacon.

"Good morning," Mark said cheerfully. "You missed the excitement."

She eyed him with misgivings. "What excitement?"

"The chef's done a runner, so I'm filling the breach. Builders, bangers, and egg-and-toast soldiers, on the way."

She frowned. "In English, please?"

"Armand's gone. I took it upon myself to assume breakfast duty." He removed the bacon to drain on a layer of paper towels. "Tea, sausages, and soft-boiled eggs with toast."

"That sounds very . . . bracing," Phaedra said. "Thank you. But why has Armand left? Has he gone to the grocery store? Are we out of eggs? Is he coming back?"

"No. Not until, and this is a direct quote translated from the French, 'Hell freezes over.' End quote."

"Oh no." Phaedra sank onto a chair at the table.

"Evidently Mrs. Overton insulted his meringues as well as his knife skills after dinner last night. I came in for a coffee and tried to persuade him to stay, but he packed up his knife roll along with his pride and slammed out the door."

"What'll I do?" Phaedra groaned. "We need a chef!"

"What about Hannah?" he asked. "Surely she can pinch-hit until you find another chef."

"She could," Phaedra agreed, "if she was still here." She rose and went to the fridge to retrieve a tray of scones waiting to be baked.

"A problem cropped up at the embassy," she told him as she set the oven to preheat, "and Hannah had to catch a flight back to D.C."

Mark scratched his chin. "I make a decent breakfast," he said doubtfully, "and I can manage the odd sandwich or cheese toastie, but as for the rest . . ."

Before Phaedra could answer, before she'd even formed a coherent thought, a high-pierced shriek echoed across the lawn and shattered the tranquil late-summer morning.

She dropped the tray of scones to the counter with a clatter as another scream pierced the stillness. Racing to the kitchen door, she flung it open.

The garden. The scream had come from the garden.

Leaving Mark and the warm, fragrant kitchen behind, Phaedra plunged out into the chilly air and raced down the path, long skirts flying, until she reached the kitchen garden. Her heart pumped wildly as her gaze swept the neatly spaced rows of herbs and marigolds.

Normally, she'd pause to breathe in the heady scents of thyme, basil, lavender, and oregano, or listen to the splash of water in the stone fountain nearby. But today, her eyes went straight to the herbaceous border.

Someone lay faceup in the rosemary. Which, had one of the guests imbibed too much sherry the previous evening and passed out, wouldn't have been quite so alarming.

But this particular guest had an arrow in her chest.

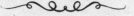

Six

It's an arrow." Eve, who'd screamed, peered between her fingers at the body.

"Actually, it's a crossbow quarrel." Phaedra couldn't take her eyes away from the horrifying sight.

Eve lowered her hands. "Is she—"

"Dead?" Phaedra met her gaze. "Yes. I'm afraid she must be."

"It's her, isn't it?" Eve's shocked blue gaze returned to the victim. "It's that author lady."

Phaedra knelt down. "Yes. It's Harriet Overton." The fresh, piney scent of rosemary reached her. She summoned the courage to press three unsteady fingers to the woman's neck and felt . . . nothing. "She's dead. There's no pulse. We need to call the police."

"On it." Eve fumbled in a pocket for her phone and pressed it to her ear.

"What's happened?" Mark asked as he joined them.

In all the excitement, Phaedra had forgotten he'd been in the kitchen when Eve screamed. "Mrs. Overton," she said as she straightened on unsteady legs. "She's dead. Eve found her just now. Someone . . . someone's shot her in the chest with a crossbow."

"Good God." He paled as he saw the woman lying there. "Have the police been called?"

"Yes, I've just called them," Eve told him. "I was on my morning run when I found her."

"She's surrounded by rosemary," Mark noted as he studied the herbaceous border planted along the base of the garden wall, and knelt down, frowning. "'There's rosemary, that's for remembrance; pray, love, remember . . .'"

"Ophelia's soliloquy," Eve murmured. "From *Hamlet*."

"Perhaps whoever did this meant to send a message," Phaedra said slowly. "'Pray, love, remember.' But remember what, exactly?"

"It's a common enough quote," Mark said. "It might mean something. Or nothing."

As she gazed at Harriet's body, scarcely believing someone had murdered the poor woman, Phaedra noticed ripples in the fabric. Something marred the smooth silken drape of the author's gown over one generously sized hip. Something crumpled. What was it?

She knelt down once again. The corner of what appeared to be a sheet of paper was visible through a small slit in the side seam. Being careful not to disturb the body, she reached in with two gloved fingers and eased it out.

"I didn't realize Regency gowns had pockets," Mark said.

"They didn't. Don't." Phaedra's reply was distracted as she turned the folded sheet over. "But a woman sometimes tied a 'loose pocket' at her waist, with an opening at one side of the gown for access. The pocket eventually became the reticule. Which is basically a loose pocket carried in one's hand."

"Like that tiny drawstring bag you carry."

She nodded and focused her attention on the crumpled paper she held. She smoothed it and carefully unfolded a single page.

"What is it?" Eve asked, edging closer.

"It's a note, written in calligraphy. Signed 'an ardent admirer.'" She stood and met Mark's eyes. "It asks Harriet to meet in the kitchen garden at midnight."

"Is it from the murderer?" Eve's eyes grew even wider, if such were possible.

"Most likely, yes."

Mark frowned. "I'm surprised whoever killed Harriet didn't take the note. Rather careless on their part."

"Perhaps she slipped it into the loose pocket before she came to the garden," Phaedra surmised. "If so, the killer may not have noticed it. It was dark, after all, and easily overlooked."

"What's easily overlooked?"

The question drew Phaedra's attention to the graveled garden path. "Detective Morelli."

"Professor Brighton," he said as he joined them. "Why am I not surprised?" His eyes gave nothing away as he knelt beside Harriet's corpse. "Who's the victim?"

"Harriet Overton," she said. "She was a guest at the inn."

"When did you last see her alive?"

Phaedra frowned. "Nine thirty or so last night. We all had a glass of sherry before the guests retired."

"Did you find the body?"

"No, I did," Eve said, and stepped forward, hugging her arms against the morning chill.

If Morelli noticed her shiny fall of straight blond hair or anxious blue eyes, he gave no sign. "And you are?"

"Eve Kowalski. I'm with the Laurel Springs Players."

He rose and flipped his notepad open to jot down her name. "In what capacity?"

"I'm Mary Musgrove."

He paused. "I thought your name was Eve."

"It is. But I'm acting the part of Mary Musgrove from *Persuasion*. She was a bit of a hypochondriac," she added, her nerves inducing her to chatter. "I'm also a server. My husband, Dave, is Captain Wentworth."

Plainly out of his Austen depth, Morelli grunted. "How did you discover the body?"

"I woke early and went for a run. Dave—my husband—was still sleeping."

"Do you normally take the same route every day?"

She hesitated. "Normally, no. I detoured through the kitchen garden," she added, "on a whim."

"A whim."

"Yes. It's just . . . I love the scent of rosemary and thyme. Mint, too. It's invigorating."

"And that's why you decided to run through the kitchen garden." Skepticism flickered in his eyes.

She nodded. "And that's when . . ." She drew her sweater closer. "When I found Mrs. Overton."

"We heard Eve scream," Phaedra chimed in, glancing at Mark, "and ran out to see what was wrong."

Morelli eyed Mark. "Who are you?"

"Mark Selden. I'm an English professor on the faculty at Somerset University. And a guest."

"What were you both doing up so early?"

"I was getting the morning tea ready," Phaedra replied. "Warming the teapots, filling the kettle, and baking scones for our guests. Mark was making breakfast."

"The professor doubles as a chef?" Disbelief was plain on the detective's face.

"No," Mark said, irritation sharpening the word. "Chef Armand quit abruptly early this morning and left Phaedra in the lurch. I stepped in to help put breakfast together."

"Why'd he take off? Trouble in the kitchen?"

Mark glanced at the body. "Mrs. Overton insulted his meringues last night, as well as his knife skills. Which, for any chef, is tantamount to a slap in the face."

"So, he was angry at the victim."

"Furious," Mark confirmed.

Phaedra frowned at Morelli. "You don't honestly think Chef Armand killed Harriet, do you? That's preposterous."

"Was he on the premises last night?"

"Well, yes, he has a bedroom off the kitchen, but—"

"Then he's a suspect." He turned to Mark with his pen poised. "What time did the chef enter the kitchen?"

"Very early, half past five or so. I came down for a cup of coffee."

"And he told you he was quitting and left?"

"That's right."

"Did he seem surprised to see you? Startled?"

Mark frowned. "No, not really. But it was plain he wasn't in the mood for a chat, either."

The detective turned his attention to Phaedra. "Any idea where the crossbow came from, Professor?"

"None. We had archery practice yesterday afternoon, on the back lawn. But everyone used a bow and arrow." Her brow puckered. "I have no idea where the crossbow came from. Or the quarrel." Her gaze went involuntarily to the shaft buried in Harriet's chest.

"What's that in your hand?" Morelli, ever alert, eyed the folded paper she clutched against her skirts.

She held it out to him. "I found it on the body just before you arrived. And before you take me to task," she added, seeing anger darken his already dark eyes, "I saw the paper sticking out of a side pocket. When I slid it out, I didn't disturb the body. I'm wearing a pair of—"

"Gloves." He snapped on a pair of blue latex gloves and snatched the note. "Nevertheless, you shouldn't have touched it, Professor. This is a crime scene. Understood?"

She nodded mutely.

The garden was quickly cordoned off as the coroner and other members of the crime scene team arrived.

"You're both free to go," Detective Morelli informed Eve and Mark. "But don't leave the grounds. You," he added as Phaedra turned to leave, "stay. I have a few questions."

Of course he did.

"Will you be all right, Phaedra?" Mark asked, and glanced at Morelli. "Shall I stay?"

"No, I'm fine. Go. I'm sure my aunt will need help getting breakfast on the table."

"Right." With a curt nod to the detective, he left.

She watched him leave and envied him his freedom. "How can I help you?" she asked, turning to Morelli, who was studying the note with a frown.

"You said this paper was on Harriet Overton's person?"

"Yes, tucked in a pocket tied at her waist. I noticed her skirt was ridged along one hip. I eased it out because I thought it might be important."

"Could be." He lowered the page. "Which is why you should've left it alone."

She waited, refusing to defend her actions. She'd done what she'd done, and it was too late for apologies.

"But at least it won't be overlooked," Morelli added grudgingly, and slid the note into an evidence bag. "So, thanks for that."

It was the closest she'd get to an apology from him and they both knew it.

"Did you notice anything last night?" he asked. "Anything unusual?"

Phaedra recalled the sound of throaty laughter and the figure she'd spied outside the guesthouse. *Was* it her aunt Wendy she'd seen? Had she met Brian for an assignation . . . or had she, perhaps, seen the murderer?

"Professor?" he prompted.

As much as she wanted to say, "No, nothing," and change the subject, she couldn't. Withholding information in a murder investigation was a criminal offense.

"I thought I saw someone on the back lawn of the inn last night," she admitted. "When I let Wickham out. But I can't be sure. It was dark, and the yard was in shadow."

"Was the figure male? Female? Where exactly did you see it?"

"Near the guesthouse. I saw a woman. Or thought I did. As I said, it was dark, and it was only a glimpse. I probably imagined it."

"Is anyone staying in the guesthouse at the moment?"

"Yes. Brian Callahan. He's a real estate broker and an old friend of my aunt Wendy's."

He noted the name and tucked the pad back into his pocket. "I'll question Mr. Callahan."

His attention returned to Harriet Overton and to the coroner who knelt beside her body.

"Is there anything else?" she inquired.

"I need a guest list. We'll want to interview everyone. And I'll need the chef's contact information."

"Of course."

"Tell me about Harriet Overton. She was a guest here?"

She nodded and told him about the immersive Jane Austen Murder Mystery week. "Harriet is . . . was," she corrected herself, "a popular Regency romance author."

"She's also a great big pain in the patootie."

They looked up as Wendy marched toward them, an oven mitt on one hand. "Wendy Prescott," she informed Morelli before he could ask. "I own the inn. What's going on? Why are the police here?" She turned to Phaedra. "Where's Chef Armand? Has he absconded with the silver?"

She caught sight of the yellow crime scene tape first, the body of Harriet Overton second. All the color fled her face and she dropped the oven mitt on the gravel. "Sweet baby in the manger . . . is Harriet *dead*?"

"I'm afraid so." Phaedra shot her a warning look and willed her not to say anything further.

"Someone—someone shot her? With a bow and arrow?"

"A crossbow." Detective Morelli looked up as the county coroner straightened from his position kneeling beside Harriet's body and ambled toward them.

"She's dead," he confirmed.

"How long?"

"Roughly five or six hours."

"So, time of death was midnight to one a.m.?"

The coroner nodded. "Twelve thirty. That's what I put

on the death certificate. The pathologist may be able to pin it down more precisely in the lab."

"Thanks." He turned back to Wendy. "You stated that Mrs. Overton was difficult, Ms. Prescott. How so?"

Wendy lifted her pale face to his. "She . . . she was a complainer, and a stickler for authenticity." Warming to her subject, she added, "The inn wasn't Georgian. The food wasn't proper Regency-era food. The other guests didn't take the immersive nature of the event seriously enough."

"In what way?"

"Tory Sutton refused to surrender her cell phone. Said she needed it for work. Felicity wouldn't participate in the archery competition. And Rollo declined to wear a costume."

Morelli eyed her in puzzlement. "Costume?"

"It's an immersive murder mystery week," Phaedra explained. "Everyone dresses as a character from Austen's novel *Persuasion*. There are no cell phones, and no communication with the outside world."

"Did Mrs. Overton get along with everyone? Any conflicts?"

"She didn't get along with anyone," Wendy said flatly.

"She had a strong personality," Phaedra interjected, and cast her aunt a warning glance. "She was very . . . opinionated."

"Opinionated?" Wendy crossed her arms against her chest and let out a huff. "That's putting it mildly. I pity her poor husband," she added, "putting up with her constant criticism—" She clapped a hand to her mouth. "Oh, my goodness! Her husband! Someone has to tell poor Tom that his wife is—is—"

"Is what?" Tom asked as he wandered down the path to join them, a smile on his face and a cup of tea in hand. "What's my dearest Harriet done now?"

Seven

Maybe we should scrap the murder mystery," Elaine said, her words sober. "Under the circumstances."

It was midmorning, and Phaedra and Elaine sat at the kitchen table as James, Wendy's newly hired chef, began preparations for lunch.

"Tom's devastated," Elaine added, "and everyone's upset. And with the police questioning the guests—"

"Suspects," Phaedra said.

"Suspects, how can we go forward with—" She drew in a shaky breath. "With the murder? Pretend or otherwise?"

"Reality's proven far more sobering than anything we could've dreamed up," Phaedra agreed. "Still, let's not table our plans just yet. Perhaps we can revisit the idea later."

To say Harriet's death had cast a pall over the day was an understatement. Rollo, normally quick with a witty riposte, answered Detective Morelli's questions in a subdued monotone. No, he hadn't seen Mrs. Overton after they'd all gone upstairs to bed. And no, no one could confirm his alibi. He'd been alone in his room all night.

Tory, who'd reportedly argued with Harriet earlier on

the evening before her murder, faced intensive police questioning.

"What was the argument about?" Morelli asked her.

"Nothing. Harriet didn't like me, that's all. She looked down on me."

"Rollo stated he saw the two of you on the terrace after dinner. Said you both looked"—he flipped a page on his pad—"'quite heated.'"

"It was nothing," Tory insisted.

"Then why were you so upset? If it was nothing?"

"Because she was infuriating! She criticized everything I did. The way I dressed. My deplorable manners. My unladylike behavior."

"Why would she do that?"

Tory sighed. "She didn't like me, that's all. And the feeling was mutual. When you're attractive," she added with a careless shrug, "other women hate you. They can't stand to see you happy." Her eyes flashed with remembered anger. "So yeah, I admit I didn't like her. But I didn't *kill* her."

Brian stated he'd gone back to the guesthouse after dinner to work and hadn't seen or heard anything. "Of course," he added with an apologetic smile, "I had my white noise machine on. I take it with me whenever I travel. Nothing short of a bomb going off would've disturbed me."

How convenient, Phaedra couldn't help thinking. Her aunt might find Callahan attractive, and she couldn't deny he was a charmer, but he struck her as a man who wouldn't hesitate to bend the truth—or his version of the truth—to suit his own needs.

Felicity, like Wendy, claimed to be in her room all night, just as Dave and Eve Kowalski were in theirs. Elaine spent the night in her apartment above the costume shop.

Now, as Phaedra stirred her tea, she lifted a troubled gaze to her friend. "No one did it. Yet someone did."

"It's disconcerting," Elaine agreed, "to say the least. Knowing someone under this roof is a murderer."

"Who would want to kill Harriet?" Phaedra wondered.

"Good question." Elaine set her cup down. "She didn't exactly endear herself during her stay. But I can't imagine anyone here actually doing away with her."

"Maybe it really was Chef Armand," Phaedra ventured half jokingly. "He did her in after she insulted his meringues."

"And questioned his knife skills." They shared a quick, guilty smile.

"Sorry." Elaine sighed. "It's not the least bit funny. Poor Harriet. And poor Tom."

"Have the police questioned him?" Phaedra knew Detective Morelli had set up a makeshift interrogation room in the parlor.

"Yes. I overheard him just a few minutes ago, saying he didn't hear a thing. He took a sleeping pill."

"And Harriet can't provide his alibi because she's—"

"Dead," Elaine finished.

"I still can't believe it." Phaedra shook her head. "I'm sorry the murder mystery thing didn't work out. I was looking forward to it."

"Maybe it's just as well," Elaine said as she thrust her chair back and stood. "I have plenty to do and a costume shop to run. The police said I'm free to go as long as I stay in town." She rolled her eyes. "Like I can afford to go anywhere else."

"Not jetting off to Saint-Tropez, then?"

"Right now, I can't even afford a bus ticket to D.C." She sighed. "At least you'll have Dave and Eve for the rest of the week," Elaine added as she headed for the door. "Good servants are *so* hard to find these days, you know."

The kitchen door had barely swung shut after her when Phaedra heard voices down the hall, growing louder.

"—can't believe this," Wendy sputtered. "It was a *joke*, detective. An offhand remark made in private."

"I have to follow up every lead, Ms. Prescott."

"This isn't a lead, it's an invasion of privacy."

Phaedra stood as Morelli held the door wide and waited for her aunt to sweep into the kitchen. Wendy marched straight to the coffeepot, poured a cup, and spooned in sugar with short, jerky movements.

"What's going on?" Phaedra asked.

"I need to question Ms. Prescott." The detective indicated the kitchen table. "You, too. Please."

Seeing his quick sideways glance at the coffeepot, Phaedra took down a mug, poured a cup—black, no sugar—and wordlessly handed it over. He nodded his thanks and waited as the two women sat down.

"Tell me exactly what you said to your niece last evening in the kitchen," Morelli said, pen poised.

"I've explained," Wendy huffed. "I told Phaedra I'd like to stick her in a cannon, that she did nothing but complain and find fault."

"Her? Meaning Harriet?"

"Yes. Phaedra had remarked that Mrs. Overton was a stickler for staying true to the Austen canon."

At Morelli's blank look, Phaedra said, "The canon refers to Jane Austen's body of work, and the fan fiction sites where writers utilize her canon, particularly *Pride and Prejudice*, to create their own fictional variations."

"Write their own stories, you mean. With Jane Austen's characters."

"Exactly."

He turned back to Wendy. "What did you do last night after the guests went upstairs to bed?"

"I took a tray of sherry glasses from the parlor to the kitchen and set them in the sink."

"Can anyone confirm that?"

"If you're asking if anyone was with me last night," she said, her eyes like flint, "the answer is no."

"Where is your bedroom located?"

"On the first floor. There are two bedrooms behind the kitchen, former servants' quarters, separated by a pantry. Chef Armand has . . . had one, and I have the other."

"Are you asking everyone these questions," Phaedra asked pointedly, "or is my aunt a suspect?"

Morelli closed his pad. "Just questions, Professor."

"Fair enough." She leaned forward. "Now I have a question for you. Who told you about our conversation?"

"Eve Kowalski," Wendy said before he could answer, her words grim. "The little sneak was eavesdropping outside the kitchen door."

"She wasn't eavesdropping." Phaedra remembered Eve pushing the swing door open the evening before to speak to Wendy. "She stuck her head in to tell you the guests wanted coffee. She must've overheard us talking."

"Overheard, eavesdropped—same thing."

"It's not the same thing at all. One is accidental, one is deliberate."

"All right, ladies. That's all for now." Morelli stood and tucked his pad in his back pocket. "I have more statements to obtain. And I'll need that contact info for Chef Armand," he reminded Wendy.

"I'll see that you get it before you go."

"Thank you." His glance flicked to Phaedra. "Both."

He'd barely left the kitchen when Eve, clad in her black servant's gown and clutching a tray of dishes, hurried in and set the tray by the sink. "I'll wash these up after I finish clearing the table. For such a meticulous bunch of ladies," she complained, "they certainly know how to make a mess."

"Wait."

Wendy's voice rang out, sharp and commanding.

"Ma'am?" Eve turned to face her.

"How could you?"

Confusion passed like a cloud over her face. "How could I what?"

"You told Detective Morelli what I said about Harriet. Don't deny it."

"I don't understand. Tell him what?"

"Did you repeat my aunt's comment from last night,"

Phaedra asked, "about wanting to stuff Harriet in a cannon?"

Shock registered on Eve's face. Her eyes grew wide, and her mouth parted in surprise. "No! Of course I didn't. I swear I didn't!"

"But you heard me say it," Wendy accused. "Last night, when you came in to tell me the guests wanted coffee."

"Yes, I heard you say it." Eve's pale face grew, if possible, paler. "But I didn't repeat what you said to that detective." She hesitated. "He did ask me a few questions, though," she admitted. "Later."

"What sort of questions?"

She twisted a corner of her starched white apron in her hands. "About you. If you got along with Mrs. Overton or not."

"And what did you say?"

"I had to tell him the truth." Eve regarded each of them in turn. "He was persistent, as if he knew I was holding something back. I . . . I told him you didn't care much for Harriet Overton."

"Making me a murder suspect into the bargain. Thanks."

She tilted her chin up. "I also told him that no one else liked her, either. And that you have a quirky sense of humor, and if you said anything unkind, anything at all, you were only joking." Eve's eyes brimmed as she fixed a pleading gaze on her employer. "I'm sorry."

"Oh, for heaven's sake. Don't be sorry," Wendy grumbled, and stood to give Eve an awkward hug. "You told the truth, I didn't like her. And please don't cry. You're pregnant, after all. Crying's not good for the baby."

The young woman's eyes widened as she drew back. "How did you know?" She turned to Phaedra. "Did you tell her?"

"I didn't need to." With a smile, Phaedra smoothed her green muslin skirts. "Your hormones gave you away."

Eve swiped at her tears with the back of her hand. "Is it that obvious?"

Wendy nodded. "You turned green once or twice at dinner last night, and your emotions are all over the place. Which is perfectly normal. Why don't you go take a nap? Phaedra and Dave and I can manage lunch service."

"I didn't sleep very well last night," she admitted.

"Did you see or hear anything unusual?" Phaedra asked.

"No, sorry. I watched TV on my tablet for a while, so I had my earbuds in. Dave snores," she added, and yawned. "I could do with a couple of hours' sleep."

"Go," Wendy ordered. "Sleep now while you still can."

"I'll be back in time to serve afternoon tea," she promised. "Thanks."

As Eve pushed through the door to go upstairs, Phaedra turned to her aunt. "You know what this means, don't you?"

"It means Eve is hormonal."

"No." Phaedra shook her head firmly. "Eve told Morelli that if you'd said anything unkind, anything at all, you were only joking. Which means," she added, "someone else must've told him what you said."

"About stuffing Harriet in a cannon?" Wendy frowned. "But who? We were the only ones in the kitchen. Who else could've heard me say that?"

"I don't know," Phaedra replied. "But someone did. Someone who wanted to throw you under the bus."

Eight

As if dealing with a barrage of questions and a sheriff with a search warrant wasn't enough punishment, Phaedra's mother, Nan Prescott Brighton, stopped by the inn in her Sunday best. Phaedra opened the door to her mother and her pug, Fitz.

"What's going on?" Nan demanded as Fitz settled on his haunches at her feet. "Police cars everywhere, and that local television reporter stuck a microphone in my face—"

"There's been a murder." Phaedra shut the door firmly as Willa Wilkins, the aforementioned reporter, rushed up the front porch steps with a cameraman close behind her.

Ignoring her shouts of "Press!" and "Just a quick word, please," Phaedra led her mother into the small parlor and shut the doors behind them.

"A murder?" Nan echoed, rooted to the spot. "How . . . how awful."

"Eve found one of the guests in the kitchen garden early this morning." She met her mother's shocked gaze. "She was dead."

"*She?* Oh, my goodness. How? Who? Why?"

"I can't say, I can't say, and I don't know."

"Oh, for heaven's sake. You can't tell me who she is?"

"No, Mother. It's a police investigation. Sorry."

"I saw the county coroner's van leave." Nan unsnapped Fitz's leash with an unsteady hand and sank onto the sofa. "At least it isn't anyone we know. Is it?" She looked up sharply. "You said 'she.' So it can't be that rude French chef Wendy hired. "

Fitz allowed Phaedra to scratch him behind his ears. His tongue lolled out, and he snorted in canine pleasure. "No. Chef Armand is alive and well."

"Was the poor woman shot? Stabbed? Strangled?" Nan glared at her. "Oh, never mind, I can see from your expression that you have no intention of telling me." She shot to her feet and snapped the pug's collar to the leash. "Let's go, Fitz. We'll learn more on the evening news than we will here."

"Sorry, Mom, but I really don't know much at this point."

"Fine. Goodbye, then. I'm meeting Malcolm for brunch. I went to church this morning." She paused. "Alone," she added. Pointedly.

"Sorry. I always mean to go, but . . ."

"You and your father! Two of a kind. Well, you know what they say about the road to hell. It's paved with—"

"Good intentions." Phaedra sighed and followed her to the front door. She bent down to give Fitz's ears an affectionate ruffle. "I know. Maybe next Sunday."

His curly tail waggled. Nan gave her a curt nod, flung the door open with one gloved hand, and left.

With breakfast out of the way and her mother safely en route to brunch, Phaedra took the opportunity to don her bonnet, left the inn, and walked to the Poison Pen, where she could peruse the Sunday morning newspapers in peace.

Her costume, a slim-skirted Regency gown of palest green, gloves, and ballet flats, and a reticule hanging at her wrist, earned her a few curious glances. But most of the locals knew her and gave her a friendly nod.

Arriving at the bookstore, she scarcely glanced at the Victorian town house or the potted topiary trees flanking its narrow front doors. She climbed the porch steps and bent down to retrieve the Sunday morning editions of the *Washington Post* and the *Richmond Times-Dispatch*. Once inside, she set the papers aside and locked the doors behind her—the Poison Pen was closed on Sunday—and paused at the foot of the staircase as she untied her bonnet. "Anybody home?"

As she'd expected, there was no answer.

Newspapers tucked under her arm, Phaedra headed down the hall to the reading room, her ballet flats silent against the polished wooden floor.

The glassed-in room, formerly a sunporch, was empty. Her parents normally spent their Sunday mornings back here, sharing the long table that formerly graced her father's law office, sipping coffee, reading the newspapers, and doing the Sunday *Times* crossword puzzle.

The click-clack of toenails behind her heralded Fitz's arrival, and she dropped the papers on the table with a thump and knelt to rub his head. "All by yourself, boy?"

Fitz's reproachful look plainly said that he was.

Phaedra straightened. "We can keep each other company until they get back. How does that sound?"

He wagged his tail, waited as she pulled out a chair, settled with a grunt at her feet, and promptly fell asleep.

She reached for the *Dispatch* and flipped through until she found the entertainment section. She wanted to read Rollo's review of Harriet's latest book without guests interrupting her or Detective Morelli questioning her.

Just how badly, she wondered, had Rollo trashed *The Duplicitous Duke*?

"Book reviews," she murmured, and turned to the back of the entertainment page. "Ah, here we are."

Placed prominently at the top, and accompanied by a photo of Harriet Overton, was Rollo's review.

A ROMANTIC, ROLLICKING REGENCY, the headline proclaimed. LOCAL AUTHOR DELIVERS AN-OTHER WINNER.

Phaedra's brows drew together. *No one deserves success more than Harriet Overton*, Rollo had written. *Hard work and talent collide in Ms. Overton's latest,* The Duplicitous Duke. *This, her first national bestseller, is deservedly flying off the shelves.*

Her frown deepened. *The only way this book is flying off the shelves*, Rollo had informed Harriet only yesterday, *is if your readers throw it off.*

Perplexed, she lowered the paper. What had changed Rollo's opinion of Harriet's book so dramatically, and in such a short time?

He'd filed the story yesterday afternoon. Which meant he'd already written his review, and had taunted Harriet needlessly. Unless . . . had he rewritten the review later and resubmitted it?

And if he'd changed it, *why* had he changed it?

As Fitz snored, she went upstairs to fix herself a cup of tea and carried it back downstairs. She took a sip and settled down to catch up on local and international news.

The front door opened a short time later, and her parents' voices drifted down the hallway. "Fitz," her mother called out. "We brought treats from Woofgang's."

The pug scrambled to his feet with a snort and raced down the hall. He loved the dog bakery's savory peanut butter pumpkin cookies far more than Phaedra's company.

"What are you doing down here, buddy?" Phaedra heard her father inquire.

"Blame me," she said as she joined them. "I was in the reading room, looking at the Sunday papers."

"Anything in particular?" Malcolm Brighton asked.

"A book review. How was brunch?"

"Wonderful. We went to that new Cajun place, Lagniappe."

"I've heard good things. How was it?"

"Marvelous," Nan pronounced as she set her handbag

aside. "I'd suggest you and that Shakespearean scholar have dinner there one night, but I wouldn't want to be accused of *interfering*."

As she marched upstairs, her back stiff, Fitz capered after her, his turned-up nose twitching in anticipation.

Phaedra's father turned to her with a half smile. "Mother annoyed with you again?"

"Is she ever not?"

He indicated the hallway that led back to the reading room. "Have time for a talk?"

"For you? Always."

Once they were seated, he saw the open entertainment section of the *Times-Dispatch* and the photo of Harriet Overton. "Ah. Was this the book review you were reading?"

She nodded. "She's . . . one of Wendy's guests."

"And you didn't want to talk about it in front of your mother."

"I can't put anything past you, can I?"

"Nope."

"You know how Mom is."

"Yes." He sighed. "I certainly do."

"This has to stay between us," Phaedra warned. "Can I rely on your discretion?"

"Of course." He paused. "I assume it has something to do with whatever took place at your aunt Wendy's this morning. The place was crawling with police."

"One of the guests was shot, Dad. With a crossbow."

He paled. "Accident?"

"No. Very definitely murder."

"Ah." He knitted his brows as his glance strayed to Harriet's photograph. "And was Ms. Overton the victim?"

"Yes." Phaedra lowered her voice. "The police are questioning the guests and getting statements."

"As they should be."

"One of the guests is a journalist, Rollo Barron. He wrote a review of Harriet's new book."

"Hence your desire to read it." He glanced again at the paper. "From the headline, it seems he liked it."

"That's just it. He hated it. Or at least, that's what he told us yesterday." She relayed Rollo's less-than-complimentary comments in front of the other guests at afternoon tea, and his promise to print a two-and-a-half-star review of Harriet's latest. "Her husband Tom practically challenged Rollo to a duel over the shrimp salad. But the published review praises Harriet to the skies and lauds her for her hard work and talent."

"That's quite a turnaround," Malcolm agreed. "Why is that, do you suppose?"

"No idea. He'd already filed the story before—" She paused. "Before Harriet's murder. So it wasn't that."

"Not a case of deciding to soften his words in the aftermath of her untimely death, you mean?"

"Exactly. Their dislike went too deep. They'd known each other for years, and I sensed bad blood between them."

"Then that's where I'd start," her father suggested. "What ignited their dislike? Was it her fault, or his? If you can find the answers," he said as he stood and ambled down the hall, "you'll likely find a motive."

Nine

Phaedra returned to the inn in plenty of time for afternoon tea.

Eve met her at the door, refreshed and rosy cheeked after her nap, while Chef Armand, minus his white jacket and toque and making no secret of his displeasure, waited with ill-disguised impatience in the front hall.

"Chef Armand," Wendy said as she came downstairs. "You're here. Thank you."

"Yes, I am here, madame," he informed Wendy brusquely. "Where is this detective who wishes to speak to me?"

"Here." Morelli appeared in the parlor doorway and gestured him inside. "Thanks for coming. This way, please."

Wendy scowled at his retreating back. "I wouldn't be at all surprised if Armand fired that crossbow at Harriet, with that Gallic temper of his. But never mind." She fixed a gimlet eye on Phaedra. "We have a problem."

"We," Phaedra said as she untied her bonnet and tossed it aside, "have several problems." She waited until Chef Armand strode into the large parlor and Morelli shut the doors behind them. "The police presence, for starters. It doesn't help the inn's image."

"There's nothing can I do. I can't ask them to leave."

"No. All we can do is cooperate." Phaedra turned to her aunt. "Has the medical examiner arrived?"

"While you were gone." Wendy glanced up the front stairs and lowered her voice. "They took Harriet's body to be autopsied."

"Is that the problem? Because that's normal in a homicide."

"No. The problem is Bella."

"Bella?" Phaedra echoed. "Harriet's cat?"

"Yes. As in, what's to become of her, now that Harriet's . . ." She grimaced. "Dead."

"I'm sure Tom will take the cat when he leaves. Won't he?"

"That's just it. He's refused. He apparently dislikes cats and has a serious phobia. He only put up with Bella because—" She paused. "Well, because of Harriet."

"I can certainly understand that," Phaedra murmured.

Wendy fixed her with a pleading look. "I thought perhaps, since you already have a cat—"

"No." Firmly. "Wickham is male and he's very territorial. He barely allows *me* in the carriage house."

"What about one of your friends? Lucy, or Marisol?"

"Lucy's allergic. And Marisol couldn't take care of a goldfish, much less a pampered feline like Bella."

"Well, then, I have no choice. The Poison Pen it is."

Phaedra shook her head. "Fitz won't like it. Not to mention Mom. You won't get that cat carrier past the front door."

"We'll see about that. Besides, it's just for a few days," Wendy said, her mind made up. "Until I can find a permanent home for Bella."

She hurried off to call Nan, while Phaedra paused to check her appearance in the hall mirror. Her topknot was secure and ringlets framed her face becomingly. She'd become adept at arranging her hair into a variety of Regency hairstyles, from basic chignons and twists to more elaborate ringlets and curls. And despite the day's humidity, there was nary a sign of frizz.

Thank goodness for extra super-hold hair spray.

"*Oui.*" Chef Armand's voice boomed forth from behind the parlor's closed doors. "Madame Overton's husband came downstairs for a glass of water, to take a sleeping pill."

Phaedra edged nearer to the door.

"What time was this?" Morelli asked.

"Last night. About eleven."

"Was he alone?"

"Quite alone. He said the old witch—*pardon*, I mean his wife—was sleeping. And snoring," he added. "That is why he could not sleep."

Which meant, Phaedra mused, that Harriet was alive and snoring at eleven last night, if Tom could be believed. Had he told the truth? Or was his trip to the kitchen deliberate, a way to provide himself with an alibi?

"What did Mr. Overton do after he took the sleeping pill?" Morelli questioned.

"He went back upstairs, I suppose. I went to bed."

"Meaning you didn't actually see him go upstairs."

"*Non.*"

"Did you notice if Ms. Prescott was in her bedroom?"

"Her door was closed. That is all I can say. Whether she was inside or not, who knows? Perhaps yes; perhaps no."

Hearing the voices growing closer, Phaedra hurried down the hall and through the swinging door into the kitchen before the detective caught her eavesdropping.

"Ah, Phaedra, just in time," Wendy called out as she came in through the back door with an empty tray. "We're ready to serve tea. Will you bring out the blackberries and clotted cream? And the Victoria sponge?"

"Of course." She was just arranging the requested items on the tray, along with a stack of clean linen napkins, when the kitchen door whooshed open.

"Professor Brighton," Morelli said.

She looked up in feigned surprise. "Detective! I didn't realize you were still here."

"I saw you disappear into the kitchen." He eyed her

without expression. "Indulging in a little eavesdropping again?"

"No, of course not. As you can see," she added as she picked up the tray, "we're in the middle of tea service."

"I won't keep you. I hope you'll be available for any further questions."

"Of course."

"I'll stop by later this afternoon."

"You're leaving?" Her surprise was genuine this time.

"There are other crimes in Laurel Springs, Professor."

"Has there been another robbery?"

He nodded. "A B and E, on Main Street."

She didn't ask for details on the breaking and entering; he wouldn't provide them, anyway. "Has the murder weapon been found?" she asked instead.

"Not yet." He paused. "But we'll find it. And I'm sure I don't need to tell you to keep this under your hat. Or bonnet, as the case may be."

"My lips are sealed." She headed for the back door and waited as he reached out to open it for her. "Thank you, Detective." She favored him with a demure smile. "Would you like a cup of tea before you go? Perhaps a slice of Victoria sponge?"

"No, thanks. I'm not much for tea. Or sweets. Goodbye, Professor."

"Goodbye."

Not much for tea or sweets? She shook her head in bemusement as she headed across the back lawn to the terrace.

Another reason why she and Detective Morelli could never truly become friends.

Halfway through tea on the terrace, as the guests' conversation waned, Felicity Penrose glanced at Tom Overton's empty place.

"Where is Harriet's husband?" she asked. "I feel so bad for the poor man." Sympathy warmed her voice.

"He's holding up," Phaedra said. "Staying in his room."

"Grieving," Felicity murmured, and nodded. "I'm sure he wants nothing more than to leave this all behind. But under the circumstances," she added ruefully, "he can't."

"Have the police questioned Tom?" Rollo asked. "If I were investigating the murder, I'd start with him."

"Why do you say that?" Phaedra reached for the teapot.

"Any investigator worth his or her salt always looks for the money trail. Who benefits from Harriet Overton's death? Her husband."

"Or her sister," Wendy pointed out. "Tom told me he asked Harriet's sister to take Bella, but she refused. She's allergic."

"Harriet wasn't close to her sister." Rollo spoke dismissively. "And she and Tom have no children. As her husband, I've no doubt he'll inherit her entire estate. Including," he added with a lift of his brow, "all of those lovely publishing royalties."

"You make an interesting point," Phaedra conceded. It was worth looking into. "More Darjeeling, Mr. Barron?"

He shook his head. "I imagine this is difficult for you as well, Professor. The murder . . . well, it's rather spoiled your immersive Austen week, hasn't it?"

"Not completely," she said, although it nearly had. A real murder definitely wasn't in her plans for the week's activities. "We'll carry on with our roles, play a few hands of whist and faro, practice our dancing, compete in an Austen quiz, and enjoy a recital later this evening."

"A recital?" Tory lowered her teacup. "Who's playing? Not one of those god-awful harpists, I hope."

"Actually," Phaedra said, "Felicity has graciously agreed to perform a piece by Mozart on the piano for us."

"Ooh, I can hardly wait," Tory muttered.

"If Harriet were here," Rollo said, "she'd say Liszt and Beethoven were more popular during the Regency period."

"But she's not here." Felicity thrust her chair back. "So, it hardly matters whether I play Mozart or Liszt, does it, Mr. Barron? Either way, you'll just have to suffer through it." She glared at Tory. "Both of you."

With that she stood, bright eyed with anger, excused herself, and strode back to the house, long skirts swishing.

"Wow. Touchy, much?" Tory rolled her eyes. "Talk about a diva. Who cares which composer she plays? They're all equally boring. And equally dead."

"Really, Ms. Sutton," Rollo scolded. "You might at least pretend to enter into the proper spirit of things."

"I am," she protested. "And it's Miss Musgrove," she pointed out primly, "not Ms. Sutton."

"Miss Musgrove makes an excellent point," Elaine said. "Let's all make an effort to assume our assigned roles from here on out, shall we?"

"Someone needs to tell Anne Elliot over there, then."

They followed Rollo's gaze to Felicity, just disappearing into the kitchen.

"Do you think it was Felicity?" Eve wondered. "Maybe she did it."

"She's certainly a drama queen," Tory agreed.

"What makes you say that, Eve?" Phaedra asked, curious.

"You can't deny she has a temper. Maybe losing her role to Harriet hit her harder than any of us realized."

Phaedra shook her head. "I doubt it. Even if that were true, it hardly constitutes a motive for murder."

Elaine shrugged. "People have killed for less."

"You've all heard about the infamous short story contest, right?" Rollo said.

"No," Tory said, an avid gleam in her eye as she leaned forward. "Do tell."

"Well, I'm not one to gossip," he prefaced his remark, "but I've known Harriet for years. After her initial success as an author, she served as a judge in a short story contest for unpublished writers. The first prize was publication in a major magazine."

"Nice," Elaine approved. "Who won?"

"I don't recall. But it wasn't Felicity." He leaned back, pleased to have their undivided attention. "She had a pen name. Arabella something or other. Anyway, she entered a fan fiction variation based on *Pride and Prejudice*. Her stories were quite popular online. Harriet read it, critiqued it, and offered it up to everyone at the contest as a prime example . . ."

They waited, riveted on his words.

". . . of how *not* to write. She trashed the story so thoroughly the poor girl never wrote another word."

And that, Phaedra couldn't help but think as she helped Eve begin to clear away the tea things, certainly provided Felicity with an excellent motive for murder.

Ten

"Wickham? Where are you, Wicks? I'm home!"

Phaedra glanced from the sitting area to the dining room and the recently remodeled kitchen, but there was no sign of the finicky feline.

Wickham liked to play hard to get. No surprise there. She closed the carriage house door, tossed her bonnet and gloves aside, and eased out of her ballet slippers. Her feet ached, and after today, she truly understood the meaning of the phrase "bone weary."

"Wickham," she called out again, more loudly. "Dinnertime." That usually got his attention.

Sure enough, he appeared at the top of the stairs leading to the loft, paused, and padded down the steps at a leisurely pace.

"I see you're in no hurry," she told him as she went into the kitchen and took down a can of salmon. "You know you're about to be fed, don't you? Spoiled boy."

I guarded our domain from mice and intruders all day, didn't I? his blue eyes seemed to say. *Isn't that enough?*

With a dish of kibble topped with salmon in front of

him, Wickham settled down to the serious business of eating, and Phaedra left him to it.

She'd just reached into the freezer for a microwave meal when someone knocked sharply on the front door. Her hand froze in midair.

Normally she wouldn't give a nine o'clock visitor on Sunday evening a second thought. Her mother, her aunt, Lucy, even Hannah popped by unannounced when she was in town. But she'd already returned to D.C. And with a murderer on the loose, one couldn't be too careful.

Phaedra closed the freezer door and crept to one side of the sitting room window to peer out. She didn't see a car out front, or much of anything, unfortunately. She'd forgotten to turn on the outside light. The realization brought a pinprick of unease. Perhaps whoever was at the door thought the house was empty and planned to break in.

After all, according to Morelli, there'd been an unsettling rash of robberies in town of late . . .

"Professor Brighton? Are you in there?"

At the sound of the familiar British accent, so warm and male and unexpected, all of her reservations fled, and she opened the door. "Mark! You startled me. I thought—" She waved him inside. "Never mind. Come in, please."

"Thanks." He stepped inside and held up her reticule, dangling incongruously from his finger. "You left this behind in the sitting room. I thought you might need it."

"I do! My phone is inside. While I dislike technology on principle, I'd be lost without it. Thank you."

She set it aside and preceded him into the living room. "Can I offer you a cup of tea for your trouble?"

"No trouble. And no, thanks. I've drunk enough tea today to float a battleship."

She clasped her hands in front of her. "How's your work on the monograph going?"

"It's going well. I made decent progress today, despite Detective Morelli grilling me for nearly an hour."

"I didn't realize he'd questioned you."

"Routine stuff. Where was I last night, when did I last see Mrs. Overton, how well did I know her, et cetera. I'm afraid I wasn't much help." He slid his hands into his trouser pockets and glanced around. "So," he mused, "this is where you live."

"This is it."

"Reminds me of my first term at Oxford. One bedroom, sitting room and kitchen, and a half-dead philodendron someone left behind on the windowsill."

"I think every dorm has one."

"I loved it, though. It was the first place I could truly call my own."

"Virginia Woolf got it right. There's nothing like a room of one's own." Phaedra gestured to the sofa. "Please, sit."

"Thanks, but I've been sitting behind my laptop all day." He wandered over to the breakfast bar and came to a stop when he saw the microwave meal. "My apologies. You were about to fix dinner. I should go."

"No, please. Stay. I don't really want it, at any rate." She returned the box to the freezer and reached into the fridge for a carton of eggs and a packet of baby spinach. "Are you hungry? I make a decent omelet."

"Tempting," he admitted. "But only if you let me chop the spinach. I have mad chiffonade skills."

She handed him the package. "Prove it."

A short time later, as they ate in companionable silence, Wickham approached, tail twitching.

"This must be the infamous Wickham," Mark said.

"You remembered. I'm surprised."

"Yes, of course I remember. I stopped by the Poison Pen during your father's open house and asked if you had a Yorkshire terrier named Mr. Darcy. You informed me—rather coldly, as I recall—that you did not."

"What a thing to say! You knew I was a Jane Austen scholar, so you assumed, quite wrongly, that I just had to have a cute little dog named Darcy."

"I suppose it was a bit condescending of me."

"A bit?"

"But to be fair," he pointed out as he stood and carried their plates to the sink, "you insulted my plaster bust of Shakespeare and accused me of trying to be—" He winced. "Hip."

Phaedra choked back a laugh. "I did, didn't I?"

"You did."

He grinned, and she smiled, and suddenly she realized she liked this man. A lot. He was smart, and funny, and—

And she had to nip this—whatever *this* was—in the bud, right now.

Mark was attractive and clever, and she liked him immensely, but like her, he was a faculty member. A coworker. She had a long-standing policy of not mixing business with pleasure, and she wasn't about to change it now.

Not even for Mark Selden.

"Leave the dishes." She stood and ran hot water into the sink, followed by a liberal squirt of dishwashing liquid. "I'll do them later. Or in the morning."

He nodded and returned the butter and carton of eggs to the fridge and shut the door. "I should go."

"I'll walk you out."

At the door, he paused. "How's the investigation into Harriet's death going? Any leads thus far?"

"If so, Detective Morelli isn't sharing them with me."

"Standard police procedure, I imagine."

"I know. It's just that . . ." She shook off her thoughts. "Never mind."

"No. Tell me. Any insights? You've spent more time with the guests than anyone. I'm sure you've formed a few impressions by now."

She hesitated. "At tea yesterday, Rollo told Harriet his review of her new book would be published today. He made no secret of the fact that it wasn't favorable." She frowned. "But when his review appeared in the *Times-Dispatch* this morning, it was stellar. Five stars."

"Perhaps he only wanted to taunt her. What is it you Americans say? Make her sweat?"

"Maybe." She wasn't convinced. "But that wasn't the only odd thing I noticed."

"Oh?"

"Elaine assigned everyone a role from *Persuasion* to assume during the week. Felicity's role was Anne Elliot."

"The heroine, and Captain Wentworth's one true love." She lifted her eyebrow. "You do know your Austen."

"Enough to get by. Did Felicity not want the role?"

"She didn't seem to care one way or the other. But when Harriet learned she was to be Lady Russell, she demanded that Elaine switch their roles. She refused."

"And I'm guessing," Mark ventured, "that Elaine relented and gave the role of Anne Elliot to Harriet."

"Yes. Which makes me wonder . . ."

"If Elaine and Rollo changed their minds willingly?"

"Or if they were—pardon the pun—persuaded."

Mark frowned. "You're suggesting that Harriet . . . had something on the two of them?"

"I can't help but wonder," Phaedra admitted, "if perhaps Harriet wasn't blackmailing them."

The next morning, everyone discussed Harriet's murder over breakfast. The guests were intrigued to find themselves in the middle of a real murder mystery.

"I hardly slept a wink last night," Tory grumbled as she poured maple syrup on her Belgian waffles.

"I'm sorry to hear that." Phaedra noticed a diamond tennis bracelet glimmering on her wrist. "What a lovely bracelet." As she sipped her Lapsang souchong, she wondered how the girl could afford such extravagances on an administrative assistant's salary. Did she have a trust fund? Or did she finance her lifestyle on plastic?

"Thanks." Tory extended her arm to admire it. "A friend gave it to me."

"Why couldn't you sleep?" Rollo asked her. "Guilty conscience?"

"I kept tossing and turning," she admitted, "hoping we won't all be picked off, one by one."

"This isn't a horror movie," Rollo said, dismissing Tory's comment with a wave of his wheat toast. "Or an Agatha Christie novel."

"*And Then There Were None*," Elaine intoned, and let out a throaty laugh.

"It's not funny." Tory repressed a shudder. "We could all be killed in our beds."

"Those of us who *stay* in our beds," Eve muttered.

Before Phaedra could wonder at Eve's remark, Wendy appeared in the doorway. "May I speak to you, Phaedra? It's important."

"Of course." She stood and turned to the guests. "Today, we'll be painting watercolors en plein air."

"In plain what?" Tory echoed.

"Air painting," Felicity informed them.

"Thank you, Felicity." Phaedra smiled. "We're painting outdoors. You'll find easels, watercolors, and a jar of brushes on the front porch. Enjoy."

With that, Phaedra joined her aunt in the hall and closed the dining room doors behind her. "What is it?"

"That detective is back," she said. "Morelli. He's got a diver with him and they want to search the pond."

"Does he have a warrant?"

"Yes. It's all very official." Wendy crumpled the skirt of her bright yellow sundress in one hand. "He's waiting on the terrace. I have breakfast service still to finish. Would you mind . . ."

"Don't worry. I'll take care of it." She paused. "How was your date with Brian last night?"

"It was perfect." Wendy sighed. "After a candlelit dinner, a strolling violinist stopped at our table and played 'It Had to Be You.' I half expected to find an engagement ring in my tiramisu."

"Were you disappointed you didn't?" Phaedra asked.

"A little," she admitted. "But I can hardly expect a proposal after three dates. We're still getting reacquainted." She frowned. "And he smokes. He says he's trying to quit."

"I'm sure it isn't easy. Did he smoke back then?"

"No. He acquired the habit and now he's trying to quit."

"Good for him. I hope he succeeds."

"He's very determined once he makes up his mind. That hasn't changed. I wouldn't be surprised if he really *does* pop the question, and soon."

Phaedra was silent.

"After dinner," Wendy added, "he did make a proposal, of sorts. A business proposal." She paused. "He suggested I consider selling the inn. To him."

If Phaedra harbored any doubts about Mr. Callahan before—and she most definitely did—she was more convinced than ever that his single-minded determination had nothing to do with marrying her aunt, and everything to do with getting his hands on her property.

As her aunt hurried back to the kitchen, Phaedra made her way to the terrace and greeted the detective. Today he wore khakis and a white polo shirt, along with a shoulder holster and sidearm.

"I'm afraid my aunt is busy at the moment," she told him. "How can I help you?"

He held up a document. "I have a warrant to search the grounds for the murder weapon. I'd like to start with the pond."

Her glance flicked to a man in a wet suit waiting nearby. "Of course. It's not very large, as ponds go. It's barely six feet deep in the center."

"Makes our job easier. With your permission, then?"

"By all means." She followed him down the slope to the pond. Ringed on one end by woods, it was small, less than half an acre, its surface quiet in the still, humid air.

The diver put on a pair of fins and a snorkel mask and

waded out to the center of the pond. A moment later, he disappeared beneath the surface.

"A crossbow should be fairly easy to find," Phaedra ventured as they waited. "It's large and bulky."

"Should be," Morelli agreed. "It's definitely not in the house. Which means it's got to be out here somewhere."

Twenty-five minutes later, after surfacing several times, the diver returned empty-handed.

"Nothing," he reported. "An old boot, a tire . . . and a whole lot of muck. But no crossbow."

"Okay, thanks." Morelli turned to Phaedra. "I appreciate your cooperation. We'll take a closer look around the grounds before we go."

"Professor Brighton," Mark Selden called out. He crossed the terrace, mug of tea in hand, and made his way down the slope to join them. "Has the weapon been found?"

She shaded her eyes against the sun and wished she'd taken the trouble to put on her bonnet. "No. A diver searched the pond but all he found was a boot and a tire."

Mark glanced at Morelli. "Whoever hid that crossbow did an excellent job of concealment."

"Yes." The detective met his eyes. "Any ideas as to where it might be, Professor Selden?"

"Me? None whatsoever. Perhaps the killer hid it in plain sight." He glanced at Phaedra. "Like Minister D—in Poe's 'The Purloined Letter.' I take it you've searched the house, Detective?"

"From top to bottom."

"There's a dumbwaiter in the dining room," Phaedra offered. "It hasn't been used for years. The original owner had an extensive wine cellar. He stationed a servant in the cellar during meals to send up bottles as they were needed."

"We've already checked it out," Morelli said. "No crossbow. No room for more than a couple of bottles."

Mark lifted his mug to his lips. "I'm afraid I have no

other ideas. Unless there's a secret panel or a hidden staircase, I can't imagine where—"

He lowered his mug and squinted at something in the distance.

"What is it?" Phaedra asked, following his gaze.

He handed her the mug. "There's something in one of those oaks over there."

He strode toward several trees separating the carriage house from the rear of the inn, Phaedra and Morelli trailing after him, and came to a stop at the base of a pin oak. "Up there," he said, and pointed. "The sun glinted off something metallic just now. I couldn't help but notice. Do you see anything?"

"I'll be damned," Morelli muttered, peering upward. "You're right. It's a crossbow. Someone's wedged it in one of the branches."

"I only noticed it when the sunlight hit it."

"It might've remained up there for years," Phaedra said slowly. "But how did the killer get up there? It's halfway up the tree. And that's a really *tall* tree."

"There aren't any low-hanging branches," Morelli said.

"Yet they managed to get the crossbow up there," Phaedra pointed out. "How?"

"A rope ascender," Mark said. "And a carabiner clip." He glanced at Morelli. "Used to do a bit of climbing."

"Do any of the guests happen to be recreational climbers, Professor?" the detective asked. "Aside from Professor Selden?"

"I've no idea." Phaedra set the mug aside. "There's a ladder in the basement. I'll go see if it's still there."

"No," Morelli said firmly. "We'll handle it. I don't want potential evidence contaminated."

"Fine." She folded her arms under her bodice. "Then how do you suggest we get the crossbow down?"

He took out his cell phone. "Thompson? Go to the local hardware store and buy a ladder. The longest ladder they have. Bring it back here. And make it quick."

He returned the phone to his back pocket. "Thank you both for your help. We'll take it from here."

"If they used a rope or a bungee cord," Phaedra suggested, "it may still be out here somewhere." She studied the flower beds. "Hidden in the grass. Or concealed in the kitchen garden."

"Thank you, Professor." His tone left no doubt as to his desire for her—for both of them—to leave. "In the meantime, one of your, ah . . ." His gaze rested on the retaining wall at the far end of the property. "Guests, requires your attention."

Phaedra followed his bemused frown to the eight-foot wall. A graveled path ran along the base of the wall, veering off into the kitchen and rose gardens before winding around the side of the house.

Atop the wall, sitting with her tail curled around her, was Bella. Wendy must've lost her battle with Nan to give the orphaned cat a temporary home at the Poison Pen.

She eyed Phaedra now with sphinxlike regard.

"Bella?" She walked toward the Persian. "What are you doing up there?"

As she drew nearer, the cat rose to her haunches, and with a quick, graceful leap, darted up the slope and disappeared into the neighboring property.

Eleven

Bella? Come back here this instant!"

When it became clear that the fluffy white Persian was not coming back, Phaedra hurried around the side of the house, skirts swishing against her ankles, and came to a stop outside the neighbor's gate. It was tall, ornate . . . and firmly closed.

"Shall I help you look?" Mark called out as he rounded the corner behind her.

"Would you? She isn't mine and I shouldn't care, but I can't let her wander off. She's an Instagram star."

"You can't be serious. She's a *cat*."

"She has over ten thousand followers. She belonged to Harriet Overton."

"Isn't she Mr. Overton's problem, then?"

"Technically, yes. But he hates cats and wants nothing to do with Bella. Wendy's trying to find her a home." She glanced hopefully at him. "I don't suppose—"

"No. Furnished condo. Rental. No pets."

She struggled to lift the latch, but it didn't budge. "It's stuck."

"Here, let me try."

After a vigorous jiggle and a muttered expletive or two, the latch gave with a rusty groan, and they were in. He glanced around. "We may never find your cat in this jungle."

The house, a two-story Craftsman bungalow, was empty and for sale. Its state of neglect—climbing vines and overgrown bushes, peeling paint, broken window-panes, and missing shutters—had so far put off any prospective buyers.

"It's no wonder the place hasn't sold," Mark observed.

"It's been on the market for ages. Old Mr. Taylor wants too much money and refuses to budge on the price, even though the house needs a new roof and a new kitchen, not to mention it's riddled with rot and water damage."

"I'm guessing it doesn't have central air, either," Mark said as he noticed a window unit shoved in an upstairs window.

"No." Phaedra raised the hem of her gown and made her way cautiously forward. "Bella? Where are you?"

No answer, not even a meow.

"There." Mark pointed to a thicket of vines in one corner of the yard. "I saw a flash of white."

"Bella?" Phaedra coaxed, moving closer. "Here, kitty." When her soft calls garnered no results, she let out a breath of frustration. "I wish I had a treat in my pocket. Or a sardine."

"I'm rather glad you don't."

"Sardines are the only way to persuade Wickham to do anything."

"Perhaps he needs a feline friend. You should take Bella home. You could rename her Lydia."

"Wickham is a confirmed bachelor. And this is no time for jokes." She cut a glance at him. "Will you help me look for Bella or not? If not—" She broke off. "There she is! On that old stone wall by the garden shed."

Bella eyed them warily but didn't move as Phaedra stepped closer. Her tail twitched, and her paw rested atop something. It was bright red on one end and shiny on the other.

"What's she got?" Mark asked as he joined her.

"I'm not sure." Phaedra drew closer to the cat. "What've you found, Bella? May I see it?"

Slowly, so as not to startle the Persian, she edged nearer, crooning reassuringly all the while. As she reached out a tentative hand to demonstrate that she meant no harm, the cat leaped from the wall, streaked across the yard, and disappeared into the house.

Whatever she'd been toying with fell into the grass.

"She's gone into the cellar." Mark pointed to a shallow flight of stone steps leading down to a basement door. The door was ajar.

"Mark, look at this."

Phaedra knelt in the grass to pick up the object Bella had knocked to the ground when she jumped. "Good thing I have my gloves on." It was a large metal clip, red on one end, and she held it out on her outstretched palm. "It's a carabiner, isn't it? Like climbers use."

He nodded. "Used to connect apparatus to a bungee cord or rope."

"Could the killer have used it to haul the crossbow up the tree?"

"Possibly." He knelt beside her. "It looks brand new."

"Yes. Which tells me it hasn't been here long." She straightened. "And it wouldn't be here at all," she added, "if someone hadn't tossed it over the retaining wall."

"Give it to the police when we get back. If you're right, and I'm sure you are, it's potential evidence."

"I will." Phaedra curled her fingers around it. "But first, we need to find Bella."

She wished, not for the first time, that her Regency-era gown had a proper pocket. Clutching her find tightly, she followed Mark down the steps, wrinkling her nose as the smell of mold and damp earth assaulted them.

At the bottom was a door, open just enough to allow

Bella to squeeze through. Mark turned the knob and gave it a push. It shuddered but didn't budge. "Something's blocking it."

"Give it a good shove."

He glanced at her over his shoulder. "You know this is breaking and entering," he reminded her. "Technically."

"We're on a search and rescue mission. I'll take full responsibility if we're arrested."

"Better not say anything about this to your detective friend."

"I won't. And he isn't my friend."

"Just like Bella isn't your cat."

"Exactly."

Squaring his shoulders, Mark pushed against the door. It gave a few inches.

"Harder," Phaedra urged. "We have to get Bella out of there." She glanced at a pile of moldering leaves with distaste. "There could be snakes. Spiders. Rats."

With another, more forceful shove, the door creaked open, groaning in protest, and they found themselves in a small, dirt-floored root cellar.

"It's literally a root cellar," Phaedra said. "With roots. In the walls."

"They stored apples and onions down here during the winter months," Mark said.

"It's so dark." Phaedra could see little beyond the light provided by the open door behind them. "No windows. I wish we had a flashlight."

"Hold on."

Mark took his cell phone out and activated the flashlight, then cast it around the room.

There were a couple of wooden barrels—one of which partially blocked the door—a few empty burlap sacks, and an assortment of rakes and hoes propped against one wall.

But Bella was not in evidence.

"Stairs." Mark illuminated a set of wooden steps in the far corner. "Leading up to a door. Kitchen, probably."

"It's open. Wide enough for Bella to squeeze through, at any rate." She brushed past him and moved forward.

"Wait." He caught at her arm. "You said the house is riddled with rot. Test each step before you put your weight on it. Better yet, let me go up first."

"I'll be careful." Phaedra was already halfway up. "The treads are okay. But we'll need that flashlight," she added as she emerged onto the first floor. "It's dark up here. The windows are all shuttered."

He followed her up, and the first thing he noticed as he joined her was the smell of . . .

"Bacon!" Phaedra exclaimed. "That's odd."

"Recent, too, I'd say."

They exchanged an uneasy look. "Do you think someone's here?" she asked in a low voice. "Living here, I mean?"

"It's possible. We got in, which means someone else could've, too." He pointed at a fast-food wrapper crumpled on the floor. "Kids, most likely."

"The neighborhood children stay away from this place. They swear it's haunted."

"Kids say that about all empty, old houses."

Phaedra knew he was right, and she didn't sense anything sinister about the old house, beyond a frightening amount of dirt and neglect. But the thought of someone lurking nearby, waiting in one of the rooms for the intruders to leave, unnerved her.

Another thought occurred to her. What if Harriet's killer hadn't merely flung the carabiner into the yard to hide it? What if he or she were in the house, right this minute? Living here? She edged nearer to Mark.

The kitchen, a galley design, was long but narrow, and the appliances, a stove and a refrigerator, were decades out of date and coated with grease and grime.

"I'm sure neither of them works," she said. "There's no power. So how—"

Mark pointed to the kitchen counter. "There's your answer. A camping stove. Brand new, from the looks of it.

And a cooler." He frowned. "Someone's camping out on the premises. Which might explain the bungee clip Bella found."

Phaedra uncurled her fingers and stared down at the carabiner in dismay. "You're right. Which means it may not have anything to do with the murder weapon at all."

Before she could ponder who might be living in an abandoned, boarded-up house with ghosts and spiders and a camping stove for company, or why, a soft thud in the next room was followed by an outraged feline howl.

"Your cat," Mark said.

"She's not my cat." Phaedra brushed past him into the adjoining dining room. "Bella," she called out, her voice low but firm as she eyed the cobweb-festooned corners. Only a dining table, thick with dust, remained. She half expected to see Miss Havisham looming at the head of the table, clad in a tattered bridal gown. "Where are you?"

Perhaps having decided that she'd had enough adventure for one day, Bella darted out from beneath the table and all but leaped into Phaedra's arms.

Mark smirked. "Like I said. Your cat."

After returning to the inn, Phaedra set the Persian down in the hallway. She meowed plaintively and allowed her rescuer to administer a brief scratch behind her ears before darting upstairs. A suitcase stood near the door.

Which wasn't surprising. Someone was always coming or going at the Laurel Springs Inn.

"Professor Brighton." Detective Morelli, phone pressed to one ear, emerged through the kitchen door. His dark gaze flickered from Phaedra to Mark. "Find anything? Aside from the cat?"

"As a matter of fact, we did." She held out the carabiner. "Or should I say, Bella did."

"Where?"

"On the adjoining property."

"You found this," he repeated as he studied the metal clip with a frown. "Just lying in the grass."

"It was under Bella's paw, actually. And don't worry," she added, "I had gloves on when I picked it up." She wriggled her fingers. "No fingerprints. At least, none of *my* fingerprints."

He put his phone away. "I'll have forensics look it over. Thanks." His glance flicked to Mark. "Both of you."

She wanted to tell him about the camping stove and fast-food wrapper they'd found in the kitchen, along with the smoky scent of bacon in the air, indicating a recent—very recent—trespasser on the property, but refrained. Admitting they'd entered the house without permission wasn't the best idea.

And she'd promised Mark she'd keep silent. So, keep silent, she would.

Besides, it was too late. Detective Morelli had left.

Mark returned to his room to work on his monograph, nodding briefly to Wendy as she descended the stairs.

"Phaedra, there you are. I see Bella's back."

"Yes, she decided to run into the yard next door. Mark and I had to chase after her. I thought you were taking her to the Poison Pen."

"I did. But she and Fitz got into a spat, and Bella won. Nan sent her packing." She shifted the pile of clean towels in her arms. "Will you ask Eve to take a tea tray up to the bridal suite, please?"

"Oh? Have the newlyweds arrived?"

Wendy hesitated for a fraction of a second. "Yes."

"I noticed a suitcase by the door."

"Dave's coming to carry it up."

"Don't newlyweds normally have more than one suitcase?"

"Already upstairs," Wendy replied. "There were so many, Dave couldn't manage the last one."

Phaedra, her thoughts occupied with camping stoves, crossbows, and carabiners, nodded distractedly. "I'll make a tray and carry it up myself."

"Let Eve do it. It's her job, after all."

"Don't you think you're being a bit lady-of-the-manor?"

Wendy regarded her in surprise. "What do you mean?"

"This isn't Downton Abbey. Eve's an actress, a *pregnant* actress, not a servant. And she and Dave were staying in that suite. Until you tossed them out."

"I didn't toss them out! The bridal suite was reserved two months ago. They knew that up front, and they were fine with it. And it's not as if they don't have an apartment right down the street."

"Sorry." Phaedra sighed. "It's just that you seem a little flustered. Let me take the tray up. I really don't mind."

"I'm sure you have other things to do." Wendy's words were firm. "They're newlyweds, Phaedra. They want privacy."

Recognizing defeat, she acquiesced. "Of course. I understand."

"I knew you would." Wendy patted her on the shoulder and hurried away into the kitchen.

What, she wondered, was her aunt up to? Why the secrecy surrounding their new guests? And why had she refused Phaedra's offer to carry the tea tray upstairs? Something odd was definitely afoot.

Abandoning her suspicions for the moment, Phaedra resolved to stay out of it, and smoothed her skirts as she headed to the front porch to check on the progress of her budding artists.

"I now call this meeting of the Jane Austen Tea Society to order."

It was the first Monday evening of the month, and Phaedra had readied the Poison Pen's reading room to discuss their latest book club selection, *Persuasion*.

Lucy Liang sat at one end of the table, across from Marisol Dubois, Phaedra's high-energy teaching assistant. Mari had a cup of tea and Lucy a glass of chardonnay. A plate of jalapeño cheese straws and another of shortbread cookies waited in the middle of the table.

"Does everyone have a copy of the book?" Phaedra asked.

They nodded. "Mine's a little dog-eared," Marisol said. "I bought it for Mr. Singleton's ninth-grade English class. I still have notes scribbled in the margins."

"Remind me never to loan you a book," Lucy said.

Phaedra went to the whiteboard and scrawled out the title. "*Persuasion* was Jane Austen's last fully completed novel. It was published six months after her death, in 1817. Let's begin our discussion with Anne Elliot." Phaedra put the dry erase marker down. "What did you think of her?"

"She was a complete doormat," Marisol complained. "I really struggled to understand her. She put everyone else first, every single time. She was selfless to a fault."

"I agree." Lucy reached for her glass. "Anne was almost *too* good. But at the same time," she added, "her respect for duty and desire to make a suitable match demonstrated that she was responsible, and practical, and steadfast in her affections. Nothing swayed her from her love for Frederick Wentworth."

"Nothing except Lady Russell." Marisol bit into a cheese straw. A drift of buttery, cheddar-cheesy crumbs showered her vintage seventies blouse, a recent thrift store find, and she brushed them quickly away. "Wow. These are amazing, Phaedra. The jalapeños take it to a whole new level. I want the recipe."

"Mom thought you might. She printed it out and put a few copies beside the plate."

"Why didn't we meet at your place tonight?" Lucy asked as she reached for a cookie.

"I have an unexpected houseguest."

"Oh? Is Hannah back from D.C.?" Marisol asked.

Phaedra shook her head. "I wish. We could certainly use her skills at the inn right now. But she's still at the embassy. The prime minister arrives tomorrow, and Hannah's providing the pastries for his welcome tea."

"No pressure there." Marisol selected another cheese straw. "Just tea and all the trimmings for the British prime minister."

"At least the queen won't be there," Lucy said. "Even so, it sounds pretty nerve-racking."

"Hannah's stressed to the max," Phaedra agreed. "But I have no doubt she'll sail through it with flying colors. She always does."

"Back up for a second." Lucy set her wineglass down and frowned. "If your houseguest isn't Hannah, who is it?"

"Is it the Shakespearean dreamboat?" Marisol asked hopefully. "Please tell me it's him."

Color warmed Phaedra's cheeks. "Professor Selden is a colleague, Mari. He's widely respected in his field."

"So are you. That's why you're perfect for each other."

"Sorry to disappoint you," Phaedra informed her firmly, "but my houseguest is female. Her name is Bella."

"She's Italian?" Lucy queried.

"Persian. She's a cat."

"How on earth did you end up with another cat? Wickham must be spitting mad to have his territory invaded."

"He's not happy," she admitted. "Bella belonged to Harriet Overton."

The words had barely left Phaedra's lips when she realized her mistake. She'd flung the door open to a subject she'd steadfastly vowed to avoid.

"Harriet Overton?" Marisol leaned forward. "The author who was murdered at your aunt's inn?"

"Yes. She brought her cat along, and her husband Tom doesn't want it, so we're trying to find poor Bella a home. Wickham definitely isn't pleased. But it's only for a day or two, until I can convince Mom to take her."

"I don't see that happening," Lucy said. "And I don't see Fitz exactly welcoming a cat with open paws, either."

"That's why I need to try to convince my mother. Difficult, since she's annoyed with me at the moment."

"She's always annoyed with you."

"Bella's a beautiful cat," Phaedra said, adroitly sidestepping the subject of her prickly relationship with her mother, "with fluffy white fur, blue eyes, and a wonderful disposition—"

"You can save the hard sell," Lucy said firmly. "I have enough trouble taking care of myself."

"Same," Marisol echoed. "No pets allowed at my apartment, anyway. And I don't want cat fur on my vintage clothing. Sorry."

"Oh well. It was worth a try. If you know of anyone who might be interested, let me know." Phaedra picked up her marker and turned back to the whiteboard. "Now. Let's get back to the book. What are your thoughts on Frederick Wentworth? What trait makes him unique when compared to other Austen heroes?"

"He was a self-made man." Lucy leaned back in her chair. "His family wasn't wealthy, or aristocratic. He distinguished himself in the Royal Navy and returned a hero. You know this isn't going to work, don't you?"

"What isn't going to work?"

"You can't sidetrack us with a book discussion now. Not after the M-word came up."

"The M-word?"

"Murder," she and Marisol chorused.

Twelve

Everyone in town knows Harriet was found toes-up in the kitchen garden with a crossbow quarrel in her chest," Lucy said.

"In a patch of rosemary," Marisol added. "Which, come to think of it, might be a telling detail. 'There's rosemary, that's for—'"

"Remembrance," Lucy cut in. "And that's Shakespeare 101. Everyone knows Ophelia's famous soliloquy. Just like everyone knows the murder weapon hasn't been found."

Phaedra started to correct them, to tell them about the crossbow Mark had spotted in the tree only that morning, but hesitated. She'd promised Morelli to keep the particulars of the case to herself.

"What I want to know," Marisol mused, "is how Harriet ended up in the kitchen garden at midnight. Why? What on earth was she doing there?"

"Hold that thought." Phaedra put her dry-erase marker down and went to close the reading room's door. "I'll tell you both everything I know so far. But it needs to stay between the three of us."

"Doesn't it always?" Marisol pointed out. "We didn't

breathe a word when you clued us in on the details of William Collier's murder case, did we?"

"No," she admitted. "You were the souls of discretion."

The murder at Marling made national headlines when Collier, who'd recently inherited the historic Georgian home, was found dead in his claw-foot bathtub.

"We'll keep our mouths shut." Lucy leaned forward. "Just like last time. And if we put our heads together, we can share our thoughts and ideas. Discuss suspects. Brainstorm. Like we always do."

Lucy made a valid point. Three heads were better than one, particularly when it came to solving a murder. And Phaedra not only valued her friends' opinions, but trusted their integrity implicitly.

"All right." She returned to the whiteboard. "Listen up, because I'm about to tell you something you won't read about in the newspapers."

They waited, their expectant gazes locked on Phaedra as she brought them up to speed on Harriet's murder.

"You found a note? In Harriet's pocket?" Marisol asked. "On her *dead body*?" She shuddered. "But Regency gowns don't normally have pockets."

"They don't," Phaedra agreed. "She'd tied a loose pocket at her waist."

"I've heard of those," Lucy said. "They were worn under a lady's gown. They were a precursor to the reticule."

Phaedra nodded. "I noticed Harriet's silk gown was ridged at the hip. The fabric was crumpled, as though something was thrust underneath."

"The note." Lucy nodded. "And you took it out. What did it say?"

"It asked Harriet to meet the sender in the garden at midnight, and it was signed 'an ardent admirer.'" Phaedra could still see the beautiful, flowing script. "A calligrapher penned it, on paper similar to parchment."

Marisol tapped a pen against her notepad. "Maybe Harriet thought the note was a clue, a part of the faux murder.

That would explain why she rushed off to meet a stranger in the garden in the middle of the night."

"And it was written in calligraphy," Lucy agreed. "On old-fashioned paper. It fits in perfectly with the *Persuasion* theme."

"'Dare not say that man forgets sooner than woman, that his love has an earlier death,'" Marisol quoted. "'I have loved none but you. Unjust I may have been, weak and resentful I have been, but never inconstant.'" She sighed. "Now, *that's* true love."

"Harriet was nothing if not competitive. She'd do anything to win." Phaedra remembered the author chastising her husband during the archery competition, accusing him of boasting when he mentioned his days on the college archery team. And she remembered the curdled glare he'd given her when Harriet won, as well.

Resentment, brief but unmistakable, had twisted his normally genial expression into something harsh and ugly.

Had Harriet pushed him too far? Did Tom pen the mysterious note? Did *he* fire the quarrel that killed her?

"Can calligraphy be analyzed?" Marisol asked Phaedra. "Like handwriting?"

"According to Detective Morelli, it can. He's already turned it over to an expert in the field. Hopefully, he'll share whatever he learns."

"I wouldn't count on it," Lucy said.

"What about the crossbow you found?" Marisol wondered. "Were there any prints?"

"I don't know. Probably not." Phaedra picked up the marker. "Whoever our killer is, he or she is clever. Clever enough to conceal the weapon up a tree and clever enough to lure their victim to the garden with a mysterious note."

"The murderer has to be physically fit," Marisol said. "To get the crossbow up there, they had to climb the tree—"

"Unless they used a ladder," Lucy pointed out.

"And they had to carry the weapon up, too."

"We found a carabiner in the yard next door," Phaedra

said. Seeing Mari's look of confusion, she added, "It's a metal clip used by climbers to attach equipment to a rope or bungee cord. And it was brand new."

"So, the killer, what?" Lucy frowned. "Carried the crossbow up, clipped to a cord?"

"Something like that."

"It sounds like a gothic novel," she said. "More *Northanger Abbey* than *Persuasion*. Cloak-and-dagger stuff."

Marisol shrugged. "It's simple, really. Find the calligrapher, and you've found the murderer."

"It's not that easy, Mari," Lucy said. "The killer isn't going to admit to being an expert calligrapher. And it doesn't prove anything, anyway. The note could've been written by anyone. A genuine admirer, for instance."

"No way," Marisol scoffed. "That's ridiculous."

"Maybe the killer saw the note before Harriet did, and hid in the garden to wait."

"That's even more ridiculous."

"It's called brainstorming. That's the point, to throw out ideas, no matter how crazy."

"I think," Phaedra cut in firmly, "we're all getting a little off track."

Having regained their attention, she turned back to the whiteboard and wrote SUSPECTS and underlined it twice. "Let's start with a list of the guests and see what motives we can come up with."

"We don't know these people," Marisol pointed out.

"I don't know them, either. At least, not well. But you and Lucy can offer a fresh perspective. You might think of something, or notice something, I've missed."

"Who found the body?" Lucy asked. "Let's start there."

"The newspaper said it was one of the actors staying at the inn," Marisol said. "Eve something. She found Harriet during her early morning run."

"Eve Kowalski." Phaedra put her name on the whiteboard. "She and her husband Dave are actors in Elaine

Alexander's troupe. Elaine owns the new costume shop and she manages the Laurel Springs Players."

"Does Eve normally run every day?"

Phaedra nodded. "She took a detour through the kitchen garden that morning, though. I remember Detective Morelli questioned her about it."

"And what did she say?" Lucy asked.

"Apparently, she likes the scent of rosemary and mint. She finds it very invigorating when she runs."

"She's right," Marisol agreed. "I swear by my rosemary and mint shampoo. Not only does it wake me up in the morning; it makes my hair super shiny and manageable, and it smells *so* good—"

"We're getting off track," Phaedra reminded her gently.

"Not to mention, you sound like a shampoo commercial." Lucy frowned as she toyed with her pen. "Does Eve have a motive to kill Harriet?"

"I've noticed she's a little possessive," Phaedra said. "She didn't like Harriet flirting with her husband one bit. But she's also pregnant, and hormonal. And she doesn't have a history with Harriet—at least, not that I know of. She was genuinely distraught when she discovered Harriet's body."

"She's also an actress," Lucy said. "Just saying."

"Good point." Phaedra put an asterisk by Eve's name. And, although Eve had denied it, there was the distinct possibility she'd thrown Wendy under the bus by telling Detective Morelli about her "cannon" comment. And she'd admitted she often couldn't sleep. Had her insomnia led her down to the garden at midnight to kill Harriet?

"What about Eve's husband?" Marisol ventured. "Dave?"

Phaedra shook her head. "Harriet flirted outrageously with him, too, but he ignored her. Her behavior obviously embarrassed him, but he seemed to take it in stride."

The second name she put on the board was Tom's. "Harriet's husband is pleasant, amenable . . . and henpecked.

Years of being belittled and ordered around by his wife have taken a visible toll on him."

"Visible how?" Lucy asked.

She recounted the archery contest and the dark look Tom had given Harriet when she won the trophy.

"Is he capable of murder?" Marisol wondered.

"Anyone is capable of committing murder." Lucy shrugged. "Under the right circumstances, if someone's pushed to the breaking point, then . . ." She snapped her fingers.

"Tom may have killed his wife," Phaedra allowed, "but I doubt it. He's too timid, for one thing. And I don't think he's physically fit enough to climb a tree. At any rate, he's skilled at handling a bow and arrow. Not a crossbow."

"Aren't they the same?"

"A crossbow is far more lethal, especially at close range. The draw isn't manual like a bow and arrow. It has a horizontal bar called a tiller, and a locking mechanism."

Marisol shuddered. "Sounds positively medieval."

"They were," Lucy said. "Used during the medieval period, I mean." She paused. "Another thing to think about. Our murderer wrote the note in calligraphy. Which means he or she needed tools to do it properly. As in, pens, ink, and parchment paper."

"Which goes back to what I said," Marisol added. "Find the calligrapher, find the murderer."

Writing "calligraphy" and a question mark next to Tom's name, Phaedra added a new name underneath.

"Rollo Barron," she pronounced as she put the marker down, "is guest/suspect number two. He's a journalist from Richmond, Virginia, and he has a history with Harriet."

"What sort of history?" Lucy asked, curious.

"I'm not entirely sure. I suspect he may have given one of her books a poor review early on and earned her ire. In any case, they despised each other."

"What makes you think he's a suspect?" Marisol asked.

"He told Harriet—in front of everyone—that he'd reviewed her latest book and given it two and a half stars." Phaedra put two asterisks beside his name. "He informed her it would appear in the Sunday paper. But the published review was glowing. Five stars."

"That *is* odd," Marisol agreed. "Why did he change his mind?"

"I can think of a reason." Lucy crossed her arms loosely under her chest. "Maybe Harriet had something on Rollo. Something damaging."

"Blackmail?"

"It's possible."

Marisol frowned. "What could his secret be? It'd have to be pretty bad if he killed Harriet to keep it quiet."

"I'll ask Elaine a few discreet questions," Phaedra said. "She's an old friend from my UVA days. She was a wardrobe assistant on a big-budget Austen film several years ago, and Harriet was the script consultant. She mentioned that Rollo interviewed the leading man."

Marisol leaned forward. "Who was the leading man?"

"Richard Troy."

"The British actor? The one who's—"

"Married to Jocasta Davies?" Lucy finished. "Yes. They're known in the British tabloids as 'the happiest couple in Hollywood.'"

Phaedra had just added Felicity Penrose's name to the suspect list on the whiteboard when the doorbell rang and Fitz, barking frenziedly, hurtled down the stairs. She put the marker down.

"Excuse me. I'll be right back."

She let herself out and closed the door behind her, then hurried toward the entrance hall. The Poison Pen closed early on Mondays, at seven p.m. on the dot, and tonight was no exception. She glanced at her wristwatch with a frown. It was nearly ten.

"It's a little late for a social call," her father grumbled as he trudged down the stairs after Fitz.

He swung the door open as Phaedra peered over his shoulder. Detective Morelli stood on the porch.

"Detective," Malcolm said. "This is a surprise. Please, come in. How can I help you?"

"I won't keep you." He stepped just inside the door. "Just letting you know there's been a break-in next door."

"Brennan's bakery?" Phaedra asked, dismayed. "Again?"

He shook his head. "This time, it was the costume shop."

"Oh no." Poor Elaine. She'd barely opened her doors, was struggling to establish her new business, and now this. "Was anything stolen?"

"Not that we saw. But it's difficult to say for sure."

"Why is that?" Malcolm asked.

"The place was vandalized. Costumes are thrown everywhere, a couple of tables were overturned, and that tall, tilting mirror in the corner? It's shattered. There's broken glass everywhere."

Phaedra let out a breath of pained disbelief. "I can't believe it. That this could happen here in Laurel Springs . . ." She met Morelli's gaze. "Does Elaine know?"

"Yes. She got home a short time ago and called us right away. I'm hoping she can inventory the stuff and determine if anything's missing or not."

"I'll go over there right now. See if I can help." Phaedra moved to brush past him, but he held up his hand.

"It's best if you let her concentrate on taking inventory right now, Professor," he said. "She's upset, as you can well imagine. And she'll definitely need your support," he allowed, "tomorrow. In the meantime, we'll handle it."

She opened her mouth to argue, but at the sound of footsteps hurrying up behind her, she turned around.

"Phae? What's going on?" Lucy demanded. "We heard something about a break-in."

"Is everything all right?" Marisol asked anxiously.

"The costume shop next door was vandalized."

"Oh no." She clapped a hand over her mouth. "Isn't that your friend's new shop?"

"I'm afraid so." Phaedra turned to Morelli and introduced him to Lucy and Marisol.

"We just finished our monthly meeting," Marisol said.

"Book club," Phaedra added quickly. "We're reading *Persuasion*."

"Book club?" He turned to Phaedra. "I see. I'd hate to think you were having one of your murder club meetings."

"Murder club?" She almost laughed, taken aback by his remark, but his expression was anything but amused. "No, of course not. I can assure you," she went on, her surprise giving way to annoyance, "we were discussing Captain Frederick Wentworth and the relative merits of a self-made man until you came banging on our front door."

"I'll leave you to it, then." Morelli turned to her father. "Sorry for the interruption. Good night, Mr. Brighton. Professor."

"Goodnight, Detective," Malcolm said. "Thanks for keeping us informed." He nodded to everyone and headed back upstairs, with Fitz close behind him.

Morelli paused in the doorway as Lucy and Marisol returned to the reading room to gather their things.

"Professor Brighton, listen to me, please." His voice was low but firm. "Stay out of matters that don't concern you. Particularly police matters involving dead bodies and break-ins."

Her fingers tightened on the doorknob. "Understood. Good night, Detective."

With a curt nod, he left.

"Thanks for the goodies," Marisol said as she and Lucy returned, armed with leftover cheese straws, cookies, and promises to reschedule their next meeting. "See you next time." She turned to Lucy. "Coming, Lu?"

She looked up from her phone screen. "You go ahead. I need to answer this text."

"Is everything all right?"

Lucy's brows furrowed as she returned her attention to the phone. "Fine," she said shortly.

Marisol exchanged a quick *what's going on?* glance with Phaedra before letting herself out. "Good night."

"Okay, she's gone." Phaedra crossed her arms as the front door closed after Marisol. "So, tell me. What's up?"

For a moment, Lucy was silent, her face unreadable. "My mother." Her words were flat. "She's here."

"That's great." She eyed Lucy quizzically. "Isn't it?"

"No. Not at all. It's complicated." She hesitated before meeting Phaedra's gaze. "When I was eleven, my mother left. One day she was there, the next—" She snapped her fingers. "Gone."

"Why did she leave? And where did she *go*?"

"Who knows? She had mental health issues." She shook her head. "If not for my *ah yi*—our aunt Roz—my sister and I would've ended up in foster care."

Lucy's eyes darkened as Phaedra reached out to squeeze her hand. "She changed our lives. College. A future." Her gaze was fierce. "I owe my aunt *everything*."

"And now your mother's back."

"She wants to see me, Phaedra." Her voice was barely audible. "She wants to reconnect."

"And you don't want to see her."

"She left." Remembered hurt lurked in her dark eyes. "All these years, and not a word. Now she wants a relationship with me. With both of us. Leah can talk to her if she wants. But I have nothing to say to her. I dealt with my anger and made peace with the past. Or I thought I had. Now, I don't know. She's stirred it all up again."

"At least she's reaching out," Phaedra offered. "I'm sure she has regrets. Deep regrets."

"Too little, too late." She put her phone away. "I need to go. I'm meeting Roz at Josie's in twenty."

"Tell her I said hello. And . . . thanks."

"Thanks?" Lucy stared at her. "For what?"

"For telling me." Lu was an intensely private person who rarely offered up any personal details. Yet she'd opened up about her childhood, and her absent mother.

Lucy shrugged.

"I hope . . ." Phaedra hesitated. "I'm sure you and your mother will figure it out."

"Thanks, but I don't see it happening." She shouldered her bag and opened the door. "Not in this lifetime, anyway."

Thirteen

Phaedra returned to the carriage house a short time later, armed with leftover cheese straws and cookies, and called up the stairs to Wickham.

"Time for your evening prowl, Wicks."

He meandered out of the bedroom and paused at the top of the stairs to yawn. *I was just in the middle of a dream. Or, should I say, a nightmare. No canned sardines and no catnip to be found. I may never recover from the trauma.*

She swore the cat gave a tiny shudder.

"Where's Bella?"

I'm sure I don't know. Try the top of the refrigerator.

He followed her into the kitchen. The minute she opened the back door, Bella darted out from under the table and raced out the door past Wickham, who ignored her and headed for the low hedges bordering the property. Amused, Phaedra lingered inside the door to watch.

Wickham had feline stalking down to a fine art.

Something rustled deep within the bushes. He waited, his tail twitching ominously, and sized up his prey.

Probably a field mouse, Phaedra decided. Or Bella. She moved to shut the door when she glimpsed something dart across the shadowy expanse of the adjoining B and B's backyard. Whatever, or whoever, it was went straight to the guesthouse.

She heard the low murmur of voices, and just like before, a spill of throaty laughter . . . then the door of the guest cottage cracked open, spilling light briefly onto the tiny front patio.

Brian Callahan stood silhouetted in the door as he ushered someone into the cottage. Phaedra's eyes narrowed. She'd recognize that burly build and sandy gray-blond head anywhere. His motions were furtive, his words hushed.

Who was with him?

She pursed her lips in puzzlement. The visitor was definitely female. Her face wasn't visible, but she knew instinctively it wasn't Wendy. This woman was petite, and her hair was long, not bobbed.

Who in the world could it be? Who was sneaking out to Brian's guest cottage like a thief in the night?

The two of them shared an embrace and a brief but passionate kiss in the doorway. As the woman turned back to close the door, dark hair cascading around her shoulders and a mischievous smile curving her ruby-red lips, Phaedra clapped a hand over her mouth to muffle a gasp.

Brian's mysterious visitor was Tory Sutton.

Tory, who claimed she was at the inn to work. Tory, who refused to surrender her cell phone, shunned all immersive activities, and enjoyed mocking the Janeites.

No wonder she wasn't interested in learning archery or needlework. She was too busy majoring in hanky-panky. It didn't take a PhD to figure out what those two were doing.

Phaedra waited as the light inside the cottage blinked off. All was quiet and Brian's visitor did not reappear.

Poor Wendy. Her aunt, dazzled by her former high school flame's generous gifts of flowers and candy, swept off her feet by a shower of compliments, was being played like the proverbial violin.

She only hoped he didn't manage to sweet-talk Wendy into selling the inn.

Phaedra called out to Wickham, and after a brief, defiant exploration of the hedges, he abandoned his prey and padded disdainfully past her into the kitchen. Not wishing to be left behind, Bella raced up and darted inside.

As she closed the door, her glance flickered once again to the darkened guesthouse. All was silent. Not a creature was stirring, not even a . . .

Rat.

She locked the door and headed upstairs to get ready for bed, her thoughts troubled and her heart heavy. What to do with her unwelcome knowledge? Should she tell Wendy what she'd seen and break her aunt's heart, or wait a bit to see how things played out? Phaedra wasn't sure.

But she was sure of one thing. The only "business" going on between Tory and Brian Callahan right now was monkey business.

A thunderstorm woke Phaedra early the next morning.

She glanced at the bedside clock. Nearly seven. Time to get up, get dressed in her favorite primrose-yellow gown, and head next door to help prepare breakfast.

"I'll be glad when Hannah gets back," she grumbled.

Wickham, curled up at the foot of her bed, lifted his head to regard her balefully. *You think I enjoy getting up at such an uncivilized hour? This "early to bed, early to rise" nonsense is strictly for the birds. Personally, I prefer late nights and sleeping in.*

He leaped down from the bed and stalked downstairs to the kitchen in the highest of high dudgeon. As usual, Bella was nowhere to be seen.

After filling both food dishes with kibble and half a can of mixed seafood grill each, Phaedra glanced out the window. Rain bucketed down, battering the yard and drumming steadily on the roof. So much for her plans to take everyone to the farmers' market in the town square today.

Since colonial days, farmers and artisans had gathered in the cobblestoned Market Square to sell produce, meats, live poultry, and a variety of handmade wares.

Bounded by Federal-era buildings on three sides, the former courthouse and town hall now housed a museum and a thriving collection of artists' studios. On Tuesdays and Fridays, local craftspeople sold everything from raw honey and artisan cheese to homemade jams, soaps, quilts, and candles.

Perhaps the weather would clear by Friday and she could take everyone to the market then. In the meantime, she'd stop by the costume shop after breakfast and check on Elaine.

Ten minutes later Phaedra entered the inn's kitchen and propped her dripping umbrella by the back door. Wendy stood by the double oven, where she'd just removed a tray of piping hot blueberry muffins. The mouthwatering scent of vanilla and cinnamon perfumed the air.

"I've made the pancake batter," her aunt said, "and James is on the way to handle the rest. Professor Selden offered to help, but I can't impose on him again. He's a guest, after all. I thought we'd offer Belgian waffles as well as pancakes this morning."

"Sounds great. What can I do?"

"You can set the dining room table. Oh, and there'll be one less place setting today."

Phaedra, a stack of blue-and-white Johnson Brothers

china cradled in her hands, paused. "Why is that? Has some-one left?"

"Tom. The police cleared him to leave late yesterday afternoon. He couldn't get out of here fast enough."

"I suppose I can hardly blame him." Still, the news surprised her. "Does that mean he's no longer a suspect?"

"That's exactly what it means. Eve told Detective Mo-relli she heard Tom snoring heavily late Sunday night, un-til she finally drifted off early Monday morning. She has trouble sleeping," Wendy added. "The baby."

"And Harriet's estimated time of death was between mid-night and one a.m.," Phaedra said slowly, "so that means, if Tom was snoring—"

"Then he can't have done it."

But something bothered her as she set another plate down. What had Eve said when Phaedra asked if she'd heard anything the night of the murder? *I watched TV on my tablet for a while, so I had my earbuds in. Dave snores.*

If so, Phaedra wondered, how did she hear Tom snoring?

"What about the note I found in Harriet's pocket?" Phaedra asked as she laid out the last place setting on the dining room table and returned to the kitchen. "Have the police analyzed it yet?"

"No idea." Her aunt tilted the muffins out of the tin and tipped them into a cloth-lined serving basket. "But now that you mention it, that detective wants a handwriting sample from everyone by the end of the day."

Phaedra carried a tray of butter, jams, and maple syrup into the dining room and placed it on the sideboard. Re-turning to the kitchen, she paused in the doorway. "I'll let everyone know. Shall I leave Tom's place setting and add another one? For the newlyweds?"

Wendy shook her head as she set the bowl of batter in the refrigerator. "They're having breakfast in their suite. Lunch and dinner, too."

"They have to come out for air eventually," Phaedra

pointed out. "After all, there's plenty to see and do in Laurel Springs." She glanced at the rain sheeting down the kitchen window. "Usually," she amended. "Why would they want to spend their entire honeymoon—"

"In bed?" Wendy arched an eyebrow. "I can't imagine."

Phaedra returned to the sink without comment and filled the basin with hot, soapy water. She began washing the muffin tins, her thoughts troubled. The memory of Tory, sneaking across the darkened yard to the guesthouse and falling into a passionate embrace with Brian Callahan, was still fresh in her mind.

She rinsed the tin and set it in the dish rack to drain. While she had no desire to keep Brian's disloyalty a secret, neither did she wish to ruin her aunt's whirlwind romance with her former high school flame.

"Morning, Professor."

She glanced up as Dave Kowalski entered the kitchen dressed in full footman regalia. "Good morning, Dave. Breakfast for the lovebirds is almost ready."

"Here you go." Wendy handed him a tray laden with toast, scrambled eggs with smoked salmon, and a pot of tea.

Phaedra eyed the tray. "There's only one plate."

"They're *newlyweds*, Phaedra," Wendy said, exasperated. "They like to share their food with each other. Careful," she warned Dave. "Don't spill anything."

"I won't."

She headed for the door with a basket of muffins in hand. "I'll set these out for the other guests."

As Wendy departed, Dave set his tray down and turned to Phaedra. His expression was troubled.

"Professor Brighton? There's . . . something I need to tell you. It's important. Or it might be. I probably should've said something earlier."

She dried her hands on a dish towel, as intrigued as she was mystified. "I'm all ears."

He lowered his voice. "It's about Harriet Overton."

"Is it about the murder?"

"It could be. I'm not sure. Probably not," he back-tracked, flustered, "but I thought someone should know."

She laid the dish towel over the back of a chair. "I'm listening."

He glanced at the door and cleared his throat. "Mrs. Overton flirted with me, Professor. Nonstop. She followed me around, winked at me. She . . ." He reddened. "Well, not to sound full of myself, because I'm not, and I definitely had no interest in her, but she had it bad for me."

She suppressed a smile. "Yes, I noticed that. I think we all did. Especially Eve."

"Not only did I not return her interest," he said firmly, "I hated it! It was embarrassing. I'm happily married. And she was . . . well, old. She cornered me in the kitchen garden when I went out to dig up some carrots for Chef Armand. She said she wanted a rendezvous. That's what she called it." He grimaced. "She wanted to hook up."

"When was this?" Phaedra asked, her words sharp.

"The evening she was killed. Earlier, though, around nine fifteen or so."

"Why didn't you tell Detective Morelli about this?"

He flushed and stared at his feet, then looked up defiantly. "It was embarrassing. I was mortified. And I didn't want Eve to know. Like you said, she's jealous."

She could certainly understand that. "Go on."

"I told Harriet I wasn't interested, that I was happily married, but she wouldn't listen. Then she tried to . . ." He swallowed. "Kiss me. I pushed her away, and she stumbled, and fell back onto the grass."

"I'm sorry this happened, Dave." Concern puckered her brows. "Harriet's behavior was inappropriate. No question. You need to tell the detective about this. The sooner, the better."

He nodded. "At the time, I didn't think it was worth mentioning. She wasn't hurt," he added, his eyes fixed on hers. "She was furious, no question, and insulted. But she was alive when I ran out of there. I swear, she was as alive as you or me."

The rain fell steadily throughout the morning, turning the grounds into a quagmire and putting paid to Phaedra's plans to visit the farmers' market in the town square.

"All right, everyone," she called out to the assembled group as they finished breakfast and reconvened in the drawing room. "I've planned something special this morning."

"Building an ark?" Rollo inquired.

Ignoring him, she held up a stack of stapled pages. "I have the script for our play, *Persuaded to Die.* I thought we'd have a quick read-through."

"That's right." Felicity turned away from the window. "We're supposed to ask each other questions and solve a murder mystery, aren't we?"

"Why bother with fiction?" Rollo asked. "We have a real murderer on the loose."

"True," Felicity agreed. "Why chase after a pretend killer when someone in this very house . . ." Her glance skittered around the room.

"We're all upset by Harriet's death," Phaedra acknowledged as she handed out the pages. "We almost scrapped the theatrical because of it. But I think the play may be just the distraction we need. I'll speak with Elaine later today. She's finished our costumes."

"Where is she, anyway?" Tory asked.

Phaedra hesitated. "She had a personal matter to take care of." No point telling them the costume shop had been vandalized. Detective Morelli wouldn't approve, and Elaine wouldn't want to answer a barrage of questions later. "Do we all know our roles?"

With a rustling of pages, everyone settled down to learn their parts, Tory with a heavy sigh. Phaedra recited her lines as Elizabeth Elliot, and Rollo portrayed Sir Walter Elliot's vanity and selfishness to perfection. Tory, not surprisingly, fluffed her lines repeatedly. Only Felicity delivered her written words with conviction.

"Why can't I be Anne Elliot?" Tory flung her pages aside. "She gets all the lines."

"This isn't the West End, for heaven's sake," Rollo said. "Or kindergarten."

"I'm surprised you can remember that far back."

"Oh, that's right—it was only last week for you, wasn't it?"

Phaedra felt as if she were dealing not with a group of Jane Austen aficionados, but with unruly preschoolers. "Behave, Sir Walter," she warned, "or you'll go into the Regency equivalent of a time-out."

An hour later Phaedra called for a tea break. As everyone drifted from the drawing room and into the dining room, she caught Tory at the door. "I'm surprised you joined us, Ms. Sutton. I thought you'd be working in the guesthouse with Mr. Callahan."

"It's Miss Musgrove." She lifted one shoulder in a negligent shrug. "And Brian gave me the day off."

"Oh? Late night last night?"

"You could say that." Her lips curved into a knowing smirk. "We're all caught up. And he's having lunch with your aunt today."

Although Phaedra longed to wipe the smirk from the young woman's carmine lips and tell her she knew all about the clandestine rendezvous with Brian Callahan, she managed a polite nod. "Go ahead. I'll be along in a moment."

She glanced out of one of the tall windows, hoping for a glimpse of sunshine, but the rain continued apace. As she made her way into the dining room, she heard the phone ring in the lobby.

Her aunt appeared in the doorway a few minutes later. "Phaedra?"

"I heard the phone just now," she said as she joined her aunt. "I hope Brian didn't cancel your lunch date."

"No. The call is for you. It's Elaine." Wendy added, "She sounds upset. Is she coming in today? Our theatrical rehearsal is scheduled for tomorrow night."

Her aunt didn't know about the break-in at Elaine's costume shop the night before, and Phaedra didn't have time to explain. "I'm sure she'll be back in plenty of time." She caught the attention of the assembled group at the dining room table and promised to return shortly.

Hurrying into the lobby, she answered the phone at the front desk. "Elaine? It's Phaedra."

"Oh, Phae . . . I'm sorry to bother you, I know you've got your hands full right now, but . . ." Elaine drew in a shaky breath. "My shop's been vandalized."

"I heard. Detective Morelli stopped by the Poison Pen last night to let us know. I wanted to rush right over and help you, but he insisted I stay put. Are you okay?"

"I'm fine. The shop, however," she added with a rueful sigh, "is another matter. I stayed up half the night taking inventory to see if anything was missing. Nothing was. Not even one piece of costume jewelry."

"Who would do such a thing? Kids? Maybe the same kids who've been breaking in around town lately?"

"Possibly. But I don't think so. Like I said, no cash was stolen, nothing's missing. Even my candy bar stash in the desk drawer is still there."

"Then it must've been vandals. Or someone in desperate need of a feather boa."

Elaine hesitated. "I have a theory. I think my intruder was looking for something. Something specific."

"Like what?"

"I'm not sure," Elaine said. "Maybe they wanted the note you found in Harriet's pocket. The one you didn't tell me about."

Phaedra eyed her in surprise. "How did you know about that?"

"Detective Morelli. After he reported the vandalism, he

asked me to provide a handwriting sample. When I asked why, he said a note was found on Harriet's body."

"But why break in to your shop? Everything went to the lab for analysis. Including the note."

"I don't know. It makes no sense." She sighed. "Morelli seems to think it's a simple B and E."

"We can't rule anything out." Phaedra frowned. "But if your theory is correct, then your intruder may very well have been Harriet's murderer."

Fourteen

Shouldn't we share our theory with the police?"
Elaine asked.

"No," Phaedra decided. "We're probably grasping at
straws. And Morelli won't appreciate my interference."

"He's asked everyone at the inn to provide a handwriting sample. I promised to give him a copy of my handwritten
inventory list later today."

"Why don't you bring it over this evening?" she suggested. "We're having drinks on the terrace at seven." She
glanced out the window at the gray, sodden skies. "Provided
the weather clears."

"I'll be there." She added hopefully, "I don't suppose
you could slip over at some point, help me restore order?"

"Yes, of course I will." Phaedra sighed. "To be honest,
I'd welcome any excuse to escape. See you soon."

After stopping by the carriage house to check on Wickham,
Phaedra slid behind the wheel of her Mini Cooper and drove
into town. She parked in front of Stage Door Costumes—the
Poison Pen was right next door—and turned off the engine.

A "Closed" sign hung inside the window and yellow crime scene tape crisscrossed the entrance.

Someone had tossed a rock through the glass-paneled door, leaving a jagged hole near the doorknob.

She hastened out of the car and hurried up the walk. Rapping sharply on the doorframe, she called out, "Elaine? Are you in there? It's me. Phaedra."

A moment later Elaine, her hair in disarray and shadowy smudges under her eyes, opened the door. "Thanks for coming. Watch your step, there's glass everywhere. I haven't vacuumed it up yet."

Following her inside, tiny bits of glass crunching under the soles of her ballet slippers, Phaedra came to a stop. Although some of the clothing racks had been restored to order, a profusion of feather boas, costumes, and sparkly paste jewelry still littered the display tables in heaps of colorful disarray.

"Oh, Elaine . . . what a mess."

"Tell me about it. Trust me, last night it was much worse." She led Phaedra back to her office. "I just made a pot of double-strength coffee if you're interested. I'm in desperate need of caffeine."

"What can I do to help?" Phaedra wandered over to a clothing rail and flicked idly through a collection of Regency costumes, admiring the colorful silk and satin Empire gowns, an emerald green cloak, spencer jackets, and a couple of men's cutaway coats.

"You can sit down and give me an excuse to do the same. And you can have a cup of coffee with me. Unless you'd rather I make tea? I think there's a box of tea bags around here somewhere."

"Coffee's fine. After this morning, I could use a cup."

Elaine gestured to a chair. "Are the Janeites driving you to distraction already?"

"I thought Harriet and Rollo were a bad combination," Phaedra admitted as she sat down. "But he and Tory are far worse. They bicker constantly. About everything."

"I think Rollo just likes to bicker. And he's very good at it."

"He is. But enough about my problems," Phaedra said, leaning forward to take the mug of coffee Elaine held out. "How are *you* doing?"

"Honestly? I'm exhausted after taking inventory half the night, but otherwise I'm okay. Nothing damaged, other than some broken glass and a smashed mirror, and nothing stolen. So, all in all, I guess I'm lucky."

"Do you really think the murderer came here to search for Harriet's note?"

"Nothing else makes sense. That note is evidence. They want it back." Elaine frowned. "One thing puzzles me, though. Why not take the note after killing Harriet?"

"Maybe there wasn't time. Or they heard something, or saw someone, and took off before they were caught."

Elaine regarded her intently. "You found the note in a loose pocket tied at her waist, right?"

"Right . . ."

"We both know Regency gowns don't have pockets, but the murderer probably didn't. It was dark, they were in a hurry. Maybe they didn't realize Harriet had it."

"Possibly. Or maybe," Phaedra added gently, "Detective Morelli is right. Maybe this was just an unrelated break-in. Kids. A prank."

"I thought you liked my theory!"

"I do. But you have to admit, it's a little far-fetched. Why not let the police handle it?"

"I suppose you're right."

Phaedra took a sip of coffee and studied her friend closely. "Tell me something."

"Of course. Anything."

"Why did you give Harriet the role of Anne Elliot? After you gave the role to Felicity? At first you refused, and the next thing I knew, you caved."

"It was a small price to pay for a little peace."

"Oh? Did she hound you about it?"

"Mercilessly. Harriet wanted that role, and she wasn't about to let it go to Felicity Penrose."

"And Felicity didn't mind?"

"Not at all. She couldn't have cared less. Why do you bring it up?"

"No reason," Phaedra said, and wrapped her fingers around the warm mug. "It's just that I noticed Harriet always got her way. She wanted the part of Anne Elliot, and she got it. And then there was Rollo's book review."

"Rollo?" Elaine echoed. "I'm not following."

"He made a point of telling everyone over tea Saturday afternoon that he planned to give Harriet's newest book a scathing review. Two and a half stars."

"I'm sure even then he was being generous. I read one of her books once." She gave a tiny shudder. "Awful."

"But that's just it. When his review appeared in the Sunday *Times-Dispatch* the next day, it was glowing. And it appeared right next to a splashy interview with Harriet."

"That is odd," Elaine agreed. "Quite an about-face."

"My point exactly."

"I wouldn't read too much into it, though." Setting her coffee aside, Elaine pushed her chair back and stood. "Harriet could be very persuasive. And so can I." She lifted one brow inquiringly. "Are you ready to dive in and help me restore order to my kingdom?"

She stood as well and sketched a curtsy. "Your humble servant." Phaedra straightened, her smile fading as she glanced at her wristwatch. "I don't have much time before my budding artists finish their paintings. Let's get on with cleaning up this mess, shall we?"

Late that afternoon the rain finally stopped, and everyone gathered on the terrace at seven for predinner drinks. Detective Morelli came and went after collecting handwriting

samples from the guests, including Phaedra and Wendy, to
have them analyzed by a handwriting expert from Charlottesville.

"That should prove interesting," Rollo observed, swirl-
ing the olives around in his martini glass. "I wonder what
our dashing detective will turn up?"

"Whatever he knows, he's keeping to himself," Tory
said. "When I asked him if the police were any closer to
figuring out who murdered poor Mrs. Overton, he wouldn't
tell me a thing."

"Standard police operating procedure." Rollo speared
an olive and popped it into his mouth. "Not that I'd mind
for one minute being locked in an interrogation room with
Detective Morelli."

"Really, Mr. Barron." Felicity drew her pale brows together. "This is a Jane Austen event, after all, and we
should all behave with the proper decorum."

"Decorum?" he echoed, and snorted. "Please! Eve
stumbled over a dead body in the kitchen garden, making
us all potential murder suspects into the bargain. 'Decorum' flew out the window when that quarrel landed in
Harriet Overton's chest."

Phaedra was about to step in and steer the conversation
away from the lurid subject of dead bodies and murder
suspects to something more Austen appropriate, when
Mark Selden made an appearance.

"Is there room for one more at this cocktail party?" he
inquired as he strolled onto the terrace.

Like Rollo, he wore a dinner jacket and tie, but there
any resemblance ended. Phaedra couldn't help but notice
how well Mark's shoulders filled out his jacket and how at
ease he was in semiformal attire. All traces of the schol-
arly professor were gone. No tweed jacket, no dark-rimmed
reading glasses, no ink-stained fingers.

It was like one of those old movies, she mused, when the
prim-and-proper secretary shook out her hair and whipped
off her eyeglasses to morph into someone entirely different.

She was glad she'd worn the deep blue embroidered silk gown with cap sleeves and fastened a sapphire pendant at her throat. Not wishing to be overdressed, she'd almost abandoned the gown for something simpler.

"Please." She indicated the empty seat beside her. "Would you like a drink? My aunt made a pitcher of martinis, or there's whiskey or bourbon if you prefer."

"Whiskey on the rocks, please."

Dave, taking his role of footman seriously, poured a generous measure of whiskey over ice and presented it to Mark on a tray.

"I thought you were holed up in your room, Professor Selden," Elaine said. "Working on your monograph."

"I'm nearly finished. Just verifying a few citations and making some final changes." He glanced at Felicity. "Ms. Penrose graciously offered to edit the manuscript."

"It's my pleasure," she assured him. "And an honor."

"I understand from Professor Brighton," he said to Elaine, "that your shop was vandalized last night. I'm sorry to hear it. I trust everything is all right?"

"I've restored order, more or less." She smiled at Phaedra. "Thanks in no small part to a certain friend."

"Was anything taken?" Felicity inquired.

"Nothing. That's what makes no sense."

"Perhaps the vandal was looking for something," Mark observed. "Something in particular. Have you any valuables on the premises?"

"Not unless you consider costume jewelry or diamanté-studded platform shoes valuable, no."

"Speaking of crime and chicanery," Rollo said as he set his martini aside, "both of which Laurel Springs seems to be distressingly *rife* with, did we all provide our handwriting samples to Detective Morelli?" He gave a smug little smile. "I know I did."

Everyone nodded.

"Why do the police need to look at our handwriting, anyway?" Tory asked peevishly, and glanced at her boss.

"Brian is staying in the guesthouse. Why should he have to provide a sample? He wasn't even in the main house at the time of the murder."

"If anything, I'd say that makes him even more of a suspect." Rollo lifted his brow. "Closer proximity to the murder scene."

"He's cooperating fully with the police," Tory pointed out. "He has nothing to hide."

Phaedra sipped her sherry. In her experience, people who claimed they had nothing to hide often did.

"But *you* were in the house, Tory," Rollo said slyly.

"So were you," she shot back.

"The note was written in calligraphy," Phaedra said, determined to sidetrack another exchange between Tory and Rollo before it grew unpleasant. Honestly, it was like refereeing unruly children.

"Calligraphy?" Tory echoed. "You mean, like you see on one of those fancy wedding invitations?"

Phaedra nodded.

"Can calligraphy be analyzed?" Felicity wondered.

"I asked Detective Morelli the same question," Phaedra said. "It turns out the answer is yes. It can."

"Well, I'm curious to know what the analysis reveals," Wendy said, and stood. "Should prove interesting. Another round, anyone?"

As Wendy refilled drinks and returned to the kitchen to oversee Chef James's dinner preparations, Elaine set her glass aside.

"I'd like to know what Harriet was doing in the kitchen garden at midnight."

"Midnight in the garden of cloak-and-dagger," Rollo quipped.

"It's not a joke, you know," Felicity reproved. "Murder is a very serious business."

"Especially for the corpse."

Phaedra followed her aunt's example and rose. "Shall we all head inside to the dining room?"

Everyone stood, some still clutching glasses, and wandered inside. Everyone, Phaedra noted, except Mark.

"You're not joining us for dinner?" she asked.

"Oh, I most definitely am." He finished his whiskey and set it down. "But first," he said as he took her hand—ungloved this time—and clasped it, "I wanted to thank you."

A flush warmed her face. "Thank me? For what?"

"For being such a gracious hostess, and for preventing Tory and Rollo from assaulting each other. That's no small thing. And," he added as he released her hand, "for giving me the opportunity to finish my monograph in relative peace and quiet."

"You're welcome. I know how important quiet is when you're writing. I published a monograph of my own only last spring."

"About?"

"Jane Austen, of course."

"Of course."

His faint smirk didn't go unnoticed. "I fail to see why you find my choice of subject matter surprising, Professor Selden. I *am* an Austen scholar, after all."

"Yes, unquestionably. Your success thus far proves it."

She studied him. "You don't like Jane Austen, do you? You've made no secret of that."

"I don't have an opinion one way or the other."

"Yet every time I mention Austen, or her novels, or anything relating to either, I sense your indifference." Her admiration for the writer was a deeply felt, personal thing, inextricably tied to her livelihood and her passion for teaching.

After Donovan Wickes broke up with her, she'd been devastated. Inconsolable. It was years ago now, high school stuff. But reading, studying, and immersing herself in Jane Austen's novels helped her through a painful and confusing time.

Hate Austen, hate me. Even as the thought occurred, she knew she was being unfair. And patently ridiculous.

But she couldn't, wouldn't admit it.

"I think you're reading too much into things." He paused. "Overanalyzing. Imagining you know what I think. And what I think," he added, his jaw tensing, "is that you take yourself too seriously. Since you're offering up criticisms."

She felt a flare of irritation. "I don't—"

"You do. Just as you insist on putting Jane Austen on a literary pedestal."

"Where she deserves to be."

"You're an excellent professor as well as a celebrated scholar," he conceded. "No question. But, at least in my opinion, your judgment is flawed where Austen is concerned."

"And here I thought I'd risen in your estimation since you first arrived in town."

Puzzlement creased his brow. "I'm sorry?"

"Oh? You don't remember? I'm not surprised. I doubt you even noticed me that night at the wine bar."

"Wine bar?" Confusion darkened his eyes. "Now you've completely lost me."

"'In my opinion,'" she said, mimicking his perfect Oxford accent, "'the woman's little more than a caricature. She looks as if she stepped straight out of one of those ridiculous costume dramas.'"

He stared at her, confusion clearing as comprehension dawned. "My discussion with Dean Carmichael," he murmured. "A colleague insisted on taking me out for a drink to welcome me to the faculty."

"Yes, one of the econ professors. Brandt, I believe. He shared your low opinion of my teaching methods."

"What? I never said—"

"You did."

He scowled. "I don't remember exactly what I said."

"How very convenient."

"It was a private conversation."

"In a public place. So, not private."

"What I *do* know," he added firmly, "is that *you* were not there."

"But I was, Professor Selden. I overheard your conversation as I was leaving the ladies'. Needless to say, I left before my temper got the better of me."

He stepped closer, so near she could smell the woodsy scent of his aftershave and see the flush of anger on his cheeks. "You left too soon. Because I went on to tell Carmichael that while I don't approve of your teaching methods, your success and popularity with students are beyond reproach.

"In short," he added curtly, "I went on to express nothing but the utmost admiration for you. Now I wonder if perhaps my admiration wasn't misplaced."

And before she could reply, he strode inside, leaving her standing, alone and chastened, on the terrace.

Fifteen

In the dining room, place settings of Limoges china and antique silverware were laid out with precision on the linen tablecloth. Wendy had elected to turn off the chandelier in favor of the soft glow of candlelight.

As the footman ladled creamy pink crab bisque into their bowls, Phaedra risked a glance across the table at Mark. He sat as far away from her as possible, exchanging polite conversation with his dining companion, Tory Sutton, and studiously avoided looking in her direction.

Embarrassed by her rush to judgment and her earlier behavior toward her colleague, she forced herself to sample the bisque. It was thick with crabmeat and delicately flavored with sherry and cream. Chef James had outdone himself. Nonetheless, she managed only a few tastes before putting her spoon down. It might as well have been ashes.

She turned to Brian with a polite smile. "Are you enjoying your stay in Virginia thus far, Mr. Callahan?"

His spoon clinked against the bottom of the bowl as he finished his soup and pushed the bowl away. "Well, I won't lie. This humidity? It's like nothing I've ever seen. It rivals South Florida on the misery scale."

"It does." She touched one of her drooping ringlets with a rueful laugh. "I often wonder why I bother."

"You're an English professor, correct?" he asked. "And a Jane Austen scholar. Your aunt is very proud of you."

She offered a modest smile. "My sister, Hannah, works at the British embassy in Washington, D.C. She has a far more exciting career than I do."

"Oh? What does she do at the embassy?"

"She's a pastry chef. Today she made a Battenberg cake and catered a tea to welcome the British prime minister."

"Impressive! I'd love to meet her. I want to get to know everyone in Wendy's family." He smiled warmly at his former high school girlfriend. "I'm hoping her family becomes my family one day soon. Very soon."

Phaedra's startled glance darted to her aunt. Wendy blushed and looked away. Her expression was unreadable. Did Brian mean what she thought he meant? Had he *proposed* to her aunt Wendy?

She leaned back slightly as Dave removed her bowl in preparation for the main course. "Then you're in luck. Hannah's coming tomorrow to visit for a few days."

"I look forward to meeting her."

As Dave cleared the first course, Eve opened a bottle of wine and filled their glasses with a crisp Sancerre.

Phaedra focused her attention on the *bœuf en croûte* that Dave set before her, which was delicious, and the conversation, which proved enlightening.

"Is tomorrow night's theatrical still going on as planned?" Felicity asked Elaine. "Despite the break-in?"

Elaine nodded and set her wine aside. "We'll start rehearsing our parts tomorrow, bright and early."

"Are we assuming the roles you gave us when we first arrived?" Rollo questioned.

"Yes. You'll each have a few speaking lines. Lines that you'll need to memorize."

Tory groaned. "Memorization? Ugh. Count me out."

"Why?" Rollo said. "You're Louisa Musgrove. All you

have to do is bat your eyelashes at Captain Wentworth and fling yourself off a wall onto the pavement."

"I'm sure you'd be only too happy to give me a shove," she retorted.

He shrugged. "Anything to help a lady out."

"There's one problem," Felicity observed. "We have no Anne Elliot."

Phaedra exchanged a quick glance with Elaine. "She's right." Harriet's death left them without a leading lady.

"That's easily resolved," Elaine said. "Felicity, you had the role originally. You can be Anne. If you wish."

"Of course."

"Did you know," Rollo said as he laid his fork and knife aside, "that Ms. Alexander was a wardrobe assistant on a BBC production of *Persuasion*? It was a television miniseries in the UK, hugely popular back in the day."

Tory looked at Elaine, her eyes bright with interest. "Really? Tell us more."

"It was a long time ago. Harriet was a script consultant and she recommended me to the producer." She busied herself cutting a small piece of beef and said nothing more.

"Who played Captain Wentworth?" Tory asked. "Don't tell me it was Colin Firth, or I'll *die*. I adore him."

"He played Mr. Darcy in the *Pride and Prejudice* miniseries," Felicity pointed out. "He's never portrayed Captain Wentworth. At least, not to my knowledge."

"How do you know so much about it?" Tory demanded of Rollo. "If it was a BBC production and Elaine was a wardrobe assistant, her name must've been buried in the credits." She smiled sweetly at Elaine. "No offense."

Elaine's answering smile was bland. "None taken."

"Actually, I was on the set as well." Rollo glanced around the table self-importantly. "I interviewed Captain Wentworth himself. The star," he added, and paused for effect. "Richard Troy."

"Oh, my," Felicity exclaimed. "He's amazing."

Mark nodded. "He's one of the finest Shakespearean actors on the planet. His King Henry the Fifth was stellar."

"Wasn't he married to that English actress?" Eve asked as she began to clear away their plates. "Jocasta Davies?"

"Still is." Felicity toyed with the stem of her wineglass. "They've been happily married for years."

Elaine, Phaedra noticed, remained strangely silent during the discussion. Why?

"Unlike Harriet and Tom," Rollo observed. "I've never seen a more miserable married couple than those two in my life." He leaned back in his chair to survey his audience. "They did everything separately—travel, work, shopping, you name it. Harriet desperately wanted children, but Tom . . ." He paused to sip the last of his wine. "Well. Let's just say, it never happened."

That might shed some light on Harriet's cavalier attitude toward her husband, Phaedra mused as Eve carried out dessert plates. He couldn't produce a son or daughter, so she had no use for him. Poor man.

"Harriet threatened to file for divorce," Rollo added. "I overheard her telling Tom as much when I walked past their room Sunday night. He begged her to reconsider."

"Overheard," Tory mocked, "or eavesdropped?"

He glared at her. "Overheard, of course. Their voices were raised. I don't make a habit of lurking outside peoples' doors."

Tory let out a disbelieving snort but said nothing more.

The conversation moved on to other topics as the main course gave way to dessert. As she took a small bite of her charlotte russe, Phaedra eyed the guests ranged around the table, all of them chatting and enjoying their trifle.

Had Harriet's threat to file for divorce been the last straw for Tom? Had it motivated him to murder his wife?

And what about Brian Callahan? She'd seen a woman sneaking out to the guesthouse on the night of the murder. Was it her aunt Wendy she'd seen? Or Tory?

And Eve, who swore she hadn't told the police about Wendy's unfortunate "cannon" comment; yet she was the only one who could possibly have overheard. And she'd been only too eager to throw Wendy under the bus.

Which one of them, Phaedra wondered as she laid her fork aside and studied the guests' faces, was Harriet Overton's murderer?

After dinner, Phaedra let herself out onto the terrace. It was a still, moonlit night, and she wanted nothing so much as to escape polite conversation for a few minutes and clear her mind. Luckily, the terrace was empty.

She wandered over to the balustrade and rested her arms on the cool stone surface. The scent of wisteria drifted on the night breeze, evocative and sweet, and her thoughts drifted as well.

Her mother hadn't called. She was still annoyed, Phaedra knew, by her daughter's reticence about Harriet's murder case. Unwillingness to gossip was a cardinal sin in Nan Brighton's estimation. That her daughter was peripherally involved in an active criminal investigation didn't matter one jot.

Nor had she heard from Hannah. Phaedra drew her brows together. Was her sister still planning to return to the inn tomorrow? How had her tea for the prime minister gone? Was she still at odds with Charles?

Had Phaedra put clean sheets on the sofa bed?

The sound of the French doors opening interrupted her thoughts, and she turned around.

"Mark," she said.

At the sound of her voice in the darkness, he halted by the door. "Sorry. I didn't realize anyone was out here. I'll go back inside."

"No. Please, stay."

He hesitated, and moved across the terrace to stand beside her. "Beautiful night." The words were gruff and impersonal.

"Yes."

The silence stretched between them, fraught with tension, until she couldn't bear it any longer.

"I'm sorry," Phaedra said finally. "For what I said earlier."

He sighed. "No need to apologize. You were right."

"I was?"

"I admit I'm not partial to Austen, although I do admire her work. As far as nineteenth-century female writers go, I always preferred the Brontë sisters. All passion and angst and dark secrets." He smiled.

"Well, since we're confessing," Phaedra said, "I'm not crazy about Shakespeare."

"You're not alone in that, believe me. I'm sure my students would agree."

"Your students love you," she protested. "You're the most popular professor in the entire English Lit department. So maybe . . ." She rested her forearms atop the cool marble railing. "Maybe I'm a little bit jealous."

"You've no reason to be." He leaned next to her. "If anything, I should be jealous of you. Celebrated Austen scholar that you are."

"You once compared me—unfavorably—to Elizabeth Bennet. You said I was quick to believe the worst of you, despite not knowing you at all."

"I did say that, didn't I? I'm sorry."

She hesitated. "No. You were right. I don't know you. Not well, anyway."

"I don't exactly make it easy, do I?"

"How do you mean?"

"I've always found it difficult to talk about myself. Personal stuff makes me itch." He let out a low chuckle. "Now, Shakespeare . . . I can go on and on about the Bard for hours."

They stood side by side, listening to the call of a screech owl and the distant sound of traffic on Main Street.

"Sometimes I forget how close to Main Street the inn is," Phaedra mused. "It feels like a million miles away. I loved staying here when I was growing up. Wendy gave me and my sister the run of the place in the summer."

"I'm guessing she was the fun aunt."

"She was. Still is." She glanced over at him. "What about you? What did you do during the summer, growing up?"

"I read a lot. My father had a remarkable library. I built model planes. Avoided my younger sister."

"Didn't you go away for the summer? Visit your aunts and uncles?"

"No."

He didn't elaborate and she didn't press him. She sensed there was more to the story, something he wasn't ready to share with her. "Hannah and I spent every summer here until I started high school. I got a job at Monticello, working weekends as a docent."

"I'm sure you made an excellent guide."

"I loved it. That's when I learned to make these gowns. Necessity required it." She glanced down at her dark blue silk gown self-consciously. "We had to wear historically appropriate clothing. I bought one dress—it was all I could afford—took it apart to make a pattern, and stitched up duplicates."

"And still managed to make the honor roll and take all AP classes, no doubt."

"You're making fun of me."

"Not at all. I admire you."

"The other kids didn't think much of me." She sighed and rested her elbows on the balustrade. "I was a convenient source of derision, at least until someone else who didn't fit in became the next target."

"Kids can be incredibly unkind." He spoke as if he knew that fact only too well.

"Academia filled the void. I'd always loved to read, especially the classics. I decided to make English literature in general, and Jane Austen in particular, my life's work."

"And look at you now." Mark turned toward her in the darkness, the moonlight faintly illuminating his face. "You've shown them all, haven't you? Intelligent, accomplished . . . and beautiful."

She opened her lips to protest, to tell him she was ordinary in the extreme. But before she could utter a word, he lowered his mouth and brushed it against hers, so feather-light and brief it might never have happened.

"As I recall, things worked out rather well for Elizabeth and Mr. Darcy." He drew back. "Good night, Phaedra."

He left her standing, alone and confused, on the moon-washed terrace. Wondering if she'd dreamed the whole thing.

Sixteen

I need to speak to you, Professor Brighton," Detective Morelli said from the drawing room doorway. "Alone."

Morelli returned to the inn on Wednesday afternoon. The guests, assembled in the drawing room and engaged in their second practice run-through of *Persuaded to Die*, were only too glad for an excuse to toss their scripts and stage directions aside and take a much-needed break.

"Can't you talk to her in front of us?" Tory demanded. "We're in the middle of rehearsal."

"I'm afraid not. This is a matter of police business."

Elaine rose and clapped her hands briskly. "All right, everyone. You heard the detective. Let's take a break and head to the front porch for refreshments."

"About time," Rollo groused. "A French roll for breakfast might do for the typical Regency gentleman or lady, but I need more substantial fare. Eggs, and bacon."

"I'd say that's the last thing you need," Tory sniped.

As they trooped out to the front porch to take their tea and cake alfresco, Phaedra led the detective into the room. Scripts, several discarded ladies' fans, and a pair of prop dueling pistols cluttered the coffee table.

She eyed the folder in his hand with interest. "Is that the handwriting analyst's report?"

"It is."

"And did your expert find anything of interest among our guests' handwriting samples?" She settled at one end of the sofa and gestured for him to do the same.

He perched on the edge of a Victorian armchair.

"None of the samples yielded anything noteworthy, I'm afraid. I've no doubt our culprit deliberately disguised his or her writing. Nevertheless," he added as disappointment registered on her face, "Ms. Hendricks came up with some interesting theories about the murderer."

Phaedra leaned forward. "Such as?"

"According to her, the fact that the killer chose this particular form of writing—namely, calligraphy—indicates he or she is mindful of appearances, on the page as well as in person."

"That makes sense."

"And," Morelli went on as he opened the folder and flipped through the notes, "she says that although the writing flows and the message is flowery, there's rigid control in the formation of the letters. The author sought attention but also didn't wish to reveal too much."

"An interesting dichotomy."

He nodded. "And the pronounced slant indicates insecurity."

"Which means our murderer is controlling and insecure. And manipulative," Phaedra added. "Does Ms. Hendricks have any idea whether the calligrapher is male or female?"

"Nothing definitive either way. I tend to lean toward a female. This seems more like a woman's thing to me."

"There are male calligraphers, Detective," Phaedra pointed out mildly, "and male romance writers. Purple prose isn't confined to the female sex."

"You're right. I don't mean to sound sexist. But my instinct tells me this particular writer is a woman."

"I agree."

He regarded her with a raised eyebrow. "That must've been painful."

"I never thought we'd find ourselves on the same page," she admitted. "So to speak. But in this instance, I think you're right."

"Only in this instance?"

"Maybe once or twice before." Phaedra glanced at the silver tea service on one end of the coffee table. "I know you don't drink tea, but there's a fresh pot of coffee in the kitchen if you'd like a cup."

"I'm good. But thanks. For agreeing with me," he added. "And for your time." He stood to leave.

"Before you go, may I ask you a question?"

He eyed her warily. "What's that?"

"Is Tom Overton no longer a suspect?"

"No. He's not. Eve Kowalski stated that she heard him snoring, quite loudly, during the time frame of the murder."

"About that." Phaedra crossed her arms loosely beneath her bodice. "Eve mentioned she wore earbuds that night, to watch a program on her tablet while her husband Dave slept. He also snores."

"And?"

"If what she says is true, how could she possibly have heard Tom snoring? She and Dave were in the bridal suite, in the rear of the house. Harriet and Tom stayed in the front tower room. On the opposite side of the hall."

"She got up to go to the bathroom. Which," he added patiently, "is right next to the Overtons' former suite."

She pressed her lips together. "What about the argument Rollo Barron overheard between Harriet and Tom? She threatened to divorce him. He was upset and begged her to reconsider. Isn't that a possible motive for murder?"

"From what I understand, she threatened to divorce him on a daily basis. And as far as any financial benefit," Morelli added, "Tom Overton is wealthy in his own right. Just as well, considering Harriet left her entire estate to her only sister . . . and to a cat rescue foundation."

But Phaedra had one last card to play. "Mr. Overton was on the archery team in college."

"That doesn't make him a murderer. I was on the chess team in high school, even competed in a few tournaments. Doesn't make me Bobby Fischer."

With a sigh, Phaedra dropped her arms to her sides. She knew when she was outmaneuvered. "I'll show you out."

An hour later Phaedra found herself at Dixon's farm stand, a basket over one arm as she debated the merits of two heirloom tomatoes for the evening's salad.

"We had a good crop this year," Emmylou Dixon, owner of the farm, said. "Can't go wrong with either. Or both."

Phaedra nodded as she held up one of the tomatoes and breathed in its dusky, sun-warmed scent. "Good point. Both it is." She handed them over to be weighed. "Hannah's coming out to help us at the inn." She picked up a peach, admiring the fuzzy blush and drinking in its ripe summer scent. "Only the best fruit for her cobblers and pies."

"She's a very discerning customer." Emmylou placed the tomatoes on a scale. "Speaking of which, I saw your old boyfriend the other day."

"My old boyfriend?" Although the news startled her, she gave no sign as she inspected the blueberries and added a quart container to the basket. "You mean Donovan?"

Emmylou nodded. "You two were like pork chops and gravy back in high school. Never one without the other."

"I'm sure you're mistaken. He left Laurel Springs years ago. Last I heard he was living in Boston somewhere. The South End, I think."

"Oh, no mistake," the older woman said firmly. "It was him, all right. I know, because I spoke to him myself."

"Where?" Phaedra shifted her basket from one arm to the other, keeping her question casual. "What did he say?"

"He was with a real estate agent, looking at that empty café. Bertie's old place. It's for sale, you know."

She did know. Roberta Walsh, or Bertie, as she was lo-cally known, was gone and her café stood empty. There'd been a flurry of interest in the property from a few inves-tors but no buyers thus far.

"Why would Donovan be interested in the café?" Phae-dra asked.

"He wants to buy it. At least that's what he told me."

"But why? He's not a chef, or a short-order cook. He's a fitness instructor. He owns a gym. At least he did," she hastened to add, "the last I heard."

Emmylou bagged the tomatoes and handed them over with a shrug. "All I know is, he's interested in buying the property and opening a gym downtown. Says he's got three in the South End already. That'll be two fifty."

Phaedra reached in her reticule and handed over a ten. "Sorry. I don't have anything smaller." Donovan was here? In Laurel Springs? And looking to buy a property?

Why, out of all the Main Streets in all of the small towns in the world, had he ended up on *hers*?

Emmylou took the ten Phaedra gave her. "He wants to be 'hands on,' his exact words. And he liked that there's an apartment above the café. Said he plans to live there."

Her mood, so buoyant before, sank. "So . . . he's mov-ing back here. To stay."

Mrs. Dixon nodded as she pressed the bills and quar-ters into Phaedra's hand. "He's a catch, if you ask me. Sin-gle, good-looking, successful businessman . . . and eager to move back to Laurel Springs. Permanently."

After spilling the tomatoes and fruit on the kitchen coun-ter, Phaedra grabbed an apron and began to help James prep the salad.

"Where did you find those?" he asked as she began rinsing the tomatoes.

"Dixon's farm stand. Aren't they gorgeous?"

"Beautiful," he approved. "And perfect for what I have in mind tonight. After they're cleaned, slice them into wedges and take those mozzarella pearls from the fridge. We'll have individual caprese salads and garlic bruschetta for starters. Regency food be damned."

Ordinarily, the thought of Italian food made her mouth water. But knowing that Donovan Wickes was in town—soon to become a permanent fixture—didn't do much for her appetite. Why was he coming back to Laurel Springs, of all places?

What was he thinking?

As she went into the dining room and took a stack of plates down from the china cabinet, Phaedra wished, not for the first time, that her sister Hannah were here. Acting as a temporary sous chef wasn't really in her wheelhouse. Her scones, while passable, couldn't compare to Hannah's.

More importantly, she missed having her sister's ear. She missed the days when Hannah would sit cross-legged at the foot of her twin bed and listen as Phaedra confided her teenaged troubles du jour. Her advice was thoughtful and generally reliable.

Other than Lucy and Marisol, Phaedra had no one to confide in. No one to share her concerns or theories about the murder, no one to discuss Mark Selden's mixed messages.

She sighed, imagining herself on a riverbank, plucking daisy petals one by one. *He likes me; he likes me not . . .*

"Have you heard from your sister?"

Wendy's question behind her caused Phaedra to turn suddenly, nearly dropping the plates cradled precariously in her arms. "No. I haven't." Irritation marked her words as she began setting the plates on the table.

"Sorry. I didn't mean to startle you." Wendy opened a drawer on the sideboard and took out a stack of crisp linen napkins. "Her flight from D.C. should've landed in Charlottesville by now."

"You know Hannah. Thoughtless to a fault."

"She's busy, Phaedra. She probably hasn't had a chance to call yet. I just wondered if you'd heard from her. You know me," she added as she folded a napkin and centered it on the plate. "I worry."

"I'm sure she's fine."

Wendy nodded distractedly as she continued to fold napkins. "Yes, you're probably right. I think I'll call Chef Armand tomorrow. See if he'd consider coming back."

"Why? Chef James is more than sufficient. No histrionics, just good food."

"That's just it." She lowered her voice. "His food is good. But it isn't haute cuisine. Take tonight, for example," she added, making a moue of disapproval as she placed the last napkin on the last plate. "*Italian* food."

"What's wrong with Italian food?"

"Nothing. I love pasta even more than I love dark chocolate. But this is a Regency-themed week, Phaedra. You of all people should understand that. Nothing we've served since Armand left is historically appropriate."

"If Harriet were still here, I'd agree. But she's not. And no one's complained, so I don't see the problem."

"I suppose you're right." She didn't sound happy about that. "I'll call Armand later tonight, just the same. Couldn't hurt to put out a feeler or two."

"You'll just get a refusal and an earful of French insults for your trouble."

"I wouldn't be so sure about that." Wendy paused in the dining room doorway. "I still know how to charm a man. Which reminds me—I won't be joining you in the dining room tonight. I have an eight o'clock dinner date at Lagniappe."

The French-Creole-Cajun restaurant was the newest and, according to her mother, the finest fine dining restaurant in town. "Lagniappe," Phaedra knew, meant a gift, "a little something extra."

"That's great, Aunt Wendy," she said, and tried to mean it. "I'm sure you and Brian will have a great time."

She just hoped that Brian's "little something extra" didn't turn out to be a marriage proposal.

Seventeen

After dinner, as the rehearsal began, Hannah still hadn't shown up at the inn.

Phaedra leaned back against the kitchen counter and frowned at her phone screen. Her sister wasn't answering her calls or responding to texts, and she felt the first real pinprick of worry.

Where was she?

After dismissing her aunt's earlier concerns, uneasiness settled over her. What if something had happened? Had Hannah's plans changed? Surely if she couldn't make it, she would've let them know.

"Everything all right, Professor?"

James, who'd stayed on to watch the rehearsal, paused by the back door, his hand on the knob.

"Fine. Just waiting for my sister to arrive."

"Oh, yes. Your aunt said she's a pastry chef at the British embassy. Is she driving or flying out of D.C.?"

Phaedra dragged her gaze away from her phone. "Flying."

"The weather's been unsettled all day," James said. "Thunderstorms. Her flight was probably delayed."

"Yes. I'm sure you're right." She smiled and laid her

phone aside. "Thanks. And thanks for staying to watch our play after whipping up such a delicious dinner. Everyone loved your mushroom risotto."

He smiled modestly, bid her good night, and left.

She glanced at her watch. Ten fifteen. Not late, but past the time Hannah should have arrived. Wendy and Brian were still at dinner.

She'd give it another forty-five minutes, she decided. Then she'd try calling her sister again.

Phaedra moved to the window over the kitchen sink and peered out. The guesthouse was dark, which meant Brian and Wendy hadn't yet returned.

Suddenly unable to bear her own company or the silence of the empty kitchen one minute longer, she decided to go outside, to get some fresh air. She couldn't stand one more second of waiting and worrying.

The night air was cool and redolent with the fragrance of night-blooming jasmine as she stepped onto the terrace. No one was out.

Clutching her phone in the event Hannah called, Phaedra began to walk. It was what she did when she needed to think. And she desperately needed to think, if only to focus her thoughts and take her mind off her sister.

Twenty minutes later, after circling the perimeter of the pond, she headed back toward the house. On impulse, she detoured down the graveled path that led to the kitchen garden.

Who, she wondered as she drifted past beds of herbs and edible flowers, had killed Harriet? Who had lured her out here to the kitchen garden in the middle of the night?

A calligrapher. Probably, according to both Detective Morelli and the handwriting expert, a woman. Harriet had been shot in the chest at close range with a crossbow.

Her body was found in a patch of rosemary.

Mark's quote came back to her. *There's rosemary, that's for remembrance; pray, love, remember . . .*

Remember what, exactly? Had Harriet slighted the

murderer somehow? Was her death retribution? A warning? Or had she forgotten something, something important to the killer? Was the fact that her body was found in rosemary symbolic? Or merely a coincidence?

She paused at the site where Eve had found Harriet's body. A piece of crime scene tape fluttered in a nearby bush. What, she asked herself, did the police know with certainty about the killer? He or she was physically fit and able to climb a tree without difficulty, knew how to use climbing equipment, and had skill with a crossbow.

Those facts would seem to eliminate Rollo as a suspect. He was neither fit nor athletically inclined. His attempts to shoot an arrow into the target resulted in only one direct hit, and that had been on the outer edge, nowhere near the bull's-eye.

Dave Kowalski was in excellent physical shape. But like his wife, he hadn't taken part in the archery competition, so there was no way of knowing his skill level with a bow and arrow. She'd ask Eve about it tomorrow.

Mark was fit, she thought suddenly. And he knew quite a bit about climbing, too.

She thrust the thought aside as disloyal and unfair. Professor Selden could no more kill someone than misquote Shakespeare. Besides, he didn't know Harriet. He'd barely ventured out of his room since he'd arrived.

Nor did he know the first thing about shooting a bow and arrow or firing a crossbow.

Which brought her to Brian Callahan. He was older, early middle-aged, but in good physical shape nonetheless. He certainly could've climbed that tree. But like Mark, he didn't know Harriet. Which gave him no discernable motive to kill her.

Yes, he was a liar, and a cheat, and a rat of the first order. No question.

But was he a murderer? Hard to say.

The moon moved behind a cloud, cloaking the garden

in darkness. Phaedra glanced at the luminous dial of her watch. It was ten forty-five.

Time, she decided, to check on Hannah.

She lifted her phone, and the screen sprang to life. But there were no new messages from her sister.

"Damn it," she muttered. "Where are you, Han?"

Why hadn't she shown up yet? Why didn't she answer her phone?

That's it, Phaedra decided. *I'm calling right now.* As she pressed the phone icon, her grip slipped and the device flew out of her gloved hand to land on the ground.

Oh, drat. It was here somewhere. Had to be. But where?

The woody scent of rosemary teased the air as she knelt and began to scrabble in the dirt. With the moonlight gone, she could barely see her hand in front of her face, and gravel from the edge of the path dug painfully into one silk-clad knee. "Call me, Hannah," she muttered. "Right now. Help me find my phone."

But her phone remained stubbornly silent.

Her fingers brushed against something small and round under the bush. A berry? No, it was too hard, and too flat. A rock?

The clouds shifted and moonlight once again silvered the ground around her. The object, whatever it was, was small and a dull brown. She picked it up. A button. A crosshatch pattern was etched into the wood, and there was a shank on the back.

Where had she seen it before?

Before she could consider the question further, or examine the button more closely, she heard the stealthy crunch of gravel nearby, growing nearer, and straightened.

"Who's there?" she asked, straining to see in the silvery darkness as uneasiness gripped her. "Wendy? Is that you?"

No sound. No answer. No movement.

As she turned back around, she heard the rapid whoosh of air, and something hard crashed down on the back of her head. Pain blossomed and exploded behind her skull. She let out a muffled moan and sank to the ground as her knees folded beneath her.

Then everything went blessedly dark.

Eighteen

Phaedra? Phaedra, where are you?"

Panicked voices cut through the moonlit darkness as she regained consciousness. Wincing at the effort, she sat up. She was half-in, half-out of the rosemary bed.

What was she doing in the rosemary bed?

"I'm here," she croaked, but doubted anyone could hear her. Her throat was dry, and even those two words taxed her energy. How long had she lain here?

She remembered coming out to the garden in search of fresh air, trying to call Hannah, dropping her phone.

Her phone! Where was it?

She tried to stand, but dizziness overtook her, and she remained where she was.

"Phaedra Jane Brighton!" Wendy shouted. "Where are you?"

"I'm here, Aunt," she mumbled, and gingerly touched her throbbing head. Her fingers detected a lump the size of a Fabergé egg at the base of her neck. Who did this? Why?

Her gaze scanned the ground nearby. The scent of rosemary was strong, and its fragrance jogged her memory. In a rush she recalled the wooden button she'd found when she dropped her phone, just before someone snuck up behind her and bashed her on the head.

She looked for it now, in the dirt and under the bushes and rosemary plants, but the button was gone.

Her phone, however, lay on the path, and she stretched out her hand to grasp it. It was nearly eleven thirty.

"Professor Brighton!" Eve's voice rang out nearby, etched with concern. "Are you out here?"

"In the kitchen garden," Phaedra said again, her voice stronger this time. "In the rosemary patch."

A moment later, Eve, Wendy, and Dave gathered around her, their faces pale and startled.

"What happened?" her aunt cried, kneeling beside her. "Are you all right? I was half out of my mind with worry!"

"I'm fine," Phaedra assured her. "Other than my head, which feels like the inside of a timpani drum. How was your dinner with Brian?"

"How was my *dinner*? Is that all you can say when we find you out here, sprawled in the rosemary in the middle of the night, just like that poor woman—"

She didn't finish the sentence. She didn't need to.

"I'm not dead, Aunt. And it's hardly the middle of the night. I'm fine. Just a little woozy, that's all."

Wendy eyed her niece suspiciously. "You didn't overindulge in the sherry, did you?"

"No! It's all I can do to force down one glass."

"Then please. Tell me what happened."

In as few words as possible—her head still throbbed—Phaedra relayed her evening walk, her concern when Hannah hadn't shown up, finding the button in the dirt, and getting hit from behind.

Shock froze Wendy's features. "Who would do such a thing? And why?"

"I wish I knew. It might have something to do with the button I found."

"What button?"

"It's gone," Phaedra said, frustration undercutting her words. "I found it lying under a bush."

"I'm calling your sister."

"Why? There's nothing she can do. Besides, she's not answering."

"I spoke with her earlier. Her flight was delayed." Wendy reached for her own phone. "And there was a mix-up with the rental car. But it's all straightened out now and she's on her way. After I call an ambulance, I'm calling Hannah. And the police."

"What? No!" Phaedra struggled to her feet. "I told you, I'm fine."

"You were hit on the head by an unknown assailant. You might be concussed."

"I'm not concussed. No nausea, no dizziness, no blurry vision. Just—" She touched the lump on the back of her neck. "A slight headache."

"You should be examined. What if you fall asleep and slip into a coma?"

"I won't slip into a coma. I'm going to the carriage house to let Wickham and Bella out, then I'll take something for this headache and go straight to bed."

"I'll walk with you."

Knowing argument was useless, Phaedra took her aunt's arm, and together they made their slow way across the lawn to the carriage house.

"Are you sure you're all right?" Wendy asked as they paused outside the kitchen door.

"Fine. I wasn't out very long. Maybe twenty or thirty minutes."

"I still think an EMT should look at you. And you should tell Detective Morelli that someone attacked you."

"I will," she promised, "tomorrow. Good night, Aunt," Phaedra added as she unlocked the door. "See you tomorrow."

She called the cats, and as they shot downstairs and

streaked outside, she reached into a cabinet for a glass and a bottle of acetaminophen and swallowed two tablets.

Thankfully, Bella didn't dawdle, but did her business and returned to the door a few minutes later. Wickham was not so cooperative.

"Poor boy," she sympathized as he stalked back into the kitchen ten minutes later. "I know you're hungry. Don't worry, there's plenty for both of you."

She filled their bowls with fresh water and added extra kibble to Wickham's food dish.

He eyed Bella, delicately lapping up water, and investigated his own dish. *I don't do sharing. And I don't do roommates.*

Phaedra rubbed his ears and yawned. "Bon appétit. I'll grab a blanket and pillow and wait on the sofa for Hannah."

Leaving the light on—she had a long-standing phobia of staircases dating back to a horror movie Hannah had once insisted she watch—Phaedra trudged upstairs to the linen closet, took down a blanket, and grabbed a pillow from her bed.

Her head felt marginally better as she settled on the sofa and propped the pillow at her back. Glimpsing one of her dad's paperback mystery offerings on the coffee table, she picked up *The Circular Staircase* by Mary Roberts Rinehart and began to read.

Barely two paragraphs in, she fell asleep.

Her sleep was restless and troubled with dreams, fragments of dreams, and the beginning of a nightmare with a shadowy figure lurking outside the carriage house window.

A scraping jolted her awake, followed by a click, and she sat up and groped on the coffee table for her wristwatch.

It was twenty minutes past midnight.

Her hand froze as the tumbler on the front door lock engaged with an audible click. Someone was outside. Someone was trying to get in.

Was it the same person who'd clunked her on the head, come back to finish the job?

Not if I can help it.

She flung back the blanket with an unsteady hand and swung her feet to the floor. A weapon. She needed a weapon.

The only thing within reach was a speckled stoneware mug she'd left on the coffee table that morning. And it was half-full of cold Earl Grey.

She hesitated. While she disliked the thought of tea flying everywhere if she hit the intruder over the head, needs must.

Better a tea stain than a bloodstain.

Before she could dart into the kitchen and empty the tea into the sink, or better yet, find a more lethal weapon, the lock clicked again, and the door edged open.

Phaedra stood—a bit unsteadily—and crept toward the shadowy front hall. At least she had the element of surprise on her side.

The door creaked open, and a figure paused on the threshold. Phaedra let out a yell and launched herself at the intruder, stoneware mug upraised.

A brief struggle ensued as the trespasser blocked her attack with one arm and managed to reach out and switch on the hall light.

"Phae, have you seriously lost your *mind*?"

Phaedra lowered her arm and blinked in the bright light. "Hannah?"

"Who else would it be?" she demanded. "Never mind, I don't even want to know." She dropped her handbag on the hall table and dragged her wheeled suitcase over the doorstop. "Why are the lights on?"

"I fell asleep reading."

Hannah groaned. "Not *Pride and Prejudice* again, I hope."

"No. A murder mystery."

"That explains the lights." She frowned. "Why do you

read stuff like that, anyway? You only scare yourself. Didn't Wendy tell you I'd be late?"

"She did. She said your flight was delayed and there was a rental car mix-up."

"You have no idea. This has been the longest, worst day of my entire life."

"Why didn't you answer my calls or texts?"

"My phone was on airplane mode. When I got to the rental car counter, everything was so mixed up that I forgot to turn it back on." She eyed the blanket and pillow on the sofa. "Is that where I'm staying?"

"No, of course not." Her sister's toffee-brown hair, normally immaculate, was bedraggled, and her lips parted in a yawn for the second time. "Go upstairs and get some sleep. You must be exhausted."

Phaedra had a million questions to ask Hannah, starting with the status of her relationship with Charles. But she refrained. Nor did she mention the lump on the back of her head or how she'd acquired it. Right now, they both needed sleep. Everything else could wait until morning.

"I am. Thanks." Hannah gave her a grateful smile, grabbed the handle of her wheeled suitcase, and thumped up the stairs to the loft's bedroom.

Thursday morning Phaedra busied herself in the inn's kitchen, preparing pots of Earl Grey and Formosa oolong tea. Hannah moved with quiet efficiency from the fridge to the counter to the stove, retrieving a carton of eggs, mixing a batch of scones, and thrusting two muffin tins filled with batter into the oven to bake.

She was pale and monosyllabic, but otherwise her late night hadn't taken a noticeable toll.

Chef James focused on cooking omelets and simmering poached eggs. Toast popped up in the toaster, and Phaedra took down a serving plate from the cabinet. She set the toast, whipped butter, a jar of honey, and an assortment of jam on a tray and carried everything out to the side porch.

There was no time to talk to her sister.

Wendy came in as Phaedra returned to the kitchen, bid her a cheery good morning, and went straight to the coffeepot and poured herself a cup.

"How was your dinner date last night?" Phaedra asked.

"Wonderful." She took a sip of coffee and closed her eyes in momentary ecstasy before turning around. "We were the last ones to leave the restaurant."

"I bet the owners loved that."

"We were having such a good time we didn't notice how late it was getting until the waiter began stacking chairs. Brian asked me to go antiquing this afternoon."

"Another date? So soon?"

Wendy paused, cup halfway to her lips. "Yes. Why not? We enjoy each other's company."

"It just seems like things are moving a little fast."

"Things," her aunt said firmly, "are moving along just fine."

"Don't forget your guests. We're going downtown this afternoon to shop and sightsee, and grab lunch at the deli. Shouldn't you be there? You *are* the hostess, after all."

Phaedra had no qualms using guilt to persuade Wendy to join them. She'd do anything to protect her aunt from the questionable machinations of Brian Callahan.

"I appreciate your concern for me, Phaedra," Wendy said, her lips tightening, "but I'm a big girl. I can take care of myself." She set her cup aside to indicate the subject was closed. "How's your head doing?"

Hannah paused in the midst of creaming butter and sugar to eye her aunt with raised eyebrows. "I know Phaedra's a little eccentric, Aunt Wendy. But asking how her head's doing? That's rude, even for you."

"She's not being rude," Phaedra said. "She's concerned. Unnecessarily so," she added as she slid James's omelet and sauté pans into the sink to soak. "And to answer your question, Aunt Wendy, I'm fine. No lasting damage."

"Will someone please tell me what's going on?" Hannah demanded as she switched off the stand mixer and dusted off her floury hands. "What happened last night?"

"When I got back from my date," Wendy said, "your sister was missing. We found her lying in the middle of the kitchen garden. She'd been conked on the head from behind and left unconscious."

Hannah let out a horrified gasp and turned to Phaedra. "You got hit on the head? Why didn't you tell me? Why aren't you in the hospital? You could have a concussion!"

After reassuring Hannah she was fine and explaining she'd gone out for air, dropped her phone, and found a potential clue in the garden, Phaedra hoped that would be the end of it.

She should've known better.

"A clue?" Hannah's face turned to thunder. "Please tell me you're not investigating that Regency author's death. Tell me you haven't landed yourself in the middle of *another* murder investigation!"

"Okay. I won't tell you."

"You're a professor, Phaedra, not a sleuth! You nearly got yourself killed the last time." Hannah glared at her. "Why can't you sit at your desk and write those long, boring articles that no one but other academics read—"

"Monographs," Phaedra supplied.

"—or spend your time researching stuff in the university library? Why can't you stay out of trouble?"

Before Phaedra could answer, Wendy's phone rang. When she saw the name on the screen, her aunt's face brightened.

"Excuse me, girls. I need to take this." She abandoned them to dart out the back door.

"Bet I know who that was," Phaedra muttered.

"Who?" Hannah asked.

"Brian."

"Who's Brian?"

Eve appeared before she could answer. "We need another pot of Earl Grey, Professor."

"I'll be right there."

As Phaedra grabbed the kettle of water she kept simmering on the back burner, Hannah returned to the mixer. "You haven't answered my question."

"Which one?"

"Let's go with the first one. Why can't you stay out of trouble?"

"I don't exactly seek it out," Phaedra said in her defense. "Trouble just seems to find me."

"Then you need to do a better job of hiding from it."

After brewing the tea and taking it out to the guests, Phaedra returned to the kitchen and removed her apron. "My duties here are done. At least until tomorrow morning."

"You should try working in a professional kitchen every day," Hannah said. "You have no idea what hell is."

"Would you like some tea?" Phaedra asked as she reached for the pot of Earl Grey and poured herself a cup. "You can sit and tell me all about it."

"I'm good. Thanks."

"Suit yourself." She stirred in a touch of honey and took a sip. "Finally," she said, and sighed as she settled at one end of the table with her cup, "we have a chance to catch up. What's new? How did the prime minister's tea go?"

"Very well. The Battenberg cake was a big hit."

"I'm sure it was. Any photos?"

"Of course." Hannah rested one hip against the counter and pulled out her phone. She scrolled to a photo of herself and the British PM standing alongside a lavishly set tea table. She sported a chef's toque and a wide smile.

Phaedra was properly impressed. "Did Charles attend?"

"No. He's in London this week." She dropped the phone in her pocket and returned the egg carton to the fridge.

"How's he doing?"

"Fine, I suppose. You'd have to ask him."

She set her cup down with a thump. "Hannah, what's going on? Hasn't he been in touch?"

"What's going on?" Her blue eyes flashed. "I've just provided scones and muffins for the breakfast buffet, after very little sleep, I might add; now I'm making a Victoria sponge for afternoon tea. And no, we didn't break up. You have to be together in the first place to do that."

She turned away to disengage the bowl from the mixer stand, but not before Phaedra saw her lower lip tremble. She stood, emptied her cup into the sink, and rinsed it.

"When you're ready to talk," she told her sister gently as she turned to leave, "I'll be ready to listen."

Hannah didn't answer. But she paused as she wiped down the counter, and gave an almost imperceptible nod.

Her sister was hurting, that much was clear. Her bright, effervescent personality had gone as flat as day-old champagne. But one thing hadn't changed. She was still just as stubborn as Phaedra remembered.

As she pushed through the kitchen door into the hallway, she vowed to get the truth out of her sister before the day was over.

Halfway down the hall, telling herself she was glad she wasn't enmeshed in a relationship, with all the messiness it entailed, she collided with an unexpected and immovable object.

The obstacle was male. Dark hair, dark blue eyes—filled now with concern—and just as dangerously handsome as she remembered from high school. He was older now, like her, but age had only improved him. He was still, unquestionably . . .

"Donovan!" she exclaimed as her heart sank down to her toes. "What are you doing here?"

Nineteen

S orry. My fault," he apologized, and reached out to steady her elbow. "Are you okay?"

"Fine," she mumbled, and brushed a stray ringlet, more of a straggler now, from her face. "I'm good." He looked exactly the same. No, she decided, he looked even better than he had in high school. She drew back abruptly. "What are you doing here? At Aunt Wendy's B and B?"

"I'm staying here. I'm a guest."

"No, you're not."

He laughed. "Okay, I'm not. I'm a ghost. A figment of your imagination."

"More like a memory I'd rather forget."

The second she blurted out the words, Phaedra regretted them. Not only because they were hurtful, and made his smile slip, but because she didn't want him thinking, even for a moment, that she cared.

"Well. You haven't changed a bit," Donovan said, and tilted his head to one side. "Still honest to a fault."

"I'm sorry. I shouldn't have said that."

He shrugged. "It's okay."

"No, it isn't. It's just that you caught me off guard. Wendy didn't tell me you were arriving today."

"Actually . . ." He scratched the back of his head. "I've been here since Monday. But don't blame your aunt. She didn't tell you because I swore her to secrecy."

Phaedra stared at him, and all at once the pieces fell into place. The mysterious newlyweds and their refusal to leave their room; the single suitcase by the door; and Wendy's insistence that Eve bring their trays upstairs.

"The bridal suite!" she exclaimed. "You're one half of the newlywed couple, aren't you?"

Suddenly, she understood Wendy's reticence. There was no easy way to explain to Phaedra that her first love, who'd shattered her heart into a million jagged pieces, was staying in the bridal suite with his new bride.

"Newlywed couple?" he echoed. "Not exactly." He looked uncomfortable and suddenly a lot less sure of himself.

"What does that mean, not exactly? Either you just got married or you didn't."

He brushed a hand over his chin. A habit she remembered well, and one that meant he wasn't being completely honest. He still had that tiny mole just above his jaw. "I almost did. Get married," he explained. "But Emily backed out at the last minute. The night before."

"Emily? Endicott?"

"You remember her?"

How could she forget? He'd ditched her for Emily on the night of their senior prom. Rumor had it the pair had driven up to a lookout point on Afton Mountain in Donovan's GTO and . . . well, she'd figured out the rest.

"Of course I remember. You dumped me for her."

Discomfort flickered over his face, but he managed a cocky smile. "I don't remember it that way. *You* sent *me* packing, as I recall."

"After you ditched me for Emily on prom night." She

shrugged. "But that was a long time ago. We were seventeen. Kids."

Relief warmed his words. "Yeah. Kids. Poetic justice in the end, at least for me." He held up his hand to show her his bare ring finger. "She cancelled the wedding, returned my ring, and told every one of our two hundred invited friends that I was to blame. Serves me right, I guess."

"Oh. That's . . ." *Karma*, she almost said. "I can't imagine. I'm sorry."

"I had to cancel the wedding, cancel the honeymoon, and return our wedding gifts. But the bridal suite was reserved and paid for, and Em definitely didn't want it, so I decided not to let the room go to waste. Wallow in my sorrow for a few days." He flashed her a sad, crooked grin.

She almost fell for it. Almost. Until she recalled Emmylou Dixon telling her Donovan was in town and that he was interested in buying the old corner café building.

That didn't sound like the actions of a brokenhearted bridegroom to her.

"You'll survive, Donovan. Like you always do."

He let out a surprised laugh. "Wow. That's cynical. And harsh, even for you."

"It's not a criticism. Well, not entirely." She paused. "I guess it's true what they say. That some things never change."

"Meaning?"

"Meaning, you always find a way to make the best of a bad situation."

"What can I say? I'm a survivor." He shrugged. "That's a good thing, right?"

"I suppose. As long as your survival doesn't hurt someone else in the process."

His smile, so cocksure and charming, slipped. He sighed and lowered his voice. "Listen, I'm sorry I hurt you back then. I was a jerk, okay? No excuses. I behaved—"

"Like a cad?" Phaedra finished, as thoughts of Mr.

Wickham, Austen's handsome, red-coated scoundrel, came to mind.

"A cad? Seriously?" He shifted on his feet. "Okay, yes, I suppose I was. But that was years ago. People change."

She was pretty sure Donovan Wickes hadn't changed one iota. But although he hadn't changed, she had. And she wasn't about to let him get under her skin in the meantime. "Now that your secret's out," Phaedra said, changing the subject, "why not join us for dinner tonight? We're going on a carriage ride afterward."

"Dinner? With those Austen people?" He shook his head. "I wouldn't fit in. I barely passed high school English."

"Those Austen people, as you call them, are from all walks of life. There's a journalist, an editor, an administrative assistant . . . even a former wardrobe mistress. It'll be fun. Good food, good conversation."

"I don't know . . ."

"'My idea of good company,'" Phaedra added, quoting Anne Elliot, "'is the company of clever, well-informed people, who have a great deal of conversation.'"

He hesitated. "You mentioned a carriage ride."

"Wendy hired a pair of restored coaches to take us out to Dixon's farm for a 'moonlight and champagne' ride after dinner. You should come along. The best cure for a broken heart is getting out there again."

"Fun?" He lifted his brow. "I'm sure it will be . . . for everyone else. But I just got jilted. Dumped. Left at the altar."

Did he actually expect *sympathy* from her? He did. Proving that he was still the same old self-centered Donovan she remembered. "I'll tell my aunt to set an extra place, just in case you change your mind." She thought of Tory and added, "You never know. You might meet someone interesting."

After Phaedra led Wendy's guests on a leisurely stroll down Main Street, pausing to exclaim over a handmade quilt, a rack of couture dresses, and a collection of hammered metal jewelry, they'd just reached the Old Virginia Deli when a familiar voice called out Phaedra's name.

She turned, and surprise suffused her face. "Aunt Wendy! You made it."

Her aunt smiled at the group gathered around her. "I couldn't very well miss our outing, could I?"

"Glad you decided to join us," Rollo said, and the others nodded. "We were just about to have lunch."

"Why don't you all go inside and place your orders?" Phaedra suggested. "We'll be in shortly."

As they turned away and trooped inside the narrow brick building, Phaedra turned back to her aunt. "I thought you and Brian were going antiquing this afternoon."

"We were. But I thought about what you said, and I decided you're right."

"That he's moving too fast?"

"That I should be here with our guests," Wendy shot back. "Phaedra, I love you dearly, but please don't interfere in my love life. You don't want to turn into your mother, do you?"

She winced. "Message received. How did Brian take the news?"

"He was disappointed. But he offered me a rain check tomorrow."

"Kind of him."

"Phaedra . . ." Wendy said warningly.

"Sorry. And before we go inside and join the others, why didn't you tell me Donovan's been hiding out in the bridal suite? I had no idea. I literally ran into him in the hallway. You might have warned me."

"*This* is why I didn't want to tell you. I knew you'd be upset."

"I'm not upset. Not anymore," she amended. "But I wish you'd told me."

"He'd already reserved the suite. And when everything fell apart with Emily, he decided to keep the reservation, and swore me to secrecy. Poor man." Wendy reached out to squeeze her hand. "I should have told you. I'm sorry."

"It's okay. It was a long time ago and I shouldn't even care. I *don't* care," she corrected herself. "Let's go inside. I hear the country ham sandwich is to die for."

As she followed her aunt to the door, Phaedra's phone rang. She glanced at the screen.

"You go ahead," she told her aunt. "It's Lu. Hi, Lucy. What's up?"

"I need a distraction," Lucy said without preamble. "This thing with my mother is all I can think of."

Phaedra switched the phone to her other ear to hear better over the clink of dishes and chatter of customers seated outside. "Is she here? Did she meet with you?"

"No, not yet. But she wants to see me. And I don't think I'm ready for that yet."

"Listen, I'm at lunch with my aunt and our guests right now. I'll be home in an hour or so. We're giving everyone the afternoon off to get ready for the carriage ride tonight."

"You're kidding. Where on earth did you find a carriage?"

"From a rental company. The same one that provides rides downtown." She paused. "Why don't you come with us?"

"No, thanks. You know my feelings on that Regency stuff. Getting jolted all over the place while looking at a horse's rear end isn't my idea of fun."

"It's a coach, Lu. Not a farmer's wagon. It's actually quite luxurious inside."

"I don't care how luxurious it is. If it doesn't have an engine, satellite radio, and air-conditioning, I'm not interested. This is August in Virginia, Phae. The heat index is murderous." She added, "Which reminds me. Are you any closer to catching Harriet's killer?"

"No." Phaedra lowered her voice and moved closer to the sidewalk, distancing herself from the outdoor tables. "I found a button in the kitchen garden, very near the spot where we found her body, but when I came to, it was gone."

"Wait—what?" Lucy demanded. "'Came to' means you were unconscious. Which means someone must've knocked you out. When did this happen? And when did you plan to tell me?"

"Let's have a quick meeting this afternoon. See if Marisol's free. I'll tell you all about it then."

"Good idea. Last time, if you remember, that cute detective interrupted us. We didn't even make it through the suspect list."

"Morelli is . . . Morelli." Phaedra eyed her in exasperation. "He's a cop."

"So? Cops can't be attractive? Because he is. Even if you won't admit it."

Before she could argue the point, or deny any interest whatsoever in Detective Matteo Morelli, Lucy ended the call, and Phaedra headed into the deli.

An hour later, as Wendy returned to the inn with her guests to get ready for the evening's activities, Phaedra returned to the carriage house.

"Bella! Wickham!" she called out as she entered the front hall and put her keys in the dish. "I'm back."

Bella sauntered up and rubbed herself, purring, against Phaedra's legs. Wickham lifted his head from his perch atop the sofa and regarded her with indifference. *Am I supposed to care?* his blue eyes seemed to say. He returned his attention to a male cardinal perched in an elm tree and ignored her.

"Well, you're a grumpy boy today. I suppose you won't want a kitty treat, then."

He cocked his ears forward and leaped down from the sofa to follow her into the kitchen, where she doled out a treat to each cat. As the pair settled down to the serious business of devouring their goodies, the doorbell rang.

"Hang on, Lu," Phaedra called out. "I'm coming."

But when she opened the door, it wasn't Lucy Liang who stood on the doorstep, but Elaine.

"Glad I caught you," she said. "May I come in?"

"Of course." Phaedra stood back to let her inside and closed the door. "Has something happened? Do the police have any leads on the break-in?"

"They do." She followed Phaedra into the living room and took a seat on the edge of the sofa. "Detective Morelli reviewed the security footage from the outside camera, and it captured video of someone breaking in. Unfortunately, whoever it was had a black balaclava over their face."

"Good thing you weren't there when it happened."

"I was at Dave and Eve's place at the time. Dave's mom wasn't feeling well, and he went to check on her. Eve asked me to have dinner and keep her company until he got back. She didn't want to be alone."

"I can understand that."

She understood, too, that the intruder, whoever he or she was, must've known Elaine wasn't at home.

"Did you tell anyone about your plans?" Phaedra asked.

"No. It was spur of the moment." She hesitated. "There's something else you need to know. About Rollo."

"Rollo? What about him?"

"I should've told you sooner, but I'm not supposed to know. It may have nothing to do with Harriet's murder. But if it does, then I'm pretty sure she was blackmailing Rollo."

Phaedra leaned forward. "Okay, I'm intrigued. And you can count on my discretion."

"You know I was wardrobe mistress during the filming of *Persuasion*."

She nodded.

"Harriet was script consultant, and she recommended me. It was my first professional job." Elaine extracted a tissue from her pocket and began to twist it in her hands.

"Go on."

She eyed Phaedra. "Rollo and Richard Troy . . . they were briefly involved in a relationship."

"Rollo? And Richard *Troy*?" she echoed, when she found her voice. "But Richard's married, happily married, to Jocasta Davies. Their fidelity is legendary. They're like a modern-day Newman and Woodward."

"Which is why his secret fling with Rollo made such a tempting tidbit for Harriet. It didn't last long. If the truth came out, it would've destroyed Richard's marriage."

"How did Harriet find out? I assume the two of them were extremely discreet."

"She observed everything around her, missed nothing. Which is how she discovered Rollo and Richard's trysts."

"But she never said anything? It would've been all over the tabloids. She could've made a fortune."

"Holding the knowledge over Rollo's head was more fun. And more Harriet's style. As I know only too well."

Before Phaedra could reply, or wonder at the bitterness in Elaine's voice, the doorbell rang a second time. She stood to let Lucy and Marisol in.

"We brought cake," Marisol announced as she carried in a white bakery box and set it on the kitchen island. "Coconut cream."

"And pink moscato," Lucy added as she brandished a bottle. "Oh." She stopped short as she spotted Elaine. "Sorry. Didn't realize you had company."

"I was just on my way out," Elaine said, and rose to her feet. "I'm Elaine, I own Stage Door Costumes. If you ever need a party costume, I'm your girl." She turned back to Phaedra. "I should go."

"Stay," Phaedra invited. "Have some cake and tea."

"Or a glass of fizzy," Lucy said. "There's plenty."

"I'll have to take a rain check. I have a few things to take care of. Enjoy your carriage ride this evening."

"Carriage ride?" Marisol echoed. "Sounds fabulous!" She turned an accusing eye on Phaedra. "Why is this the first I'm hearing of it?"

"Because it's for the inn's guests, Mari." Lucy grabbed the wine opener and popped the cork. "It's part of the Jane Austen Murder Mystery week thing."

"Oh. Right. And speaking of murder . . ." Marisol registered Phaedra's warning glance. "I mean, this heat! It's been really *murderous* this summer."

"Lethal," Elaine agreed. "Well, I'm off. I have costumes to finish and ball gowns to alter for the masquerade ball on Saturday night. Have fun, ladies."

"I suppose," Marisol said with a pout as Phaedra shut the door after Elaine, "we're not invited to the ball, either."

"Of course you are." Phaedra helped herself to a glass of moscato and took a sip of the bubbly pink wine. "And you're most definitely invited to this afternoon's meeting of the Jane Austen Tea Society. And the first item on the agenda is—"

"Murder," Mari said archly. "What else?"

Twenty

. . . and that's why Elaine was here," Phaedra finished as she set her plate aside. Every delicious crumb of her slice of coconut cake had been consumed.

"Someone broke in and trashed her shop?" Marisol shook her head in disapproval. "What is this town coming to?"

"The police have video from a security camera, but the intruder's face is hidden." She didn't mention Rollo's fling with Richard Troy. That secret, if it ever came out, still had the power to damage two lives.

Lucy reached out to the coffee table to top up her wine. "Did anyone know Elaine wasn't at home that night?"

"Only Eve and Dave," Phaedra said. "He had to go to his mom's place and suggested Eve invite Elaine over to keep her company while he was gone."

"You said nothing was missing." Marisol finished her tea and set her cup onto the saucer. "So, vandals?"

"That's what Morelli thinks. But Elaine believes someone may have been looking for something related to Harriet's murder."

Marisol frowned. "Like what?"

"The note," Lucy said suddenly. "You know, the 'ardent admirer' who asked Harriet to meet in the garden. But the police have it, don't they? For analysis?"

"They do," Phaedra said. "But the intruder may not have known that."

"Are you saying Elaine's intruder was the murderer?" Marisol asked. She exchanged a sideways glance with Lucy.

"It's possible, but unlikely." She paused. "I tend to agree with Morelli."

"What else have you learned since our last meeting?" Lucy asked. "You mentioned something earlier about finding a button?"

Phaedra provided the details of finding the button in the kitchen garden and getting hit from behind, only to regain consciousness and realize it was gone.

"Was it from Harriet's costume?" Marisol asked.

"I don't think so. It was half-hidden under a bush, which is probably why the crime scene team missed it. I only noticed it when I dropped my phone and knelt down to look for it."

Lucy shrugged. "If someone knocked you out and took that button, then it has significance. Had you seen it before?"

"It looked vaguely familiar, but I don't know why."

"What about the note?" Marisol wondered. "Did the police analyze it yet?"

"Yes. They believe the sender is female, that she's insecure, and she cares a great deal about appearances."

"That," Mari said glumly, "describes just about every woman I know."

"It isn't much help," Phaedra agreed. "This case is frustrating. There aren't many clues, no fingerprints, and so far, not a trace of DNA on anything."

Lucy set her wineglass aside. "Not to mention that whack on the head you got. If it were me," she added as she stood to leave, "and if you want to preserve your skull, I'd leave any further detecting to the police. Just saying."

* * *

Halfway through predinner drinks, Phaedra glanced up to see Donovan standing in the drawing room doorway. He looked handsome in his suit and tie, but decidedly ill at ease as his eyes sought out hers.

"You decided to come down," she said as she approached him.

"Every cocktail hour needs at least one cad, right?"

"Yes," she said, and drew him forward. "Grab a drink and I'll introduce you to everyone."

He snagged a glass of wine from a passing tray and took a sip. "Lead on."

Mark saw them and stretched out his hand. "Hello. Mark Selden. I'm on the faculty with Professor Brighton at Somerset University. It's a pleasure to meet you."

"And you," Donovan said. "Donovan Wickes. I own several fitness centers in Boston. I'm looking to expand."

"Here in Laurel Springs?"

Donovan nodded. "That's the plan."

Phaedra could almost see the two sizing each other up.

"Are you an Austen aficionado?" Mark inquired.

"An Austen . . ." Donovan shook his head ruefully. "Sorry, no. Not in the least."

"Good. Then we have something in common."

A flicker of surprise morphed into relieved amusement. "Do you like cars, Professor?"

"As a matter of fact, I do. That's my Triumph TR5 out front. Fuel-injected petrol engine, the first of its kind. Nightmare to maintain, though."

"I saw it parked outside when I arrived. Wire wheels, convertible top. Sweet. A '67 or a '68?"

"A '68. I'm not in the least mechanically inclined, unfortunately, and the parts are long out of production. Luckily, there's a place in California . . ."

As they discussed engine specifications and debated the merits of stick shift versus automatic, Phaedra excused herself to join Brian and Tory as Wendy regaled her high school beau with details of their excursion downtown.

"I'm glad you enjoyed yourselves." Brian, dressed in a dark blue suit and a yellow-and-gray-striped tie, sipped his bourbon and turned back to Wendy. "Tomorrow promises to be another beautiful day. Can we take another stab at antiquing?" He gave Phaedra a brief smile. "Unless your niece here objects."

"I don't object." Phaedra forced a polite smile despite the flicker of dislike he stirred in her. He made her sound like a spoiled little girl who didn't want to share her aunt with him.

And the truth was, she didn't. Wendy could do so much better than this roguish charmer with his wandering eye and empty promises.

"Good. Then it's all set," Brian said, and linked his arm with Wendy's. "I'll pick you up at two o'clock." If he noticed the hot flare of jealousy in Tory's eyes, he gave no indication. "Allow me to escort you to dinner."

"You should join us," Wendy said as they went into the dining room. "On the carriage ride tonight."

"I'd love to, doodlebug, but I have a few business calls to make." He lifted her hand to his lips and kissed it. "But I promise you, I'll be with you in my thoughts."

"Phaedra," Donovan said as he and Mark approached, drinks in hand. "May I take you in to dinner?"

Although her first impulse was to refuse, to do so would've been petty and childish. *And I'm above that. Aren't I?* "Why, yes. Thank you, Mr. Wickes."

As she laid her hand demurely on his extended arm, she saw a glimmer of irritation darken Mark's eyes. His reaction amused her.

Which lasted until he turned to Tory and offered his own arm as he asked to escort her into the dining room.

"I'd love that," she agreed, and rested her hand on his outstretched arm. "You're quite the handsomest man in the room, sir."

"And you, Miss Musgrove," he returned politely, playing along, "are quite the most charming young lady."

After Donovan seated her at the table, Phaedra turned to her dinner partner, Rollo Barron. Although she did her best to ignore Tory's shameless flirtation with Mark Selden, knowing she only wanted to make Brian jealous, Professor Selden's reciprocal interest annoyed her.

"Everything all right, my dear?" Rollo inquired in a low voice as Dave brought in the first course.

"Yes. Why do you ask?"

He leaned forward, a gleam in his eye. "You're glaring at Ms. Sutton—forgive me, Miss Musgrove—as though she's a platter of particularly ripe Stilton."

"On the contrary, Sir Walter," she replied, "I adore Stilton. It's Miss Musgrove I can't stomach."

He laughed. "I commend your honesty. And," he added as he spread his napkin over his lap, "I completely agree."

The last blush of sunset washed the sky as everyone gathered in front of the inn after dinner to board the waiting coaches.

"Two horse-drawn carriages!" Felicity exclaimed, impressed. "With footmen, no less. They're gorgeous."

"The carriages," Tory asked coyly, "or the footmen?"

"Both." Felicity laughed. "Where are we to sit?"

"You, Dave, Rollo, and I are in the second coach," Wendy said. "Phaedra, you're with Mark, Tory, and Donovan in the first."

"Suits me," Donovan said. He turned to Phaedra. "I forgot how chilly it gets up here in the mountains at night, how the temperature drops when the sun goes down."

Phaedra nodded and drew her shawl closer around her shoulders. "I like it, though. It's a welcome change."

"I agree." Tory slid her arm possessively through Mark's. "*So* cozy."

Mark handed her up into the carriage and turned back to Phaedra. "Elaine and Eve aren't joining us?"

"Elaine's getting our costumes ready for the masquerade ball on Saturday," Phaedra said. "And Eve said the last thing she wanted was to get bounced around in a glorified wagon in her condition."

"I can't say I blame her."

Donovan held out his hand. "Your carriage awaits, Miss Elliot."

He assisted her up the fold-down step and into the plush interior of the coach, then climbed in and settled next to her, opposite Mark and Tory.

"This is fun, isn't it?" Tory said, letting the shawl at her shoulders slip slightly. "Really romantic."

Before Phaedra could reply, the footman folded the steps, closed the door, and took his position at the rear of the carriage. The driver called out to the horses, and with a jolt and a squeal of excitement from Tory, they were off.

The carriage ride, although rough by modern standards, was surprisingly comfortable. The seats were upholstered in soft, luxurious leather, and the interior was roomier than Phaedra expected.

As dusk deepened into evening and the first stars appeared, the coach rolled at a sedate pace down Main Street, keeping to the right to avoid traffic, and turned onto a side street. They soon left the bustle of downtown Laurel Springs behind and bowled unimpeded down a rarely used access road.

"Where're we going?" Donovan asked as he peered outside.

"The Dixon farm," Phaedra replied. "They're providing sparkling cider, champagne, and homemade doughnuts, square dancing, and a path lit with solar lights for those who fancy a romantic stroll."

"Square dancing?" Tory grimaced. "Count me out."

"I think you'll like it, if you give it a chance. It's based on the Virginia reel, which was popular during the Regency period in the form of English country dancing."

"Oh. Well, we'll see. Maybe I'll try it," Tory said doubtfully. "Get into the spirit, and all that." She turned to Professor Selden and tapped him playfully on the arm with her fan. "But only if Mark agrees to be my partner."

"I'd be honored. But I warn you now, I'm an abysmal dancer."

"I don't believe it." She curled her fingers over his arm and edged closer as her lips curved into a seductive smile. "I bet you're good at whatever you do."

Phaedra pressed her lips together and gazed out at the passing darkness. Did Tory have no shame? Of course she didn't. She was canoodling with Brian, her aunt's former flame, and practically under Wendy's nose, to boot; and now she was all but sitting in Mark Selden's lap.

Belatedly, she realized Donovan had spoken to her. "I'm sorry. Did you say something?"

"I asked," he said patiently, "if you'd like to take a spin around the dance floor with me."

She dragged her thoughts away from Mark and Tory. "I'd love to. But I'm no Ginger Rogers," she warned.

"And I'm no Fred Astaire."

"In that case, you're on."

The carriage slowed to turn onto another, narrower country road, and the horses picked up the pace to a brisk canter. A branch slapped now and then at the roof, and moonlight silvered the trees and fields.

It really was a beautiful night, Phaedra reflected. She could easily imagine herself as a Regency lady, traveling to a ball at a neighboring house, where she'd dance, and flirt, and perhaps fall in love with a handsome, and hopefully prosperous, young man—

"Ooh, look, over there," Tory cried, and pressed her face to the window. "I can just about see the farm. The trees are strung with little white lights. It's beautiful!"

Phaedra had barely turned to get a better look when she heard the unmistakable growl of a car engine approaching from somewhere behind them.

"What's that?" Mark said as he followed her gaze. "A car?"

"Yes," she said. "It's coming up fast." Her fingers tensed on the upholstered edge of the seat.

Their driver saw it, too. He tugged on the reins and struggled to calm the team as one of the horses let out a whinny of fear.

As the vehicle gained on them, the engine's throaty roar filled the night air. Headlights, bright and blinding, swept the interior of the coach.

Tory's face went as pale as milk. "What's happening?"

"Perhaps we're being waylaid by highwaymen," Phaedra ventured shakily, only half joking. A robbery by jack-booted criminals might be exciting on film or in the pages of a novel, but she had no desire to experience it in real life.

"Highwaymen don't drive cars," Donovan said tightly.

The vehicle was now directly behind them.

"Why are they so close?" Phaedra exclaimed, her heart racing even faster than the horses' hooves. "They're frightening the horses! Why don't they go around us?"

"Good question." Mark pressed his face to the window and eyed the darkened country lane. "They're starting to pass us. Hang on, everyone—"

He didn't finish the sentence. The horses whinnied in renewed terror as the car behind them swung out and drew up alongside them. After a brief, heart-stopping moment, the vehicle cut sharply in front of them before gunning it and disappearing into the darkness ahead.

The driver pulled hard on the reins and managed to guide the carriage to the farthest edge of the lane.

But they'd ventured too close to the pavement's edge. With a jolt, the rear right wheel came off the pavement, unbalancing the coach, and it lurched to one side.

With a groan of wood, the coach teetered precariously on the shoulder, still upright but canted at an unnatural angle. They were inches away from a ditch.

Tory clutched at Mark. "We're going to turn over!" she cried.

Twenty-One

Everyone, stay calm."

Mark spoke with quiet command. Tory subsided beside him, her hands visibly trembling.

"Donovan and Phaedra," he directed, "stay put and don't move." As they nodded, he turned to Tory. "I'll get out first and hand you down on this side. Don't make any sudden movements. Okay?"

"O-okay."

He helped her down. A moment later, with the footman's assistance, everyone dismounted safely, and the driver set out to calm the team.

"That blasted car." Donovan scowled. "It forced us off the road and nearly upended the carriage."

"If we'd ended up in that ditch," Mark said grimly as he surveyed the wheel ruts left in the muddy earth, "we would've overturned. No question."

The driver approached them. "Is everyone all right?" he called out. His face was ashen.

"I'm okay," Tory huffed, plainly annoyed as she took Mark's arm. "No thanks to that crazy driver."

"We're all fine," Phaedra assured him. "How are you? And the horses?"

"I'm good. Scared the team pretty bad. They're used to cars; we carry passengers downtown, every day. But in all my years, I never saw anything like this." He shook his head. "Glad no one was hurt and the horses are unharmed."

"You need to report this," Phaedra said. "To the police."

"Already on it, miss." He took his cell phone out to make the call, and shook his head in disgust. "Darned kids."

They followed his gaze to the side-tilted carriage, where one bright yellow wheel spun slowly in the air.

"I'll stay with the carriage and driver until the police arrive," Mark offered. "Tell them what happened."

"They'll probably want to talk to all of us," Phaedra pointed out.

The second carriage rolled to a halt behind them. The doors flew open, and Wendy rushed over with Felicity, Rollo, and Dave close on her heels.

"Phaedra!" she cried, her face set in panic. "What on earth happened? Are you injured? We saw that car go flying by. Someone, call an ambulance!"

"We're fine," she assured her aunt, and glanced at the farm in the distance. "No ambulance necessary. But we have to stay here until the police arrive."

"Police?"

"To report the accident."

A short time later a motorcycle officer arrived and took their statements. "Did anyone get a license number? Make or model? Color?"

"It happened too quickly," Mark said. "And it was dark. All I can say with any certainty is that the vehicle was a sports car. Two-seater, dark gray or black."

"Okay." He called in the accident and told them they could go. "You folks have a way to get where you're going?"

"We're headed to Dixon's farm," Phaedra told him. "It's not far. We can walk."

"Absolutely not," Wendy said firmly. "You've had a shock. You and Tory climb in our carriage. We ladies will ride up to the house in comfort. The gentlemen can walk."

Although her aunt tried to persuade Phaedra to call an Uber and return home to soak in a hot bath, she refused, and stayed on to enjoy the festivities. Emmylou found her sitting on the sidelines and took a seat next to her. "Why aren't you dancing?"

"Still a little shaken after the accident, I suppose."

"Looks like your friend hasn't let it stop her. She's having a good old time."

She followed the woman's gaze to Tory, her face flushed with pleasure as Donovan tapped on Mark's shoulder to cut in on their dance. "Tory? Yes, I'm sure she loves having two men on a string." Three, if you counted Brian Callahan.

"It's just harmless fun. Flirting." Emmylou smiled. "I remember those days." She kept her eyes on the dance floor and added, "Not jealous, are you?"

"Jealous?" Surprise colored her voice. "No, of course not. Donovan's a free agent, and so is she."

"I wasn't talking about Donovan. Anyone can see that the professor over there only has eyes for you."

As if he'd sensed their attention, Mark glanced over and threaded his way toward them. "Hello, ladies. Can I interest either of you in a cup of punch?" His eyes sought Phaedra's. "And perhaps the next dance?"

She nodded. "Yes, to both. Thank you." As he left, she added, "Now I know how a wallflower feels. It isn't much fun."

"Oh, I don't know," Emmylou said. "Sometimes it's more entertaining to sit on the sidelines and gossip." She chuckled, then sobered. "I'm just relieved everyone's all right. What happened tonight was bad enough. But it would've been far worse if your carriage overturned."

"We were lucky," she agreed.

"Strange, though, isn't it? A car racing up behind your carriage like that."

"It was terrifying. It happened so fast, I barely realized we were in trouble before we found ourselves headed for the ditch."

"Probably just teenagers, out joyriding."

"That's what the motorcycle officer said. But I'm not so sure."

"What else could it be? Do you think someone side-swiped your carriage on purpose?"

She frowned, remembering. "Whoever drove that car handled it like a pro. They ran our carriage off the road. Not Wendy's. Ours."

"Can you think of anyone who'd want to harm you?"

"No." Phaedra sighed. "It sounds crazy, doesn't it? I'm probably just being paranoid."

"I doubt that. You have good instincts, Phaedra." Emmy-lou reached out and patted her hand. "And if you're right," the older woman added gravely, "that means your 'accident' tonight may have been no accident at all."

It was late when Emmylou returned Phaedra, Mark, and Donovan to the carriage house in her battered Land Rover. The others had taken advantage of the Dixons' shuttle bus while Tory elected to call herself an Uber.

"Why not come with us?" Phaedra asked her. "We have plenty of room."

"I have other plans." She returned her phone to her tiny clutch purse. "I'll catch up with you tomorrow."

A short time later the Land Rover slowed to a stop in front of the darkened carriage house.

"Get some rest," Emmylou advised as Mark handed Phaedra down from the vehicle. "A good night's sleep works wonders."

"I will. I can feel a headache coming on. Thanks, Emmy-lou. For everything."

"Don't mention it. Good night." She lifted her hand in farewell, shifted into drive, and drove away.

"Can I get you anything, Phaedra?" Donovan asked. "Perhaps a cup of herbal tea or a glass of wine?"

"How about something useful, like an aspirin and a glass of water?" Mark suggested shortly. "You'll find both in the kitchen."

Donovan opened his mouth to argue, saw the implacability of Selden's expression, and took Phaedra's key and let himself inside.

Mark turned to her. "What did you ever see in him?"

"Donovan? What do you mean?"

"According to your aunt Wendy, he was the great love of your life."

"It was high school," she defended herself. "I was seventeen."

"You obviously grew up. I don't think he ever did."

As Mark headed for the front doorstep, her hand tucked into his arm, she glanced up at him. "I thought you two liked each other. You got on so well over drinks earlier."

"He knows a bit about cars. I'll give him that much."

"But?"

"But you and he have nothing in common. It's plain enough, to me at least, that he's not suited to you."

She leaned on him as he helped her up the front steps, and paused just outside the door. "And I suppose you know what does suit me?"

"I do," he replied, ignoring the gentle reproof in her voice. "You had a scare this evening, and although you're hiding it fairly well, I suspect it shook you up." He stepped nearer. "What I think you need at this precise moment, therefore, is—"

"Aspirin," Donovan announced as he returned with a bottle in hand. "And a glass of water. Just what the doctor ordered." He shook out a pill and eyed Mark as he pressed it into Phaedra's palm. "Right, Professor?"

"Yes. Quite."

"Well, good night then, gentlemen." Phaedra swallowed the aspirin and water. "Thank you both for making this such a memorable night."

She went inside, favored them both with a demure smile, and closed the door.

It was long past seven when Phaedra opened her eyes the next morning. She knew by the slant of the sun on her bedroom floor.

And because Wickham, tired of waiting to be fed, sat atop her chest and regarded her balefully.

She nudged him gently aside and threw back the covers. "Nearly nine o'clock! You've been remarkably patient. You and Bella must be starving."

Get into the kitchen and open a can of salmon, and I might forgive you, his blue eyes seemed to say. *A cat cannot live on kibble alone, after all.*

At least her headache was gone. Which was a good thing, since today was the last day before tomorrow night's ball, and the unmasking of Lady Russell's fictional murderer, and it promised to be busy.

She had dance steps to teach, costumes from Elaine arriving to distribute and accessorize, food preparations to oversee, and final music selections to make for the hired musicians.

Not to mention, cats to feed. And a real murder to solve.

Elaine's revelation the day before, that Rollo and Richard Troy had briefly been involved, troubled her. Not because of the nature of their relationship, but because, like the rest of the world, she believed that Richard and Jocasta were that rare thing—a true, happily married celebrity couple.

Poor Jocasta. And poor Rollo, if what Elaine had told her was indeed true. Harriet must have held the knowledge of his fling with Richard over his head like the sword of Damocles for years, threatening to reveal everything should he ever cross her.

No wonder he'd despised Harriet. She had Rollo exactly where she'd wanted him—at her journalistic beck and call. Now she understood why his published review of her latest book was glowing. He had no choice in the matter.

How he must have hated her, Phaedra reflected as she dressed in a simple muslin gown printed with tiny flowers and pinned up her hair.

But had he hated her enough to kill her?

"I'm sorry I missed breakfast service," Phaedra said as she entered the inn's kitchen twenty minutes later. "I overslept. Wickham's still put out with me."

Wendy bit into a piece of leftover bacon. "I certainly didn't expect you to help out this morning. We got home late and you were in a carriage accident. How are you?"

"Better. A long soak in a hot bubble bath works wonders."

"I'm glad you're okay," Hannah, seated at the kitchen table, said. "Wendy told me what happened."

"I'm fine. Where is everyone?"

"Elaine brought the costumes over," Wendy said. "They're trying things on in the drawing room, one at a time, and Elaine's making alterations as needed."

"Why one at a time?"

"So that no one sees anyone else's costume."

Phaedra caught her sister's eye. "What about you? Are you coming to the masquerade ball tomorrow?"

"I don't think so." She returned her attention to her phone screen, her expression unreadable. "I don't have a costume."

"I'm sure Elaine can rustle something up."

"No, thanks. I really don't have time," Hannah said, her voice edged with irritation. "I'm heading home on Monday."

"So soon? But you just got here."

"I have a life, Phaedra, surprising as it might be. With a job, and demands, and expectations. I can't hang around the inn all summer like I did when we were kids."

Wendy, sensing that an argument was imminent, discreetly disappeared.

"I understand that," Phaedra said. "But surely you can stay here for another day or two. You'd be a big help."

"I can't. I just told you, I'm busy."

"Well, I'm busy, too. I've taken on this *Persuasion* murder mystery week to help Aunt Wendy, which is more than I can say for you—"

"All hail Saint Phaedra," Hannah muttered.

"—and we've had an actual *murder* in the middle of it, I've got the fall teaching term to prepare for, the masquerade ball is looming, and I haven't even told you what a certifiable rat Wendy's boyfriend Brian is—" She stopped as Hannah's comment registered.

"What did you just call me?" Phaedra demanded. "What does that even mean?"

"It means that nothing I did ever measured up to Saint Phaedra's glorious example."

Her words hit Phaedra like a punch in the stomach—unexpected and surprisingly painful. "That's not true."

"It *is* true. All my life, all I've ever heard is how smart you are, how well you did in school. What lovely manners you have. My grades could never measure up. My boyfriends could never measure up." Her lower lip wobbled precariously. "*I* could never measure up."

"Where is this coming from?" Phaedra was perplexed. "I always thought we got along so well."

"We did. Only because you were too busy studying and leading tours at Monticello and spending every spare minute with Donovan to notice me, or how much I resented you."

"So I was, what? Supposed to fail my classes and sit at home with you and—and give you makeup tips?"

"No, of course not! But you could have hung out with me once in a while. Instead of brushing me aside like a—a mosquito."

Phaedra sank down across from her at the kitchen table. Her first instinct, to deny Hannah's accusations, died. Maybe her sister was right. Maybe she really had been that self-absorbed and clueless in high school.

Clark Mullinax had certainly thought so.

"You have a fantastic job, Hannah," Phaedra said firmly. "You work as a pastry chef at the British embassy. Last spring you were named one of the top twenty new chefs to watch by *Washingtonian* magazine."

"You're biased. You're a university professor. You teach, and publish articles, and solve crimes. I bake cakes."

"Oh, piffle. You make French pastry, Hannah. There's a world of difference. Give yourself some credit. You're every bit as smart and capable as me. No, more so. Yes, I publish monographs that no one but academics reads, but I can't whip up a St. Honoré cake or a financier. I can't even make a boxed mix without leaving out the eggs—"

"He's gone, Phaedra. Charles left." She lifted a stricken face to her sister. "And I don't know why."

Twenty-Two

Oh, sweetie." Phaedra reached out to grip her hands. "I'm so sorry. But I'm confused. Everything was good, or at least I thought it was. The two of you were so close. Perhaps you're jumping to conclusions."

"No. I'm not." She pulled her hands away. "I work ridiculous hours; he travels. He said he'd like me to be more available." Tears streaked down her face. "I'd like that, too. But my career is important to me, just as important as his is to him. His wanting to spend more time with me feels like a—a criticism. Like I should be available on his terms. Like I'm being selfish for prioritizing my job."

"Like you should accommodate him, not vice versa."

"Exactly. It's not fair. It makes me defensive," she admitted. "And crazy."

"You need to talk to him."

"That's just it. I can't." She reached for a napkin and blotted at her eyes. "He's *gone*, Phaedra. His house on Kalorama Road is for sale. He took a leave of absence and he's returned to London. And the worst part is, he never . . ." She blew her nose. "He never said a word to me."

"But that makes no sense." Phaedra leaned back in her

chair. "Are you absolutely certain the two of you didn't have an argument beforehand, or a misunderstanding of some kind? Did you give him an ultimatum?"

"I told you, no. This all just blew up out of nowhere." Hannah crumpled the napkin into a tiny ball. "Can you—can you do me a favor?"

"Yes, of course. Just name it."

"Would you talk to Mark? He and Charles go back a long way. He might know what's going on. Or he could find out."

"I can do that." She hesitated. "Do you really want me interfering in your personal life? That's more Mom's style."

"You wouldn't be interfering. I'm asking you to talk to him. Totally different thing."

Phaedra nodded. "Okay, then. If that's what you want, I'll speak with Mark today."

"Is he staying for the masquerade ball tomorrow night?"

"He is. You should come, too. You could ask him about Charles yourself."

"I don't really know him. We've never actually been introduced."

"Well," Phaedra said as she stood up, "I'll have to remedy that. In the meantime, I'll get to the bottom of this. I'm sure it's all just a silly mix-up."

A thousand different things needed doing in preparation for the ball, and Phaedra's assistance was required for all of them. Lunch service came and went, and still Mark had not come downstairs.

"Where's Professor Selden today?" Phaedra asked her aunt as she carried a tray of lunch dishes into the kitchen.

"He took breakfast and lunch in his room." Wendy looked up briefly from her perusal of a cookbook Hannah had left open on the counter. "Why do you ask? Did the two of you have a lovers' tiff?"

"A lovers' . . . " Phaedra eyed her in irritation and lowered her voice. "Of course not. We're not lovers, Aunt Wendy, we're work colleagues."

"I saw the way he looked at you last night. The man is smitten."

"That statement is so ridiculous, I refuse to justify it with a response."

"It's plain enough he's attracted to you. Donovan sees it, too. He's more than a little jealous, if you ask me."

"I didn't ask you." Phaedra set the tray of dirty dishes down by the sink and reached out to turn the faucet on. "I need to talk to him."

"Who? Donovan?"

"Mark. He's good friends with Charles. Hannah's boyfriend."

"Are Charles and Hannah having a lovers' tiff?"

She shook her head as she squeezed dish soap into the sink. "Worse. He's disappeared. He took a leave of absence from the embassy, put his house up for sale, and went back to London . . . all without a single word to Hannah."

"That *is* serious." Wendy closed the cookbook with a thump. "She really cares for that young man, doesn't she?"

"Very much. Which is why she's devastated. Since he and Mark are close, she's hoping Mark might have some insight into what's going on."

Elaine thrust her head around the door. "Sorry to interrupt," she apologized, "but I'm ready for you to try on your costume, Phaedra. Do you have a few minutes?"

"Not really," she sighed as she turned away from the sink.

"Go ahead," Wendy told her. "I'll finish washing up."

"Thanks." Phaedra untied her apron and handed it to her aunt. "I'm all yours," she said to Elaine.

* * *

Seeing her costume, of ice-blue brocade edged in broderie anglaise, Phaedra let out a gasp of pleasure.

"It's beautiful. Stunning! Did you make this?"

Elaine shook her head. "Heavens, no. The broderie alone would've taken weeks. It's a costume from last year's production of *Vanity Fair*. Suitable for Becky Sharpe," she added as she directed Phaedra to step into the gown, "and now, for Miss Elizabeth Elliot."

"I love it." Phaedra studied herself in the tall, tilt-stand mirror in the corner as Elaine stepped back. Although simple, the gown arrested the eye with its delicate detail work and classic Regency styling. "And it fits like a dream."

"Like it was made for you." Elaine regarded the gown with a critical eye. "No alterations needed, thank goodness. Now, then," she said, and turned away to navigate through a jumble of fans, shawls, shoes, and other accessories, "let's find you a silk shawl and a pair of slippers."

As she flicked expertly through a rack crowded with shawls, spencer jackets, and a dark green cloak—"that's for Anne Elliot, or should I say, Felicity—" she re-pinned the attached note more firmly and glanced up as someone knocked on the drawing room door.

"Excuse me," Mark said, edging the door open and peering around it, "but I wonder if I might trouble you for another cravat. Mine seems to have disappeared—"

He caught sight of Phaedra and the words stuck in his throat. "Professor Brighton. You look stunning."

"Hello, Mark." She couldn't help staring at him. He wore breeches, a waistcoat, and a tailcoat, as befitted a Regency gentleman attending a ball. "You don't look half-bad yourself."

"Thanks." With a rueful smile he indicated the two ends of his collar, which stood up on either side of his face.

"I'm good to go, except for this. I look like Dr. Franken-stein."

"Let's find you another cravat." Elaine took a length of white silk from one end of the costume rack and handed it over. "Here you are. Do you know how to tie it?"

"I do. Professor Brighton taught me last spring, when I assumed the role of Darcy in the Jane Austen festival at the university."

"I'm sure you made a fine Mr. Darcy. Now," Elaine added briskly, "if you wouldn't mind, Professor Selden, I'm in the middle of a fitting."

"Yes, of course. And thank you." He held up the cravat. "For this. Can't think what happened to the other, but I'm sure it'll turn up." He started to close the door.

"Mark, wait."

Phaedra stepped down from the small round dais and hurried over to the door. "Can you spare a few minutes to talk to me later today? It's important, or I wouldn't ask."

"I—yes. Certainly." He hesitated. "I'd planned to go out to dinner this evening. Why don't you join me?"

After a moment's hesitation, she agreed. "What time?"

"Seven. I have a reservation."

"Oh. I'm not crashing a dinner date, am I?"

"No, not at all. I'd planned to meet with Dean Carmichael to discuss next year's curriculum, but he cancelled a few minutes ago."

"Oh. Well, in that case, yes. I'd love to."

He nodded and turned to go. "No need to dress up," he added over his shoulder. "I'll pick you up at six thirty."

What to wear for her dinner date with Mark tonight?

Phaedra's usual decisiveness abandoned her as she stood before her bedroom closet in the carriage house and pondered the question.

With no idea where they'd be dining, she decided on a

simple beige linen shift and slipped on a pair of sandals. It
was far too warm to dress in her customary Regency attire.
Whether they went to Orsini's, Lagniappe, or the wine bar,
she'd be dressed appropriately.

As she fastened a string of pearls at her neck, the doorbell rang downstairs, and her fingers froze. Was this dinner thing with Mark a date? she wondered.

No, she told herself firmly. It was nothing more than
two friends meeting to talk over dinner. That's all.

"You're early," Phaedra said, smiling as she swung the
door open a moment later. "Please, come in—"

"Your aunt told me I'd find you here," Rollo replied,
rubbing his hands together as he brushed past her. "And
thank you for inviting me in. Don't mind if I do."

"Mr. Barron." She followed him into the living room.
"What brings you here?"

He didn't answer, but eyed the decor with a critical eye.
"I like it," he decreed. "Elegant but approachable. I love
the cozy vibe. All those built-in bookcases."

"Thank you. I'd offer you a drink, but I'm afraid—"

"I'd love a drink. Bourbon rocks if you have it. Wine if
you don't."

Phaedra shot a discreet glance at the clock. She had
twenty minutes before Mark arrived to pick her up. "Bourbon it is." As she clinked ice into his glass and poured in a
measure of whiskey, she added, "How can I help you?"

"That sounds so formal," he observed as she returned
with his drink and handed it over. "Besides which, it's not
you who can help me. It's I who can help *you*."

She gestured him to the sofa and seated herself across
from him. "I'm intrigued. And I'm listening."

He sipped his bourbon. "Has Elaine spoken to you?
About the murder?"

"Elaine tells me all sorts of things," she said, surprised
by the question. She hesitated. "In fact," she added carefully, "she mentioned that Harriet Overton had a fondness
for blackmail."

"Oh, indeed she did." He lifted his glass and took a lingering sip. "Harriet was a collector. Of facts, and damaging tidbits. Something, I suspect," he added as he set his glass down with deliberation, "that your friend Elaine knows about firsthand."

"Are you suggesting that Harriet was blackmailing Elaine?"

He leaned back against the sofa cushions and regarded her with a self-satisfied smile. "Yes, Professor. That's exactly what I'm suggesting."

Twenty-three

Would you care to elaborate, Mr. Barron?"

"Rollo, please. No need to stand on formalities." He stretched his arm expansively along the back of the sofa. "I may have mentioned that I once interviewed Richard Troy on the set of *Persuasion*."

"Yes." Several times.

"That's where Elaine and I met, although I'd forgotten all about it until we crossed paths at the B and B. She was the wardrobe mistress and Harriet was a script consultant."

"Yes, and she recommended Elaine for the job." Phaedra's glance strayed to the window. Mark would arrive soon, and she really didn't have time for Rollo's stroll down memory lane.

"Elaine and Harriet," he went on, oblivious to her inattentiveness, "had a—how shall I put this—complicated relationship. Did you know they once owned a small production company together?"

She regarded him in surprise. "No. I didn't."

"It was years ago, and the partnership didn't last long. A couple of years."

"Your point being?"

"Harriet dissolved the partnership, and quite abruptly, too. There were rumors of malfeasance on Ms. Alexander's part . . ."

Before he could elaborate, the doorbell rang a second time, and Phaedra peered outside. A vintage green Triumph stood in the driveway. Mark.

"I'm sorry, Mr.—pardon me, Rollo," she corrected herself as she stood, "but my dinner date is here. Perhaps we can talk further tomorrow?"

"Yes, yes, of course." He stood as well and followed her gaze out the window. "Ah, the Shakespearean scholar," he murmured in approval. "How lovely."

Whether he referred to their dinner date or to Professor Selden himself, she couldn't be sure.

Phaedra opened the door to greet Mark and introduced the two men.

"Ah, yes, Mr. Barron," Mark said as he clasped the shorter man's hand. "The journalist. We haven't had much occasion to speak at the inn."

"A regrettable situation we must endeavor to fix."

"Yes. Certainly."

"Don't worry, Professor, I'm just leaving. You two lovebirds enjoy dinner!" Rollo wiggled his fingers in farewell, let himself out, and traipsed across the lawn to return to the inn.

Mark indicated the door. "Shall we go, too?"

"Yes." Phaedra closed and locked the door behind them and preceded Mark to his car. "I'm sorry."

"For what?"

"For Rollo. I have no idea where he got the impression that you . . . that we . . ."

He shrugged. "He's a typical journalist, likes to fill in the blanks on his own. Even if his assumptions are completely inaccurate." He opened the passenger door. "Hop in."

* * *

Ten minutes later Mark parked the car at the curb halfway down Main Street.

Phaedra, curious as to where they were going, glanced around in puzzlement. He'd parked the Triumph equidistant between Orsini's and Lagniappe. Which one was it to be? Or did he have reservations at a lesser-known restaurant?

The mystery was solved as he led the way to the Dog 'n Draft, its tables out front packed with people and shaded with colorful yellow-and-blue-striped umbrellas.

"The hot dog place?" she asked, confused. "*This* is where you arranged to meet with Dean Carmichael?"

"He loves the Big Kahuna. It's a half smoke with everything," Mark explained as he saw her blank look. He laughed. "Don't knock it until you've tried it."

"I'm surprised you need a reservation," she said doubtfully.

"You don't. But it gets really busy on Friday nights, so they promised to hold a table for me. And there it is," he said as he indicated an empty table in the far front corner. "Unless you'd rather go inside."

Sitting on the patio surrounded by beer-drinking, sports-watching patrons was hardly ideal for a private conversation, but Phaedra shrugged. "This is fine. We can dine on our hot dogs alfresco." She preceded him to the table and slid onto the chair he held out for her.

A waiter appeared. "Would you like menus?"

"Yes," Phaedra told him. "And a sparkling water."

"I'll have the same." Mark took the menus he held out and handed one to Phaedra.

"So, you and Dean Carmichael planned to discuss the curriculum?" She hung her purse strap over the back of her chair.

"He's concerned with the financial pressures facing the liberal arts." He looked up from the menu. "Students want

STEM degrees. Science, technology, engineering, mathematics. Funding for the humanities continues to dwindle, and entire departments are being downsized. Some colleges have eliminated liberal arts degrees altogether."

"Without the humanities," Phaedra pointed out, "students won't acquire the critical thinking skills they need to find success in the professional job market."

"No argument here." He laid the menu aside. "These things go in cycles, though. Ten years from now, who knows what the academic situation will look like?"

The waiter returned, and they ordered draft beers and two Dog House Specials—a half smoke topped with sauerkraut, mustard, and onion. "I'm glad we're not really on a date," Phaedra joked.

Mark lifted his brow. "Who says we're not?"

She blushed and changed the subject.

She had to admit, when their food arrived, that it was the best hot dog she'd ever tasted—juicy, plump, and bursting with flavor.

"I can't eat another bite." With a groan, Phaedra set her half-finished dog down on the plate. "How does Carmichael manage to consume an entire Big Kahuna?"

"He punishes himself at the gym later. We both do."

"You seem to be on good terms with him. For a relative newcomer."

"I think he sees me as a sort of sounding board. I'm an outsider, so he feels he can let his guard down a bit."

Phaedra took a sip of her beer and leaned back. *You're here for Hannah*, she reminded herself. *So go ahead. Ask the question.* "Mark, can I ask you something?"

"Ah, yes. The reason you wanted to talk to me." He licked the froth from his lip. "Ask away."

"You and Charles Dalton are good friends, right?"

"Yes. We've known each other most of our lives." A guarded note came into his voice. "Why do you ask?"

"Hannah came back from D.C. recently. She and Charles are both so busy, lately they've . . . grown apart."

He nodded. "It happens sometimes."

"But that's just it. Charles and Hannah were different. They really connected, almost from the first day they met. Everything was so good between them."

"You're speaking in the past tense. Did something happen?"

She rested her elbows on the table and met his eyes. "Charles has left the embassy, Mark. He's taken a leave of absence, returned to London, and put his house up for sale, all without saying a word to Hannah. She's devastated. Understandably so."

"I'm sorry to hear that." His words were measured. "But I'm not sure how I can help."

"Can you tell me what's going on with Charles? Offer some insight? Do you have any idea why he suddenly pulled up stakes and left D.C.?"

He didn't answer right away. In fact, the question hung between them for so long, Phaedra thought perhaps he didn't intend to answer her.

"He really did it, then," he muttered. "Damn."

"Did what?" she demanded. "Did you—Mark, did you *know* about this?"

He crumpled his napkin and dropped it on his plate. "I did. Although I didn't quite think it would come to this."

Phaedra stared at him. "Please explain. My sister's hurting, and I think she deserves an explanation."

"I agree." He lifted his gaze to hers. "Charles complained to me several times that he didn't see enough of Hannah. He said they were both busy; their schedules were always at odds. They couldn't make it work. He felt . . ."

"What?" she prodded when he stopped.

"He felt that Hannah prioritized her career over him. Charles is anxious to settle down," he added, "and he thought Hannah wanted the same. But when it became apparent that she didn't, he . . ."

"He what? Decided to bail?"

Mark let out a regretful breath. "Yes. And I'm afraid I may have had something to do with that decision."

The waiter arrived to take their plates and asked if they wanted anything else. Numbly, Phaedra shook her head.

"Just the check, please." Mark waited until he left. "Phaedra, please understand. I only meant to look after Charles's best interests."

"By coming between the two of them?" She tamped down a flash of anger. "Tell me exactly what you said to him."

"I asked if they both wanted the same things out of their relationship. If Hannah was as committed to him as he was to her."

"And what did he say?" she asked, her words even.

"He felt he didn't come first with her, more a distant second. I did what any good friend would do. I advised him to put some space between them, to step back and reassess what he wanted." He frowned. "Though, I didn't think he'd take me quite so literally."

"Hannah has no idea what she's done or why he left so abruptly. Everything was fine, and still would be," Phaedra informed him, "if you hadn't interfered."

"I didn't interfere." A defensive note undercut the words. "Look, my intention was, and always will be, to look out for Charles's best interests. We've known each other for a donkey's age. He's like a brother to me. From my perspective, your sister was playing fast and loose with his heart. When he asked me what to do, I advised him to give it some space. And I wouldn't hesitate to do so again."

"Well. There's nothing more to say, then, is there?" Phaedra thrust her chair back and grabbed her purse strap. "But it seems to me," she added, her voice suffused with anger, "that *you're* the one playing fast and loose with Charles's life. Not my sister."

He rose and threw a couple of bills on the table as she strode away. "Phaedra, wait. I'll take you home."

Several customers turned as Phaedra threaded her way determinedly through the café tables to the sidewalk.

"I'll walk," she flung over her shoulder. "Thank you for dinner."

She didn't turn back. Anger carried her down the street, past couples heading for drinks and dinner and shoppers in search of handmade goods and souvenirs, her thoughts propelling her onward. Why had Mark interfered? Why hadn't he left well enough alone?

Why did she let him get under her skin this way?

Her steps slowed. She remembered the night on the terrace, when she'd accused him of disliking Jane Austen. How wrong she was, and how quick to judge. *I think you're reading too much into things*, he'd told her. *Overanalyzing. Imagining you know what I think.*

Was she doing it again?

Well, she thought with a sigh, it was too late now. The damage was done. She'd try to speak to Mark again at the first opportunity. All she could do in the meantime was offer Hannah comfort and a shoulder to cry on until she got over her short-lived romance with Charles Dalton.

She proceeded down Main Street. As the sun waned overhead and the shade cast across the sidewalk by the old oaks lengthened, she reached the Taylor place. Her steps slowed.

A Realtor's sign stood atop the steep slope of the front yard. "Under Contract," it proclaimed in bold black letters. A lockbox hung from the front doorknob, and the grass was freshly cut.

When had the house gone up for sale? So far as Phaedra knew, it had been off the market for several years. Yet someone had already put in an offer.

Who'd be crazy enough to buy a house in such dire need of bulldozing?

With a shrug she turned away. The clip-clop of horses' hooves sounded behind her, signaling the approach of the horse-and-carriage tour offered every hour on the hour from nine a.m. to nine p.m., six days a week.

She lifted a hand and waved to the driver. He was the same man who'd driven her carriage the night before, and as he nodded and lifted his hand in return, it all came rushing back—the sudden jolt and harrowing tilt of the coach as the wheels dropped over the edge of the pavement, the high-pitched whinnies of fear from the horses as they nearly overturned into the ditch.

Someone had deliberately attempted to run her carriage off the road. Who would do such a thing? And why?

Phaedra turned up the walk to the inn. She needed to ensure everything was running smoothly before she returned to the carriage house for the evening.

Wickham and Bella would just have to wait.

"Phaedra, there you are!" Wendy cried out as she entered the lobby. "Where on earth have you been?"

She closed the door. "I went out." She left it at that, not wishing to share the details of her less-than-pleasant discussion with Mark Selden. "Why? What's wrong?"

"It's Tory. Tory Sutton. She's missing!"

Twenty-Four

Missing?" Phaedra echoed, and stared at her aunt. "What do you mean, she's missing?"

"No one's seen her since last night, when she called an Uber to pick her up when we left the Dixons' farm."

Did you check with Brian? Phaedra almost said, but caught herself in time. "Are you sure she's not in her room, or out in the guesthouse, working?"

"Positive. We've checked everywhere. Her clothes and things are in her room, but she's not in the house or anywhere outside. Brian said they had no plans to work today."

"Did anyone see her come home last night?"

"No. I locked up and went up to bed as soon as we got back. Tory has her own key, like all of the guests. I don't monitor their comings and goings."

Phaedra set her purse down. "I'm sure there's a reasonable explanation," she assured Wendy. "Maybe she went to stay at a friend's place."

"She doesn't know anyone in Laurel Springs."

"Maybe she stopped for a drink on the way home and met someone at the bar."

"Wouldn't she have come back by now? Or called to let

us know where she is? No," Wendy said, shaking her head, "something's wrong. I just know it."

Phaedra couldn't argue with her logic. "I'll call the police."

"I doubt if they'll do anything. She hasn't been missing long enough."

"I'll call Detective Morelli. He'll know what to do."

He picked up after two rings. "Morelli."

"Hello, Detective. This is Phaedra Brighton. I'm at the Laurel Springs Inn, and I want to report a missing person."

"Who? And when was he or she last seen?"

She filled him in on the details. He advised her to telephone the car service to learn where and when Tory was dropped off the night before. "I'm sure it's nothing to be concerned about," he reassured her. "Any idea why she didn't return to the inn with the others?"

She explained about the carriage mishap, and the limited seating in the remaining coach. "After the dance, Emmylou offered to drive the four of us back in her truck. Donovan, Mark, myself . . . and Tory, but she said she'd call for a car."

"Why? Did she have other plans?"

"Yes, but she didn't tell me what they were."

"What about her car? Is it gone?"

Phaedra felt the first pinprick of unease as she went to one of the drawing room windows and peered out into the darkness. There was no sign of the Porsche. "I don't see it," she admitted. "But she may have parked on the side of the house. Or down the street."

"She probably came home and took off to meet someone or go clubbing. She's young. Single. Give it until tomorrow morning. If she's not back by then, I'll issue an APB."

"What if she really is missing?" She glanced over at her aunt. "Or injured? If so, every minute counts. Wendy says everyone searched the house and grounds and there's no sign of her. But her clothes are still in her room. Don't you find that odd?"

"Not necessarily. Like I said, she's young. There are any number of explanations, any number of places where she might have gone. You've done all you can do for the moment." He paused. "You sound tired, Professor. My advice? Get some sleep. I'm sure Tory will turn up soon."

"I hope you're right. Thanks." She said good night and ended the call.

"Well? What did he say?" Wendy asked.

"He said there's nothing he can do at this point and suggested we both get a good night's sleep."

But sleep—at least the good, solid, restful variety—eluded Phaedra that night. Her dreams were troubled with runaway horses and guests who couldn't be found. She felt more tired when she woke up on Saturday morning than she had when she'd gone to bed.

Worst of all, Tory still hadn't returned.

"What are you looking for?" Wendy asked as Phaedra entered the kitchen and strode to the pantry, her face set in determination as she glanced inside.

"Not what, who. I think we should organize another search for Tory. Scour the entire place. She should've turned up by now. I'm getting really worried."

"I am, too." She untied the apron from her waist. "I'll help you."

Although they searched the house from top to bottom, enlisting the help of the guests, who allowed them to come in and search their rooms, there was no trace of Tory.

It was as if she'd vanished into thin air.

Phaedra paused in the doorway of the missing girl's room. Her clothes and things were strewn everywhere; a pair of heels, kicked off carelessly, lay abandoned on the floor, and her suitcase—Louis Vuitton, of course—still rested on the luggage rack.

"Shouldn't we go in and look around?" Wendy said. "Maybe we'll find a clue of some kind."

Although that was her first instinct, too, Phaedra shook her head. "I think it's best if we don't touch anything. But something's definitely wrong. It's not like Tory to leave her clothes and suitcase behind. If we don't find her within the next hour, I'm calling Morelli and officially reporting her missing. But first, I'll get in touch with the car service and see if the driver dropped her back here on Thursday night."

When she finally got someone on the line who could answer her question, she thanked them and hung up.

"Well?" Wendy asked.

"The driver remembers her very well. She gave him a substantial tip when he dropped her off here at the inn at ten thirty."

"Ah. So, she did come back."

"According to the person I spoke to, yes."

"Then where is she?" Wendy lowered her voice. "We have to find her, Phaedra. It's bad enough she might be hurt, or . . . or worse. I hope that isn't the case. But if anything's happened to that girl, after Harriet Overton's murder in the garden, the story will be all over the local news. The notoriety will ruin me!"

"We'll find her," she assured her aunt, although she didn't hold out much hope. If Tory Sutton wasn't here at the inn, she could be literally anywhere. "I know we will."

Phaedra's eyes went to the last door on the right. It was the only room left to search, the only room whose occupant hadn't appeared for breakfast or offered to help them look for Tory.

Mark Selden.

Could Tory possibly be with him? she wondered. After all, she'd flirted with him outrageously in the carriage. She practically sat in his lap on the ride out to Dixon's farm. And although he'd looked distinctly uncomfortable, perhaps he'd secretly enjoyed the attention.

Perhaps he'd decided to extend their evening into something more.

She turned back to Wendy. "Why don't you go downstairs and call Detective Morelli? I pinned his card to the kitchen bulletin board."

"Of course. What do you plan to do in the meantime?"

Phaedra glanced at Mark's door, firmly closed. "I have one more room to visit. Let me know what Morelli says."

As her aunt went downstairs to call the detective, Phaedra drew in a breath, tilted her chin back, and knocked on Selden's door.

"Professor Selden?" she inquired. "Are you in there?"

The door opened almost immediately. Surprise turned to caution as he saw her. "Phaedra."

"May I come in? Tory still hasn't returned and we're searching the entire house."

"Oh. Of course." He widened the door and gestured her inside. "As you can see, I'm alone. Unless," he added, his voice tightening, "you'd like to check the closet, or under the bed."

"I didn't really expect to find her here."

"Obviously you did, or you wouldn't be standing here."

"We're leaving no stone unturned." Her words were stiff. "I apologize for bothering you. And for the cliché. Thank you for your time." She turned to go.

"Wait." He reached for his keys. "I can help you look for her, if you like. Drive up and down the streets and inquire in the shops."

Phaedra hesitated. "I'd appreciate that. Thanks. About yesterday," she added. "I'm sorry I left so abruptly. You were only looking out for Charles. I see that now."

"And you were only looking out for your sister."

"I hate to see Hannah hurting like this," she admitted. "But I have to trust that she and Charles will work things out . . . without any help from me."

"Or any interference from me." He gave her a tentative smile. "Now, let's go find Tory, shall we?"

She nodded gratefully and preceded him down the hall to the staircase.

* * *

As Mark zoomed off in his Triumph to search the streets of Laurel Springs for any sign of Tory, Phaedra began her own search of the grounds. The musicians would be arriving in a few hours, along with the caterers Wendy had hired to provide food for tonight's grand finale, the masquerade ball. Tomorrow the guests would begin to leave.

Not to mention, she had to don her costume.

There was no sign of the young woman in the kitchen garden or on the back lawn; only a couple of squirrels, chasing each other through the hedges, and the flash of a blue jay on the wing. Bees drowsed in the hydrangea bushes, and shade dappled the grass.

It was the perfect lazy summer day to lie back in a hammock with a book and have a leisurely doze.

Phaedra paused under the tree where she and Mark had found the crossbow, and eyed the guesthouse. Although she'd seen no sign of Brian since breakfast, she knew he was there. His car was parked in the drive, and he'd been seated on the porch earlier, sitting beside Wendy in one of the white wicker chairs as he shared amusing anecdotes. Everyone had laughed.

Everyone but Phaedra.

"Any sign of Tory?" Donovan called out as he approached across the lawn.

She shook her head. "Wendy's inside, calling the police. No one's seen her since Thursday night. Her car's gone, too." She glanced at him. "Do you know why she didn't come back in Emmylou's truck with the rest of us?"

He shook his head. "No clue." He paused and frowned. "I remember she got a call on her phone, though. Seemed happy about it."

"Any idea who it was?"

"No, sorry."

Her gaze sharpened as the guesthouse door opened and

Brian Callahan stepped out, cell phone clapped to one ear. He was dressed impeccably, as usual, in a suit and tie.

"I guess dressing down isn't his thing," Donovan observed, reading her thoughts.

Brian caught sight of them and thrust his phone in his breast pocket. "Have either of you seen Tory?" he asked as he drew nearer. "I gave her the day off—it's Saturday, after all—but I have a couple of questions about a contract she drew up for me."

"She's missing, Mr. Callahan." Phaedra's words were measured. "Haven't you heard?"

"Sorry, no. I've been working," he said. As her comment registered, he drew his brows together. "Wait. What do you mean, missing? She's gone?"

"We don't know where she is. No one's seen her since Thursday evening."

"Since—well, why the hell haven't the police been notified?" he demanded. "What are you people waiting for?"

"Wendy's calling them now. We thought . . . we hoped that Tory would turn up on her own. But she hasn't."

"My God." His face paled. "I hope nothing's happened to her. How can I help?"

"Let's split up and search the grounds," Phaedra decided. "I'll take the area behind the guesthouse and along the retaining wall. Donovan, you and Brian search the rose garden and—" She swallowed. "Check the pond."

They nodded and took off, faces grim.

She strode across the lawn toward the guesthouse, rounded the corner, and paused on the back terrace. It was small, with barely room enough for a cushioned lounger, a café table, and a pair of chairs on its flagstone surface, but it invited visitors to linger. Hanging ferns and potted geraniums abounded. It was a pleasant place to sit and read a magazine or enjoy a coffee or a glass of wine.

But there was no sign of Tory.

With a sigh, Phaedra left the terrace and struck out for the far back corner of the property. A garden grew in one corner, and tucked under the shade of a small stand of oaks was a wishing well.

It was abandoned now, its wooden bucket and metal dipper long gone, the well itself long since covered over with plywood for safety. But like the terrace, it had a certain rustic charm.

There was no one here. Only Bella, sitting on the edge of the well, meticulously grooming her paw.

"Bella!" she said softly, not wishing to startle the cat as she stepped closer. "What are you doing out here?"

The Persian gave her a momentary glance before returning her attention to her paw.

"You're every bit as rude as Wickham," Phaedra said, shaking her head. "And just as indifferent to anything but the offer of food—"

She broke off, her ears alerted to a sound. It was faint, barely audible. Almost like the mewling of a kitten.

What was it?

Listening intently, hardly daring to breathe, she waited until she heard it again. It sounded like a low moan. And it was coming from inside the well.

But that was impossible. Surely?

Her heart quickening, Phaedra approached the well and studied the boarded-up top. The plywood that she'd assumed was nailed down wasn't. In fact, it sat slightly askew. She reached out a tentative hand to move it aside, but it was thick and heavy and took some effort before she managed to slide it partly sideways.

The sound of moaning grew louder as she pushed the plywood fully out of the way and peered down into the well. Her eyes widened in astonishment.

Someone was sprawled at the bottom, some seven or eight feet down, barely conscious. A woman.

"Tory!" Phaedra cried.

Twenty-Five

Can you hear me, Tory? It's Phaedra. I'm getting help, right now!"

She pushed herself away from the well with trembling arms, ran to the edge of the garden, and shouted for help.

In a moment Donovan and Brian appeared and raced across the grass, their faces flushed as they joined her.

"I found her," Phaedra exclaimed, and pointed to the well. "I've found Tory. She's down there. She must've fallen in somehow. We've got to get her out."

"She's in the *well*?" Donovan echoed, startled. "But how . . ."

"Never mind that!" Brian snapped. "Let's find some rope. We need to go in there and get her out."

"Wait. I'll call an ambulance." Phaedra focused her panicked thoughts and groped for her cell phone. Of course she didn't have it. "Do either of you have a phone?"

"What's going on?"

Phaedra looked up to see Detective Morelli striding toward them. "Detective!" She filled him in, her words rushed, as Brian and Donovan ran to the house in search of rope.

"Is she conscious?"

"Barely." She lifted concerned eyes to his. "Do you think she's been down there since she disappeared?"

"Good possibility." He glanced at the well and turned back to her. "There's a jump bag in my car. I'll get it and get an ambulance out here. I'll need strong rope or bungee cord if you have any. If she isn't too badly injured, we'll try to lift her out of there. In the meantime, stay put."

"But—"

"Talk to her. Keep her calm until the ambulance arrives. The best way to do that is for *you* to remain calm." He pressed the phone to his ear. "Tell her help is on the way."

Brian and Donovan returned a short time later with a coil of rope, and together with Morelli they fashioned a crude harness. Morelli dropped a separate length of rope down the side of the well and secured the end around the trunk of a tree.

"I'm going in." Morelli already had one leg hitched up and over the side of the well. The harness hung over his shoulder. "See how badly she's injured. We may have to wait until the EMTs get here before we attempt to move her."

"What can we do to help?" Donovan asked.

"Spot me, and if I tell you to bring her up, you and Brian start hauling, very slowly, on that rope."

After what seemed like hours but was barely ten minutes, Morelli reappeared at the top of the well, his shirt torn and his face sweaty and streaked with dirt.

"She's badly bruised and possibly concussed, but no broken bones as far as I can ascertain. She was lucky."

"Lucky," Brian echoed.

"Okay, Tory," the detective called down into the well, his voice reassuring. "Hang on and we'll lift you out, very slowly. Okay?"

There was a faint reply. "Okay."

Phaedra held her breath as the three men tugged on the rope he'd harnessed to Tory, keeping the line slow and steady so she wouldn't bump against the rough stone sides and injure herself further.

She never imagined that the sight of the girl, who'd been a royal pain from the moment she'd arrived, would fill her with such profound relief. Her face was dirty, her dark hair matted and dank, but she was alive.

"Tory," Brian said, his face creased in concern. "We were all worried sick about you! Are you okay? Do you have any idea how you got in there?"

She shook her head, and even that tiny effort exhausted her.

"No questions," Morelli said tersely. "She needs medical attention. Phaedra, hand me the jump bag."

She did as he asked, and he cleaned and bandaged the worst of her cuts and gave her a few small sips of bottled water.

"EMTs are on the way," he told Tory. His voice was calm. Gentle. "They'll get fluids back into your system and they'll probably keep you at the hospital for observation overnight. Does that sound okay?"

She managed a tiny nod.

A short time later the ambulance arrived, and after a quick examination the EMTs transferred her carefully onto a gurney.

"Any family who'd like to go with her to the hospital?" one of the EMTs asked.

"I'll go," Brian offered. "I'm the closest thing to family she has right now."

"Her name is Victoria Sutton," Wendy added. "She's a guest here at the inn."

As the EMTs rolled the gurney to the ambulance, Brian, still visibly shaken, followed close behind. Donovan had disappeared.

Typical, Phaedra thought. *When the going gets tough, Donovan gets going.*

As if reading her mind, Morelli asked, "Where's your friend?"

"My friend?"

"Donovan. The ex-boyfriend. Looks like he took off."

Bright flags of embarrassment burned her cheeks. "To be fair, there's not much he can do. And how did you know—"

"That he broke your heart and flushed it down the toilet? Your sister told me."

She promised herself she'd deal with Hannah later. "It was high school. Ancient history."

"She also said that if Donovan ever hurt you, he'd have to deal with her."

Okay, maybe she'd give her sister a pass.

"Your timing was impeccable." She glanced at the well. "You got here just as I found Tory."

"I'm glad I did."

"Believe me, so am I. Thank you. You were a real hero today."

He turned away to pack up his jump bag. "Just doing my job. You're the one who found her, after all." He paused and eyed her in curiosity. "Tell me, Professor—how *did* you find her?"

"Bella."

"The cat?" He looked as if he didn't believe her.

"She was sitting on the ledge cleaning her paws. When I got closer, I heard Tory moan."

"Good thing," he said. "Otherwise, we might never have found Ms. Sutton." He frowned at the heavy round of plywood partly covering the well. "Was that well cover in place when you found her?"

"Partly. Which is odd."

"Why is that?"

"Wendy's ex-husband, Jack, secured that cover years ago. I watched him nail it down myself. He didn't want anyone falling in."

"Which means someone went to the trouble of prying those nails out and moving the lid aside. And I don't think it was Tory."

"No." She crossed her arms against her chest as if doing so would ward off the implications. "Which indicates that someone deliberately pushed her down that well."

A chill threaded its way up her spine. Who? she wondered. Who would do such a horrible thing?

As Morelli reached for his phone, he added, "I found Ms. Sutton's car late last night."

"You did? Where?"

"The bus station."

"What was it doing there?"

"Good question. And you can bet I intend to get an answer." He called the incident in, spoke briefly to someone on the other end, and ended the call. "Forensics are on their way. They've gone over her car, but no prints turned up. Didn't really expect they would."

Although Phaedra pressed him for further details, Morelli remained stubbornly silent. She was lucky he'd divulged as much as he had. The crime scene team arrived, and as they began investigating the well and the area around it, she retreated to the house with troubled thoughts.

Could Tory and Harriet be victims of the same person? Her instincts told her that whoever had murdered Harriet so cold-bloodedly wouldn't have left Tory alive. They would have killed her first and thrown her body down the well.

Still, she couldn't help but wonder if the two events—Harriet's murder and Tory's attack—were somehow connected. Had Harriet seen Tory sneaking out to the guesthouse one night, like Phaedra, and threatened to tell Wendy? Did Tory kill Harriet to shut her up?

If so, then who threw Tory into the well? The same person who left her car at the bus station? Phaedra frowned. Mark had said the vehicle that nearly ran their carriage off the road was a sports car, a two-seater.

Tory's Porsche fit that description.

She called Mark and left a voice message to let him know Tory had been found, and returned to the inn.

As she let herself into the kitchen through the back

door, Wendy glanced up. "Coffee?" she asked, gesturing at the pot. "There's a kettle on the stove if you prefer tea."

"Thanks." Phaedra fixed herself a mug of Earl Grey. "I just can't believe this. First Harriet, and now Tory."

"What do you mean, now Tory?" Wendy set her mug down with a frown. "She fell down the well. It was an accident."

"Detective Morelli doesn't think so." She settled at the kitchen table across from her aunt and stirred sugar into her tea. "He's called in a forensics team to examine the well and the surrounding area."

"Why, for heaven's sake?"

"Jack secured that well years ago, when I was a kid. I watched him nail the cover in place. Someone deliberately removed it."

Wendy stared at her. "First a murder, now Tory's been thrown down a well? If Harriet's death didn't shut the inn down, this will be the nail that broke the camel's back."

"That makes absolutely no sense. You mean the straw that broke the camel's back."

"You know what I mean! The notoriety, Phaedra. It'll kill off any hope I have of garnering new business. Once the local media gets wind of this—"

"They won't. At least, not right away. Morelli has no desire to publicize Tory's attack. He won't even share his theories with me."

"Maybe not, but the hospital will have to notify the police. If there's any question of foul play, that is."

Her aunt was right. It wasn't a question of *if* the media found out, but *when*. "Clark Mullinax will be all over this story."

Wendy was silent, lost in gloomy thought.

"Brian and Donovan came out to help," Phaedra said. "At least, Brian did. Donovan left at the first opportunity."

"At least Brian stuck around." Wendy chased a packet of sweetener around her place mat with the tip of her finger. "I hesitate to bring this up," she ventured, lifting her gaze to Phaedra's, "but there's something I need to tell you. Something I've been putting off."

"Oh?" Phaedra wondered how long it would be before Clark Mullinax showed up on their doorstep with a microphone and a photographer. Hard news was difficult to come by in a small town like Laurel Springs. "You haven't changed your mind and decided to sell the inn, have you?"

"No, it's nothing like that. Not exactly, anyway."

"What, then?"

Wendy hesitated. "It's Brian. He's asked me to marry him. And I'm seriously tempted to say yes."

Twenty-Six

Her statement so startled Phaedra that she nearly overturned her mug of tea. "He *what*? When?"

"The other night, when he took me to dinner."

"Did you give him an answer?" she asked, more sharply than she'd intended.

"Not yet, no. And it's probably just as well." She sighed. "With so much going on, I can't even think about marriage. Or planning a wedding. Or anything, really."

"But . . . a marriage proposal, Aunt Wendy! That's a huge deal. Why didn't you mention it before?"

"That was the night I came back and found you unconscious in the garden, if you recall. My immediate concern was making sure you didn't have a concussion. Or a cracked skull."

"I'm fine."

"I didn't know that at the time, did I?" She added tartly, "I could hardly spring the news on you when you'd just suffered a head injury. Even under the best of circumstances—and let's face it, getting knocked out is anything but—I knew you wouldn't be pleased."

The door from the hallway swished open, and Eve appeared. "Excuse me, Ms. Prescott, but the caterers are arriving. Where should I have them set up?"

As Wendy went out with Eve to give instructions to the caterers, Phaedra followed them to the lobby. "Are the musicians here?" she asked Eve.

"Not yet. Where do you want me to put them when they arrive?"

"We've opened the front and back parlors and rolled up the rugs for dancing," she replied. "They can set up in the corner."

"How many musicians are there?" Eve asked doubtfully.

"Four. Don't worry," she added, amused. "No tattoos or piercings or ear-bleedingly loud decibel levels. Wendy's hired a nice, sedate string quartet. Excuse me."

She hurried to the front door as Elaine bustled in, a pile of altered costumes draped over her arm.

"Can you believe it? In just a few hours, it'll be time for the masquerade ball!" Her face was flushed. "I hope everyone remembers their dance steps."

"I'm sure they will." Phaedra drew her aside as a pair of men trundled by with the drawing room rug hoisted on their shoulders. "Do you have a minute? To finish our talk?"

"Talk?"

Seeing the blank look on Elaine's face, she said, "At the carriage house, when we were interrupted by Lucy and Marisol. You said you wanted to tell me something. Something about . . ." She lowered her voice. "Harriet, and her fondness for blackmail."

Discomfort slid over Elaine's face. "Yes. I remember. And yes, we do need to talk. But not now. And not here."

Twenty minutes later, with a cup of tea for Phaedra and coffee for Elaine, they sat in her office at Stage Door Costumes.

"Okay." Elaine settled back in her desk chair. "You may

not know this, but I once partnered with Harriet in a production company."

"Yes, I know. Rollo told me all about it. He said the partnership didn't work out and Harriet dissolved the company."

"What else did he say?"

Phaedra hesitated. "He claimed there were rumors of malfeasance on your part."

She waited, expecting Elaine to defend herself and deny the charge. But surprisingly, she did neither.

"Good old Rollo. He can't resist a good scandal. Or sharing a juicy piece of gossip."

"In all fairness, I think he means well. Most of the time."

"Well, I deserve it, I suppose. I told you about his affair with Richard Troy, after all. And he's telling the truth." She leaned forward. "Do you remember when we met, and I told you my name was Eleanor? But I insisted on being called Elaine?"

"How could I forget?" Phaedra laughed. "'Hi, I'm Eleanor. Not Nell, or Elle, or Lenore. Eleanor. As in Rigby. But you can call me Elaine.'"

"Did you ever wonder why I didn't want you to use my real name?"

"No." She gave a shrug and sipped her tea. "Not really. Lots of people reinvent themselves in college."

"Oh, I reinvented myself, all right." Her words were bitter. "I didn't have much choice. In high school I started skimming money from my parents' dry cleaning store. For nearly two years."

Phaedra stared at her as if seeing her, really seeing her, for the first time. "You stole? From your *parents*?"

"When I worked summers at the store. I never took much. I never got greedy, so I never got caught."

"Why?" she asked, trying to reconcile the person she knew with this other Elaine. "Why would you do that?"

"UVA was a new start for me, a clean slate. I swore I'd never steal another penny from my folks, or from anyone. Which lasted," she went on, "right up until my partnership with Harriet a few years later. I was in charge of the books. Talk about putting the fox in the henhouse." She shook her head ruefully.

"Did you . . ."

"Embezzle? Yeah, I did. A little here, a little there. Harriet eventually figured it out when we had a financial audit. She didn't prosecute me. She gave me the option of paying it back, which I did. Every last dime.

"And before you judge me," she added, leveling her gaze on Phaedra, "ask me again why I did it. Why I betrayed my father and stole from Harriet."

Phaedra was silent, waiting.

"My brother. Joey. He was a gambler. He ran up debts, Phae, huge debts, to some very nasty people. People who would've burned down the store or murdered me or my parents without blinking an eye."

"You gave him the money to pay them off," she said slowly.

"More than once. What else could I do? He's a lifer in prison now. Armed robbery. But I didn't do it for him. I did it for Mom and Dad." She let out a short, raspy breath. "Am I ashamed of what I did? Yes, of course. But would I do it again, given the circumstances? I would, in a heartbeat. No question."

"You were protecting your family."

Elaine shrugged. "I doubt the Feds would see it that way. And Harriet knew it."

"I understand why you did it. I do. But why are you telling me all of this now?"

"She held it over my head, Phaedra. For years. Harriet found out every detail and used it as leverage whenever she wanted a favor. I didn't dare refuse. I knew she'd tell my parents without hesitation what I'd done. It would've broken my father's heart."

"That's why you gave her Anne Elliot's role," Phaedra murmured.

"It was such a small thing, and Felicity didn't care. So I gave in. I had no choice."

"You know," Phaedra said, and leaned back in her chair, "I'm sorry Harriet was murdered. No one deserves that. No one. But she truly was an odious woman."

Their conversation waned. What more was there to say?

"I should probably go. I have a million things to do." Phaedra stood and carried her mug into the tiny kitchenette to rinse it out in the sink. She felt bad for Elaine. What a terrible predicament to be in, forced to steal from her own father to protect her brother and save the family business. Talk about a no-win situation.

She stuck her head in the office to say goodbye. "I'll see you tonight at the masquerade ball."

"You bet." She smiled but didn't get up.

Phaedra let herself out, her thoughts subdued. She wondered what she might have done in the same situation. Would she have handled things differently? Probably not, she mused. Elaine had made the only choice she could in the circumstances.

But that choice, unfortunately, also gave Phaedra's old college friend a good reason to want Harriet Overton dead.

Twenty-Seven

The masquerade ball began at dusk.

A pair of faux gaslit torches flanked the front walkway, lending the inn a festive air. The tall windows glowed in the gathering darkness and offered beacons of welcome to invited guests as they climbed the front porch in their costumes. Laughter, music, and the murmur of conversation drifted out each time the doors opened.

Phaedra surveyed the crowd from her position at the top of the stairs and smiled in anticipation. Wendy had invited her friends, neighbors, and family. She spotted Little Bo-Peep, a cowboy, a turbaned genie, even Sherlock Holmes in a caped coat and deerstalker hat. Male servers bearing silver trays of drinks and appetizers moved through the gathering in breeches and satin tailcoats.

She came down the stairs to greet Lucy Liang and Marisol Dubois.

"You look stunning!" Phaedra stood back to admire Lucy's scarlet dress and red elbow-length gloves. A strand of rubies circled her neck.

"Every party needs a scarlet woman."

Phaedra laughed and turned to Marisol. "And look at you! Marianne Dashwood, I presume?"

"This was all I had," Mari admitted as she smoothed the demure white skirts. "From last spring's Jane Austen festival. I'd much rather be Elizabeth Bennet. Or Emma. At least she was rich."

"Handsome and clever, too," Phaedra observed. "The perfect trifecta."

"Why didn't you get yourself a costume?" Lucy asked Mari. "Elaine would've hooked you up."

"I didn't have time." Her eyes were bright with curiosity as she turned to Phaedra. "Any news on the . . ." She lowered her voice to a whisper. "Murder?"

"Actually, yes. But we can't talk here." Her gaze swept over the colorful crowd. "Let's meet up tomorrow at my place. Three o'clock? I'll make tea."

"Tea," Lucy inquired hopefully, "as in cookies and teeny little cakes and maybe a lemon tart or two?"

"Tea," Phaedra said firmly, "as in leftover fruit crumble and cookies from the bakery. I've been busy."

"Works for me," Marisol piped up. "We'll be there."

"Phaedra!" Nan Brighton called out as she wove her way toward them with Malcolm in tow. "What a wonderful party."

"Hello, Mother. You look lovely." She pecked Nan dutifully on the cheek as her friends left to mix and mingle. "I like the feathered turban. Very becoming."

"Thank you. Elaine assures me it was the height of fashion in its day. Is Mark here? I don't see him."

"He's around somewhere. Just look for Captain Wentworth in full naval regalia."

A mischievous gleam livened Malcolm's gaze. "There's nothing like a man in uniform, eh, Phaedra?"

She gave him a distracted smile but didn't answer. She and Mark were not exactly on good terms at the moment.

"And who are you meant to be?" Nan asked her daughter as she surveyed her figured blue gown and the pearls arranged artfully in her upswept hair. "It suits you."

All her mother needed was a lorgnette to peer through and she'd fit the role of a marriage-minded Regency mama to a tee.

"I'm Elizabeth Elliot, from *Persuasion*. Anne's older sister."

"Is she the murder victim?"

"No. That dubious honor belongs to Lady Russell, Anne's godmother. She learns something shocking and sets out to warn Anne."

"How intriguing. Tell me, Phaedra." Nan leaned closer. "Who is the murderer?"

"You'll have to wait and see." She glimpsed Donovan, deep in conversation with Brian at the bottom of the stairs.

"Can't you at least give me a hint?"

She sighed. "He's male. And that's all you're getting out of me."

"Fine," her mother retorted. "I'll just have to puzzle it out on my own." With that, she excused herself to visit the powder room.

Phaedra waved her fan idly in front of her face, smiling and nodding at guests as she edged closer to the drawing room. Conversations swirled and eddied all around her. Her glance strayed once again to Brian and Donovan. What could they possibly be talking about so earnestly?

Felicity, her hair dressed with a small cluster of ostrich feathers, joined her. Her dress, a dark and iridescent green overlaid with a glittery overskirt, reminded Phaedra of a peacock's plumage.

"Quite a spectacle, isn't it?" Felicity observed, easing her hold on the black silk shawl draped around her shoulders. "But it's getting a little warm, with so many people in here. I feel as though I've been plunged right into the middle of one of Harriet's Regency romances."

"My aunt did a fantastic job," Phaedra agreed. "And your gown is stunning."

"Thank you. Elaine stitched it up specially. It reminds me of Lady Dalrymple's ball gown in *The Duplicitous Duke*, 'all shimmer and ostentation.'"

"Harriet's last book?" Phaedra asked. "I haven't read it yet."

"Oh, you should. No one could write quite like Harriet." She indicated Elaine, threading her way through the crowd toward them. "Here comes our dressmaker now."

Elaine's Empire-waist gown of white satin was trimmed in gold braid, and a necklace of emeralds sparkled at her throat. "You look stunning," she said as her gaze swept over them. "Both of you."

"Due in no small part to your nimble fingers." Felicity smoothed her skirts.

"You've done a fantastic job on our costumes," Phaedra agreed. "Harriet didn't want Lady Russell's role, but you've made it your own. You look very regal."

"Thanks. It's not too much, is it?" She glanced down at herself doubtfully.

"No. It's perfect. Is Mark here? Can't perform the play without Captain Wentworth."

"Or William Elliot," Elaine pointed out, and added, "Our murderer. Good thing Dave took on the part when Tom left."

"He's a hero *and* a villain," Phaedra agreed.

"If you'll both excuse me," Felicity said, "I think I'll duck out to the terrace for a smoke."

"Felicity!" Phaedra gave a guilty start. "You're so quiet, I nearly forgot you were there."

"People often do." She withdrew a cigarette and lighter from her beaded clutch. "I worked out the murderer's identity ages ago. But don't worry. I won't breathe a word."

"Thanks," Elaine said. "We appreciate your discretion."

She turned to go. "Have fun, ladies."

"I see your aunt headed this way," Elaine told Phaedra. "See you later."

"Thanks for the warning. Have fun."

As she departed, Phaedra turned to greet Wendy. Although not dressed in costume, she wore a black fitted cocktail dress and a double strand of pearls around her neck.

"You look very chic." Phaedra stood back to admire her aunt's stylish outfit. "Like Holly Golightly in *Breakfast at Tiffany's.*"

"Thanks. You don't look half-bad yourself."

Her gaze moved past her niece and the costumed guests around them, to Brian Callahan and Donovan Wickes.

"I wonder what those two are talking about?" Wendy asked.

"Exactly what I was wondering." They stepped aside to allow a group of guests to flow unimpeded into the front parlor. "Have you given Brian an answer yet?"

"An answer?"

"Yes, you know. When he popped the question."

"Oh, that. No." She fiddled with the pearls at her neck. "No, I haven't. But I can't put him off much longer."

Phaedra frowned. "I hope he's not pressuring you."

"He isn't. But he's leaving on Sunday and he'd like my decision before then."

One of the caterers hurried up to Wendy. "Excuse me. Can someone move that big old Cadillac from the driveway? We need to back our truck out and it's in the way."

"That big old Cadillac," Wendy replied curtly, "is mine." She turned to her niece. "Phaedra, would you be a dear and move the car? I need to speak with Brian. The keys are on a hook behind the reception desk."

"Where they always are." Phaedra touched her on the arm. "I'll take care of it."

As the string quartet launched into a waltz, she made her way outside, leaving behind the sound of laughter and a champagne cork popping as she headed down the front porch to the drive.

It was almost fully dark. Thank goodness for those fake

gaslit torchères, Phaedra thought as she made her way down the length of the drive to the Cadillac. If not for the flickering light they gave off, she couldn't see a thing.

As she rounded the back of the car, keys in hand, her gaze went to the rear left tire. It looked alarmingly low.

She reached the driver's-side door and inserted the key, surprised to find it was already unlocked. Wendy must've forgotten to lock it. She glanced once again at the rear tire.

It wasn't just low, she realized. It was flat as a pancake.

"Great," Phaedra muttered, and glanced down at her blue satin skirts. Changing a tire was the last thing she felt like doing. She was dressed for dancing, not removing lug nuts.

There was nothing for it but to go inside and see if she could prevail on one of the men to change the tire for her.

"Professor? What are you doing out here?"

She looked up to see Detective Morelli approaching, hands thrust into his pockets. "I could ask you the same thing."

"Just wrapping up our search of the grounds."

"Find anything?"

"You know I can't answer that." He glanced at the Cadillac. "Nice Caddy. Yours?"

She gave a mock shudder. "Please. No, it's Wendy's. She asked me to move it so the catering truck can back out, but . . ." She glanced over at the rear tire. "It's got a flat. And I'm not exactly dressed for changing a tire at the moment."

"I'd say not." A flicker of amusement warmed his eyes. "You look great, by the way."

A flush of mingled pleasure and embarrassment warmed her cheeks. "Thanks."

"I'll take care of the flat. Is there a spare?"

"Should be, in the trunk." She leaned into the car and pressed the release button on the dashboard.

"My dad had a Deville just like this when I was a kid," Morelli said as he surveyed the interior from the passenger's side. "In Dad's mind, it meant he'd arrived. He was living the American dream."

"The car belonged to Jack. My aunt's ex-husband," Phaedra added in answer to his quizzical glance. "He got the brand-new Lincoln when they split up. She got this."

"Was this what she wanted?"

"Only because she knew Jack wanted it more."

He grinned. "Remind me not to get on your aunt's bad side."

"Is there any word on Tory?" she asked as they both drew back and shut the car doors. "I'd like to visit her at the hospital tomorrow if she's up to it."

"She's hooked up to all kinds of intravenous fluids but resting comfortably. I tried to get a brief statement, but she was pretty loopy from the pain meds, and the doc ran me out."

"Does she remember anything? Like who shoved her into that well?"

"Not a thing," he said as he rounded the car and lifted the trunk lid. "Could be a result of trauma, or a concussion." He gazed down into the trunk's interior. "I'm hoping, given time, she'll remember a few salient details." He frowned. "Well, well. What's this?"

Phaedra hurried around the side of the car to join him. "It's a champagne coupe," she said as she caught sight of the saucer-shaped, stemmed glass lying on the carpet.

"I know what it is. But what's it doing back here?"

"I'm not sure. Wendy mentioned there's a coupe missing from the set she keeps in the butler's pantry."

"When did it go missing?"

She wrinkled her brow in thought. "Thursday afternoon. Why?"

"Because Tory Sutton was drugged at some point before someone shoved her down that well. Her doctor called me with her test results a few minutes ago."

"Drugged!" She stared at him in disbelief.

"I'd like to take this in for analysis," Morelli said as he

reached into his pocket and pulled on a pair of latex gloves. "With your permission."

On instinct, Phaedra opened her mouth to refuse, to protect her aunt in the unlikely event the glass turned up something damning, like Wendy's fingerprints; but she and her father had discussed the "plain view doctrine," an exception to the Fourth Amendment's warrant requirement, many times.

Morelli already had a warrant to search the grounds. And he had probable cause to suspect a crime had been committed on the property, which allowed him to search Wendy's vehicle. He'd spotted the coupe during a lawful observation.

Besides, her aunt had nothing to hide.

Did she?

Twenty-Eight

"May I have this dance, Miss Elliot?"

As Phaedra returned to the party a short time later, her thoughts troubled, she looked up to see Mark Selden standing before her.

Or rather, Captain Wentworth.

Her ability to form words fled. From his bicorn hat and dress blue coat to his white breeches, stockings, and black buckled shoes, he looked every inch the dashing Regency naval officer. His gaze, steady and serious, collided with hers.

It would be so easy to lose her heart to this man. Poor Anne Elliot never stood a chance.

"Miss Elliot?" he repeated. "Would you like to dance?"

"Of course." She smiled, well aware of her mother's keen eye on them. "I'd be delighted, Captain."

He clasped her gloved hand in his and led her onto the dance floor. As everyone acknowledged their partners, the familiar strains of "The Blue Danube" filled the air, and the two of them began to waltz around the perimeter of the room.

"It's been years since I danced," Mark said.

"I never would have guessed."

They moved together well, Phaedra admiring the swirl of the ladies' skirts and the spectacle of the colorful costumes. Neither spoke. She caught a glimpse of her mother, nudging her father in the ribs as she pointed the two of them out.

"We've been spotted." She nodded her head in the direction of her parents. "My mother will be expecting a proposal of marriage from you by evening's end."

Mark lifted his brow. "I thought that was the case only if the gentleman and lady danced together three times."

"Under Regency rules, yes. Under my mother's? We're as good as married."

He smiled as his fingers tightened on hers. "I can think of worse fates."

With a blush, Phaedra returned his smile. She longed to enjoy the moment and savor the romance of being transported to a Regency ballroom with the gallant Captain Wentworth as her dance partner. Whirling around the ballroom in Mark's arms was magical. Intoxicating. She never wanted it to end. But it was imperative she find Wendy and tell her about Detective Morelli's discovery in the trunk of her Cadillac.

Not only that, Tory haunted her thoughts, too. Who had shoved her into that well? And why?

The dance ended and they drew apart. "Is everything all right?" Mark asked. "You seem preoccupied."

"Do I? Sorry. I'm fine," she assured him. "Just a little distracted."

"Anything you'd like to share?"

She hesitated. "It's Tory. I can't stop wondering who pushed her into that well."

"Let the police figure it out. That's their job, after all," he reminded her. "Not yours."

"You're right." Phaedra forced her dark thoughts aside for the moment and gave him a dimpled smile. "Perhaps some refreshment, Captain?"

"Excellent idea."

They headed for the dining room. Halfway along the crowded hall someone tapped her on the shoulder, and Phaedra turned. Donovan, strikingly handsome in scarlet regimentals, white breeches, and black boots, bowed and fixed her with a roguish smile.

"Lieutenant Wickes at your service, Miss Elliot."

She inclined her head. "Hello, Lieutenant. We're just on our way to the buffet. Who knew all of this waltzing could make a girl so hungry?"

He glanced at Selden's retreating back. "I'm glad to see you're enjoying yourself."

"I am. Aren't you?"

He didn't reply. "Do you have a minute? I'd like to talk to you. Outside, if possible."

"Now?" She eyed him in dismay. "Can't it wait?"

"Ordinarily, it could. But I've just learned something. And it's something I think you should know."

"Okay. Let me tell Mark, and I'll be right back." She turned to go.

"No need," Donovan said, and laid his hand on her arm. "Won't take a minute." His eyes scanned the room, searching the faces around them. "Your erstwhile swain can wait."

"He isn't my swain. Erstwhile, or otherwise."

"I saw you two dancing. Captain Wentworth might not agree."

"If I didn't know better, Donovan, I'd almost think you were jealous."

"Please, Phaedra. It won't take long."

With a sigh she followed him, retracing her steps down the hall, out the front door, and onto the porch. "Where are we going? Can't you tell me whatever it is you need to tell me, right here?"

"Too risky. I don't want us to be overheard. Come on." He took her hand and tucked it in the crook of his arm.

Phaedra allowed him to lead her around the far side of

the house and down the path, gravel crunching under their feet, until they reached the rose garden.

She drew away. "Seriously, Donovan, what's this all about? Mark will be wondering where I am."

He indicated a stone bench and gestured for her to sit, then sat down and angled himself toward her. The hilt of his sword clanked against the stone.

"It's about your aunt's high school boyfriend, Brian Callahan," he said. "He's not what he seems."

"If you're about to tell me he's been two-timing my aunt Wendy with Tory Sutton," she said, leaning forward, "there's no need. I already know."

"Wait—what?" Surprise lifted his brows. "I mean, I suspected he was seeing Tory on the sly, but I wasn't sure. Sometimes she can be pretty . . . um, indiscriminate."

Phaedra chose not to comment. Her mother had drummed the old "If you can't say something nice, don't say anything at all" adage into her head, and it was a rule she tried to live by. Mostly.

Instead, she changed the subject. "Why am I here? And why the secrecy?"

"I came back to Laurel Springs for a couple of reasons. I didn't want to lose my deposit on the bridal suite, for one thing."

"And the other?"

He rested his hand atop the hilt of his sword. "I'm planning to open a gym downtown. Stationary cycles, treadmills, ellipticals . . . boxing and yoga classes. I need an affordable commercial property. I contacted Berkshire Hadley and they recommended a broker. Brian Callahan."

"And did he find you a property?"

"He did." He frowned. "Great location, fair price, right on the corner of Main and Spring Street."

"Main and Spring?" Phaedra echoed. "That's where Bertie's Café used to be. It's been empty for months."

"It isn't ideal—it has plumbing issues, and I'll have to tear out the kitchen to put in a smoothie bar—but for the right price, it's feasible. And Callahan offered me a very good price."

"I'm sorry, but I don't see the problem."

"You know what they say. If it seems too good to be true, it probably is. I did some checking, and I learned Callahan's Maryland real estate license was revoked."

She frowned. "Revoked? Why?"

"Mortgage fraud. Which can be tricky to prosecute. Anyway, none of the charges stuck. As a broker, he doesn't need a license." He glanced at her. "There's a contract pending on the place next door."

"The Taylor house." She nodded. "I saw the sign."

"I'll give you one guess who's buying it."

She stared at him in dawning dismay. "Not—"

"Yes. Wendy's beau. Brian."

"But why does he want the Taylor property? I don't understand."

"He's after the land. He brokered a deal with a Charlottesville property developer to build a mixed-use shopping center on the site."

Her face went slack with shock. "They're putting in a shopping center? *Here?* But that means—"

"He plans to raze both houses and clear the way for the new Laurel Springs Towne Center."

"Why, that lying, sneaky, two-faced polecat!"

"There's more." He hesitated. "You can't let your aunt marry him."

"I'm not about to let that happen. But . . . why not?"

"Because he's already married."

Phaedra stared at him. "Married," she repeated. "Of course. It all makes sense now."

"What makes sense?"

"Last Saturday, we hosted our first dinner at the inn. Harriet insisted she recognized Brian. Halfway through the first course, she remembered seeing his real estate signs."

"So?"

"She was about to tell everyone, including my aunt, that he was married." Phaedra shot to her feet. "And a few hours later, she was murdered."

"Phaedra, you can't just assume—"

"I have to warn Wendy. She needs to know her ex-boyfriend is worse than a cheat and a liar. He may be dangerous."

"I'll go with you."

"No. It's best if we go back separately." Phaedra glanced across the lawn toward rear of the well-lit inn and turned back to Donovan. "We can't let Brian know we suspect him. You go ahead. I'll wait a few minutes and follow you back."

"I don't like leaving you out here."

"I'll be fine." As he stood, Phaedra added, "Act like everything's normal. Mix and mingle." She lifted her eyebrow. "You used to be pretty good at that."

"Still am." He hesitated. "I told you, Phaedra, I know I messed up. I miss you," he added. "I miss us."

"There is no 'us,' Donovan. You dumped me, and we both moved on, that's the bottom line. It was high school. We were kids."

"Yeah. Yeah, I guess. Still, I wish—" His voice grew husky and he cleared his throat. "Never mind. Okay, I'm off. See you in a few, Miss Elliot."

As he crossed the darkened yard, sword clanking, and headed for the house, Phaedra lingered in the garden. Night jasmine blooms filled the air with scent, and she breathed deeply. Stars winked overhead like tiny pearls against a velvet sky.

Such a beautiful night was made to share with someone special.

Someone like Mark, she thought, remembering with a pang of guilt that she'd left him without a word. He'd be worried. She raised her hem to make her way across the lawn and return to the inn, when she heard a small sound behind her. A snap, like a twig breaking.

She whirled around, her eyes searching the darkness, but nothing moved. All was still.

"Hello?" she called out sharply. "Who's there?"

There was no answer.

After a moment she shrugged and headed across the lawn toward the house. The air had grown chilly.

She drew her silk shawl closer around her shoulders and glanced over at the Taylor house. Most of the windows were boarded up, and the house was empty and dark.

Why, then, did she see the gleam of a flashlight moving around behind one of the windows?

Phaedra watched, mystified, as light glinted and swooped behind the boarded slats covering the kitchen window. Who was prowling around inside at this hour?

She decided to investigate.

Fingers tightening on her shawl, she hurried to the garden shed and grabbed a flashlight from the storage bin near the door. She switched it on to make sure the batteries worked, then turned it off again. With any luck she could let herself in via the cellar door, just as she and Mark had done when they followed Bella into the house.

But luck wasn't with her. When she arrived at the cellar door, it was not only locked; there was a padlock hanging from the doorknob. Time to come up with a plan B.

Evidently, Brian had already secured all of the entrances.

She tried the kitchen door next, but it was also locked. There had to be another way in somewhere. She remembered seeing one of those old-fashioned coal cellars, with a slanted entrance and double wooden doors, when she was here before.

Following the flashlight's beam, she illuminated a tangle of bushes and weeds obscuring the foundation. She cast the light over the back of the house until it came to rest on her target—the old coal cellar entrance.

Bingo.

She only hoped the doors weren't locked.

They weren't. But a heavy wooden bar dropped into

place barricaded entry. She set her flashlight aside and wrestled with the bar until she managed to lift it. She opened one of the old wooden doors and pulled it outward with a loud, protesting creak.

She retrieved the flashlight and cast its beam down a shallow flight of stairs to a small, dirt-floored space. There was no coal piled up in readiness for the coming winter, only a rusted hoe and a slatted wooden basket once used to store apples and other produce.

Nor was there an entrance from the coal cellar into the house itself. Just a small, inhospitable room with a musty smell that housed only memories. And possibly mice.

Phaedra reached for her shawl, but it was gone. She must've dropped it somewhere. It was time she returned to the party before Mark and the others started to worry. She'd been gone for quite some time.

She'd just turned to reach out and close the door when footsteps, stealthy but unmistakable, sounded behind her. Before she could whirl around, or open her mouth to scream, a pair of strong hands shoved her on the small of her back, sending her tumbling down the steps into the coal cellar.

And closed both doors before dropping the barricade into place behind her.

Twenty-Nine

It was dark. Dusty. And it smelled faintly of apples.

Phaedra sat up, very slowly. Her head ached. How long had she been down here? A few minutes? A few hours?

She wasn't sure. She felt a little woozy. Had she hit her head when she fell? Or did someone knock her out? Either way, she was, quite literally, in the dark.

Her flashlight. Where was it? She'd had it in her hand when her assailant thrust her into the cellar. With no windows and the doors firmly shut, the darkness was impenetrable. She held up her hand but couldn't see it, even inches from her face. Perhaps if she groped around on the floor, she might find her flashlight.

While she didn't relish the thought of discovering first-hand what insects or creatures might be lurking down here, or worse, of touching one, she needed light if she had any hope of getting out of this cellar.

And she was determined to get out.

She skimmed her hands across the packed-dirt floor, regretting the ruination the headlong tumble had made of Elaine's beautiful costume, and wondered who had shoved her. No one knew she was here. Not even Donovan.

Besides, he'd returned to the house. He couldn't have followed her and pushed her into the coal cellar. Could he?

Unless he'd doubled back and crept up behind her.

"Stop," she said, her voice firm in the darkness. Donovan had no reason to harm her. Someone else had done this. Someone who must've overheard them talking.

But who?

She couldn't have been missing long, she reasoned, or they'd all be looking for her, calling her name.

But it was as quiet as the grave down here.

"Okay, not helping," she said aloud.

She tried to think positively, but found it nearly impossible. She wasn't on the inn's property, after all; she was next door. Why would anyone think to look for her here?

Before her thoughts spiraled into complete panic, her hand brushed against something. Gingerly, she touched it again, and her fingers closed over a smooth metal cylinder. Her flashlight! She scrabbled to pick it up and switched it on with trembling fingers.

She'd never been so glad of a flashlight beam in her life.

Wasting no time, she pushed herself to her feet and illuminated the shallow wooden steps that led up to the entrance. Perhaps the doors were closed, not barricaded. If so, all she had to do was climb the steps and give a good, hard push . . .

She thrust upward as hard as she could, but the doors didn't budge. They were firmly secured.

What now? Phaedra wondered, swallowing real fear. There was no one to help her. No one knew she was here, not Mark, not Donovan. She'd have to figure this out on her own.

Why hadn't she done as she'd promised and returned to the party? She'd be safe now. Instead, she'd allowed herself to be lured over here to the empty Taylor place. It might be hours before she was found. *If* she was found.

Obstinate, headstrong girl . . .

She fisted her hand and banged hard on the door. "Help!"

she shouted. "I'm in the coal cellar. Someone, please, let me out!"

When the echo of her pounding fists died away, the only answering sound was silence and the ragged rise and fall of her breathing.

No one was coming for her. At least, not anytime soon. She fought down panic and swept the flashlight beam around the perimeter of the room. At least she could see. Maybe there was a hatchet somewhere, or a pickax, and she could break the door down. Or—she glanced at the dirt walls—maybe she could dig her way out?

But there was nothing. No tools, other than the hoe, which was so rusted it would probably come apart after the first few whacks.

Think, Phaedra. Think!

Her brain worked feverishly to come up with a plan of escape. Perhaps there was an air duct of some sort that led up into the house above? If it were wide enough, she might be able to climb inside and inch her way through to freedom—

She froze. The smell of coal dust and apples gave way to a newer, stronger odor. Smoke.

Was the house on fire?

"Please, no," she whispered, and turned back to the doors in mounting dread. The acrid scent was stronger there, and as she reached out to lay her palm against the rough wood surface, it felt warm to the touch.

The Taylor house was on fire. And she was trapped down in this coal cellar, where no one would find her, with no viable means of escape.

Perspiration dampened her skin as she banged on the doors with renewed fervor.

"Help!" she screamed. "I'm in the coal cellar! Please, someone, please help me!"

In desperation, she focused the flashlight's beam at the doors, waving it back and forth in hopes that someone outside might see the light gleaming like a beacon in the crack between the doors.

The light, she thought suddenly. That's what brought her to the property in the first place. She'd seen a light moving inside the house, behind the boarded windows. Which meant someone had been there.

Were they still here? Would they help her if they heard her screaming? Had they been engulfed by the fire?

Or had the intruder—or intruders—*set* the fire?

Her breathing grew more labored. Was it her imagination, or was it getting harder to breathe? Was the supply of oxygen already growing shorter?

If only she'd taken her cell phone, she could call for help. But she'd left it behind in the carriage house, tucked in her reticule. Probably wouldn't get any cell reception down here, anyway—

Her flashlight batteries chose that moment to waver and die.

"No, no, *no!*" she groaned, and felt her throat thicken with incipient tears as darkness settled around her. She couldn't cry now. She didn't have that luxury. There simply wasn't time.

"Help!" she shouted again, and slammed her fists against the door until they ached. "Please, someone, let me out!"

The heat had intensified and the wood had grown warmer, too. The smoky darkness wrapped itself around her like a cloak, thick and heavy and inescapable. She began to cough.

"Help," she cried out again, her voice coming out in a croak from her Sahara-dry throat. "Let me out!"

She felt dizzy and light-headed. Another fit of coughing overtook her, but she continued to pound on the doors. Pinpricks of red danced before her eyes, and the heat had grown unbearable.

"Please," she croaked one last time, the word ending on a sob. "Help!"

With that, her legs crumpled beneath her, and she slid down against the door. Well, she'd done what she could. Once smoke inhalation got her, she'd lose consciousness, and she'd die in here, alone and helpless . . .

thirty

Shouts rang out nearby. Someone was out there!

Phaedra rallied enough to sit up and struggle to her feet, and began a thunderous pounding on the doors. "Help! In here! Help me, please!"

"Hang on!" a voice called back. "I'll get you out of there."

She heard a heavy clunk as the wooden barricade was lifted, and one of the doors flew open, letting in moonlight and fresh air. And smoke.

A lot of smoke.

Her rescuer reached in and grabbed her arm. "Hurry. The kitchen is on fire."

She stumbled out, leaning heavily on his arm, coughing and choking as her legs buckled beneath her. She couldn't see though the smoke. "Th-thank you. You saved my life—"

"Never mind that. We need to get away from the house," he urged. "The fire's starting to spread."

She focused on the dark-haired teenager, and her jumbled thoughts cleared. "Billy? What are you doing here?"

"Lean on me." He led her to the front yard, where

neighbors and onlookers had gathered, to a grassy spot under an oak, and held up his phone. "Fire and rescue are on the way."

With every breath of fresh night air, Phaedra felt clarity returning. Like her, Billy smelled strongly of smoke, and his face was streaked with soot. "Were you in the house?" she asked, her eyes widening in concern. "Are you okay?"

"Yeah, fine. I was inside, but I got out in time."

"Thank goodness. And thank goodness you heard me screaming. I was trapped in that coal cellar, and I thought . . ." She drew in a breath. "I'd just about given up."

"I saw something in the grass when I ran out. A shawl. I picked it up and that's when I heard you."

In the wake of a pair of fire trucks, a police car pulled up to the curb, blue lights flashing, and behind it, an unmarked car came to a stop. A dark-haired man unfolded himself from the passenger seat and slammed out of the car.

Morelli's eyes swept the scene and came to rest on her. "Professor Brighton?"

She nodded, unable to reply, and waited as he strode toward them.

"Are you okay?" he demanded. "What are you doing here?"

"I saw something," she choked, and coughed. "A light. In the Taylor place."

"Fire?"

She shook her head. "No. Before that. A flashlight. Moving around inside the house." She coughed again. "Why . . . why are you here?"

"The scanner. I heard there was a fire at the Taylor place. I know it's next door to your aunt's B and B, so I decided to swing by." He knelt down. "Have either of you been checked out by the EMTs?"

"Not yet."

He turned to Billy. "What happened?"

"I found Professor Brighton in the coal cellar. Someone had shoved her inside and barred the doors."

Morelli turned back to Phaedra, his face like thunder. "Care to tell me what you were doing hanging around the coal cellar?"

"Billy just told you. Someone pushed me in."

"Who?"

"I don't know." She cleared her throat. "I was in the rose garden earlier, and I saw a light moving around in the house. I came over to check it out, and—"

"And what?" he prodded.

She couldn't tell him she'd tried to break into the house to investigate. Not unless she wanted to face charges for attempted breaking and entering.

"I went around to the coal cellar," she said instead, "to have a quick look around. It was empty. I was about to call the police when someone came up behind me and pushed me in."

Morelli's dark brown gaze shot to Billy. "How do you fit in? What were you doing over here?"

A guarded look crossed his face. "Nothing."

"Nothing." The detective plainly wasn't buying it. "Try again."

"Look, I don't want any trouble, okay?"

"Tell me the truth, and you don't have to worry. You got Professor Brighton out of that coal cellar, correct?"

He nodded. "Yeah. As soon as I heard her screaming."

"So, you saved her life. Which means," Morelli added, "that if you've been squatting in the Taylor place—" He ignored Billy's startled expression. "I'd be inclined to overlook any charges of trespassing or B and E. But you need to be straight with me in return."

He shoved his hands in his pockets. "I stay in the house sometimes. Temporarily."

"Are things bad at home?"

Billy shrugged. "No. It's just . . . since Dad died, Mom won't let me leave the house or have friends over when she's at work. And she's always working. It's like being in jail."

"She worries about you," Morelli pointed out gently. "She wants to keep you safe."

"I got a part-time job after school, at the Coffee Stop. Figured I could help out a little. I thought she'd be happy. But she said no. Says my schooling is more important than a few extra dollars."

Phaedra and Morelli exchanged glances. She suspected, and he probably did, too, that the boy was behind the recent rash of thefts of petty cash from local shop owners.

"I pick up a few odd jobs here and there," Billy added. "Cleaning windows, mowing lawns. I bought a camping stove and some canned stuff so I could hang out in the house. Get away."

"I understand," Morelli told him. "But think about your mom. You're all she's got. Taking off without warning only adds to her worries. Is that what you want?"

"No," he said, and sighed. "I guess not."

Phaedra's heart went out to him. She wanted to wrap him in a hug and offer to help, but knew instinctively he wouldn't welcome it.

"How'd the fire start?" Morelli asked. "Your camping stove?"

"What? My . . . no!" Alarm widened the boy's eyes. "The fire wasn't my fault. I'm always careful when I use the stove."

"Okay. Then tell me what did happen."

Billy shifted from one foot to the other. "You—you probably won't believe me. *I* wouldn't believe me."

"Try me."

In hesitant, halting words, the story tumbled out. "I was in the house, about to heat up a can of ravioli, and I heard footsteps. Someone was in the house. I got scared and hid in the pantry."

"Did you see anyone?"

"A guy. At least, I think it was. Hard to tell, with the ski mask he wore. You know, the kind with eyeholes, that covers your face? Like a cartoon burglar."

"A balaclava."

"Yeah. He wore all black. Except his shoes. They were brown. Expensive looking."

Morelli nodded. "And you didn't hear anything before that? No breaking glass or the sound of someone jimmying the door?"

"No."

"What happened next?"

"He stood in the kitchen, looking around. He saw the camp stove and the can, and he must've wondered if anyone was in the house. If he'd searched the place, I'd have been busted, but he didn't. Seemed like he was in a hurry. He turned his back, and I couldn't see what he was doing. I heard a scratch, like a match striking. I figured he was lighting a cigarette."

"But he wasn't."

"No. He picked up a burger wrapper I left on the floor"—Billy had the grace to look embarrassed—"held the match to it, and dropped it when it caught fire. He was laughing," he added, shaking his head in disbelief. "Like it was funny or something. Then he left. And the minute he did, I got out of there. That's when I heard Professor Brighton screaming."

"Did you recognize his voice? When he laughed?"

"No."

One of the EMTs approached. "Were you two inside?"

"Someone pushed Professor Brighton into the coal cellar behind the house," Detective Morelli said. "This young man heard her screaming and got her out. They both need medical attention."

"I'm fine," Phaedra protested, and coughed.

"Not up for discussion, Professor." Morelli stood by, arms crossed, as she and Billy were examined and treated for mild smoke inhalation.

Phaedra thanked the EMT and insisted she was okay. "I have to get back to the inn. My aunt will be worried."

"Worried? That's an understatement! Where have you

been, Phaedra?" Wendy cried as she hurried up to them, Mark and Donovan in her wake. "I was frantic. We all were. What happened? Are you hurt?"

"No. It's a long story. But thanks to Billy, I'm fine."

"You said you were coming back in." Donovan eyed her in reproach and turned to Mark. "That's what she told me."

"We looked everywhere," Mark told her. "But you'd vanished. When we heard the sirens, we rushed over to see what was going on, and saw the fire trucks."

"I'm sorry." Her words were contrite. "I didn't mean to cause all this fuss. I saw a light moving around inside the Taylor place, and I had to check it out."

"Well, whatever the case, I'm glad you're all right." After a brief hesitation, he turned and left.

"Go back to the inn with your aunt," Detective Morelli said. "Get some rest." He helped Phaedra to her feet and lowered his voice. "And just for once, Professor . . . try and stay out of my investigation. Deal?"

She nodded. "Deal."

"Good." His hand remained, warm and solid, on her elbow. "You had a serious scare tonight, one that could've ended up a lot differently."

Her throat tightened. "I know."

"Are you sure? That you're all right."

"Positive." She met his dark, reassuring gaze. "Thank you for asking. And for getting here so quickly." After a moment's hesitation, she added, "You're not charging Billy, are you? For trespassing?"

"Ordinarily, I would. But if he hadn't been in that kitchen tonight, you probably wouldn't be standing here."

He released her elbow and let his comment sink in.

"He saved my life." She cleared her throat. "You didn't tell the firefighters that Billy was in the house when the fire started."

"When I take Billy's statement, I'll make sure he includes that fact. He was eyewitness to an arson attempt.

And I'll make sure it's understood that his actions saved your life tonight."

"Thanks, Detective. For everything."

"You bet. Good night, Professor."

It was late when Phaedra returned to the carriage house. Wickham, nestled atop a discarded shawl on the sofa, lifted his head to regard her with condemnation.

Don't mind me, his blue eyes seemed to say. *I'm just the cat. Overlooked, once again.*

"I'm so sorry, Wicks," she crooned as she closed the door and joined him on the sofa. "Did you miss me?"

Miss you? Why would I miss you when you're never here? Is it any wonder I've developed separation anxiety?

"Would you like to go out, handsome boy?"

As she knew he would, he leaped to his feet and padded haughtily alongside her into the kitchen and out the back door. She refilled his kibble and put the kettle on for a cup of chamomile. "Bella?" she called out softly.

The fluffy feline lifted her head to eye her but didn't stir.

Phaedra was tired, but a strange restlessness gripped her. So much had happened. Tory's disappearance, the champagne coupe in Wendy's trunk, not to mention her own near brush with death in the coal cellar tonight.

What did it all mean? Were the incidents connected to Harriet's murder?

Phaedra sat at the kitchen table to wait for the water to boil and picked up a paperback copy of *Persuasion*. Anne Elliot, the overlooked and underappreciated heroine of Austen's novel, was the subject of a question on her Austen quiz earlier in the week. Felicity Penrose came up with the correct answer and won first prize.

She'd been pleased for Felicity, since, like Anne, she seemed content to fade into the background. Putting the book aside, Phaedra spotted a small stack of well-worn paperbacks and drew them toward her. All were Regency romances, and all were written by Harriet Overton. There was a sticky note atop the stack.

"'Found these in Harriet's dresser drawer,'" she read aloud. "'Thought they might be of interest. W.'"

Picking one up, she skimmed it, flipping idly through the pages, stopping to read a few lines here and there. The earlier novels were written in a florid, overdone style. The newer ones were a vast improvement—so much so, it felt as though someone else had written them.

The kettle whistled and she stood to take it off the burner. She fixed her cup and stood by the sink to gaze out at the darkness beyond the kitchen window.

Who had shoved her headlong into that coal cellar? Was it the same person who'd pushed Tory into the well?

She had no idea. But as she set her cup down and let Wickham back in, she knew she had to find out soon.

Before whoever it was decided to strike again.

Thirty-One

P haedra had just taken a bracing sip of English Breakfast tea and tied an apron at her waist when the doorbell rang.

After her uncomfortably close brush with death, she'd slept surprisingly well and returned to the inn on Sunday morning, ready to face the final day of the Jane Austen immersive murder mystery week.

By this evening, the guests would all be gone.

One more breakfast to serve, one more lunch, and the week would officially be over.

"Who could that be, and so early?" Wendy, her hands encased in oven mitts, glanced at Eve. "Will you go and see who it is, please?"

Eve nodded and left.

They heard the front door open, followed by a murmur of voices, and Eve returned with Detective Morelli.

"Sorry to disturb you so early on a Sunday morning," he said, "but in light of recent events, I'd like your guests to remain here at the inn until further notice."

"But this is the last day of our murder mystery week," Wendy protested. "Everyone's leaving this afternoon."

"I'm afraid that's not possible. This is still an open murder investigation. With the attacks on Victoria Sutton and Professor Brighton, we need to question everyone again."

"How long will that take?" Phaedra asked.

"We'll try to wrap it up today," he said. "In the meantime, I have a few questions." He glanced at Wendy. "I'll start with you. If I might have a word? In private?"

She nodded, flustered, and removed the oven mitts. "We can talk in the front parlor."

"And before you object," Morelli added as he met Phaedra's eyes, "I'm not here to charge your aunt. Or arrest her."

Yet. The unspoken word hung in the air between them.

"It's all right, Phaedra," Wendy assured her. "I haven't done anything wrong and I have nothing to hide. I'll do whatever I can to help. This way, Detective."

She preceded him through the swinging door and into the hallway just as Hannah arrived.

"What's going on?" her sister asked. "When I woke up, you were gone. And why is that detective here again?" She opened the cupboards to gather the ingredients for scones. "Has something happened?"

"What hasn't happened?" Phaedra went to the fridge to load butter, cream, homemade jams, and crème fraîche onto a tray for the dining room table. "He's just informed us that no one can leave until everyone's been questioned."

"Questioned? About what?"

"Someone pushed me into the coal cellar next door."

"What?" Hannah whirled on her, aghast. "When?"

"Last night. You really should've gone to the ball. There was a fire at the Taylor house."

"There was a *fire*?" She searched Phaedra's face with anxious eyes. "Are you all right?"

"Fine. Billy Roberts heard me screaming and got me out."

"The boy who mows Wendy's lawn?"

Phaedra nodded. "He saved my life. Like I said, you missed a lot."

"I didn't feel like socializing. I still don't. This thing with Charles . . ." She sighed and returned her attention to the mixing bowl, breaking an egg against the rim. "Is the house a loss? Or were they able to save it?"

"It's mostly okay, thanks to Billy. He called the fire department right away, and they managed to put out the flames before they spread. Kitchen's gutted, though."

"What were you doing hanging around the coal cellar?"

Briefly, Phaedra filled her in on the previous night's events. ". . . and when I saw a light moving around inside the house, I had to see what was going on."

"And nearly got yourself killed in the process," Hannah finished, shaking her head. "Am I getting warm?"

"Warmish."

"Phaedra—"

"Someone was in the house. I saw a flashlight moving around. I was concerned."

"Someone creeping around in an empty house with a flashlight? That usually screams 'burglar' or 'intruder' or, at the very least, someone who's up to no good."

"It was Billy," Phaedra said. "He's been camping out in the kitchen. But I didn't know that at the time. I had to check it out."

"No, you didn't. You're not a detective, or a private investigator. You're a college professor. You can't keep doing this stuff. One day, you'll get into a fix you can't get out of. End up in serious trouble."

"You're right." Phaedra sighed. "I know you are. But you just reminded me of something."

"What?"

"When Donovan and I talked last night, I heard a noise behind us. A snap, like a twig breaking. I think someone was listening."

"Who'd want to eavesdrop on you and your old high school boyfriend? What were you talking about, anyway?"

"Donovan mentioned that the Taylor place is under contract. He said . . ." Her hands stilled on the pitcher of cream. "He said Brian Callahan bought it."

"Why would Mr. Callahan want to buy that old dump? It'll cost a fortune just to make the place livable again."

"It's not the house he wants." She glanced over her shoulder at the door and lowered her voice. "He's after the land it stands on. For a property development deal he's brokering." She pressed her lips together and untied her apron. "With everything going on last night, I nearly forgot. I need to tell Morelli. And warn Aunt Wendy."

"Warn her about what?"

"That her former boyfriend isn't what he seems," she said, and flung her apron aside. "She can't marry him."

But when she arrived at the front parlor, expecting to find the door closed, it was open and the parlor was empty.

Where was her aunt? Where was Detective Morelli?

She hurried back to the kitchen and retrieved the tray. "I need to leave for a few minutes. I'll put these on the sideboard on my way out. Can you and Eve and Dave manage breakfast?"

"Yes, of course. James is already on his way. Where are you going?"

Phaedra didn't answer. She was halfway down the hall, tray in hand. *The champagne coupe*. Had the lab returned a forensics report on the glass Morelli had found in Wendy's trunk? Was that why he was here?

He hadn't said anything about charging her aunt, though. Or arresting her. In fact, he'd stated he was only here to question her. Which was encouraging. It also meant that something else was going on. But what?

She glanced out of the dining room window, reassured to see Morelli's car still parked outside. He hadn't left.

Setting the tray on the sideboard, Phaedra retraced her steps to the kitchen and went out the back door, nodding to James as he arrived. Finding Wendy was her first priority. She deserved to know the truth, that Brian's reconnection with her after all these years was purely self-serving. Even though she knew the news would devastate her aunt.

Her steps faltered. The last thing she wanted to do was hurt Wendy. But nor could she stand by and allow Brian to coax her aunt into marriage when he already had a wife. She loved her aunt too much to let someone like Brian willfully break her heart.

Picking up her pace, Phaedra moved purposefully down the graveled path that circled the kitchen garden and struck out across the lawn to the guesthouse. As she drew closer the sound of raised voices reached her ears.

"—lied about everything, didn't you? Including your so-called feelings for me!"

She recognized her aunt's voice, livid with anger.

"Now, doodlebug," Brian soothed, "you know that isn't true. You need to calm yourself down."

"Don't," Wendy gritted out, "tell me to calm down. Never in the history of the world has telling someone to calm down ever calmed them down. And don't you dare call me by that nickname, ever again. You have no right."

"Wendy, honey—"

"You never wanted *me*, did you? You wanted my property. Phaedra was right," she added, her words choked with emotion. "She warned me about you, but I didn't listen."

"Phaedra," he bit off, as if spitting out a watermelon seed. "Meddlesome girl. It's no wonder she's not married. No man wants a woman who thinks she's smarter than he is."

There was a brief, shocked silence. "Careful, Brian," Wendy said evenly. "Your misogyny's showing."

"Look, I'm sorry, doo . . ." He cleared his throat. "Wendy. Listen, please. I care for you. You know I do! I guess I'm more upset by all of this than I realized."

"All of what?"

"The murder, Tory's disappearance, and now, finding out someone pushed your niece into that coal cellar—"

Edging nearer the window, Phaedra risked a glance inside. Brian was flinging clothes into an open suitcase as her aunt looked on, arms crossed against her chest.

"What are you doing?" Wendy demanded.

"Leaving."

"No one can leave until the police question everyone."

"I'll take care of it on my way out."

"Oh, please. We both know that's a lie."

"Believe what you want." He slammed the suitcase shut. "Either way, we're done here. Now get out of my way."

With that, he grabbed his suitcase and thrust past her. She stumbled and fell back on the bed.

Furious, Phaedra flew up the path to the front door to confront Callahan. Footsteps sounded behind her as Morelli caught up to her and grabbed her by one arm.

"Don't even think about it," he warned in a low voice as he pulled her aside.

"But—"

"Listen to me, Professor. Go back to the house. Now."

"I need to tell you something. About last night. About Brian."

"And I'll listen," he promised. "But right now, I need you to leave. Okay? This is a police matter."

Reluctantly, she complied. She felt his eyes on her as she turned away, gravel digging into the soles of her silk slippers.

He rapped twice on the half-opened cottage door. "Brian Callahan?"

Phaedra, her curiosity piqued, slipped behind a hydrangea bush and peered cautiously around it. What was going on?

Wendy's former beau appeared in the doorway, suitcase in hand. "Yes?"

"Detective Matteo Morelli, Homicide Division, Somerset County." He held up his badge. "I need to ask you a few questions."

"I'm sorry, Detective, but as you can see, I'm in a bit of a hurry at the moment—"

"It'll have to wait. As I said, I have questions."

A uniformed officer came up the path to join him.

"This is outrageous!" Callahan blustered. He fumbled in the breast pocket of his suit jacket for a card and extended it with a scowl. "I refuse to answer anything without my lawyer present."

"Fine. You want to lawyer up, that's your prerogative. In the meantime," he added, "you leave me no choice. I'm detaining you for questioning."

"What? You can't do that!"

Morelli's gaze flicked to the suitcase and back. "I'm afraid I can. Because it looks to me like you're planning to go somewhere. That makes you a flight risk."

He glared but made no reply.

"We can either question you here, Mr. Callahan, or we can do it at the station. You decide."

Thirty-Two

What do you mean, we can't leave? What is this, the Hotel California?"

Rollo Barron set his cup of Darjeeling onto the saucer with a rattle of china and glared across the breakfast table at Phaedra.

"I'm sorry," she calmly informed him, "but Detective Morelli wants us to remain here at the inn until everyone's been questioned."

"But I can't afford to stay any longer," Felicity fretted. "My budget is stretched to the limit as it is."

"You won't be charged for the additional stay," Phaedra assured her. "None of you will." There was a murmur of relief around the table. "Perhaps Detective Morelli can take your statement first, Felicity. In the meantime, I ask all of you to please cooperate with the police."

"Where's Mr. Callahan this morning?" Elaine wondered as she spread cream cheese on a bagel. "And your aunt?"

Phaedra hesitated. What to say? "She has a personal matter to take care of." It was the truth, more or less. She didn't have the energy to explain that her aunt was barricaded in her room, heartbroken by Brian's betrayal.

"Not to gossip," Rollo said, "but just before I came downstairs, I saw the police put Brian in a cruiser and take him away."

"Brian?" Eve lowered the pitcher of cream onto the table with a thump. "But he seems like such a nice man. Was he arrested? Whatever for?"

"He wasn't arrested," Phaedra replied. "He's been taken in for questioning."

"Why not question him here?" Elaine asked. "Like the rest of us?"

"I was at the guesthouse when Detective Morelli arrived," she replied. "Brian refused to say a word without a lawyer present."

Rollo shrugged. "He's perfectly within his rights. Although it does look a trifle suspicious, refusing to answer a few routine questions."

"Unless they weren't routine," Felicity mused.

Elaine leaned forward. "What do you mean?"

"Maybe the police know something we don't."

"Like what?" Phaedra asked.

"Maybe Brian had something to do with Tory's disappearance. She was his assistant, wasn't she?"

"Yes. But that doesn't mean he had anything to do with it."

"You know what they say." Felicity stirred milk into her tea. "The simplest explanation is often the best."

"Occam's razor." Phaedra nodded as she reached for her tea. "Don't make more assumptions than absolutely necessary."

"Well, I hope for your aunt's sake that you're both wrong in assuming Brian had anything to do with Tory's disappearance." Elaine exchanged a glance with Phaedra. "Aren't he and Wendy an item?"

"They had dinner a couple of times. That's all."

"Oh. I was under the impression it was a little more serious than that. Glad to hear I was wrong. How awful for her if Brian really is mixed up in all of this."

Phaedra didn't reply.

"Not that I'm one to talk," Elaine added with a rueful laugh. "When it comes to bad judgment, I wrote the book."

I wrote the book. Distracted by the phrase, Phaedra let the conversation flow around her as she remembered the stack of paperbacks Harriet had left behind in her room. She darted a discreet glance across the table at Felicity.

Rollo claimed that Harriet had once publicly trashed the budding writer's fan fiction so badly she never wrote another word. *No one could write quite like Harriet.* That's what Felicity had said at the ball last night.

"How's Tory doing, by the way?" Elaine asked her. "Any news on her condition?"

"She's being released today," Phaedra said. "I'm picking her up after breakfast. More tea, Rollo?"

"Yes, please." As she refilled his cup, he mused, "Do you suppose that Callahan murdered Harriet? Maybe that's the real reason the police took him in."

Felicity cast him a disapproving glance. "Really, Mr. Barron. That's a reach."

"Well, someone did it. Why not Brian? He stayed out in that guesthouse, after all. Much easier for him to slip out and kill Harriet without being seen."

"It's possible." Phaedra set the silver teapot back on the sideboard as she considered the question. "But unlikely. One could argue that he had opportunity, I suppose. But he doesn't have means, or motive. He and Harriet were complete strangers."

"True. Then again," Felicity pointed out, her words measured, "if Brian really *did* push Tory Sutton into that well for reason or reasons unknown, then who's to say he didn't murder Harriet as well?"

There was an uncomfortable silence.

"And on that cheery note," Elaine said dryly, easing the

tension as she pushed her chair back, "I need to get going. Phaedra, I'll clear those costumes out of the front parlor later today. Sorry I haven't done it yet, but I haven't had a chance."

"No hurry. They're not in anyone's way," Phaedra assured her. "Leave them here as long as you need to."

Mark Selden entered the dining room as Elaine left. Giving Phaedra an inscrutable glance, he poured a cup of coffee at the sideboard and seated himself at the table. "I understand we're all to be kept here for another day."

He didn't sound particularly happy at the prospect, Phaedra noted. So much for their magical evening together. Evidently any romantic feelings he'd harbored for her were as fleeting as their spin around the dance floor. "I apologize for any inconvenience, Professor. The inn will cover any additional expenses."

He pressed his lips together but made no reply.

Just before lunch, Phaedra drove to the hospital to pick up Tory Sutton. She loaded the girl's overnight bag into the trunk and helped her into the passenger seat.

"How are you feeling?" Phaedra asked as she slid behind the wheel and started the car. Bruises and cuts still marred her skin, and a pair of crutches lay on the back seat.

"Hungry for real food." Tory rested her head against the headrest. "I'm sick to death of soup and gelatin and mashed potatoes without salt. I want a cheeseburger. With mayo, and fries. And a chocolate milkshake."

"I think we can arrange that."

As they emerged from the local drive-through a few minutes later, Tory dug into the bag and withdrew a crinkle-cut french fry. Her face registered bliss as she bit into it. "*So* good. Want one?"

Phaedra shook her head. "I'm glad to see your appetite's back."

"I'm just glad to be out of that hospital."

"Did Brian come to see you?"

"A couple of times. I only talked to him once, though. The first time I was still out of it."

"And the second time?"

For a moment, the only sound was the crackle of Tory's fast-food wrapper. "He threatened me," she said finally.

Phaedra regarded her in shock. "He *threatened* you?"

"I told him I remembered what happened."

Her fingers tightened on the steering wheel. "What did you remember, exactly?"

"He called me Thursday night, after the carriage ride, and asked me to get an Uber. He said he'd pay the driver when I got back. And then he invited me in for a drink."

"And did you go?"

She put the burger, half-eaten, aside. "Yes." Her eyes darkened. "I can't believe I was so stupid. I trusted him. I thought he cared about me. But all he did was use me."

Phaedra signaled a turn and focused on the road. She didn't want to push the girl; her story would come out in its own time. After a moment, her patience was rewarded.

"He drugged me," Tory said finally. "He put something in my champagne."

That explained the missing champagne coupe, Phaedra thought. Brian must've planted it in Wendy's trunk. "What happened after you drank it?"

"I started to feel strange. Woozy. He suggested we go for a walk. Clear my head."

"And you ended up by the wishing well?"

She nodded. A tear squeezed from her eye and slid in a slow zigzag down her cheek. "I don't remember anything after that, but he m-must've pushed me in."

"The man's a monster," Phaedra said softly.

"He asked me to help him. When we first arrived."

"Help him, how?"

"After Harriet's murder, he got this idea. He wanted to make it look like Wendy did it. That way, even if she refused to marry him, she'd be arrested and the inn would close. She'd be forced to sell, and he'd buy it. Probably at a bargain price."

Although she'd suspected as much, hearing Tory share the facts of Brian's duplicity in stark detail angered her. He'd taken advantage of a young, foolish woman, not so different from herself at that age, and very nearly killed her.

Had he murdered Harriet, too?

"You overheard Wendy's 'canon' comment about Harriet in the kitchen, didn't you?" Phaedra asked, with a sidelong glance. "And you told Detective Morelli about it."

She hesitated, then sighed. "I was in the hall when Eve opened the kitchen door, and I heard your aunt say it. I decided to tell that detective. Throw her under the bus, like Brian wanted me to do."

As Phaedra turned onto the road that led to the inn, she mentioned the champagne coupe in Wendy's trunk. "Was planting evidence part of Brian's plan, too?"

"What do you mean?"

"Detective Morelli found a champagne glass, presumably the one used to drug you, in my aunt's trunk." Phaedra glanced over at her. "Someone let the air out of Wendy's tire. When I reached in to get the spare, there it was."

She shook her head. "I don't know anything about that."

"You said Brian threatened you. At the hospital."

"Yes. He—" She paled. "He leaned really close, and said if I told the police he shoved me into that well, he'd deny it, tell them I had a drug problem . . . and then he'd kill me."

"Do you think he meant it?"

"No question. Underneath the charm and those expensive suits, the man's got a legit scary side." She shuddered. "I'm glad he's in jail."

"He's not in jail, but he's been detained." Phaedra tapped a fingernail against the wheel. "Detective Morelli turned the champagne glass over to forensics for testing. He can't charge Callahan without proof."

"I hope he gets it. Because if he doesn't . . ." She sucked in a breath.

"The police will charge him. Don't worry."

Despite her reassurance, Phaedra felt a niggle of doubt. Morelli could detain Callahan for forty-eight hours. After that, he'd have to charge him, or cut him loose.

"I'm sorry," Tory said, turning a pale, exhausted face to hers. "I owe you, and especially your aunt, an apology. Getting involved with Brian was a mistake. A big mistake."

"He fooled a lot of people." Including her aunt Wendy.

"At first it was fun. The two of us, no strings. I'd sneak out to the guesthouse late at night. It was exciting." She pursed her lips. "But when he started seeing your aunt, I didn't like it. I mean, here's this older lady, divorced, and he's more interested in chasing after her than me?" She shook her head. "It was insulting."

"It wasn't serious."

"No. But he wanted her to believe it was."

"Because he wants the inn." Phaedra nodded. "I know."

Tory glanced at her. "You don't know the half of it."

Her pulse quickened. "Then why don't you tell me."

"Last Saturday, when you were all downstairs having sherry after dinner"—she made a face—"Brian went back to the guesthouse, and I took my wine out to the terrace. Harriet followed me."

"Why?"

"She said someone should tell your aunt Wendy what was really going on." Tory folded her arms. "I said I didn't know what she meant, that Brian was my boss, nothing more. She laughed. Said she saw us herself, in the guesthouse, when she chased down an arrow during the archery contest."

"I remember," Phaedra said slowly. "Dave said he'd go get it, but she insisted on retrieving it herself."

"Yeah, so she could snoop. She must've seen us together. I was furious. I told her Brian wouldn't like her spreading lies about us. She laughed again. I warned her that if she said anything to Wendy, she'd be sorry."

"Sounds like a threat." And it also sounded like a possible motive for murder.

"It was just talk. It worked, though. She didn't say a word. To anyone." Tory smirked. "She never got the chance." As the implications of what she'd said sunk in, her smirk faltered, and her eyes widened. "Wait. I didn't mean . . . You can't honestly think that I . . . *killed* her?"

"I think you should tell Detective Morelli about this as soon as we get back."

"What if he arrests me? I didn't kill her! I swear!"

"He can't arrest you without evidence, Tory."

"No." She sagged back against the seat. "Okay. I'll talk to him."

"*Did* you sneak out to visit Brian? No judgment if you did. I won't tell Wendy. I'm just curious."

"No. Not that night, anyway." Her gaze slid away. "That first night, I was tired. I went upstairs and took a sleeping pill and went to bed early. Around ten thirty. Between the wine and the pill, I was done."

If she was telling the truth, then whoever Phaedra had seen slipping out to the guesthouse later that night wasn't Tory. It had to be someone else.

"Why does it even matter?" Tory asked.

"Because if you're telling the truth, and you weren't outside the guesthouse that night," Phaedra said slowly, "then whoever I saw was probably Harriet's murderer."

thirty-three

When Phaedra returned with Tory, Morelli's car was parked out front. Why was he here? Shouldn't he be at the station, questioning Brian Callahan?

She helped Tory out of the car and up the porch steps. "Eve," she called out. "We need a hand, please."

As Eve arrived and helped Tory upstairs, Phaedra headed into the kitchen, where Hannah was just clearing up the afternoon tea dishes.

"Why are the police here?" she asked her sister.

"No idea. They spoke to Wendy. They have a warrant, so they're looking for something."

"Evidence." Phaedra gazed out the window overlooking the backyard. The forensics team, wearing plastic booties and protective clothing, examined the well and the area around the rose garden. Detective Morelli spoke with one of them, his face set as he gestured at the muddy ground.

"What kind of evidence?" Hannah asked. "Something to do with Harriet's murder?"

"No." Phaedra nudged her out of the way and filled a teakettle with water. "Brian Callahan's been detained for questioning. Morelli can't hold him much longer without charging him. And he can't charge him without evidence."

"Charge him for what?" Hannah dried the cup in her hand and set it in the dish drainer. "What's he done?"

Phaedra told her about Tory's claim that Brian drugged her on Thursday night and pushed her into the well.

Hannah stared at her, appalled. "That's horrible. Do you believe her?"

"I do, yes." She filled a carafe and put it on a tray along with cream and sugar. Her glanced strayed to the window. "Think I'll go and see if anyone wants coffee."

"Stay out of it, Phae. That's my advice."

"I don't know what you mean. Is there any cake left?"

With a sigh, Hannah put several toffee-and-chocolate-chip cookies on a plate. "Will these do?"

"Perfect." Phaedra added the plate to her tray and carried everything outside to the terrace.

"Detective," she called out to Morelli as she lowered the tray to the wrought iron table. "Could you and your team use a coffee break?"

He spoke to the team but they shook their heads. He tucked his pad into his pocket and strode across the grass to the terrace.

"Thanks, Professor."

"You're welcome." She poured him a mug of strong coffee and added a generous splash of cream. "Just the way you like it. Can I interest you in a cookie?"

"I wouldn't say no." He accepted the mug and took a sip. "I know what you're doing, by the way."

"Doing?"

"You're fishing for information." He picked up a cookie and took a bite.

"Did Tory talk to you? About Brian?"

"She did." He brushed crumbs from his fingers. "She gave me her statement yesterday morning, in the hospital. She remembered a few more things today."

"Good. Now you can arrest him."

"Not without evidence to tie him to the scene."

"Then you have to find it!" At his startled glance, she dragged in a calming breath. "Sorry. Tory's scared, and Wendy's upset. Learning that her former boyfriend not only lied to her, but drugged and attacked a young woman . . ."

"Allegedly," he corrected.

"Oh, come on, Detective!" Phaedra retorted. "You have Tory's statement. Not to mention the champagne coupe from Wendy's trunk. I'm sure Brian's prints all over it."

"Actually, no. The coupe was wiped clean." He set his coffee mug down. "Which is good news for Wendy. Even better news for Brian."

"He's up to his eyeballs in this." There wasn't a trace of doubt in her mind. "I knew he was up to no good from the start."

"Based on what?"

"Call it a bad vibe." She tucked the empty serving tray under her arm. "He's been cheating on Wendy, for one thing. With Tory."

"Oh? Are Wendy and Brian seeing each other?"

"Yes. It was getting serious. But my aunt's pretty cautious when it comes to men. After Jack, she hasn't gone out on dates very often."

"The ex-husband who owned the Cadillac."

She nodded. "He not only cheated on her, he cheated her out of money. He skimmed from the inn's books for two years before she caught him."

"Not the best judge of character, is she?"

Phaedra thought of Donovan, and how hard she'd fallen for his charm and dark good looks, once upon a time. "It runs in the family, I suppose."

"Are you certain Callahan's cheating on your aunt?"

"Positive. I saw someone sneak out to the guesthouse one night. A woman."

His gaze sharpened and he took his notepad out. "When was this?"

"The night of Harriet's murder, around eleven o'clock. That was the first time. I assumed it was Wendy."

"But it wasn't?"

She shook her head.

"You mentioned the 'first time.' You saw someone else after hours at the guesthouse? Someone other than Callahan?"

"Yes. Tory. She admitted as much."

"Why didn't you mention any of this before?"

She sighed. "I didn't think it was relevant at the time."

He returned the pad to his pocket. "I'll look into it."

"There's something else."

He lifted his brow. "You're full of revelations today, Professor. Go on."

"Last night, Donovan told me Brian put a contract on the Taylor house next door. He's partnered with a Charlottesville property developer."

"Interesting. But hardly illegal."

"Donovan's looking to buy commercial property in Laurel Springs. Brian offered to broker a deal on Bertie's Café. Donovan did some checking and learned Brian lost his Maryland real estate license due to allegations of fraud. He also learned," she added, "that Callahan is married."

"Again, not illegal."

"It will be, if he asks someone else to marry him and she says yes."

"Let me guess. Your aunt Wendy?"

She nodded. "He's pushing her to say 'I do' when he's already got a wife in Maryland."

"Maybe he's separated. Or in the process of divorce."

"Or maybe he's romancing my aunt in hopes of getting his hands on her inn as well as the Taylor property."

"A package deal?"

"Exactly. He told Donovan he plans to raze both houses and sell the site for a mixed-use shopping center."

He let out a low whistle. "Big bucks, no question. Callahan's morals may be sketchy, but unless he actually marries your aunt, there's nothing inherently unlawful in what he's doing."

"What about shoving someone into a coal cellar and setting fire to the house above it? That's assault. And attempted murder."

"Wait a minute." Morelli regarded her intently. "Are you suggesting Callahan pushed you into that cellar and started the fire in the Taylor house?"

"It's certainly possible. I heard a twig snap behind us when Donovan and I were talking. Wendy said Brian sneaks a cigarette sometimes. I think he overheard us. Who's to say he didn't follow me next door and shove me inside?"

"Okay, let's say he did. Why would he do that?"

Before she could answer, one of the forensics team approached. "Detective? We found something."

"What is it?"

He gestured to a muddy spot behind the rosebushes. "A couple of cigarette butts. And a footprint. One behind the well, and another in the garden. From the size and width, I'd say it's a man's shoe."

Thirty-Four

At three o'clock the carriage house doorbell rang, and Wickham lifted his head from his perch on the sofa to eye Phaedra in disapproval.

Visitors, again? So much for my afternoon snooze. He leaped to the floor, every hair of his silky fur bristling with indignation, and stalked upstairs.

"Sorry, Wicks," she called after him. Bella promptly claimed his spot on the sofa. With a quick check of her appearance in the hall mirror, Phaedra answered the door.

"Looks like I'm the first to arrive for our meeting," Lucy said as she entered the hallway and set her purse aside. "As usual, Mari's late. Do I get a prize?"

"Would you settle for a cup of tea?"

"If you have green oolong, you've got a deal."

"I do. Follow me."

"I see Bella's made herself at home." Lucy followed Phaedra to the kitchen island. "How does Wickham feel about that?"

"Mostly, he ignores her."

"Are you planning to keep her?"

"No. I'm still working on my mother. She's coming around to the idea."

As she poured hot water over the tea leaves to allow them to unfurl and steep for a few minutes, Phaedra eyed Lucy. "Heard anything more from your mother?"

"Not since Roz told her I don't want to see her." She slid into a seat at the breakfast bar. "No surprise there."

"Is she still in town?"

Lucy shrugged. "I don't know. And I don't care."

Before Phaedra could suggest that she might consider giving her mother a chance, the doorbell rang again. She left to answer it and returned a moment later with Marisol.

"Hi, all," Marisol said by way of greeting. "And before you say it, Lucy, yes, I'm late. Sorry."

Normally quick with a retort, Lucy merely shrugged.

"Lots to discuss today," Phaedra said as Marisol slid her purse strap off and joined them at the kitchen island. "We're running out of time to solve the murder."

"Oh, right! Today's the last day of the Jane Austen Murder Mystery week, isn't it?" Marisol said.

"It would've been," Phaedra corrected, "if not for recent events." She filled them in on the details of Tory's assault. "No one can leave until the police question everyone."

"Do they have any idea who did it?" Lucy asked.

"They've detained Brian Callahan."

"Your aunt's high school boyfriend?" Marisol asked. "Wow. Is he behind it?"

"Tory says he is. And I believe her."

"How's Wendy taking it?"

"Not well," Phaedra admitted. "He's not who she thought he was. She's devastated."

"He pushed Tory down a well," Lucy said slowly. "Why?"

"He planned to talk Wendy into marriage and get his hands on the inn." Phaedra poured tea into Lucy's cup. "Tory agreed to help him, but she changed her mind and threatened to tell my aunt."

"Uh-oh. I see where this is going," Marisol murmured.

"After our carriage ride on Thursday night, Brian invited her to the guesthouse for a drink."

"Was it drugged?" Lucy asked.

Phaedra nodded. "Most likely. When she lost consciousness, he shoved her into the well."

"Poor Tory." With a shudder, Marisol poured herself a mug of coffee. "I'm just glad you found her."

"With an assist from Bella." Phaedra settled across from them with a cup of tea and a notepad. "Help yourselves to Hannah's blackberry crumble. Now, where'd we leave off last time?"

"Suspects," Marisol supplied as she consulted her minutes. "Eve and Dave, Harriet's husband, Tom, and Rollo."

"Right." Phaedra stirred honey into her tea. "Who's left? Brian, Felicity, Elaine . . . and Wendy."

"Why's your aunt on the list? We know she didn't kill Harriet," Lucy pointed out.

"No. But we have to be objective. Wendy's on the police's suspect list."

"Because she said she'd like to stuff Harriet in a cannon? Please." Lucy snorted. "The murder weapon wasn't a cannon; it was a crossbow. Wendy's never fired a crossbow in her life. Or a cannon, for that matter."

"Detective Morelli found a champagne coupe in her trunk," Phaedra said. "After Tory disappeared."

"The same one Brian used to drug Tory?" Marisol asked.

"Most likely. But it was wiped clean."

"No surprise there." Lucy shook her head. "Anyway, your aunt would never leave the evidence in her trunk. It's obviously a plant."

"Exactly what I said."

"Besides," Marisol pointed out, "Tory's assault has nothing to do with Harriet's murder."

"It might." Phaedra told them about Tory's confession.

Lucy frowned. "Wait. Harriet threatened to tell Wendy that Tory and Brian were having an affair?"

"Yes. Which gives Tory a possible motive to murder Harriet," Phaedra said. "Brian, too, for that matter."

"And," Lucy added, "he convinced Tory to help him throw Wendy under the bus for Harriet's murder. So even if the romance didn't pan out, he could buy the inn if she was convicted." She snorted. "Some ex-boyfriend he turned out to be."

"Did I leave out the part," Phaedra added, "where Brian's already married?"

Twin gasps met her ears.

"Your poor aunt," Marisol sighed.

Lucy scowled. "What a lying, cheating, greedy, dirtbag piece of—" She let out a huff of disgust. "Well, you get the idea."

"How did you find out?" Marisol asked. "That Brian's married?"

"From Donovan. He told me in the garden, last night," she added. "Someone was eavesdropping. The police found a footprint, and cigarette butts."

"Brian?" Marisol asked.

"I'm sure of it. Tory says he sneaks a cigarette now and then." Phaedra frowned. "But then, so does Felicity." She shook the thought off. "Problem is, it doesn't prove anything. He could've gone out to smoke at any time. But I *am* sure about one thing. Whoever eavesdropped on us followed me next door and shoved me into the coal cellar."

"If you're right," Marisol said, "and it *was* Brian, it makes me think he might be Harriet's murderer. He had motive. And opportunity."

Lucy shook her head. "I'm not so sure. Whoever killed Harriet at close range with a crossbow was pretty cold-blooded. They wouldn't have left Tory alive in that well. They would've killed her first and dumped her body inside."

"She was unconscious in the bottom of an abandoned well," Phaedra reminded her. "With the lid in place. Her attacker left her there to die. The intent was the same."

"Let's get back to the suspects." Marisol set her cup aside. "Who haven't we discussed yet?"

"Felicity," Lucy said. "And Elaine."

"Okay, Felicity, then. What makes her a suspect?"

"Well," Phaedra mused, "she's young, and physically fit. She would've had no problem hiding the crossbow up a tree."

Marisol frowned. "She's an editor, right? Which means she's probably fairly well-read."

"What does that have to do with anything?" Lucy said.

"Think about where Harriet's body was found," Marisol replied. "In the rosemary patch. It might have significance. 'There's rosemary, that's for remembrance; pray, love, remember . . .'"

Lucy made an impatient gesture. "We talked about this before, Mari. Remember what, exactly?"

"I don't know. But it can't be a coincidence."

"When I came to, after my assailant knocked me out," Phaedra said slowly, "I was lying in the rosemary patch."

"And when Eve found Harriet's body," Lucy added, glancing at Phaedra, "she said she detoured from her normal run and ran through the kitchen garden. Because she loves the scent of rosemary and thyme."

"So do I." Marisol shrugged. "Doesn't mean I murdered Harriet."

"And it doesn't mean Eve or Felicity did, either," Phaedra agreed. "Still, Marisol makes a good point. We can't rule either of them out."

"Which leaves Elaine." Lucy helped herself to a cookie. "You've known her since college, Phaedra. What can you tell us about her?"

Phaedra stood to put her cup and saucer in the sink. "She's loyal, outspoken, and very good at what she does. I'd trust her with my life."

Lucy bit into her cookie. "I hear a 'but' coming."

"But she made a choice, years ago. A bad choice that

nearly cost her everything. Harriet found out," she admitted, "and she blackmailed Elaine."

"What did she do?" Marisol asked, eyes wide with curiosity. "Whatever it was, it must've been pretty bad."

"It was. At the time, she did the only thing she could to handle it." Phaedra would never disclose Elaine's decision to embezzle from her parents to protect her brother from serious injury, possibly death. "Unfortunately, her actions left her open to blackmail. Harriet knew it, and took full advantage."

"Giving Elaine a motive to kill her."

"Maybe, but . . ." Phaedra shook her head. "I find it hard to believe that she could kill Harriet. Or anyone."

"What about her costume shop? Maybe the vandal was someone connected to Elaine's past," Lucy suggested.

"Could be," Phaedra allowed. "She thinks that whoever trashed her shop may have been looking for something. Something specific." Phaedra returned to her seat. "Like the note I found on Harriet's body."

"From 'an ardent admirer,'" Lucy said with a nod.

"If so, that would mean the intruder was also the murderer," Marisol said. She rested her elbows on the breakfast bar. "I still think if we identify the calligrapher, we've identified the killer."

"Good luck with that." Lucy stood and carried her cup to the sink. As she rinsed it, she added, "I have to run. I promised to meet Aunt Roz for a drink at Josie's. See you both later." She dried her hands on the dish towel. "Thanks for the tea, Phaedra. Tell Wickham he really needs to work on his social skills."

"I have to go, too," Marisol said. "Thanks, Phae." She reached out to give her a quick hug. "Don't worry," she added earnestly. "You've unraveled one murder already. You'll figure out who did this. You always do."

Thirty-Five

Dinner at the inn that evening was subdued. Everyone focused on their food, and conversation was sporadic.

Felicity, wearing a glittery, blue-green sequined jacket over a teal-blue cocktail dress, stood out like a peacock in a flock of sparrows.

"Cheer up!" she reproved as she lifted her wineglass and surveyed their glum faces. "No need to look so dismal. Here we are, staying at this lovely bed-and-breakfast, enjoying a delicious meal, and we can't leave." A smile curled her lips as she took a lingering sip of pinot grigio. "That's my idea of heaven."

"Well, it isn't mine," Rollo said. "I have deadlines to meet and people to interview."

She lifted her shoulder. "That's what email and cell phones are for."

He ignored her and turned to Wendy. "Any word on when we'll be allowed to return home?" The question hung over the table like an accusation.

"None, I'm afraid," Wendy replied. "You'll have to ask Detective Morelli."

"Personally, I'm happy to stay," Tory observed, and cast

a glance of solidarity at Felicity. "It isn't costing me a penny. And the sooner the police figure out who killed poor Henrietta, the better."

"It's *Harriet*," Rollo pointed out irritably, "not Henrietta. Your concern for justice is commendable, but it would be far more convincing if you actually knew the victim's name."

"Well, pardon me." Tory's voice oozed sarcasm. "Harriet, Henrietta . . . what's the difference? She's dead, either way. And you knew who I meant."

Phaedra pushed her chair back and stood abruptly. "If you'll all excuse me," she said, "I'm quite finished."

"Chicken," Wendy muttered as Phaedra brushed past.

She made no comment but headed down the hall to the kitchen and pushed through the swinging door.

"Those people!" she exclaimed as she grabbed an apron. "They're driving me mad. They can't wait to leave." She knotted the ties at her waist. "And I can't wait until they go."

"Shh," Hannah warned, glancing back at the door. "One of them might hear you."

"At this point I don't think I care."

"You should care, for Aunt Wendy's sake. This whole murder thing hasn't exactly helped business, you know."

Phaedra joined her sister at the sink and grabbed a dish towel. The truth of Hannah's words sank in, and as she dried a serving platter, she sighed. "You're right. It can't be much longer before the police let everyone go."

"Let's hope so."

They worked together silently, Hannah washing and Phaedra drying, until every dish was returned, sparkling clean, to the cupboards.

"I'm out of here," Phaedra announced as she untied her apron and hung it up on a peg. "I can't take another minute of the complaining and whining or the incessant demands to go home." She glanced at the clock. Nearly eight thirty.

"Heading back to the carriage house?"

"No. I think I'll go to the bookstore and visit Mom and

Dad first." Guiltily she realized she hadn't stopped by since the night Elaine's costume shop had been vandalized. When was that? Monday?

"I'll go with you," Hannah decided as she dried her hands on a paper towel. "If you don't mind company."

"Of course not. And if I did, would that stop you?"

"Probably not."

They were heading for the front door when Mark Selden came down the stairs. "Phaedra. Glad I ran into you. Might we talk for a moment?"

She turned back. He wore dark-washed jeans and a black Henley, the sleeves pushed to his elbows. She couldn't read his expression, but she didn't need to. He looked serious and wary and irresistibly handsome. As he always did.

She kept her expression neutral. No matter how attractive she found his rumpled, professorial appearance—or his dinner-jacket-and-tie appearance, or his current jeans-and-Henley, can't-be-bothered appearance—she refused to succumb to his charm.

She couldn't forget that his interference had come between Charles and Hannah, to disastrous effect.

"I'm sorry," she said politely, "but we're on our way out. Perhaps later?"

He looked, just for a moment, as if he might challenge her; but with a shrug and a quiet, "Of course," he turned away and headed up the stairs.

"You should talk to him," Hannah said as she closed the door after them and followed Phaedra down the porch steps. "Hear him out. He looked very serious. And contrite."

"He always looks serious. He is serious. He hasn't a humorous bone in his body." Which wasn't fair, Phaedra knew, but shoved the thought aside. Her sister didn't need to know that Mark Selden had a unique, quirky sort of humor, a sense of the absurd not unlike her own, that others didn't always appreciate but that she quite liked.

Right now, he was the man who'd come between his best friend and her sister.

"It's good to get away," her sister confided as they walked up Main Street. "Not from baking, but thinking. About Charles. About my job at the embassy."

"Wait. What about your job?" Phaedra frowned. "I thought things were going so well. I thought you loved your position as pastry chef."

"They are. I do."

"Then what's the problem?"

"I can't stay much longer, Phae, or I'll lose my job. I'm needed at the embassy, and if I don't return after tomorrow, they'll fire me."

"But it's not your fault." Phaedra eyed her in consternation. "Did you tell them the inn is a crime scene and the police aren't letting anyone leave?"

"I did." She sighed. "They're sorry, and they understand, but bottom line, they need a pastry chef. A pastry chef who's in the kitchen, baking for embassy functions, not being detained by police in Virginia."

They stopped at the corner and waited for the light to change. "And if you don't get back in time?"

"They'll fire me." Hannah shrugged. "I'll pick myself up, dust myself off, and find something else."

The light changed and they crossed the road. "You don't sound all that upset by the possibility."

"If I'm being honest, I don't much like the job anymore," Hannah admitted as they turned up the walk to the Poison Pen bookstore.

"But it's all you ever dreamed of! You were ecstatic when you landed the position."

As they neared the wedding boutique, she nodded. "I still can't believe they chose me over all those other applicants." She sighed. "Charles may have had something to do with that."

"Don't," Phaedra said firmly, stopping to face her. "You did it all on your own, on your own merits. He may have put in a good word, but you got the job based on your own skills and qualifications."

Hannah paused to peer into the boutique's window. "I love that art deco gown. It's elegant and simple, but the rhinestone detailing makes it sparkle."

"Maybe you'll get something sparkly from Charles," Phaedra said. "One of these days."

"I heard from him, Phae. Yesterday."

"You did?" She regarded her sister in surprise. "Why didn't you tell me?"

"He wrote a letter, a very long letter, detailing his feelings for me and his reasons for 'taking a break.' That's what he called it," she added. "Taking a break. From us."

"Oh, Han . . . I'm so sorry."

"No, it's okay." Hannah fell into step beside her as they resumed walking. "I think Charles is right. Maybe a break is exactly what we need."

They arrived at the Poison Pen and climbed the steps to the front porch. Phaedra wondered, as she unlocked the doors, ignoring the "Closed" sign, if Mark had kept his word. If he'd spoken to Charles. Maybe that's what he'd wanted to tell her earlier.

"Call him, Hannah." She tapped in the key code to disable the alarm. "Tell Charles exactly how you feel. Don't let a misunderstanding ruin what the two of you have."

"That's your advice?" Hannah asked skeptically.

"That's my advice. If it's worth saving," Phaedra added firmly, "then you need to save it."

From somewhere in the depths of the house, Fitz began to bark.

"Better tell Mom it's us," Hannah warned her, "before she calls the police to report another break-in."

"Good idea. Mom," Phaedra called up the stairs as she set her reticule down, "it's me. And Hannah. Are you here?"

A moment later, Fitz trotting behind her, Nan Brighton appeared at the top of the stairs. She wore pajama bottoms and a faded purple-and-gold JMU T-shirt. "This is an unexpected surprise."

"Sorry," Phaedra said as she reached the top of the stairs and kissed her mother's cheek. "We didn't get a chance to talk much last night."

"No, we didn't. I'm glad you're both here." She led the way into the kitchen. "And before you ask, Phaedra, your father isn't home. He went to Winchester this morning to visit your uncle Frank."

"Is he okay?"

"Yes, yes, he's fine. He had a couple of first editions to show Malcolm. I think your father's hoping to convince him to sell a few of them. How about some hot chocolate?" Nan offered.

"In the middle of August? Sure. Why not?" She and Hannah settled at the breakfast counter as their mother assembled the ingredients.

"What brings you both here?" Nan asked as she stirred cocoa powder, sugar, and milk into the pan, along with a generous pinch of salt.

"Do we have to have a reason?" Hannah said.

"Your sister usually does. Have you and Charles patched things up?"

"Actually," Phaedra said as Hannah hesitated, "I wanted to pick Dad's brain about the murder case."

"I have a brain, too," Nan pointed out. "And a degree in anthropology from James Madison University to prove it."

She and her sister exchanged glances. "No one's questioning your intelligence, Mom. But I want to talk to him about a criminal matter. And I know how much you dislike talking about unsavory subjects like murder."

"What kind of criminal matter? You're referring to that poor Overton woman's death, aren't you?"

"Yes. I can't understand why the police aren't any closer to solving her murder. They have a limited number of suspects, all under the same roof. The inn's roof." Phaedra took the mug her mother handed her with a nod of thanks. "Yet they're no closer to making an arrest than the day Eve found Harriet's body."

Everyone had a motive, some stronger than others. All of them had had the opportunity to kill her. Means . . . well, that was the sticking point, wasn't it? Who owned the crossbow? Who hid it in the branches of the oak tree?

And who among them was a skilled calligrapher?

"Did you ever find that button?" Nan asked as she sat down. "The one you found in the kitchen garden when someone conked you on the head?"

Phaedra shook her head. "No. I can still see it, though. Wooden, with a crosshatch pattern, and a metal shank." She'd knew she'd seen it somewhere before. Where?

"Shank buttons are usually sewn onto jackets," Hannah said. "I hated sewing class, but I remember that. The shank ensures the button doesn't sit too close to heavier-weight fabrics. Helps it go through the buttonhole more easily."

"Look at you," Phaedra teased. "Queen of the domestic arts."

"Just a piece of useless trivia I remembered."

The conversation moved on to other topics, but Phaedra only half listened as she pondered her sister's words.

The female guests at Wendy's wore lightweight, summery fabrics, and draped shawls or pashminas around their shoulders when the evenings grew cool. Even Rollo favored seersucker and lightweight linens when he wasn't in costume. No one wore a jacket in one of the hottest months of the summer.

So where had that button come from?

Unless . . . Phaedra straightened. She knew of one person who wore a suit jacket.

Brian Callahan.

Thirty-Six

After accompanying her sister back to the carriage house, Phaedra returned to the inn. As she closed the front door behind her, a yawn escaped her lips. She glanced up at the old regulator clock behind the reception desk. Half past ten.

She wanted nothing more than to go home, let Wickham and Bella out, take a long bubble bath, and tumble into bed. But first she needed to check on Wendy and her guests to make sure all was well.

The front parlor and drawing rooms were empty and quiet. Only the mechanical ticking of the regulator interrupted the silence.

Apparently, everyone had decided to spend the evening at the bed-and-breakfast closeted in their rooms. She could hardly blame them. With no more planned activities, no carriage rides, elaborate teas, or archery contests on offer, why come downstairs?

"Phaedra." Wendy descended the staircase, a basket of laundry resting on one hip. "Where've you been?"

"Sorry, I should have told you. Hannah and I went to see Mom."

She reached the bottom of the stairs. "Yes, she said Malcolm left for Winchester this morning and she was a little nervous about staying alone tonight. What with all of the break-ins lately."

A pang of guilt pricked Phaedra. Her mother hadn't said a word about being afraid to stay on her own. "Maybe I should've offered to spend the night."

"She'd just send you back home." She set the basket down. "Nan will manage, trust me. If anyone breaks in, I feel sorrier for the intruder than for her. Oh, and before I forget—someone left a note for you."

"A note?" she echoed. "For me? Who's it from?"

"No idea. Eve found it on the front desk a little while ago. Someone left it after dinner, I suppose."

She followed Wendy to the reception counter and took the envelope from her aunt. A single word was scrawled across the thick white vellum.

Phaedra.

No one at the inn called her by her first name. Only Wendy and Hannah. And neither of them had left the note. The only other person who sometimes used her given name was . . .

Mark. Her frown cleared. He'd asked to speak with her earlier, when she and Hannah were headed out to the Poison Pen.

That must be it, she decided as she slid her finger under the sealed flap. He'd convinced Charles to share his feelings with Hannah, and now, perhaps, he was attempting to do the same with her.

She unfolded the single sheet. Even before she saw his signature at the bottom, she recognized Mark's rushed scrawl, barely legible and full of loops and swoops. She smiled. He was a brilliant scholar, but his handwriting was atrocious. But as she read the message, her smile faded into a frown. He asked her to meet him at midnight. In the kitchen garden.

*WE CAN TALK PRIVATELY THERE,
WITH NO INTERRUPTIONS.*

Why midnight? she wondered. And why meet in the place where Harriet had been murdered? Something felt off.

"Well?" Wendy prodded, not hiding her curiosity. "Who's it from?"

Slowly, Phaedra folded the page and dropped it onto the counter. "Professor Selden. He wants to meet me tonight in the kitchen garden. To talk about . . . things."

"Sounds romantic. Are you two an item?"

"No." She hesitated. Should she share her doubts about the note? Wendy would certainly advise her not to go. She probably *shouldn't* go. But despite her reservations, Phaedra's curiosity was roused. "We had an argument. About Hannah."

Her aunt's brows rose. "What about Hannah?"

Briefly, she filled her in on Mark's interference in the relationship and Charles's subsequent disappearance and decision to give them both "space."

"No wonder Hannah's been walking around like a wilted flower lately," Wendy said.

"Charles wrote her a long letter and said he needs some time. She's optimistic that they'll work it out." Phaedra sighed. "I hope she's right. I just wish Mark had stayed out of it."

"I don't think he intended to break up the relationship. He was being a good friend, that's all. And that's hardly a crime." Wendy bent down to pick up the laundry basket. "Maybe you should hear him out."

Or maybe I should trust my instincts. Ignore the note and go home.

Phaedra glanced once again at the clock. It was nearly eleven. By the time she returned to the carriage house to feed the cats and catch up on her email, it would be time to meet Mark. Or whoever had sent that note.

She'd take her cell phone along, she decided. Just in case.

"Yes," she agreed. "Maybe I should."

Her aunt was right. Mark probably wanted to apologize for interfering in Hannah and Charles's private lives. She thrust her doubts aside and headed for the door.

"Don't forget to take along a flashlight." Wendy called after her.

Wickham wove himself around her ankles, purring deeply as Phaedra entered the carriage house a few minutes later. She dropped her mail on the hall table along with her reticule and knelt to ruffle the cat's ears.

"That's quite a greeting," she whispered, glancing at Hannah's sleeping form on the sofa bed. "Did you miss me? What would you like first? Food, or a quick forage outside?"

His tail twitched as he eyed her. *Both. Light on the kibble and heavy on the salmon. This boy needs protein.*

"Where's Bella?"

Who knows? And more to the point, who cares?

She let him out the kitchen door and lingered on the back step with her arms crossed as he vanished into the shrubbery. Her glance sought out the guesthouse next door.

All was dark. At least there'd be no more secret assignations for Tory and Brian.

Returning to the kitchen, Phaedra opened a can of mixed grill and spooned half onto his kibble. "You, Mr. Wickham," she muttered, "are one very spoiled cat." She topped up Bella's dish as well.

Halfway through responding to emails on her laptop, she heard him mewling at the back door and got up to let him in, shaking her head in amusement as he beelined for his food dish and began devouring the mixed grill.

With time still remaining before her meeting with

Mark, Phaedra decided to go upstairs and have a bubble bath. And maybe a glass of wine?

Although the thought was tempting, she decided against it. She needed a clear head when she met with Mark.

A few minutes later, up to her neck in warm water and bubbles in the standalone tub, she rested her head back and closed her eyes. Instead of relaxing thoughts, questions plagued her.

Had the same person who'd knocked her out taken the button? It seemed likely. Her suspicions kept returning to Brian. He had a motive, after all. Donovan had warned her about Callahan's shady development deal. A warning Brian may have overheard.

Would the footprints forensics found in the garden match Callahan's? Had he pushed Tory into the well and shoved Phaedra into the coal cellar?

And the most important question of all—had he fired the crossbow that killed Harriet?

Brian definitely had a motive. Harriet had recognized him from his Realtor signs and nearly told everyone at the dinner table, including Wendy, that he was married. Overturning his wineglass bought him a temporary reprieve. The only permanent way to keep Harriet Overton from talking was to kill her.

Phaedra couldn't overlook the fact that Tory claimed he'd drugged her and pushed her into the well, leaving her there in an act of ruthless premeditation. Surely such a man was capable of murder.

And what about Tory? She and Harriet Overton despised one another. Had the author's threat to reveal Tory's affair with Brian to Wendy prompted the young woman to silence Harriet herself, by deadly means?

It didn't seem likely. Tory wasn't the bow-and-arrow, sporty type. She hated hiking and horseback riding and favored pointy high heels. If she'd murdered Harriet, there would've been mud on her shoes, divots in the grass from her spiked heels. Forensics had found nothing of the sort.

Phaedra leaned forward to pull the plug. Harriet had allegedly blackmailed Rollo and Elaine, holding her knowledge of their missteps over their heads to ensure she got what she wanted—repayment, in Elaine's case, and more recently, a starring role in the inn's theatrical; and an unending supply of five-star book reviews from journalist Rollo.

She stepped out of the tub and wrapped herself in a large towel. Maybe Hannah was right, she decided as she padded into the bedroom to dry off and choose an outfit. Let the police and Detective Morelli figure out who the murderer was, and stay out of it.

At any rate, it was time to get ready for her rapidly approaching rendezvous with Mark Selden. Another niggling doubt gave her pause. This whole thing was so unlike him. Perhaps she'd call him, let him know she was on her way.

But the call went straight to voice mail.

A chorus of crickets filled the warm night air as Phaedra returned her phone to her pocket and let herself out the back door a short time later. Knowing the phone was tucked in her pocket reassured her as she crossed the yard onto the adjoining property.

With no desire to fuss with a chemise or a Regency gown, she'd pulled on a pair of jeans and a silk T-shirt. Her hair, normally pinned up, hung in a loose braid down her back.

She moved past the hedges, her ballet slippers making no sound in the grass as she skirted the corner of the inn and found the path leading to the kitchen garden. The scent of late-summer roses hung heavy on the air.

As she reached the entrance to the walled garden, still now and deep in shadow, she hesitated. She glanced back over her shoulder and realized the inn was in complete darkness. Even Mark's upstairs window was dark.

His words the night she'd fallen asleep in the front parlor came back to her. *I often stay up late. I get my best work done then.*

Why, then, was his room dark now? And why hadn't he picked up his phone?

Every night after dinner, and on the rare occasion when he joined them downstairs at the table, he toiled into the wee hours on his monograph. But he'd told her he'd finished it.

He'd probably turned off his lamp and his phone when he came downstairs to meet her in the garden. He was already there, waiting. That must be it.

Still, an uneasy feeling gripped her. It wasn't too late to melt back into the shadows, forget about all this cloak-and-dagger stuff, and return to the carriage house, and bed . . .

Just inside the garden, she paused. Too late; someone was already there. A figure stood in shadow beside the fountain and faced away from the entrance.

"Mark?" she called out softly. "Is that you?"

He didn't answer. Perhaps he hadn't heard her over the sound of the crickets. They were certainly noisy tonight. She moved forward, suddenly hesitant, her slippers crunching on the gravel path as she drew nearer.

"Mark?" she said again. "It's me. Phaedra."

The figure turned and lifted a moonlight-gilded face.

"Hello, Phaedra. You're right on time. I've been waiting for you."

Felicity Penrose smiled. She wore a dark green cloak, the same one Phaedra remembered hanging on the costume rail in Elaine's office. A bit of moonlight picked out the distinct crosshatch pattern on the button fastened beneath her chin.

The button just below it was missing.

"It was you." Phaedra's voice was barely audible. "You knocked me on the head that night; you took the button I found. You knew it was evidence. Evidence that you killed Harriet."

"Clever girl. Brava!"

At her side, Felicity held a crossbow.

It was fitted with a quarrel. Phaedra's eyes widened in shock as she raised the weapon and pointed it straight at her heart.

Thirty-Seven

For what seemed an eternity but was barely a moment, Phaedra stood fixed to the spot. Her brain could barely process what her eyes were seeing.

"Felicity," she choked out. "What are you doing? Why are you . . . why are you pointing that thing at me?"

"Isn't it obvious? Your interference and snooping simply can't go on. You'll lead the police straight to me, and I can't have that. After tonight, I'll be gone. Free and clear. While you, alas, will be . . ." She gave Phaedra a regretful smile. "Dead."

"Why?" she asked, forcing out the words despite her fear. "It was you, wasn't it? Why did you kill Harriet?"

"It would take all night to list my reasons." She lowered the crossbow ever so slightly. "But we don't have all night. It boils down to one thing, really. Recognition. That's all I ever wanted from Harriet. But I never got it."

"Recognition? For what?"

Felicity laughed, low and harsh. "A very good question! For what, indeed." A bitter note entered her voice. "Do you know, she didn't even remember me?"

There's rosemary, that's for remembrance . . . Phaedra's glance went involuntarily to the rosemary patch they stood beside. Marisol had been right all along about the significance of the location of Harriet's body.

"Why should Harriet remember you?" she asked, struggling to keep her voice even and calm.

"Why, indeed? I've been married and divorced since those days, and I have a different surname. A different appearance." Her smile was brief. "I used to be a mousy, forgettable girl. No one you'd notice in a crowd."

Even I overlooked her, Phaedra realized guiltily. *Last night, at the masquerade ball, when she stood right at my elbow.*

"Everyone thinks Harriet's criticism of my fan fiction all those years ago left me so distraught I never wrote another word," Felicity went on. "That losing that silly writing contest destroyed me." She let out an unladylike snort. "Hardly. No, Harriet did something much, much worse. Something I couldn't forgive her for."

"What—what was that?" *Keep her talking. Keep her talking, and edge closer to the fountain.*

"I wrote a book for a proposed Regency romance series. It was damned good, too. But I had no agent, no published stories under my belt. I knew it would be difficult to get it in front of the right people. I went to Harriet and asked her to look at it. Give me her honest opinion.

"And do you know what she said?"

Phaedra shook her head mutely.

"She said it was 'nothing special.' Not bad, not good. Nothing special." Her lips twisted into a smile. "And that might've been the end of it, if Harriet hadn't stolen the book and published it under her own name. It went on to become her first bestseller."

"I'm sorry." Phaedra regarded her in mingled dismay and sympathy. "That must have been awful. Did you confront her? Threaten to sue?"

"And who do you suppose the publisher, the lawyers, the public would've believed? A nobody fan fiction writer, unpublished and unknown? Or Harriet Overton, author of half a dozen Regency romances and a bestselling author?"

She had a point. "You could've fought her in court."

"She altered it just enough to pass it off as her own. Changed the characters' names and the settings, that sort of thing. A little fictional sleight of hand. And she got away with it."

"You could have proven that the work was yours, that she stole your idea."

"I threatened to do just that. In the end, she agreed to compromise, and paid me to ghostwrite her books. But after writing seven of the damned things, I was tired of the pittance she paid me. I wanted a writing credit or a larger cut of the profits."

"I'm guessing Harriet refused both."

"Yes. And her refusal came at a deadly cost." Felicity lifted the crossbow and aimed the quarrel squarely at Phaedra. "Just as your interference will cost you."

"You planned to kill her. To make her pay." She edged, very gradually, nearer to the fountain in the center of the garden. There was a rock lying at the base of the low stone wall. If she could just reach it . . .

"*Planned* to kill her?" Her laugh was derisive. "No, I only wanted her to apologize, to admit what she did and give me restitution for everything she took. But before I could confront her, she recognized me," Felicity said. "She noticed the mole on my index finger—I knew I should've had the stupid thing removed—and threatened to tell your aunt I was an imposter."

"Because she knew you as Arabella, your pen name." Phaedra struggled to keep her voice calm. "Hardly reason enough to kill her, though, was it?"

"No. But when I demanded she at *least* acknowledge she'd stolen my book, she refused! I was livid. So I decided to kill her. And the murder mystery week presented the perfect opportunity. Everyone playing a role, wearing costumes. I wrote her a note—I learned calligraphy years ago—and signed it 'an ardent admirer.' I knew the silly woman would assume it was a love note from Eve's husband, Dave, or a clue in the murder mystery. And she did. *So* predictable." Her fingers tightened on the crossbow. "It made killing her a simple matter. Now," she added, jerking her head to one side, "move away from the fountain, and that rock you have your eye on."

Phaedra hesitated.

"Move!" Felicity snapped. "I'm calling the shots tonight, Professor." Her laugh was low and devoid of mirth. "So to speak."

As Harriet's ghostwriter aimed the crossbow once again at her chest, Phaedra's thoughts raced. There had to be something she could do, some way out of this. She'd hit the ground, she decided in desperation, roll into the shadows.

She tensed, and terror seized her heart as Felicity steadied the tiller to shoot. Before she could aim and release the quarrel, a sound drifted on the night air. Someone was singing in a loud and drunken voice.

I asked this fair maid to take a walk,
Mark well what I do say
I asked this maid out for a walk
That we might have some private talk.

It sounded like Mark, singing an inebriated rendition of an old sea chantey. For a moment, she stood frozen, so unexpected and bizarre was the interruption.

I'll go no more a rovin, with you, fair maid.
A roving, a roving, since roving's been my ru-i-in,
I'll go no more a roving, with you, fair maid.

She stared in disbelief as a drunken figure staggered into the garden. He wore the bicorn hat of a British sea captain. Captain Wentworth, to be precise. In his hand he brandished one of Elaine's prop dueling pistols.

"Evening, fair ladies," he drawled, and swept them both an unsteady bow. "A fine night it is."

Felicity's grip loosened slightly as she gazed in bemusement at the interloper. "Professor Selden?"

Phaedra used the distraction to dart forward and knock the crossbow from Felicity's unsuspecting hands.

She flung Phaedra aside with a snarl and lunged down to snatch up the crossbow. She straightened and whirled.

And this time, she aimed the quarrel at Mark.

"Run, Phaedra," he shouted. "Get away while you can!"

But she wouldn't leave him alone to face a sure and certain death. His wool jacket would never withstand a quarrel at such close range; he'd die instantly. As Felicity focused on her quarry, her lips turned up in an ugly smile, Phaedra saw a hoe leaning against the garden wall. She pelted toward it just as Mark charged forward.

He flung his bicorn into Felicity's face. She flinched but didn't waver in her determination to shoot him. He didn't stand a chance unless Phaedra stopped her.

Grabbing the hoe, she heaved it like a javelin at Felicity as she prepared to fire. The hoe knocked her crossbow askew, but not before the quarrel shot free. Mark stumbled forward and fell.

Phaedra let out a cry of mingled anguish and fury as she wrestled Felicity to the ground. All she could think of as she and Harriet's murderer tumbled and rolled over the grass and gravel was Mark, lying just yards away. Was he dead? Had Felicity killed him?

Had his attempt to save her cost him his life?

As she rolled atop Felicity, her breath heaving and her hands pressing the writhing woman's shoulders hard into the ground, she heard a shout behind her.

"Phaedra! Is that you?" her aunt Wendy called out. "What's happened? Are you all right?"

A pair of strong yet gentle hands drew her back and

helped her to her feet. Detective Morelli. He jerked his head at Felicity as she struggled to stand up. "Cuff her," he ordered a Somerset County PD officer. He turned back to Phaedra. "Are you okay? Did she hurt you?"

"She tried to kill me," she said in a rush, "and she murdered Harriet. She confessed. I'll explain it all in my statement. But not right now. I need to go."

"Go? Go where? You can't leave. This is a crime scene, Professor."

"She shot Mark! I'm afraid—" She let out a choked sob and pushed past him. "I think she might've killed him."

Morelli followed her to the prone figure and knelt down. "Professor Selden? Can you hear me?" He pressed two fingers to his wrist. "He has a pulse."

Dazed, Mark muttered something, and sat up. "Of course I have a pulse," he said irritably. "I'm not dead."

"You're all right!" Phaedra exclaimed. "I thought—we thought—Felicity shot you!"

"No, the shot went wide." He rubbed the back of his head. "Thanks to you."

"Then why did you hit the ground?"

He scowled at a nearby paving stone. "I'm embarrassed to admit I tripped on that bloody thing." He ignored Morelli's outstretched hand and pushed himself to his feet. "But I'm flattered to know you care."

As Phaedra impulsively stretched up on her toes to brush her lips against his cheek, she realized she did care. Very much.

"I'm just glad you're not hurt," she told him. "Or dead."

His grin was wry. "*I'm* glad I'm not dead, too." His arms came around her, and his forehead touched hers as he added softly, "Very glad."

Thirty-Eight

F elicity Penrose," Detective Morelli stated, "you're under arrest for first-degree murder in the death of Harriet Overton, as well as the attempted murders of Professors Phaedra Brighton and Mark Selden."

As a sheriff recited Felicity's Miranda rights, Wendy joined Phaedra and Mark. "What a night! What on earth happened out here? I heard shouts, and drunken singing, and then the police showed up, and—"

Phaedra turned to the detective. "Speaking of which, how did you manage to get here, just in time?"

"Professor Selden called," he replied. "He said Felicity Penrose was the murderer and that she'd lured you out to the garden with another note."

Mark picked up the story. "I finished my monograph, and I must've fallen asleep at my desk. When I woke, I came downstairs. I wanted to apologize to Phaedra for . . ." His glance shot to Morelli and back, and he cleared his throat. "For my interference in a personal matter."

"No wonder you didn't answer my call," Phaedra said.

"I wish I had. I would've told you the note wasn't mine. When I saw it on the front desk in the lobby, I—well, I picked it up and read it," he admitted. "And I'm very glad I did."

"What made you call the police?" Morelli asked.

"The handwriting, for one thing. Even though she did an excellent job copying my hand, I recognized it immediately as Felicity's, from the editorial comments she'd made on my monograph earlier in the week. And I knew *I* hadn't written it."

"And the second thing?"

"There were a few sequins on the floor. Glittery and blue-green, exactly like the jacket Felicity wore at dinner. I knew then," he finished, "that she wrote the note, and lured Professor Brighton out to the garden, just as she must've lured Harriet. I ran into the parlor and grabbed the dueling pistol. I saw my costume hanging on the rack—Captain Wentworth's naval uniform—and clapped the bicorn on my head. I thought it might serve as a distraction. Then I ran out to the garden in hopes that I wasn't too late."

"He came staggering down the path," Phaedra informed Morelli, "pretending to be drunk, singing some ridiculous old sea chantey—"

"'Maid of Amsterdam,'" Mark corrected her. "Also known as 'A-Roving.'"

"—and basically, saved my life. If not for Mark, I couldn't have knocked the crossbow from Felicity's hands or wrestled her to the ground, and she would have killed us both."

Detective Morelli holstered his weapon. "Good job, Professor Selden," he told Mark. "You helped us take Ms. Penrose down. You can interfere anytime you like." He turned to Phaedra. "I'll need statements from you both."

"Of course," she agreed. "What about the footprint forensics found in the garden? Was it Brian's?"

"Yes. It was an exact match to his size twelve custom-made Italian loafers. We found a few more prints leading to the Taylor place, but the fire and rescue workers churned up the ground there pretty badly, and any usable prints near the house were destroyed."

"What about the champagne coupe?"

"No usable prints, but the glass contained traces of Rohypnol. Street name, roofies. It's a date-rape drug that causes temporary memory loss in its victims."

Phaedra exchanged a glance with her aunt. "Is that enough to convict him?"

"Without prints, no. But your hunch that Callahan followed you to the Taylor property last night got me thinking. Why follow you, why go to the trouble of pushing you in the coal cellar and setting fire to the house, unless he had something to hide?"

"Good point," Phaedra said. "I assumed he intended to commit insurance fraud. Burn down the house for a payoff, since he only wanted the land."

"That was the plan, and he nearly pulled it off. Firefighters combed the house, but they were looking for proof of arson. Which is why I obtained a search warrant."

"Did you find anything?"

He nodded. "In the kitchen, where Callahan set the fire. The old refrigerator was charred but still intact. Inside I found a half-empty bottle of champagne and a blister pack of Rohypnol tablets. One tablet was missing and Callahan's prints were all over the bottle and the package."

"He must've assumed no one would search an empty house," Mark said. "And the fire he set would've destroyed the evidence." He extended his hand. "Good work, Detective."

"Yes. Very good work." Admiration warmed Phaedra's voice.

"Thanks to Billy's statement, we've added one count of arson to the charges against Callahan," Morelli added. "If the wooden bar on the coal cellar door yields any prints, we'll get him on another count of attempted murder."

"Sounds like Brian will be spending the rest of his life in prison," Mark said.

Phaedra excused herself. Wendy stood slightly apart from the others, a bereft expression on her face as Felicity was led away in handcuffs.

"How are you holding up, Aunt Wendy?" she asked quietly. "This must be a terrible shock for you."

She shrugged. "I guess there's no fool like an old fool. And I was an Old Fool with capital letters."

"No, you weren't." Her words were firm. "You fell in love with Brian, or at least, with the man he used to be. You had no way of knowing he'd changed so much."

"You were right about him all along."

"Believe me, I wish I wasn't." She reached out and hugged her aunt tightly. "I'm just glad he's behind bars."

"How could I be such a poor judge of character?"

"He was clever, and an excellent salesman. He sold you on the image of the man you wanted him to be, not the man he really was."

"I suppose you're right."

"You dodged a serious bullet." Phaedra squeezed her hand. "Consider yourself lucky you didn't marry the guy."

"At least my money problems are over. With all of the notoriety of the past couple of days, bookings are up eighty percent. Can you believe it?" She patted Phaedra's arm. "You'll have to conjure up another dazzling event for the inn. Maybe that *Titanic* tea weekend you suggested?"

Phaedra bit back a groan. Another week like this one would send her screaming into the night, never to return. "We'll see," she hedged. "As long as it doesn't involve a mystery. Or a dead body."

"I'd best go in and put a pot of coffee on. Looks like the rest of our guests are awake."

Phaedra followed her gaze. Sure enough, Donovan, Rollo, and Tory had wandered out onto the terrace to see what was going on, wearing robes and varying expressions of bafflement and curiosity. Hannah, yawning, joined them.

"I'll be back in a minute," Phaedra told her aunt. "There's something I need to take care of first."

As Wendy headed back to the house, Phaedra followed the flash of blue and red lights around the side of the inn to the front yard, where two Somerset PD vehicles blocked the road. She found her quarry standing a little apart from the others, a phone pressed to one ear.

As he saw her, he ended the call. "Professor Brighton. I'll get your statement in a moment."

"No problem. I'm not going anywhere." She crossed her arms against the late-evening chill. "Thanks again for showing up when you did."

"Thank Professor Selden. His quick thinking saved your life. And his."

Phaedra didn't object as Morelli grabbed a Somerset County PD jacket from the back seat of his car and dropped it around her shoulders. "Thanks. What about Billy?" she added tentatively. "He won't be charged with trespassing, will he?"

"As the property owner, Brian Callahan could file a charge against him, but he's got his own problems to deal with right now. Like a long prison sentence. So, short answer? No."

She let out a sigh of relief. "Good. I'm glad, because Billy saved my life. If he hadn't been there . . ."

"But he was."

Morelli's voice was firm, and hearing it reassured her.

She drew the jacket he'd given her closer. "I'll speak to his mother, try to persuade her to let Billy get a part-time job. If he promises to keep his grades up, I think she'll relent."

"It's worth a try." He studied her. "You're good people, Professor Brighton."

She canted her head slightly. "So are you, Matteo Morelli. Not unlike a certain Captain Frederick Wentworth."

"Who?"

She smiled. "Never mind. Now—if you're ready, I'd like to give my statement."

Thirty-Nine

A single suitcase stood by the front door.

"Leaving?" Phaedra asked Donovan as he descended the inn's staircase the next morning.

She'd come over to say goodbye to the three remaining guests. Mark had departed the previous night, after giving his statement to Detective Morelli. Rollo and Tory were gone as well, on their way to Charlottesville to catch their respective flights home.

That left Donovan.

"I am," he confirmed, his lips curving into an easy smile as he adjusted the strap of the carry-on bag at his shoulder. "It's certainly been . . . interesting."

"This place is normally the definition of dull."

Wendy pushed through the kitchen's swing door in capris and a crisp white shirt and joined them. "Bite your tongue, Phaedra Jane Brighton," she scolded. "Your public relations efforts could use some work."

"No worries, Ms. Prescott," Donovan assured her. "I had a great time. Thank you for your hospitality, and—" He darted a quick, sideways glance at Phaedra. "Thanks for keeping my secret."

"You mean the fact that you were a runaway bride-groom?" Phaedra teased.

"How'd you figure that out?"

"When you told me Emily dumped you the night before the wedding, you did that thing."

"What thing?"

"That thing," she said patiently. "You always do it. When you brush your hand over your chin."

"I don't do that," he said, knitting his brows together as his hand strayed up to his chin.

Amusement danced in her eyes. "No. Never."

He laughed. "Guess I'm busted. As it happens," he added, "Em and I have worked things out. She's agreed to give me another chance."

"That's wonderful," Phaedra said, and meant it. "I'm happy for you. Both."

"I think you really do mean that." He couldn't quite keep the surprise from his voice.

"I do. We're grown-ups now. Different people. We . . . we were kids back then and we both behaved badly."

"Yeah. I'm sorry for that. I acted like a jackass, ghost-ing you on prom night, and I always regretted it. I hope—" He dropped his gaze, lifted it to hers once again. "I hope we can at least be friends."

"Of course." She walked with him to the front door and folded her arms against her chest. "How would you feel if Hannah made your wedding cake? If the wedding happens?"

"Hannah? The girl who put up 'Wanted' posters with my picture all over town, calling me a lying liar?"

Phaedra's eyes widened, and she laughed. "I forgot about that. She was really mad at you."

"Probably still is." His smile was rueful. "You honestly think she'd bake my wedding cake?"

"She's already volunteered to do it."

"Tell her thanks. I'd be honored if she made our wed-ding cake."

She reached for the doorknob. "I'm curious. Did you manage to find a property while you were here?"

"Nope. The café was the closest I came, but it's already been leased."

"Someone else beat you to it?"

He gave a *what can you do?* shrug and picked up his suitcase. "It's okay, though. I'll have to locate my new gym somewhere else. Bealeton, maybe, or Warrenton."

"Best of luck to you," Phaedra said, and smiled. "Keep in touch."

"You, too." He leaned forward to brush his lips briefly against her cheek, his gaze lingering perhaps a moment too long. As if he wanted to say something more.

A horn tooted twice outside as a silver SUV pulled in front of the inn. A pretty, dark-haired girl wearing oversized sunglasses sat behind the wheel.

"There's my ride," he said, unnecessarily. "Em."

"Well, don't keep her waiting. Safe travels."

She waited on the porch as he stowed his suitcase on the back seat and slid into the passenger seat, and waved as Emily backed the SUV out onto the street.

"Bye, Donovan," she said softly as she watched the vehicle head away down Main Street.

She went back inside, still smiling, and closed the door.

Forty

Someone banged loudly on Phaedra's front door.

"Phae!" Lucy called out. "I know you're in there. Yard sale today, remember? We have to set up. Open the door!"

"I'm coming," she called back, and hurried down the stairs. This time, she wasn't lying in bed, dreaming of Mr. Darcy. This time, she was ready.

"You're headline news again," Lucy informed her as Phaedra opened the door. "Front page of the *Laurel Springs Clarion*." She thrust a copy of the morning edition at her.

"Clark Mullinax?" she asked as she grabbed it.

"Who else? He did a good job, though. He's actually turning out to be a decent crime reporter."

"Miracles never cease."

"I brought doughnuts," Marisol said, coming up the walk brandishing a white bakery box from Brennan's. "Maple bacon, your favorite."

"That's *your* favorite," Phaedra pointed out.

"Don't be a hater. And don't get too stuck into that news story, or there won't be any left."

"Thanks. I won't," she answered, already distracted as she skimmed the article. "I made coffee, help yourselves."

As she and Lucy brushed past and made their way into the kitchen, Phaedra scanned the story.

SOMERSET UNIVERSITY PROFESSOR
FOILS MURDER ATTEMPT

"So, why did Felicity what's-her-name kill Harriet, anyway?" Lucy called out. "She ghostwrote most of her books, didn't she?"

"Seven." Phaedra tossed the paper aside and followed her friends into the kitchen. "It started years ago, when she gave Harriet a book proposal for a Regency romance. Harriet read it, told her it was nothing special and, after changing the setting and the characters' names, stole it."

"Ouch." Marisol winced. "That's cold."

"When she realized what Harriet had done, Felicity threatened to sue, and Harriet offered her the ghostwriting gig to shut her up. And it worked, for a while. But Felicity's resentment built, and when she read about our Jane Austen Murder Mystery week and saw Harriet Overton listed as a guest, she decided to sign up, too. At first she only wanted to confront Harriet. Get her to admit she stole the book. She refused."

"And Felicity decided to kill her," Lucy said.

"She was the mysterious calligrapher," Marisol mused. "And the crossbow expert. Where did she learn that particular skill, I wonder?"

"She lived on a farm out in Oregon somewhere. Detective Morelli said she got the property from her ex-husband as part of their divorce settlement. She practiced target shooting every weekend and got quite good at it."

"I still don't understand how she managed it," Marisol said. "Murdering Harriet practically under everyone's noses like that."

"It was simple enough," Phaedra said, and shrugged. "She wrote the note and lured Harriet out to the kitchen garden."

"So, what happens to Felicity now?" Lucy asked.

"A long prison term, I imagine. I hope she looks good in orange."

For a few minutes, the three were silent, sipping coffee and nibbling on doughnuts, each lost in thought.

A sharp knock sounded on the back door, and Phaedra got up to let her sister in.

"Hannah?" She gazed at her in mingled surprise and confusion. "I thought you were halfway to D.C. by now."

"Nope." She was all smiles in a pair of jeans and a T-shirt, her hair caught back in a ponytail. "I'm reporting for yard sale duty."

"What about your flight? Your job? You said you'd be fired if you didn't return today."

"Oh, that." Hannah waved her hand in dismissal. "I quit. I didn't like working at the embassy much, anyway."

Phaedra regarded her in dismay. "But . . . that job was your life! It's all you ever talked about."

"That job," Hannah said firmly as she helped herself to a doughnut, "was Mom's dream, not mine. Sure, it was great. I met a lot of interesting people and made tons of valuable contacts. But it was stressful, too. Long hours. It just wasn't for me."

"But what'll you do now?"

"Move in with you, for starters. Just for a while." She licked maple glaze from her fingers. "Until I get my bakery up and running."

"Wait, what?" Phaedra eyed her as if she'd just sprouted fairy wings and zipped around the kitchen. "What bakery?"

"Is it you?" Lucy let out a yelp of excitement. "I noticed the 'For Lease' sign's gone from the corner café. Are you—"

"Yes. I'm the owner of Laurel Springs' soon-to-be newest—and only—patisserie." She dabbed a napkin to her lips. "Brennan's is about to have a little competition."

After congratulating Hannah, Lucy and Marisol left to begin hauling folding tables outside.

"Doughnut break's over," Lucy said over her shoulder. "Let's go, girls."

"Be right there," Phaedra promised as she turned back to her sister. "I'm happy for you, I really am. If you're sure this is what you truly want."

"I'm sure. You don't mind if I crash here for a little, do you?"

"Not at all. Actually, I'd love the company. Wickham's great," she added as the finicky feline stalked into the kitchen, "but unlike Bella, he's not very sociable."

I'm not antisocial, he seemed to say as he wandered to his food dish to inspect it with disdain. *Unlike Bella, I'm particular about choosing my acquaintances.*

"What about you and Charles?" Phaedra asked. "Is there any hope there?"

"Oh, sorry, I thought you knew. We're back together."

"Han, that's wonderful! Congratulations." She hugged her sister, then pulled back and smacked her lightly on the arm. "You should've told me."

"I just did. There's something else, too." A smile blossomed on Hannah's lips. "Looks like Donovan isn't the only one getting a wedding cake soon."

"What do you mean?"

"I mean, we're engaged. Charles has asked me to marry him. And I've said yes."

By nine o'clock, tables piled with gently used items lined the front yard as the first customers arrived for Phaedra's yard sale. They flicked through racks of clothing and inspected Elaine's discarded costumes, browsed through piles of books, and admired the assortment of pots and pans and dishware.

"Marisol's in her element," Lucy observed dryly from her position behind the cashbox. "She brought an armful of her vintage castoffs and she's sold every single one. She really should open her own vintage clothing store."

"She should," Phaedra agreed. "She's a natural, and very knowledgeable. By the way," she added, lowering her voice and choosing her words carefully, "did you ever talk to your mother?"

For a moment, Lucy said nothing, only gazed into her cup of green tea with a frown. "I did," she said finally, and lifted her face to Phaedra's. "We're meeting up with Auntie Roz for dim sum tomorrow."

She smiled. "Good." Deciding to leave it there, Phaedra couldn't resist adding, "You know what 'dim sum' means, don't you? 'Touch the heart.'"

"Don't read too much into it," Lucy retorted. "It's a chance to share shrimp dumplings and *lop cheung bao.* That's all."

"Still, it's a start."

"'A journey of a thousand miles begins with a single step'?" Lucy scoffed. "Please."

Wisely, Phaedra let it go.

"Since we're sharing personal stuff," Lucy said, "what about you and the Shakespearean dreamboat? Any action there?"

"Lu!" she protested, laughing. "What a question."

But Lucy wouldn't be put off. "Well? Are you two ready to quit pretending you despise each other and take things to the next level?"

Phaedra hesitated. Seeing a paperback copy of *Persuasion* lying atop a pile of books, she felt her doubts melt away, and smiled. "You never know," she said. "I just might be persuaded."

Acknowledgments

A book, like a good recipe, requires quality ingredients, patience, and attention to detail. I'm grateful to the team at Berkley, particularly my wonderful editor, Sareer Khader; as well as my copyeditor, Angelina Krahn; and production editor, Stacy Edwards. I'd also like to thank cover illustrator Victoria Fomina; cover designer Farjana Yasmin; and art director Rita Frangie for collectively providing another gorgeous cover. Kudos to Michelle Vega for liking my Regency-gowned professor and amateur sleuth, Phaedra Brighton, as much as I do.

Gratitude to my agent, Nikki Terpilowski, for her hard work and faith in me over the years, and to the online community for their continued support and encouragement.

And a special shout-out to talented indie writer Lisette Brody for sharing her enthusiasm for *Pride, Prejudice, and Peril* . . . and for introducing me to her adorable canine sidekick, Bentley.

Don't miss Katie Oliver's next riveting entry in
the Jane Austen Tea Society Mysteries . . .

Cyanide and Sensibility

*Available soon in paperback
from Berkley Prime Crime!*

Ready to find
your next great read?

Let us help.

Visit prh.com/nextread